BOOKS IN THE CATHELL SERIES

Into the Darkness
The Taming

Into the Darkness

Into the Darkness

A.M. Rycroft

Mighty Quill Books
Pittsburgh

First Printing: 2015
Second Printing: 2016

ISBN 978-0-9860884-4-5

Mighty Quill Books
www.mightyquillbooks.com

Special discounts are available on quantity purchases. For details, contact the publisher by email at info@mightyquillbooks.com or at the following address:

Mighty Quill Books
c/o Mighty, LLC.
370 Castle Shannon Blvd., 10366
Pittsburgh, PA 15234

This book is dedicated to anyone who had a dream they just couldn't shake.

And, to Erin – all my thanks for letting me run with my dreams and for supporting every one of them. This means more to me every day.

A special thanks to my editor Anne for pushing me to get every last drop of blood out on to the page. I mean that in the best possible way. This edition is all that it is thanks to your help.

My thanks also to Katherine for once again putting up with my endless cases of "one more thing…" and telling me when the reader doesn't *actually* need to see everything.

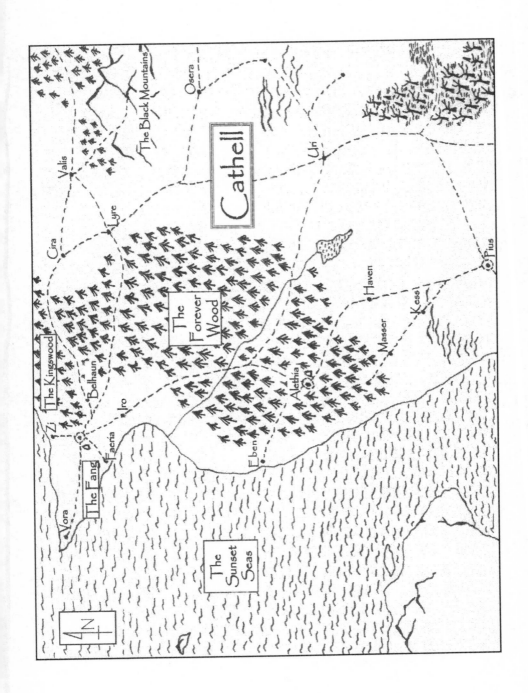

INTRODUCTION

Welcome, my friends, to the second edition, the special edition, even, of my dark fantasy/horror novel *Into the Darkness*. If you've never read it before, I think you're in for a great ride, and if you have read it before, I think you'll find some interesting new tidbits tucked into the story as well as in the bonus material at the end. But, first, a little history.

For anyone who doesn't know, *Into the Darkness* started out as a literal dream.

It feels like a lifetime ago to me now, but I was once in art school for a little over a year and half, before I made what must have seemed to my family to be a very sudden decision that the life of an artist just wasn't for me. I did this about three months prior to graduation. If you're a parent, you can probably understand how much that frustrated mine. It was actually a decision that was a long time coming, however; I just hadn't bothered to share the thoughts leading up to the decision with anyone else until I'd made the decision.

Fast forward to a few months after my exit from art school and I was working in the mailroom of a mortgage company while I tried to figure out what was next in my life. The job was as mind-numbing as it probably sounds to you, but the upside was that it gave me plenty of time to think. In all honesty, I had absolutely no idea what I wanted to do with my life. Then, one night, I had a dream.

I dreamed about a sell-sword walking through black-walled caverns lit only by torches, and though she never spoke, I knew she was looking for something. The dream was extremely vivid to me. I could feel the cold damp air, smell the dirt on the cavern floor, and feel the heat of each torch as she passed it.

For days, this dream poked at my consciousness. I just couldn't shake it, just couldn't stop thinking about it. Eventually, I started writing it down.

I'd always dabbled in writing, starting from the time I was very young, but up until that moment, I hadn't written anything at all since long before graduating from high school. As soon as I started writing, though, the character of Aeryn Ravane started to take shape. I knew she had a story to tell me, and I knew I wanted nothing more than to hear that story. I suddenly knew what I wanted to do with my life: I wanted to write.

Soon after, I enrolled in the University of Pittsburgh's English program. Over the course of getting my bachelor's and beyond, a period of seven years, I worked on my epic dark fantasy/horror story until it became the novel known as *Into the Darkness*.

The idea for this edition of *Into the Darkness* came to me after the release of the second book in the Cathell series, *The Taming*. More and more, I was getting asked questions about whether *The Taming* was part of an ongoing series (yes), and people really wanted to know more about the world itself. So, in this edition of the book, you'll find not only the novel that kicked off the Cathell series, but also in-depth information about the world of Cathell and the beings in it.

Besides the addition of the bonus material at the end, readers of the original printing of the book will notice a few differences in this printing. Most notable of the changes is the absence of the prologue that previously appeared at the beginning. I realized after its original publication that the story the prologue presents isn't crucial to the reader's understanding of the events in the rest of the novel, and it really would work best as a stand-alone story. So, in this edition, the prologue has been given new life as the story "The Fall of Tynan Selvantyr", found in the bonus content.

I now present you with *Into the Darkness*, the special edition. I hope you enjoy reading it as much as I enjoyed putting it together for you. — *A.M. Rycroft*

INTO THE DARKNESS

1

The old, grizzled drover and his mount guided the sell-sword and her stallion down from the steep mountain passage into the barren valley. The intermittent gusts of wind and rain slapping against the hood of the sell-sword's cloak told her that the rage of the Northlands' storm season was coming a full month earlier than its usual late autumn arrival. It promised to make getting back out of the valley just as treacherous as the trip to the valley, if she even made it that far.

The drover looked back over his shoulder periodically, a grim look on his face, as the pair picked their way to the valley's base. He knew her purpose for being there, and she knew this old friend of her father's did not approve. Once at the bottom, the drover turned his horse to face hers and studied her for a moment. She pushed back her cloak hood, uncovering her dark hair, and studied him with gray eyes that matched the storm clouds above. She knew what he was going to say.

"This is where I leave ye, Aeryn Ravane." He squinted at her and grimaced in the face of another biting gust of wind. "I don' feel good 'bout it. Yer father wouldn' approve, ye know."

"This was what he wanted," she replied. She had hired Phineas because he knew her father and knew his way through the Black Mountains and past some of the recent rockslides the locals in Valis warned her of. She had not hired him to lecture her.

He shook his head. "Once, mayhap, as a young man. I think he'd disapprove o' his only daughter takin' up this foolish idea of breaking the curse in his stead. I only agreed to take ye here to this gods-damned place because I knew no one else would, and ye'd come anyhow on yer own. Ye're just as damned stubborn as he was, and it's like to get ye killed."

Aeryn smiled slightly at the backhanded compliment. She pushed her cloak aside so that she could untie a pouch attached to her belt and nudged her red-brown stallion closer to him. "As agreed, the rest of your payment. Thank you for your help. May you have safe passage back."

The drover took the coins and said, "Don' thank me. It jus' makes leavin' ye here all the harder." Phineas looked sidelong at the rest of the valley. "I don't expect ye to make it out o' here alive, honest. Even if ye manage to set foot in those caverns, ye'll be dead like all the rest 'fore you. Likely, I won' get to spend this 'fore bad happens to me, as well."

"Believe what you wish. I put no stock in superstition."

"That's what they all say, whens they come here lookin' to test that curse." Phineas looked down at her horse. "Ye leavin' the stallion? I can take it back with me to Valis, if ye'd like."

She shook her head. "No, thank you. Fare thee well, Phineas." She tried to move their farewell along. She wanted to be on her way, for good or ill.

"I'll have a drink to the memory of yer father and ye tonight, Aeryn, if I live so long. Luck be with ye." The old drover kicked his horse into a gallop back toward the path up the mountainside.

Aeryn watched him retreat for a moment and then turned her attention to the wide, windswept valley surrounding her, a vague sense of anxiety prickling in her stomach. The Valley of Death seemed a much better name to her now that she was looking at the place once known as Night Valley. The long-ago massacre, and all the mysterious deaths that followed, were not the only reasons for the renaming, she suspected. Most plant life, with the exception of some scrubby bushes and short, tortured-looking trees, seemed unwilling to grow in the valley.

She frowned as she surveyed the valley, looking for a suitable place to leave Rowan. This was the only thing she had been unable to plan ahead of time. She decided that leaving him near one of the trees was best, and she turned him in the direction of the tree closest to the entrance to the caverns. He walked slowly, as though he, like the drover, felt anxious just being in the valley. This uncharacteristic behavior had started the moment they left Valis the day before, and she wondered what had gotten into him. His strange mood did little to reassure her that her quest would end any differently than those of the adventurers and treasure hunters who came before her seeking to break the curse on the Black Caverns and unlock its secrets.

Aeryn pulled Rowan to a halt next to one of the low trees and dismounted. She draped his reins over a branch of the tree, not needing to tie him to it, and then opened her saddlebags. She removed an apple, a heavy blanket, and a short length of rope. She draped the blanket over the stallion to shield him from as much of the rain as possible and loosely secured the blanket with the rope so that it did not blow away. Rowan whickered at Aeryn, and she offered him the apple. He neatly bit it in half.

She smiled and patted his rain-dampened neck. She told him, "I'm sorry to leave you in such an inhospitable place, my friend. Father likely would've scolded me for doing so, but I'm afraid I have no choice in the matter. I cannot risk something happening to you in the caverns if my plan doesn't work. I couldn't forgive myself for that."

Aeryn offered the rest of the apple to Rowan, and he devoured it. She stroked his head one last time and then said, "If the weather worsens, or I don't return before sundown, get yourself out of here. Find your way to someplace better."

The horse nudged her shoulder with his head, and Aeryn could not help but feel he understood her. Rowan was her father's horse before he became hers, and her father always said Rowan was smarter than some humans. Aeryn did not disagree. She knew he could get his own reins loose if he needed to, so she tried not to worry about him.

Aeryn untied a leather pack that hung to the side of her saddlebags and slung it over her shoulder, next to the pair of sword sheaths on her back. She turned away and trekked up the side of Nightstone Peak. Rowan neighed behind her, but she kept walking without looking back.

She picked out her destination on the mountainside without any trouble. The entrance to the caverns was not well-hidden. Her pulse quickened the closer she came to the boulder that served as the Black Caverns' door. She felt the weight of all those who died in the valley and in the caverns before her and it slowed her steps.

When she stopped in front of the boulder, Aeryn gently bit her lower lip. Try as she might to relax, her stomach tightened. She reached under the clasp of her cloak to draw out a small amulet with a ruby at its center, hanging from a sturdy silver chain. The elf from whom she got the amulet simply called it "the key." The amulet came at a high cost, and she hoped it was worth the price she paid. Trion admitted it might not work for her, since it was created for his son alone, and there was a chance the amulet would reject her. If so, she would not know until it was too late to turn back. Tynan's curse on the caverns remained strong more than a century after its inception.

Aeryn stared at the closed entrance of the caverns, hesitant still to test her fate. The wind gusted behind her and blew more rain at her and strands of long hair into her eyes. She shook off her fear. She smoothed her hair back from her eyes and stepped forward to lay her hand on the boulder. She read the inscription on the back of the amulet aloud and then offered a silent prayer to Morghell, protector of the dead, that the curse did not immediately strike her down for what she had come to do.

2

Reaching under the clasp of her cloak, Aeryn drew out a small amulet with a ruby at its center, hanging from a sturdy silver chain. The elf from whom she got the amulet simply called it "the key". The amulet came at a high cost, and she hoped it was worth the price she paid. Trion admitted it might not work for her, since it was created for his son alone, and there was a chance the amulet would reject her. If so, she would not know until it was too late to turn back. Tynan's curse on the caverns remained strong more than a century after its inception.

Aeryn stared at the closed entrance of the caverns, hesitant still to test her fate. The wind gusted behind her and blew more rain at her and strands of long hair into her eyes. She shook off her fear. She smoothed her hair back from her eyes and stepped forward to lay her hand on the boulder. She read the inscription on the back of the amulet aloud and then offered a silent prayer to Morghell, protector of the dead.

A deep rumble heralded the opening of the entrance, and the boulder rolled back into a recess inside the caverns. Its absence revealed a black hole. No light penetrated the caverns. Again, Aeryn hesitated. Many before her had reached this point—an intonation to open the caverns' entrance, different from the one on the back of the amulet, was common knowledge among adventurers. However, of those who went in, none came back out.

Aeryn closed her eyes and stepped into the darkness of the caverns. Solid ground met her boots. She opened her eyes again and found herself looking down a corridor lit by torches. She took another step forward. Nothing stopped her, and no pit opened below her. Aeryn allowed herself a moment of relief. Behind her, the boulder rumbled back into place and sealed the exit with a sharp crack of stone on stone.

The sound echoed down the corridor in front of her.

With the daylight behind her cut off, Aeryn could see better by the light of the torches. Their flames burned low, as though they were somehow aware their master had passed on long ago, and this saddened them. The sepulchral silence inside was broken only by the sound of her breathing and the occasional drip of water from somewhere in the caverns.

She slipped the small pack off her shoulder and laid it again the wall. The caverns were much warmer than she expected, so she removed her cloak as well. She readjusted her shoulder plates and the pair of sword sheaths that hung on a baldric of woven leather from her right shoulder down to her left hip in the style common to warriors in the Northlands. Only one of the sheaths contained a sword. Just below her blue tunic, a dagger rested against each thigh.

Aeryn set her cloak next to the leather pack in the hopes it might dry, and then knelt down to rummage through the pack. She moved aside a lantern and a vial of oil, neither of which she now needed. Her fingers brushed against the roll of sheepskin parchment, which she extracted, and then located the stick of drawing charcoal. Getting lost in the Black Caverns' labyrinth was the last thing she wanted.

A familiar whisper tickled at her mind, but she shoved it aside, unrolling the sheepskin. Using the charcoal, Aeryn started her map with a sketch of the entry chamber. Then, she rolled the sheepskin and tucked it and the charcoal away. Before she rose to her feet, she also took a small coil of rope from her pack, in case she found a fork in the caverns. Aeryn threw the rope over her left shoulder and started down the corridor that led away from the entrance at a gentle, downward slope. She counted her paces while she walked; she wanted an exact map.

Aeryn noticed neither the small pool of water forming behind her nor the smaller cloak that appeared out of thin air and dropped down next to her own cloak. Small, wet boot prints followed after the sell-sword at a safe distance. The boot prints became less and less wet the farther they went, until they were hardly visible at all.

3

Aeryn continued down the corridor, intrigued by the handiwork of the caverns' creator. Farther down the corridor, Aeryn caught sight of a blue glow. As she drew closer, she realized the glow came from blue runes carved into the obsidian walls in sporadic groups, which slowly turned into organized lines. Though not a magik user herself, Aeryn recognized the runes as wards of some kind from protection wards she had seen in other places. The rune lines continued on, unbroken, when the corridor ended at a three-way junction. Aeryn paused, considering each of the three options.

Her destination lay somewhere in the center of the cavern, but neither of the passages facing her now went straight—one branched off to the left, the other to the right. Her hand rose, and she fingered the thin white scar over her left eye. The scar split her eyebrow in two. After a moment, her hand dropped again, and she chose to go right. She marked this on her map, but did not lay down her rope. This, she reserved in case the path became more complicated.

The runes followed her into a passage lined on either side by wooden doors. Each one was massive in height, and she wondered how they got to the caverns. According to the legend, the adventurer Tynan Selvantyr created the caverns on his own, without the aid of other people. Aeryn supposed he might have used his fabled magik abilities to transport the doors there, fourteen of them altogether. She admired the workmanship of the intricate carvings that decorated each one. Each door's carvings depicted a different scene: a war, a hunt of some kind, the creation of a god whose artifacts she did not recognize. Looking closer at this last scene, she realized that the carving of the god's head bore scratches and scars, as if someone tried to obliterate it from the wooden door. Aeryn stepped back and wondered what lay beyond this particular door. She decided it was best not to find out.

Each of the scenes depicted on the doors from that point forward became darker and darker. One of the scenes showed a religious sacrifice, though she could not tell what the sacrifice was—a small animal or a child? Aeryn shuddered, a sense of deep discomfort washing over her. She wondered why these doors were here and what story they were meant to tell. She thought back to the stories her father told her and the stories she read about Tynan on her own, and could think of nothing in Tynan's history that these scenes might depict. The lack of an explanation for these scenes caused a small knot of apprehension to form in her stomach. She decided it was best to move on.

She picked up her pace until she reached a large, circular chamber at the end of the hall of doors. The contents of the room reflected the torchlight a thousand times over. Open chests arranged around the room overflowed with gold and silver coins and jewels of all colors. Coins covered the floor in miniature gold mountains.

Aeryn walked to the middle of the room and turned around slowly to take everything in, amazed at the wealth contained in this one room. Her spine tightened a moment later when she heard someone gasp behind her.

4

Aeryn spun in the direction from which the sound originated, drawing her sword in the same motion. Coins slid and scrapped underfoot. She ignored them.

"Show yourself," she commanded to whomever she had heard.

The gasp had been the briefest of sounds, just loud enough for her to hear, but Aeryn knew she had. The sound caused the hairs on the back of her neck to stand at attention. She studied the room with steely eyes, body still and sword at the ready. She waited for any betraying movement from her unseen watcher that she could pounce on.

Time stretched on, but no one appeared. With reluctance, Aeryn admitted to herself that she might have imagined the sound, although the lasting tingle on the back of her neck told her otherwise. She resheathed her sword anyhow, knowing she had no choice but to move on and wait for her watcher to make themselves known in their own time. She exited the room through the door opposite the one she had entered. Her sword hand remained near her dagger hilt.

The new passageway had no doors, but other passages and open chambers branched off from it. Aeryn focused on her destination and her map, marking each new room and corridor on her map as she came to them. She stayed alert for additional sounds that might give away her watcher.

Her boots, though thick-soled, were broken in well enough they made little noise on the stone floors of the caverns. Her long strides carried her past libraries filled with tomes among which she knew her father would have loved to have gotten lost. Though he chose the life of a soldier, he appreciated the value of knowledge as much as a good sword arm and spent every evening reading one of a handful of books he carried with him. Seeing the vast rows of bookshelves made her feel his absence once again.

Aeryn continued on, since the books were not her purposed for being there. As she walked, she wondered how many of the books Tynan wrote himself. A few of his journals were available in the library at Valis, and his entries chronicling his own and his company's adventures displayed an impressive attention to detail and a bent toward long, flowery prose. Aeryn guessed by his accounts that he felt no one could tell his story quite as well as he could.

After reaching the end of yet another passageway, Aeryn began to wonder whether she had taken a wrong turn and missed the passage that would lead her to the center of the caverns—the most likely place to find Tynan's remains. She stopped and unrolled her map. She examined it to look for where she might have gone down the wrong path.

A scream of definite human origin tore through the passage, and Aeryn froze. The sound came to her from one of the passages behind her. She crammed her map in her belt and again drew her sword. She jogged down the passage in the direction of the scream, looking into one room after another. A second cry accosted her ears, this time a distinct cry for help. This cry gave Aeryn a better sense of where it was coming from, and she picked up her pace.

She passed a room with pieces of antique weaponry hanging upon the walls and then stopped and turned back. A young girl hung from the ceiling, bound from neck to knee in white, ropy webbing. A black spider the size of a bear cub crept toward her. It emitted a hissing sound as it advanced on the girl. The girl writhed in an effort to free herself, but the webbing held her fast.

Aeryn ran between the girl and the spider, her longsword gripped in both hands. The spider skittered a few paces backward and studied her with its eight black eyes. Its mandibles snapped while it decided what to do with her. Aeryn thrust her sword at it to help it make up its mind. The spider reared up on its hind legs.

Behind Aeryn, the girl shrieked, "Look out!"

The spider spit a blob of webbing at Aeryn. She dove aside to avoid it. The blob of sticky material flew past her and hit the girl. When Aeryn hit the floor with a clatter, she switched her sword to her left hand and flicked one of her slim daggers with her right. The dagger flew true and hit its mark. The spider squealed in pain. Green slime bubbled up around the dagger blade buried in the spider's back.

Aeryn rolled to her feet as the beast lunged and snapped at her. Aeryn knocked it back with the flat of her sword. She thrust her longsword at the spider again, striking its body. Slime bubbled out of the wound again, this time spattering Aeryn's arms. The spider made a screaming sound. It scuttled forward in a rage.

Aeryn's boots slid on the slime that coated the floor as she backed away from the advancing spider. She skidded and cursed while she fought to stay upright in the face of the charging beast. She brought her sword's blade up again and intercepted the spider's mandibles, which snapped around it. Her muscles strained to keep the spider at arm's length. When her boots gripped dry ground again, Aeryn shoved the spider back, swung her sword, and brought it down on the spider's head, cleaving it in half. The spider fell. Its legs twitched once before it stilled completely.

"Gods be damned," Aeryn muttered. "I hate spiders."

5

The viscid slime that had sprayed her bare arms remained stuck there, though Aeryn shook both her arms in an attempt to get it to come off. She looked around the room for something to wipe the goo off with, but the only thing her gaze landed on that was not metal was an ornate, woven leather sword belt, similar to her own. Without anything else suitable at her disposal, she went over to the sword belt, flipped it to its back, and used the braided leather to scrape the bits of slime off. When she finished, Aeryn turned the sword belt right side out again, though there was no one around to care, and turned her attention back to the dead spider. She retrieved her dagger from the spider's side and cleaned it off on her leather leggings, just above the top of her boot. She did the same with her sword before she resheathed it.

The girl hanging from the ceiling cleared her throat, reminding Aeryn that she was still stuck in the spider's webbing. Aeryn turned and looked at the girl, studying her for a moment before she walked over and removed the webbing that had conveniently landed on the girl's mouth.

The moment Aeryn removed the webbing, the girl started talking. "Help me down already? I think my head might pop if I hang here much longer."

Aeryn crossed her arms over her chest. "You've been following me."

Defiance planted itself on the girl's face. "How do you know? Wouldn't you have seen me if I was?"

"Perhaps."

The girl raised an eyebrow. "Maybe I've been here all along. I could be a nymph. If you get me down, I'll grant you three wishes."

Aeryn guessed the girl to be no more than ten years of age, and her hair and face could use a good wash. She wondered how the girl got into the Black Caverns on her own, and why she was there. Then, something on the floor caught her attention.

"Nymphs don't grant wishes, djinn do," Aeryn muttered.

She picked up the object that had caught her attention and held it up. "I'll hazard a guess and say this had something to do with your little invisibility act."

The girl's hazel eyes shifted to look at the torn leather bracelet in Aeryn's hand. "What is it?"

One of Aeryn's eyebrows rose. She admired the girl's pluck. Telling lies seemed second nature to her. The silence between them stretched on, and Aeryn grew impatient for the girl to drop the act. She turned away.

"Wait," the girl called after her. "Alright, yeah, I followed you. Don't just leave me here, *please.*"

Aeryn turned back. She knew she could not leave the girl on her own. She sighed and pulled her sword loose from its sheath again; she sliced through the webbing holding the girl. It broke with a crack, setting the girl loose to crash to the stone floor.

"Don't try to catch me or anything." The girl glared up at Aeryn.

Aeryn knelt down and cut the rest of the girl's bonds. She looked the reed-thin girl in the eye when she got up and asked her, "What do you suggest I do with you?"

A smile full of charm fell into place on the girl's face. "I'll just come with you."

Aeryn asked her, "Am I apt to end up with a knife in the back if you do?"

The girl frowned. "Where am I going to go? I've already gotten lost once, and you saved my hide. I'd call it rude to stab you after that."

Whether she wanted one or not, Aeryn now had someone else to look after. "Alright. But don't get underfoot, don't stray, and don't get into any more trouble. Understand?"

Nodding, the girl dusted off the oversize flax shirt and wool pants she wore.

"What is your name?" Aeryn inquired.

"Theo."

"Do you have a family name?"

The look of insolence returned. "What does that matter to you?"

Aeryn rolled her eyes. "I am Aeryn Ravane."

"Nice to meet you, I suppose. Where to now? I don't much like this place anymore."

Aeryn could not argue with her. Her enthusiasm over having successfully breached the caverns without being felled by the curse was also starting to wane. "Let us not get ahead of ourselves. How did you get here?"

Theo sighed. "I'm from Valis. I stole the bracelet out of some guy's shop in Middle City a while back. I was playing around with it, and I heard you in one of the local taverns asking around for someone to guide you through the Black Mountains and the Valley of Death. I figured you were another one of those adventurers trying to get into the caverns. Everyone knows the caverns are filled with gold, so I hitched a ride with a caravan that passed near the valley and hiked the rest of the way."

Aeryn felt like this was only half the girl's story, but for now, she let it go. She asked, "You did not fear the curse?"

Theo shrugged. "I thought the curse couldn't get what it couldn't see. But then, that spider somehow saw through the illusion, and the bracelet broke when it attacked me. I don't even know where that thing came from. You'd think I'd have heard it or something."

Aeryn nodded. She wondered if the girl was telling the truth, but her story seemed as logical an explanation of what she was doing in the caverns as any. Greed drove many to brave Tynan's curse. "Alright then, let us go on."

She turned out of the room and headed back in the direction of the passage she had been in when she heard the girl scream. While they walked, she asked Theo, "How did you plan to get back to Valis again?"

"What makes you think I want to go back?" was the girl's reply. "Anyways, I figured if the curse got you, I'd just take your horse wherever I wanted to go."

At least the girl was honest, Aeryn told herself. They passed the point she had reached in the passageway the first time. A dancing golden light filled the end of the passage, coming from something in the next room. A strange sensation washed over Aeryn at the same moment she heard Theo exclaim in wonder behind her. Something in the room beyond made Aeryn want to turn back and yet also drew her in.

6

The end of the passageway opened into a large, irregular-shaped room with a vaulted ceiling; it burned with the light of hundreds of golden runes carved into the walls and ceiling. Off to the side stood a stone altar to Wersal, the god of benevolent magik, also decorated with the golden runes. Another archway on the opposite end of the room led out of the chamber, but Aeryn stopped just outside the chamber, staring into it.

A section of dull rock on the opposite side of the room from the altar drew her attention. That section of wall was straight, whereas all of the other walls in the chamber were curved. The texture of the rock looked nothing like the graceful, satiny obsidian throughout the rest of the caverns. It seemed to suck in the golden light of the runes and kill it. It looked dead. It drew Aeryn into the chamber, toward it, even as her sense of unease increased the closer she got to the dead stone.

"This place is creepy," Theo whispered behind her.

Aeryn barely heard her, her attention was so consumed by the wall. Additional runes, larger and in a different style than the others, covered the dead rock but did not glow as bright. Aeryn felt an almost imperceptible hum being emitted by something in the rock. The subtle throb hurt her head. Her hand rose and touched the wall. The moment her skin touched the stone, the runes shifted like snakes on the surface of the wall, and a death-like cold seeped into her outstretched hand and crawled its way up her arm.

In her head, Aeryn heard her father's voice. *"Where were you?"*

Aeryn cursed aloud and yanked her hand away from whatever force pulled her to the dead rock. She staggered back several steps and turned away, holding her hand close to her. She closed her eyes, massaging the cold out of her hand with the warmer one.

Theo went to Aeryn, her eyes wide and anxious. "What happened?"

Aeryn turned and looked back at the strange wall. The runes were back in their original places, causing her to wonder if she imagined that they moved. She replied, "I do not know."

And she decided she did not want to know. Aeryn shuddered, thinking of her father's voice coming to her as clear as if he stood beside her. She turned her back on the wall and crossed to the altar at the other end of the chamber.

"I felt . . . something. I do not know what it was."

Behind her, the girl said, "I think we should get out of here."

Aeryn nodded. She had never been the religious type, but she said a brief prayer to the god all the same before she turned away from the altar. There was no reason to tempt any gods to look upon them in disfavor because of a sign of disrespect, Aeryn told herself. When she turned back to look at Theo, the girl was chewing on an end of the cord that laced the collar of her shirt.

The girl let the damp cord drop and set her mouth in a frown. She repeated, "Something feels wrong in here. We should go."

Aeryn agreed, but glanced back at the wall of dull, black stone once more before she turned toward the doorway that led out of the strange chamber. She beckoned for the girl to follow, though she did not need to; the girl was close on her heels.

7

Theo could still feel the presence of the eerie golden-runed room, though they were far from it now. Ever since the sell-sword touched that strange wall, she swore it felt as though something followed them, dogging their steps. She shuddered at the idea. Theo, for her part, wished she had never come to this place, but she had no choice in the matter, she had to come.

To distract herself, Theo did what she did best—she started talking. "Where are we going anyhow?"

Aeryn stopped. An intersection of four passages faced them: the one that had just ended and three others. Theo knew what came next even before Aeryn unrolled her sheepskin map. Each time they reached a new passage, the sell-sword stopped to make notations on her map. She was obsessive about it. This time was not different. The sell-sword sketched out the passage just finished, made additional notations, and then drew the intersection. Theo stifled a yawn.

The woman mumbled while she made her notations, "The center of the labyrinth."

"Why?"

"I am looking for something," Aeryn said. She rolled the map and tucked it into her belt again.

She already knew what Aeryn sought, but she asked, "What? Treasure?"

The sell-sword shot her an annoyed look. "I am no treasure-hunter or adventurer."

"Then why come here?"

Aeryn started walking again, choosing the center path, as she had at every other intersection. Aeryn seemed to be trying to go in a straight line. This passage, however, started curving to the right not far along, and no doors or doorways lined it, nor were there passages that branched off from it. Aeryn slowed her pace, to Theo's relief. Her legs could use the rest. The sell-sword's legs were much longer.

A door appeared farther down the passage. When she passed it, Theo wondered what could possibly be behind it. It appeared to be made of iron, rusted over now. No holes or decoration marred its flat surface. It had nothing on it other than a handle and a padlock the size of her head. She crossed behind Aeryn to the sell-sword's other side, keeping the sell-sword between her and the iron door.

Theo asked Aeryn again, "Why did you come here?"

Aeryn sighed. "My father wanted to break the curse."

"Was he an adventurer?"

"No. He was a soldier, but he loved Tynan's legend, and he considered the curse to be an interesting puzzle to defeat. He enjoyed puzzles."

Theo considered this. She supposed it was a good puzzle. Most people just wanted the gold. "Who was Tynan anyhow? I know he died a long time ago . . ."

The sell-sword nodded. "Nearly a century and a half ago. Tynan Darius Selvantyr, adventuring great. At least for his time."

"What made him so great?"

Aeryn shrugged. "According to the journals I found and my father's stories, Tynan and his adventuring company, the Seven, were very successful. As you've seen, he amassed great amounts of wealth and knowledge. I suppose that is the definition of success, if ever there was one.

"I couldn't say what captured my father's imagination about the old stories of Tynan's adventures. Maybe it was just how he died, ambushed by his greatest nemesis, the Order, but breaking free from them so that he could reach the caverns and leave a curse to guard them in his stead."

Theo commented, "He must have really loved his gold and books."

Aeryn made a noise and nodded. "Legend says, on the day Tynan died, although he was pursued by more than thirty men, he escaped into the caverns and locked them out. Then, a great storm appeared out of a blue sky, and the heavens turned black. Lightning and brimstone bore down on them. Only one man, a coward who hid under the bodies of fallen mates, escaped the slaughter. This man made it out of the valley and back to Valis on foot, but when he got home, his hair and beard had gone white. He told of what he saw in the valley and then died that very night. No one knows what killed him."

The sell-sword made a fair storyteller, Theo decided. The tale gave her the chills.

Aeryn stopped short and frowned at the path in from of them. Now, three corridors faced them, but the one across from them was caved in. No more going in a straight line. The sell-sword annotated her map and then turned to the left-most passage.

Theo looked up at the ceiling, wondering if the obsidian rock was likely to come tumbling down on them. In studying the ceiling, she noticed that some of the runes did not glow, like they had burnt out, as a torch might. Plenty of torches continued lighting their way, but Theo wondered what might cause a rune to burn out.

Theo asked, "So, if the curse is so terrible, how is it we aren't dead? And where are the bones of the others who've made it into the caverns? I've heard some have, but they never returned."

"Strange, I know," Aeryn agreed. "It's like the caverns swallowed them whole."

Theo's eyes grew wide. When she looked over at the sell-sword, however, the woman looked back at her with a half-smile on her face.

"Funny," Theo said and glared in return.

Theo decided she would find some way to get back at Aeryn for trying to scare her like that. Then, they entered the mural room, and all such thoughts vanished from her head.

Like the hall of doors carved with frightening scenes that Theo saw while still following the sell-sword, the mural room held a series of painted murals on each wall depicting scenes even darker than those on the doors. The first mural showed piles of corpses of peasants and soldiers alike strewn across a red field. A robed figure stood alone at the center of the carnage, a sky full of black thunderheads above him. She could tell the figure was male but not what he looked like—dozens of scratch marks obscured his face, all but his eyes. They stared out at her with twisted glee.

"What is this place?" Theo whispered.

At first, Aeryn said nothing, but then she replied, "Let us keep moving."

Theo nodded and turned away from the mural. Something tugged at her, daring her to look back again, but she resisted. She kept her eyes on the sell-sword's back and followed her out of the room. She felt no desire to see what was on any of the other murals.

She remained silent for a time while she walked next to the sell-sword, still feeling the same strange presence following them. She wondered what the dead adventurer was doing in these caverns when he lived. Theo considered asking the sell-sword her opinion, but then a silver light coming through the open doorway next to her caught her attention.

Forgetting the sell-sword's warning that she needed to stay close to her, Theo slowed to a halt and went to the door to see where the light came from. She discovered five small pools filled with what looked like mercury, set into a stone platform. Theo wondered what they were and ran into the room to investigate further. The moment she crossed the room's threshold, however, a deep rumble came from somewhere below the stone floor.

Theo froze in the inane hope this would help her. Her feet

disobeyed her when she told them to take her back out of the room. She glanced down at them and saw tiny fractures appearing under her boots.

8

Aeryn grabbed her shoulders and yanked her out of the room and back into the passageway. She fell back against the sell-sword, panting. The rumble ceased and the floor stayed in one piece.

"I told you not to stray, did I not?" Aeryn admonished her.

Theo bent over, trying to catch her breath. "Excuse me for being curious."

"Curiosity might be the death of you in this place," Aeryn said.

"What was that anyhow?"

"A trap, likely. Come, let us keep going." Aeryn looked down and nodded in the direction they had been walking.

"What do you think those pools are?"

Aeryn shrugged. "Scrying pools, perhaps. Tynan was a magik user. It seems like something he might have made use of."

Theo nodded and followed after the sell-sword again. That made sense to her, though she had no experience with any such thing. Her exposure to magik was limited to an item here and there she filched from other people, like the bracelet. Her brother Brien knew more about such things than she did.

"Do you think what happened back there was the curse?" she asked Aeryn.

"Perhaps." The sell-sword did not look at her. She seemed distracted by something else.

"Why didn't it kill us?"

Aeryn glanced over at her. "Perhaps it is this." She waved a small ruby amulet hanging around her neck at Theo. It looked valuable.

"What is it?"

"A protection amulet of some kind. I was told Tynan had it

created for his best friend, Rimen, so that the traps he laid to protect the caverns from marauders did not harm him. I do not know how it works, but it seems to have gotten us past the traps and the curse alike. I've no need to look further than that. Just heed my instructions to stay close by."

Theo found herself no longer bored; she thought about how much that amulet might be worth. "Does the amulet work for anyone who wears it?"

"Not likely."

The gold coins stacking up in Theo's head shattered.

"Frankly, I'm surprised that it has worked for me."

"How did you get it?"

Aeryn frowned and said, "It's a long story." She said nothing more about the amulet.

They walked in silence for a time and then a faint sound reached her ears from up ahead. At first, she thought she might have imagined it, but it grew more distinct. "Do you hear that?" she asked Aeryn.

Aeryn said, "Wind perhaps."

Theo frowned. Was there another opening into the caverns no one knew about?

The passageway snaked to the right and then again to the left. A separate glow from that given off by the blue runes emanated from farther down the corridor. A breeze soon accompanied the sound of wind. When the corridor branched off, it split right and left, with each branch passage curving away from them.

Directly across from them was a silent blue waterfall, originating from somewhere above a stone archway dozens of feet high. The translucent water flowed over it like a curtain. Both of them approached the archway, and Theo saw a yawning chasm beyond the waterfall. The wind came from there.

Aeryn touched the sparkling blue water. Her hand passed right through it without breaking the stream. "It's an illusion," she said.

Theo put her hand into the illusion as well. It turned her hand brilliant blue as it passed through the middle and out. On the other side of the waterfall, there sat a wide ridge of stone. Aeryn stepped through the illusion and down onto the ridge. Theo's heart leapt into her throat but she gingerly stepped out onto the ledge next to Aeryn. In spots, the ridge had crumbled away, and Theo was unwilling to move any closer to the chasm. She did not want to look over the edge; she hated heights.

Instead, Theo looked across the chasm and saw two other archways on either side, identical from the one behind them. The arches appeared to stand at cardinal points. She guessed there was a fourth, but a cream-colored stone tower atop an obsidian column that rose from the center of the chasm blocked the view across the divide. The light stone of the tower gleamed amid the obsidian of the rest of the caverns. An entry point into the tower faced them across the chasm.

"What is that?" Theo asked.

Aeryn responded, "The tower—Tynan's favorite place in the caverns. This is what I searched for."

The sell-sword stepped off the ridge, onto a wide stone bridge leading from where they stood to the tower beyond. Theo's heart leapt into her throat. A section of the bridge was missing from the middle, and only one of the bridge's ornate iron railings, elven in design, still clung to the side of the bridge. When Aeryn laid a hand on the railing, it let out a long, aged moan and broke away from its rusted fittings, tumbling into the black chasm below.

Theo started backward. *"Kellen above,"* she cursed, invoking the god of thieves.

Aeryn shrugged and looked back at her. "It was over a century old."

"How are we going to get across with that gap in the middle?" Theo asked.

Aeryn did not reply. She walked to the middle of the bridge without waiting for Theo. Muttering more curses, Theo stepped out onto the bridge as well, putting one foot in front of the other with great effort.

26

The sell-sword was crazy, she told herself. She kept imagining the bridge groaning under their combined weight, but it held.

Aeryn paused in front of the gap in the middle and then—to Theo's horror—she hopped over it. "Only a foot or so is missing," she called over her shoulder.

"Only a foot or so. Right," Theo muttered.

She tried to keep moving but made the mistake of looking down into the chasm. It looked huge to her, and she only had an ancient bridge between her and certain death. When a gust of air touched her face, Theo fell to her hands and knees and crawled the rest of the way to the gap. At the gap's edge, Theo stopped altogether. She heard Aeryn sigh on the other side, but she could not go further.

Theo was unsure what she was going to do next, since staying where she was did not seem like a good option. She closed her eyes. She felt like she could not breathe. Something slapped her hand. Cracking open her eyes, she saw it was the end of a length of rope.

"Tie it around your middle. If you fall, I will pull you up," Aeryn told her.

"Or we'll both be pulled over," Theo called back.

"At least you won't die alone," was the sell-sword's response. Theo was unsure whether this was meant to be comforting.

"Easy for her to say, she's standing on the other side," Theo muttered to herself. Taking the rope in hand, she slipped it around her waist and knotted it, but she still did not move from where she was.

Finally, Aeryn called, "I think you're too far from the amulet's influence. I hear the bridge cracking."

Damn that amulet. Theo whimpered and got to her feet again. She took a deep breath and leaped across the gap in the bridge. To her amazement, she landed safely on the other side, and almost ran into the sell-sword. Aeryn caught her first.

"Is it still cracking?" Theo asked, turning back to look at the other half of the bridge. It looked fine to her.

"It wasn't cracking. I just wanted you to hurry up. Come on," Aeryn said.

Theo stared after the sell-sword, incredulous. Then, she loosened the rope from around her waist and followed Aeryn into the tower. She hoped there was a better way out of the tower than the way in. The inside of the tower was the same cream-colored stone. On closer inspection, Theo found flecks of what looked like diamonds in the stone. The flecks reflected the light from the torches on the walls and the chandelier hanging from the vaulted ceiling. Off to one side was a neatly arranged sitting area and a spiral staircase that disappeared into the ceiling. Chips of rock lay scattered across the floor and furniture. Next to the staircase, a skeleton lay sprawled alongside a sword stuck, point first, into a slotted stone.

Theo assumed this was Tynan's skeleton, well-preserved for being a century and a half old. She felt a little bad for him, looking at these unburied remains. "Should we say something?" she asked Aeryn.

Aeryn tilted her head to the side and stared at the remains. "I do not know what to say, other than I am honored to have made it so far."

The sell-sword walked toward the remains. But rather than reaching out to touch the skeleton, Aeryn's fingers brushed the pommel of the sword. The sword also held Theo's attention. She had found it.

She went to stand next to the sell-sword, wondering if the sword was heavy enough to keep her from escaping with it before the sell-sword could catch her. The blade gleamed as if just polished, as did the pommel, the multi-faceted onyx set into the pommel, and the crossguard. The leather-wrapped grip showed no cracks. A series of seven runes were lined up on the tang of the double-edged blade and bore no signs of dust or age.

Before she could make up her mind, a movement behind the sell-sword caught her eye. She looked to see what it was and then her mouth dropped open with disbelief. She gasped, prompting Aeryn to look behind her too.

28

"What is it?" she asked as she turned—and then visibly stiffened. The person behind them spoke. "As you should be honored. Welcome."

9

Aeryn almost dropped her sword. Not more than ten feet from them stood a man dressed in red silk and dark suede—and yet, he was also not a man. The wall behind him was visible *through* him.

The ghost's sky-blue eyes registered his amusement. His gaze fell on the amulet Aeryn wore. "I see you found the key to safe passage through my home. It feels like both a short time and a long time indeed since I last saw Rimen wearing the amulet you wear," he said.

When neither Aeryn nor Theo spoke, the ghost's brow furrowed. He tried again. "You do know who I am, do you not?"

Aeryn blinked and found her voice. "Yes, sir. One hundred and fifty years have passed since your death."

The ghost sighed and folded his hands behind him. "Has it been so long? Yet, here I remain. Imagine my surprise when I woke to find myself separated from my corporeal form.

"I have had quite a long time to think upon this problem, and I believe the curse I set in motion may have also proved my downfall. You see, I wanted the Black Caverns sealed and protected—I could not bear the thought of my home and my possessions laid bare for any half-wit marauder. I went to quite a lot of effort to amass all that you see within my caverns. Somehow, my soul was sealed and bound here as well."

Theo snorted. "You got stuck, because you wanted to keep thieves out of your stuff? Good work."

"Quiet," Aeryn hissed and glared at the girl.

The ghost offered them a sad smile and held up a hand. "I suppose I deserve that. However, I am satisfied that the amulet has accepted you as worthy to walk freely in my caverns. Tell me—how did the amulet come to be in your possession?"

"Trion Orinthwend."

One of Tynan's eyebrows rose. "By the gods. He still lives? Ah, well, elves are long-lived, but I thought for sure the hatred he harbored toward me after Rimen's death would have killed him long ago. It was not my fault, of course, but as they say, parents were not meant to outlive their children. I might be surprised that he took the amulet off his own son's body before his burial pyre, but then, perhaps he had plans for the amulet at one time. How did you find him?"

"Your journals," Aeryn replied. "I knew Rimen was your best friend, and he stayed in the caverns with you from time to time. I thought there might be a secret that Rimen knew about the caverns, so I traveled to Alethia to find out if any of Rimen's family still lived, and I found Trion."

Tynan nodded and did not ask more questions about the amulet, to her relief. "What prompted you to come here, if you do not mind my asking? Have you come seeking a little adventure, a little treasure?"

Aeryn realized he wanted to know if she was the very type of person he tried to keep out of his caverns with his curse. She told him, "My father, sir. He was intrigued by the stories about you and about the curse. He died a year ago, so I decided to break the curse in his honor, as he once wanted to do."

Tynan paused, and for a moment, Aeryn wondered if he believed her. Then he said, "Ah, he was an adventurer like me. I might have done the same, were I in his shoes. You have honored him well, I think."

"He was a soldier by trade, but no less a seeker of adventure, sir."

"Please, address me as just Tynan. Where are my own manners? Clearly, I am too unused to having guests in my caverns. What may I call each of you?"

"I am Aeryn Ravane, and this is Theo."

"Well met, both of you," he said, and then his gaze lit on his sword. "Since you mention your father was a soldier, my sword would

31

have been a nice prize in his eyes, do you not think so? I noticed your interest in Aric earlier. You went right to it. You have taken no other items in my caverns. A lesser person's back would be bent with all the gold they might carry from my vaults, but that does not seem to be your goal. Have you come here for something else perhaps?"

Aeryn hesitated only a moment. She saw no point in lying to a dead man. "I came for Aric."

"Why?"

"You're right that it would have been a nice prize in my father's eyes. I thought that finding the sword might be a fitting tribute to him. He was a brave man."

Tynan nodded. "You clearly loved your father very much to risk your life to come here for nothing more than my sword. It is a fine sword, of course, given to me by the dwarven god of forging."

Theo interjected, "It's a great sword. Got it. Will you give it to her or not? Too much has happened in this place, and I want to be gone from here."

A frown crossed Tynan's face. "To what do you refer?"

"There's those creepy doors and murals, and something happened to Aeryn in that creepy gold altar room."

For the first time, Tynan's pompous attitude fell away. He asked Aeryn, "Did you touch anything in there?"

His tone startled her. "I was drawn to the wall of rock across from the altar. I touched it, yes."

"You must leave," Tynan told her. "I will see you safely over the chasm again."

The shift in his behavior piqued her suspicion. "Why must we leave?"

For a moment, Aeryn thought she saw fear register in Tynan's eyes. "Please do not ask me to explain. Trust me that you must leave as soon as possible for your own safety."

His gaze went to his sword again. "However, I believe you

should have Aric, as you came for it."

Aeryn was taken aback that he was so willing to pass it on to her. "Are you sure?"

"I am. I have no use for Aric now. It is better in the hands of someone living. I know you will care for my sword as few others might, and the sword will serve you well."

Aeryn laid her hands on Aric's hilt and slid it free from the stone in which it sat. The sword was lighter that she imagined, and its grip warmed in her hand. She slid the sword into the empty sheath on her back. "Thank you, sir. It is an honor."

Theo coughed from the tower entrance before Tynan could respond. He smiled at Theo with a patience Aeryn did not feel toward the girl. Tynan walked to the entrance as well. He said to Theo, "Very well then, little one, I shall see you swiftly on your way now."

Tynan closed his eyes and muttered words Aeryn could not understand. Shifting sand and stone whispered and clattered as they gathered on either side of the gap and elongated and stretched until the bridge became whole again.

The ghost stopped muttering and opened his eyes, looking down at Theo. "Is that more to your liking?"

The girl nodded. "Not bad."

Theo put one foot out to test the bridge before she set the other down on it, too. Satisfied she was not about to plunge to her death, the girl walked the rest of the way to the other side. Tynan gestured at Aeryn to precede him. On the other side of the bridge, he took the lead and led them back to the room with his scrying pools, but from this point, his route diverged from their original path. It did not escape Aeryn's attention that his route bypassed the mural room, leaving no opportunity for her to ask Tynan directly about the murals or the strange scenes carved onto some of the wooden doors. She wondered if his fear about what had happened to her in the altar room was related to any of these things.

Aeryn broke the silence between them and asked Tynan, "How did you build the caverns, if you do not mind my asking?"

Tynan looked back at her and smiled. "Of course not. Even at nineteen summers, I possessed immense powers as a mage. As I wrote in my journals, when I discovered the winding passages, I knew this would be a magnificent place to store the trophies from my adventurers and to reside."

"Rimen stayed here with you until his death, did he not?"

He smiled. "Indeed he did. I miss him dearly to this day. Before you go, I would like to show you something."

Tynan changed direction suddenly and strode down another unfamiliar corridor, leading them past stone doors twice Aeryn's height. After passing several such doors, he stopped before one with elven designs carved into the stone face. He uttered another spell, and the door swung open on unseen hinges. Golden light spilled through the doorway into the passage, cast by runes similar to those in the altar room. At the center of the vault sat a long rack loaded with several pieces of elven-made weapons, while similar racks positioned around the room held various kinds of elven armor.

Tynan stepped through the doorway and said, "Please, come in, look around."

"What is this place?" Theo asked.

Aeryn wondered the same.

"Rimen was an avid collector of weapons and armor, as was I. These are many of the pieces he collected. I kept them all and moved them to this vault after he died. I left a preserving spell behind to ensure nothing tarnished or gathered dust." Tynan beamed at them and gestured at the various racks filled with artifacts of Rimen's life.

Theo caught Aeryn's eye as she passed her and raised her eyebrows. Aeryn ignored this. She felt a twinge of sympathy for the ghost; the vault made clear how much he cared for his friend. Yet, Theo was right that there was something unsettling about the golden shrine

Tynan built to his dead friend.

"Come, now," Tynan told them, going to the vault door. "We must continue on."

The ghost resealed the vault and turned down the passage again. He seemed in a hurry once more.

With Tynan's clipped pace, their journey back to the entrance to the Black Caverns seemed to end much sooner than Aeryn expected, though it was hard for her to tell without her map as an aid just how far they traveled. Both her and Theo's cloaks, still damp from the rain outside, lay by the entrance where they had left them, alongside her pack.

Aeryn slipped on her cloak and shoulder pack, and then she turned to Tynan. "I am glad to have had the honor of meeting you, sir, and my sincerest gratitude for the gift of Aric. I only wish there was something I could do for you in return. It seems a sad state for you to be trapped here so long."

Tynan nodded. "Yes, but as I have learned already, we cannot always choose our own fate. I will see mine out until the gods decide it should change."

"Farewell, Tynan."

"Fare thee well, Aeryn Ravane and Theo."

The ghost turned in the direction of the boulder that sealed the entrance. He gave it a quizzical look and said, "If you do not mind, I would like to see if the entrance will open for me. To tell you the truth, I have traveled very little through the caverns beyond the confines of the tower since my demise. I am somewhat surprised I even made it this far. I assumed I was confined close to where I died, and I never had a reason to test the theory."

"By all means," Aeryn told him.

Theo yawned while she donned her cloak.

Tynan recited the spell to unseal the entrance. Only a moment's silence passed between his intonation and the deep rumble that indicated the spell was successful. The boulder rolled back and revealed the Valley of Death beyond the cavern's entrance. The storm appeared to have died down for the time being, but roiling dark clouds still blanketed the sky, threatening to resume their siege.

Aeryn stepped out through the opening and exited the Black Caverns. Then, she realized they were not alone. Fifteen or so armed men and women stood just off to the side of the entrance. One of them—a stubble-faced man—stepped out from the rest of the group. His demeanor told Aeryn this was the leader.

He grinned at her. "It's 'bout time you came out o' there. We thou' we'd be waitin' forever."

10

The bandits were unkempt and smelled of unwashed flesh. However, judging by their armor and the horses hobbled at the bottom of the ridge, enough for each of them, these were not ordinary ruffians. Someone was paying them.

Aeryn opened her mouth to respond to the leader of the group, and then she realized his focus was not on her. He looked past her at Theo, now standing behind her.

"Where is it?" the leader hissed at the girl.

Theo cursed at him and said, "You weren't supposed to come here. That wasn't the deal."

"What can I say? We got tired of waiting in those damned woods, and we don' trust you." His gaze shifted from the girl to Aeryn and back again. "Wit' good cause, I'm thinkin', 'cuz you didn' keep your side o' the arrangement."

Anger flashed in Aeryn's eyes. She kept them trained on the man in front of her, but she growled at the girl behind her, "What arrangement?"

The man barked at her, "Quiet, bitch. This i' 'tween me an' the wee-un."

However, he then seemed to take an interest in the swords slung across her back. "Then again, looks like ya've got what we came here for. We'll be a'takin' tha' sword now." He hissed out what sounded like a chuckle.

The leader gestured over his shoulder, and the rest of the ruffians shuffled to life with bloodlust in their eyes. Aeryn felt a small hand tug on her cloak, but she batted Theo's hand away and then pulled Aric from its new sheath. The cold steel rasped against the scabbard. Several other blades answered the call as the ruffians pulled out their own weapons.

Aeryn charged them, taking aim at the leader first. Aric sliced open the leather armor protecting the man's stomach. He went down, and a pair of redheaded women, twins, wielding war hammers, took his place. Aeryn feinted toward the woman on the right and then slid left and disarmed the other. She spun around and swept Aric across the woman's upper arm. She fell, too, clutching at her bleeding limb. Her sister let out a high-pitched screech. She bullrushed Aeryn and wrapped thick, muscular arms around Aeryn's arms and torso, lifting her off the ground. Aeryn managed to retain her hold on Aric even as she felt the life being crushed out of her. The twin's hot breath hit her neck, and twist as she might, Aeryn was unable to free herself from the woman's death grasp. To her horror, the other twin rose to her feet and hefted her war hammer, despite the blood pouring from her wound.

Everywhere she looked, Aeryn saw only the dirty faces of the bandits. They howled at her with glee. Aeryn felt the hate and dark excitement pouring off of them in waves. She could not breathe. She needed help. The noise from the mob faded into a thick buzz as she started to black out. Then, something struck her captor from behind; she dropped Aeryn.

Aeryn landed on the ground, gasping for air. She looked up in time to see Theo hit the other sister in the back of her knees with the dead leader's spear before the woman could help her fallen twin.

Theo ran over to her and grabbed her arm. She pleaded, "Come on, you gotta get up."

The rest of the bandits were frozen in shock over something near the cavern entrance.

Aeryn sat up and asked, "What happened to the other twin?"

"Tynan."

"What?"

Theo pointed at the entrance to the Black Caverns. "There."

Aeryn turned back and spotted Tynan by the entrance, readying a

38

spell. She looked again and then realized he was not *at* the entrance, he stood *outside* the entrance. The ghost stepped into the spell, and a bolt of lightning arced from Tynan's outstretched hands to strike a bandit creeping toward them. The man's back arched when he was hit, and then he fell to the ground, smoke rising from the scorch marks Tynan's spell left behind.

Tynan glanced in their direction. He shouted, "Go while you can!"

Aeryn did not argue. She disengaged herself from the girl and scrambled down the mountain slope in the direction that Rowan still waited. Only a handful of the bandits still had enough fight in them to try to stop her. She cut them down as they came. With the addition of Tynan to the fray, however, most of the bandits turned tail and ran for their own horses.

Suddenly, something behind them at the cavern entrance exploded.

Aeryn and Theo both ducked at the crack of the sudden explosion. Aeryn whirled around, thinking Tynan miscast a spell, but when she turned back, he was looking back toward his caverns.

A murky, black mist slithered out from the mouth of the caverns. It writhed and grew in size. The mist formed into a thick cloud that twisted in the direction of the bandits. The cloud moved with malevolent intentions. Tynan backed away from what was left of the cavern entrance.

"Tynan, come on," Aeryn called to him.

"Forget him, he's a *ghost*," Theo told her and took off down the mountain.

Tynan turned and waved her away. He shouted, "Run! The dead cannot die a second time."

Aeryn scrambled down the mountainside again. When she reached Rowan, she found Theo already there, cowering next to his large form. Aeryn gave him a brief pass to make sure all of her gear was there and in good order. Satisfied it was, she strapped her shoulder pack onto her saddlebags and then climbed into her saddle.

"Take me with you," Theo pleaded from the ground.

"You set me up."

"It wasn't supposed to be that way. Not exactly," the girl whined.

Theo looked back in the direction of the still-growing black cloud. It chased after the remaining bandits. She yelled at Aeryn, "We don't have time to argue now!"

Aeryn knew the girl was right, and though it was against her better judgment, she lowered her hand so that Theo could grab it. The girl clambered up onto Rowan's back behind Aeryn's saddle.

"Hang on."

Theo wrapped her arms around Aeryn's waist and clung to her. Reins in hand, Aeryn turned Rowan and kicked him into a gallop across the valley, in the direction of the mountain pass. Behind them, several bandits screamed in pain or terror, or both.

11

Once they passed beyond the mountain ridge and entered the woodlands beyond it, Aeryn guided Rowan off of the path Phineas used when he brought her to the Valley of Death, on the chance he was also connected to the band of thugs that ambushed them on Nightstone Peak. She kept Rowan at as fast a pace as he could manage across the rocky and uneven terrain, straight through the remainder of the day into nightfall. She wanted as much distance between them and whatever emerged from the Black Caverns as she could get.

When the light grew too dim for her to safely guide Rowan through the woods, Aeryn turned Rowan toward a small clearing covered by the thick branches of several elderwoods. This place would make a good place to stop until first light. Valis lay not far from them, less than half a day's ride.

She offered Theo her arm so that the girl could slide off of Rowan's back. The girl had remained awake and alert throughout their flight from the valley. Now, she frowned at the stones and dead branches that covered the ground.

"Couldn't you have picked someplace softer?" Theo asked.

"This will do," Aeryn said and dismounted.

Aeryn walked Rowan to one of the thick-trunked elderwoods. She chose not to hobble him, as he rarely wandered far from her. She removed her saddlebags and saddle from his back and then the remainder of her tack. Rowan whickered at her when she finished, expressing his appreciation. She would brush him down as soon as she started a fire. The dark was closing in too fast for her comfort.

She cleared a portion of ground at the center of the small grove and then set about making a fire. Within a few tries, the kindling and leaves she had gathered caught fire, and orange flames licked at the firewood. Aeryn nurtured the fire until it burned brightly enough to illuminate the circle of elderwoods.

Opposite her, Theo crouched with her arms wrapped around her knees. She stared at the growing flames then met her gaze. "Where are we supposed to sleep?" she asked.

Aeryn nodded at the branches still strewn about the clearing. "Start picking those up and distribute them outside the clearing."

"Why?"

"Do you like sleeping on dead branches and rocks? Also, the branches will alert us to anyone who approaches our camp," Aeryn told her. She did not mention it was also a precaution against Theo getting away without her noticing.

The girl looked into the darkness beyond the circle of firelight and then rose. "I didn't come out here to do manual labor," she muttered while she bent to pick up the branches.

Aeryn went to her saddlebags again and took out Rowan's brush. She set to brushing him down. She said to Theo, "Be glad I took you with me at all. You are the one who set me up."

Theo pouted, "I told you it wasn't supposed to work that way."

"So you say."

The girl fell silent but continued to clear away the branches, leaves, and rocks.

Aeryn decided she would save interrogating Theo about her connection to the bandits to the morning. She continued to care for Rowan. When she finished, she offered him a pair of apples from her pack, both of which he devoured. She gave him a good pat and then picked up her blanket roll. She untied the leather straps binding it and unfurled a pair of thick wool blankets.

"Here," she said when Theo finished clearing away the branches. She offered the girl one of the blankets.

"I'm sorry, but I only have one to offer you. I did not anticipate having a tagalong."

Theo took it and wrapped it around her narrow shoulders. "Thanks. Is there nothing to eat?"

Aeryn nodded and then took some hardtack from her saddlebags and tossed part of it to Theo. She ate the rest herself. Then, she found her waterskin and rinsed the hardtack down. She passed the waterskin to Theo.

The girl took a deep pull from the waterskin and then handed it back. She asked, "What do you think that thing was that came from the caverns?"

Aeryn shook her head. "I know not. Right now, I do not care either. It seems not to have followed us." She rubbed her stiff, tired shoulders.

Gathering her blanket around her, she found a suitable spot near the warmth of the fire and sat down. She tossed a few pieces of kindling on the fire to keep it burning a little longer. Then, she said to Theo, "I'm going to sleep. I suggest you do the same. We leave at daybreak."

Aeryn lay down and closed her eyes. She heard Theo grumble, but then she also settled down. Fatigue muddled her thoughts, but not before she again saw the black cloud pouring out of the Black Caverns and the way Tynan fell back from it. She wondered if the cloud was related to why he seemed so eager for them to leave the caverns. She wondered just what else hid in those caverns beyond gold.

12

Morning broke just as cold as the night before, but even as clouds of steam puffed from Rowan's nostrils, Aeryn did not notice the cold. An odd taste sat on the air and unsettled her. Tendrils of gray light filtered through the bone-like branches overhead, but it remained darker than it should have for the morning being past first light.

Her stallion seemed to feel an urgency to be gone from this place as well. After Aeryn buckled his saddle into place, keeping one eye on the woods on either side of them, Rowan nudged her shoulder with his head. Aeryn ran a soothing hand over his soft coat and whispered to him. From somewhere she could not see, something watched them.

Aeryn continued to gather up her things. She saw Theo stir and went to the girl's side, nudging her awake. Before Theo could speak, Aeryn pressed a hand over the girl's mouth. Theo's eyes flew open.

"Quiet," the sell-sword hissed and then took her hand away. "Do not argue, just do as I tell you, and say nothing until we are clear of these woods."

The girl gave her a sullen look but obeyed, grabbing up her blanket and wrapping it around her.

A branch snapped behind them.

Aeryn and Theo spun in unison, but there was nothing there. Theo's hand grabbed the hem of Aeryn's tunic, but she said nothing. Her eyes were wide and anxious.

Another branch snapped off to the side.

It was time to go. Aeryn grabbed the girl's arm and pulled her in Rowan's direction. She stuffed the last of her things into her saddlebags and mounted, pulling Theo up behind her. The girl wrapped her arms around Aeryn's waist, gripping her tightly. Aeryn turned Rowan in the direction of the road to Valis and kicked him into a hard gallop. Only when he broke into his full stride did she hazard a look behind them. Elderwoods flew past, but still she saw nothing but an unnatural darkness in the receding woods. She told herself it was her imagination that it seemed to be spreading.

13

When woods gave way to the gentle hills and fields outside Valis, Aeryn slowed Rowan's pace to a trot and then a walk. He deserved a rest. Theo immediately spoke up.

"What in the hells was that in the woods?"

Aeryn shook her head. "I know not. Perhaps nothing at all." She did not believe that, but she had no other explanation to offer Theo.

She again regretted not questioning Tynan further when she had the chance. Her gut told her that he held the answers to what it was that came out of the caverns and what stalked them in the woods.

As if Theo read her thoughts, she grabbed Aeryn and cried out, *"The ghost!"*

"What of him?"

"He's back."

She turned her head to ask Theo what she was talking about and saw the transparent shape of a man walking beside Rowan. He became less transparent with each step. Rowan seemed to notice Tynan's presence, but he did not shy from him. Theo, however, cursed at him.

"Where in the hells did you come from? Don't you haunt those damned caverns?"

Tynan let out a short laugh. "My, you have a mouth on you, little one."

"It's a fair question," Aeryn told him.

Tynan bent his head in acquiescence. "True. It would appear that I am not confined to the Black Caverns after all. I know not why."

This new development distracted Aeryn from her previous questions. "Is it possible you're trapped between realms?"

Tynan clasped his hands behind his back as he walked next to

Rowan, a pensive look upon his face. "That is the definition of what being a ghost is: trapped between the worlds of the living and the dead. However, I have never heard of a ghost able to travel outside the confines of the location to which he is bound."

Aeryn suggested, "Perhaps one of the priests or sages in Valis can shed light on why you are able to do this."

Tynan nodded. "I thank you for your wise suggestion."

"Of course." Aeryn decided she would put off her questions about the caverns at least for the moment.

They were now within sight of Valis's gates. The four Valisian guards at the city gate watched their approach. Aeryn felt Theo begin to squirm behind her. Turning her head, she saw the girl duck down. Before she could ask Theo what she was doing, one of the guards hailed her. She brought Rowan to a stop short of the gates. The guards wore gray-and-green tabards, the city colors, with their chainmail, and all four were well armed.

"State your business in our fair city, swordswoman," one guard said to her.

He approached Rowan and looked over each of them in turn with his beady, dark eyes, while the other guards stood on either side of the city gate. He wore a solid armband of dark green, indicating a higher rank in the city watch than the other three.

Aeryn considered calling Valis a "fair city" to be a stretch, but she smiled at the man and said, "I am here for rest and to restock my supplies."

The guard's gaze kept returning to Tynan. "Is the shade with you?" he asked.

"He is."

"Is it good, evil, or neutral?"

Tynan looked indignant, but Aeryn answered with a simple "Good."

The guard paused and then nodded. "Alright. He's your

47

responsibility, though, and we don't take kindly to people who bring evil spirits into Valis." He made a sign of protection when he looked at Tynan once again.

He then turned his attention to Theo. The girl was still hunched down behind Aeryn, under her blanket. "Now, what do you have back here?"

He gave Theo a sharp poke and she yelped. He yanked off the blanket with one hand and laid the other on the hilt of his short sword. When he got a look at the girl, though, the guard grinned. "Well, well. It looks like you caught yourself a pint-size thief."

Aeryn glanced back at Theo, then the guard. "You know her?"

"Aye. Half the guard in the watch have run into this one."

The other three chuckled, and a growl more fit for an imp than a girl escaped Theo.

The guard asked her, "What'd she get you for?"

"Nothing yet," Aeryn told him. "Not for a lack of trying."

The guard nodded and threw the blanket back at the girl. "We'll take her off your hands if you want. She seems to keep making her way back to us. Maybe you like us, eh, little thief?"

The leer that followed this question made Aeryn's skin crawl. "No, that's alright, gentlemen. I'd rather deal with her myself. How much to enter Valis?"

The guard's grin faded, but he shrugged. "Suit yourself. It'll be two silvers for you, another pair for the shade of questionable origin, and six for the thief, 'cause we really don't want her back."

It was a much steeper price than she had planned for, but Aeryn decided paying it was better than leaving the girl with the guards. She took the requisite amount from her coin pouch and clinked the ten coins into the guard's hand. He turned away, gesturing to his compatriots to let them pass.

Aeryn nudged Rowan forward under the massive arch of the portcullis, into Outer City. The area between the outer and inner city walls was dirt turned to mud from the rains. Rowan's hooves sunk into the muddy road; he snorted with displeasure. Aeryn patted his neck. Tynan as well peered down at the mud and pools of filthy water with distaste, even though he was not actually touching the ground.

Past the inner wall, Aeryn guided Rowan through the squalid streets of Outer City. The city's poorest citizen eyed her and her stallion with open envy. It bothered her the way Valis treated the people of Outer City no better than they treated vermin. Though it was one of the largest cities in the north, Valis was not the most enlightened.

As they passed through Outer City, Tynan commented, "Valis has fallen since my living days. The Seven and I stayed here many times. Our favorite inn was here."

Theo snorted, "You've been dead a long time. This is all I've known Valis to be."

Aeryn gathered from this exchange that Outer City was her home. She felt a twinge of empathy for the girl, having spent her younger years in a similar situation, though nothing as bad as Outer City. It made her wonder about Theo's family. What of her parents? Was she an orphan? She did not ask, however, not wanting to make Theo uncomfortable.

Aeryn guided Rowan onto the gravel streets of Middle City, in the direction of the stables in which she had quartered Rowan the last time she stayed in Valis. She stopped Rowan just outside the Red Iron Smithery and Stables and gestured to one of the stable hands, who sat on a stool by the main gate, outside of the beehive of activity inside the stable yard. Around him, boys and young men groomed horses and other pack animals and serviced a handful of wagons and carriages.

At her gesture, the young man on the stool whistled to two other boys. The boys, grimy from their work, dashed out to meet her. As soon as Aeryn and Theo dismounted, the boys went to work removing the saddlebags and pack, which Aeryn took from them. She patted Rowan on the flank and then nodded at the boys, tossing each of them coins. They nodded in turn, smiled in thanks for the coins, and led Rowan off in the direction of the stables.

Tynan said, "If you do not mind, I am going to seek out a cleric at the local temple to Morghell. Tell me, is there one nearby still?"

Theo nodded toward a side street. "That way. Stay on Garodin and walk for about five blocks. The temple's sometimes closed during the day, though."

Tynan nodded, and Aeryn wondered why the girl knew this. She did not strike Aeryn as the religious type.

"I will find my way there, then, and wait until dusk if I must."

Aeryn asked him, "Shall I meet you there?"

Tynan offered her a slight bow and replied, "My lady, I would be honored if you did. Unfortunately, you are likely the only living souls I know now."

"Lucky us," Theo said.

Aeryn nudged her. "Well enough. We will join you after I settle up with Mulkin."

Tynan nodded.

Just then, Mulkin bellowed out her name. "Aeryn Ravane!"

She turned to see him come out of the high entrance to the stables, crossing the yard in a matter of a few lumbering steps. He was a good two heads taller than she, with broad, muscular shoulders and thick arms. Sweat from the heat inside his blacksmith and ironworks shop coated his dark skin. He wiped it from his face and shaved head with a clean towel as he walked. When he reached her, he smiled broadly and extended one of his hands to her. It swallowed hers in a firm handshake.

In the same instant, Theo turned and took off in a sprint away from the stable yard before Aeryn could stop her. Aeryn, Mulkin, and Tynan watched the girl run up the main street and then disappear down a side street.

"Did I do something to scare your friend?" Mulkin asked Aeryn.

"I wish I knew," Aeryn answered. She stared after the girl,

wondering what made Theo bolt now, after all of the chances she had before.

"A pity, and she did not even give you thanks for bringing her back to Valis," Tynan said. "She filled her pockets with plenty of gold and jewels in the caverns. Offering to help pay for your horse's boarding would have been the polite thing to do."

14

After Theo escaped from Aeryn at Mulkin's stables, she did not stop running until she was back at the outskirts of Middle City. Not only could she not risk Mulkin recognizing her, she needed to report back to Pythun. Nothing in the caverns had gone according to her plan. She needed to know what to do next, since Aeryn still possessed the sword Theo was ordered to retrieve. She had to see if there was another way to pay her debt.

When she reached Wimmel Street, Theo slowed to a walk. She continued down the street until she reached a building marked Collectors' Guild. Theo rapped three times on the door, paused after the third knock, and then knocked thrice more. After a few moments, the door opened, and a burly man in thick leathers stood on the other side and peered down at her with suspicious, pig-like eyes.

"We've been expecting you," was all he said before he grabbed her by the front of her shirt and yanked her into the building. The door slammed shut behind her.

The burly man dragged Theo past rooms filled with long tables stacked high with papers, piles of jewels, jewelry, and other, more easily sellable items. Silent boys and girls, most of them older than she, sorted through the wards and made notations on ledgers. Not one of them looked at her or the man when they passed by.

The man deposited her in an office at the back of the building, where he again slammed the door behind her. Once she heard the door lock, Theo picked herself off the inlaid wooden floor and straightened and smoothed out her clothes.

"Nice to smell you again, Bartok," she muttered under her breath.

Theo was not surprised by her reception. It differed little from what she experienced all of the times before when she visited the Thieves' Guild. She did not rate better treatment in the eyes of the guild's master.

Nothing about the office had changed since the last time she found herself here. A wide desk of carved mahogany stood at the center of the room, with a high-backed, calfskin upholstered chair behind it. She knew from experience that all of its drawers were sealed with locks that would not yield their contents to her lock picks. Theo did not have long to contemplate trying, however.

Only moments after Bartok had deposited her in the office, the door was unlocked, and the guild's master and his personal bodyguard entered. Red silk robes flowed around the master as he walked to his chair.

"Hello, Pythun. How is everything?" Theo plastered a smile on her face even as her left hand began to twitch.

Pythun did not smile in return. His thin face remained impassive while he studied her with his green eyes, which possessed an abnormally bright hue. Then, he sighed and ran both hands through his thick ebon hair, smoothing it back from his thin face. Tension built in the room like an electrical storm.

Theo told him, "I swear I can explain what happened."

"Stop talking." The words were almost whispered, but they thundered in Theo's ears. Her mouth clicked shut.

She forced herself to swallow the thick lump in her throat, and she nodded. Pythun placed his elbows on the desk and folded his fingers over each other in front of him, resting his chin on them.

When he spoke again, his voice was low and dripped with venom. "My men are dead. Not by your hand exactly, but I hold you responsible. For that alone, I should kill you now. On top of that, you have not brought me the sword."

Theo forgot herself and cried out, "It wasn't my *fault*. If Russin

53

had waited in the woods outside the valley, like he was supposed to, and just let me carry out my part of the deal, then they wouldn't—"

"*Shut up!*" Pythun slammed both his fists on the desk and stood up so fast that his chair flew backward onto the floor with a thud.

Theo backed up from Pythun's desk until the wall behind her stopped her.

Once he calmed himself again, Pythun waved a hand, and the chair righted itself. He sat down once more. "None of your feeble excuse interest me at all. All I care about is that you cost me men, and you did not even bring me what I requested.

"True, Russin did not follow his orders either, but since he is no longer alive, I cannot punish him for his incompetence. I like to judge success or failure by the merits of the group rather than just the individual, and seeing as you are the only remaining member of that group, the blame falls on you. Do you understand me? Just nod your head if you understand."

Theo nodded.

"Excellent. I love it when I am perfectly understood. What *I* do not understand is how you did not work harder to accomplish your mission, given that I hold your brother's fate in my hands. Funny—I would have thought that would motivate you."

Theo cleared her throat. "About that. I snatched a bunch of gold and stuff from those caverns. Maybe you can take those for my brother's freedom instead?"

Pythun frowned. "Your brother tried to cheat me, stole from me. Gold will not fix that. Getting the sword from that bitch sell-sword will. You have until dawn tomorrow, or you and your sibling will find out what stinking hell is reserved for lazy, dirty little thieves like you. Is that clear?"

"Yes, sir." She felt like she was suffocating. How was she supposed to find Aeryn again and get the sword from her by dawn?

"That is what I thought." To the thug, he said, "Please show our

54

young friend the way out."

Theo held up a hand and turned toward the door. "No need, I know the way."

A hand clamped onto her shoulder, and she froze.

Pythun chuckled behind her. "Have a nice day."

15

Aeryn told Tynan that she would accompany him to the temple to Morghell, god of the dead and the underworld. Though Tynan knew she meant to question him more about what had happened at the Black Caverns, he still welcomed her company. He spent so much time alone without anyone to talk to that he found he craved the companionship. He even missed the girl to some small degree, despite her incessant chatter.

After Aeryn settled the terms for her horse's boarding with Mulkin, an absolute bull of a man, they followed Theo's directions to the temple. While they walked, as he dreaded, Aeryn started to ask him questions.

"Sir, do you know what it was that came out of the Black Caverns after the bandits attacked?"

Tynan tried to put her off by saying, "A strange thing, that was. I have never seen anything quite like it."

His binding spell likely did little to contain what emerged from the caverns, as his powers had diminished greatly when he died. Tynan sensed Aeryn's suspicions and knew it was only a matter of time before the truth about the caverns could be held back no longer. However, his immediate problem lay in finding an explanation as to why he never crossed over when he died, and how he was now able to pass outside of the caverns. Once he found his answers to those things, he would worry about finding a way to explain himself and the truth about the caverns to Aeryn without her losing all respect for him. For reasons Tynan could not explain, he actually cared what the sell-sword thought of him.

Around them, vendors and street performers filled the streets, and even in the middle of the afternoon, a number of women selling more illicit services called down to the crowd from their silk-draped windows high above the street. As he and Aeryn made their way the crowds, Tynan reflected on just how much the world had changed from when he last saw it. The clothing and hair styles were foreign to him, and so many of the citizens were armed in one way or another. Valis, too, seemed to have doubled its size, and many of the buildings were multistoried masonry structures, rather than the more common timber of his day.

"Aeryn, how is it that Valis has changed such since my day?" he asked her.

She replied, "Valis is a trade hub in the Northlands. I believe Karoc was prior to that, but a great fire broke out and demolished the city some fifty years ago. My father told me of that."

"In my time, there was only Valis—no Outer, Middle, or Inner City. Never did so many poor exist in Valis either. Perhaps the changes have not been so positive for Valis," he commented.

Aeryn nodded.

He thought of what the others from the Seven might have thought of these changes and then wondered if his dwarven and frost elf companions might still live. "Do any of my adventuring companions still live? What of Rafin and Kendril?"

The sell-sword shook her head and replied, "No. I hoped that they still lived as well, but sadly, according to my research, the Black Order killed the Seven."

Tynan hung his head. After so many clashes against the mercenaries of the Black Order for the way they strong-armed honest adventurers and sell-swords out of the Northlands, the Black Order represented the Seven's greatest of enemies. A group of them ambushed him outside his caverns and brought about his own death, and it seems that they also succeeded in destroying his adventuring company.

"How could such a thing happen?" he asked.

"I gathered that when the Seven heard of what happened to you, they attempted to hunt down the surviving Black Order factions as

57

retribution. However, they were cornered in Blood Ridge by the remaining few Black Order members, and the rest of the Seven were killed."

Tynan then asked, "Do those blackguards still exist in this time?"

"No. The Black Order had the misfortune of getting into a skirmish with a group of vampyres in that region shortly after they murdered the Seven, and they lost their lives as well."

He grunted. "That is the first time I have heard of vampyres playing the heroes in such a story."

Aeryn said, "It is perhaps more common now than your day. Vampyres played a significant role in pushing back the hordes of undead raised by Untok the Despised so that he could overthrow the baronies of The Fang. The vampyres helped to destroy Untok and his hordes during the year of the Wolf."

Tynan fell silent again. So much had changed since his time. Vampyres could be heroes, and the once-quaint town of Valis was both a hub of commerce and a den of iniquity.

He and Aeryn continued walking for another block before Tynan spotted the temple to Morghell, a narrow three-story building with a placard above the heavy wooden door bearing the three faces of Death: the Neutral, the Satisfied, and the Tortured. Tynan paused and then turned to Aeryn.

"I believe you are better suited to announcing us than I, seeing as how I have no solid limbs."

Aeryn nodded and stepped forward. She used the iron knocker that hung at the door's center to strike three times. She waited.

"State your business," requested a disembodied voice close to Aeryn's right shoulder.

Unfazed, Aeryn replied, "My friend wishes to speak with a cleric about crossing over."

After a moment of silence, a click came from the other side of the door, and it opened a crack. Aeryn looked back at Tynan before she pushed open the door and walked into the temple, but Tynan hesitated before following her, wondering now if visiting a cleric was the best idea. In his experience, it was hard to hide things from clerics. They seemed to see straight through to a person's core, and Tynan was uncertain he wanted to open himself to such exposure. He sighed, knowing Aeryn's presence complicated the idea of his turning back now, leaving him with little choice other than to go into the temple and speak with someone.

Tynan entered the temple, and the door closed hard behind him. The sound echoed from every corner of the vaulted entry corridor. Tynan was pleased by the familiar sight: dozens of skulls, many with expressions of happiness or sadness created by magiks, stared down at him from the vaulted ceiling, dimly lit by candles set inside some of the skulls. Wooden tiers of votives lined either side of the corridor, guiding worshippers into the spacious main hall. At least temples to Morghell had not changed so much from his day.

Aeryn seemed transfixed by the skulls, but she tore her gaze away and walked toward the worship hall. Tynan followed her. More skulls stared down at them in the worship area, all of them lit from within. The light did nothing to dispel the darkness and gloom that hung in the air, however. If he was human, he was sure gooseflesh would cover his arms.

Rows of black pillows lined the main hall, but only four monks knelt on the front row of pillows. Their eyes were squeezed shut, and their frantic prayers, whispered and indecipherable. Tynan doubted the monks even noticed anyone stood in the room with them.

Aeryn pointed out a set of stairs tucked back against the far wall. "Perhaps we will find the priest upstairs?"

Then, a man's voice addressed them from behind the altar area. "Why do you seek him?" Though not loud, the voice reverberated off the high ceiling and walls.

Tynan and Aeryn spun in the direction from which the voice originated, and Tynan watched a figure separate itself from the shadows behind the altar. A thin man in billowing, midnight-blue robes stared down at them from the raised altar, a bone staff in his hands. His skin held such a deep pallor that Tynan wondered if he still breathed.

The man addressed them again. "What is your business here?"

"We seek the priest, sir," Aeryn replied.

His dark eyes shifted to the sell-sword. "I am Sevnor, priest of Morghell."

Aeryn looked at Tynan and then back at Sevnor. "My friend seeks your advice."

Sevnor turned his gaze from her to Tynan. "Come. Let us speak in private, sir ghost." He gestured toward the staircase with his bone staff.

"Do you wish me to go with you?" Aeryn asked.

Tynan shook his head. "No. I will return after I speak with Sevnor."

He followed Sevnor up the stairs. The priest led him past the monks' living quarters on the floor above the worship hall, and then up to a room at the top level that was part study, part throne room dedicated to Morghell. On one side sat a desk surrounded by bookshelves filled with ancient texts, some of which were religious tomes, others magik-related. The addition of potions among the shelves indicated that Sevnor probably dabbled with magik in his spare time. A half-circle stone bench and a small throne of rough-hewn stone dominated the other side of the room, neither designed for comfort.

Sevnor stepped up to the dais upon which the throne sat and arranged his midnight robes around him before he sat on the throne. The ghost chose a spot on the stone bench and frowned as he looked around the room.

The priest remarked, "You do not approve of the furnishings."

"I wonder if all these bones and skulls and stones are not

60

overdone."

"Morghell is ruler of the underworld, the afterlife, ruler of death. What better way to pay homage than with the trappings of the dead? It discomforts some, but Morghell teaches us that those who live too much in comfort are punished in the afterworld for their excesses, while those who live with pain or torment can be rewarded."

"Your place in the afterlife must be secure then," Tynan quipped.

Sevnor's face remained unchanged. "It is up to my god to decide my fate. I see you have picked up one of your companions' habits of sarcasm to hide your fear, Tynan Selvantyr."

"Reading my mind? Quite the liberty for a priest of Morghell." Tynan crossed his arms.

"I read just whatever sits at the edges of the mind. To be truthful, however, I find you to be unusually opaque." Sevnor leaned forward and stared into Tynan's eyes. "Normally, I get a sense of a person on the very surface of their mind. You are different. You are actively blocking me, I think. Why come here if you are not open to the ways in which I can help you? What is it you wish to hide?"

Tynan smiled. "Some things I simply prefer to keep to myself."

"Why?" The priest leaned back on the throne again.

"I have my reasons." Tynan's smile faded. "Are you going to help me or analyze me?"

"You want to cross over."

"Eventually. My immediate concern lies more in the realm of why I did not cross over when I died."

Sevnor nodded and rubbed a hand over his pale, receding chin. "To truly be able to answer that, I must go into your past and explore your memories. You must let me into your mind for this, Tynan."

The ghost thought about this. His apprehension increased. "This is the only way?"

"The only way."

In the beginning, when Tynan found himself trapped as a spirit in his caverns, he felt at peace. But it was not his idea to leave behind his physical body or his possessions. Peace turned to restlessness with the passage of time, one relieved by the arrival of Aeryn and Theo. Seeking out a cleric was Aeryn's idea, but he had to admit he felt some curiosity about what held him to the mortal world. Was it a mistake, unfinished business, or something altogether different?

Finally, Tynan nodded. "Let us begin."

16

Theo left the Thieves' Guild in the same way she entered: being dragged. At the front door, Pythun's thug tossed her onto the road. She skidded to a stop on her knees and felt the gravel on the road cut through her breeches to the skin on her knee. Theo waited until the door of the guild house slammed behind her before she made a move to get up. She did not bother to brush the dirt off of herself. When she looked down at her knee, however, and saw blood on the cloth of her pants, Theo cursed out loud.

"Damn it all!"

The few people on the guild's street stared as they passed her. None of them asked if she was hurt, which angered her even more.

She shouted at onlookers, "What are y'all looking at? Don't you have better stuff to do?"

Then, she turned back to the Thieves' Guild. She grabbed the largest piece of gravel she could find off the road and pitched it at the guild house. It struck and broke one of the windows. She frowned.

"Kellen's balls," she muttered.

Before anyone could come out and pound her for breaking the window, Theo took to her heels and sprinted back down Wimmel Street the way she had come. She continued running until she was three blocks away and sure no one was in pursuit. She ducked into an alleyway to think on what she was going to do next, since Pythun gave her until morn to find the sell-sword and Aric for him.

Panic made her thoughts jumble and cloud over. She told herself she *had* to find Aeryn again. Then, Theo remembered that the ghost, Tynan, wanted to seek out a cleric at the temple to Morghell. She figured she might be able to intercept them there, if she hurried. The temple was a jog from where she was, but Theo told herself she could make it.

She ran out of the alleyway and straight into someone. She bounced off them, and the other person grunted at the force of their impact. Theo stumbled and landed on her behind on the gravel road. She readied another curse, but it died in her throat when she realized the person she ran into was her own father. He squinted at her, but did not offer to help her up again.

"Tha' is you, girl. Thought so," he said. "Though, you need to be watchin' where you're goin'."

Theo stared up at him a moment before she picked herself up. "It's Theo, Rem," she told him, calling him by his nickname, short for Remmer. She had not called him "Father" or "Da" in longer than her ten-year-old mind could recall. Certainly, not since her mother died.

Rem Weldon grunted again while she dusted herself off. The disheveled and stained state of his clothing did not escape her attention any more than did the wineskin he held in a death grip behind his left leg. She wondered for a brief moment what he was doing away from the shack he called home in Outer City, as well as where he got the wineskin, and then she decided she did not care.

"I need to go," Theo told him, and then she tried to brush past him.

He caught her with his empty hand. "Where're you runnin' off to? Haven' seen you in a while." He slurred his words.

"I don't have time for this," Theo said through gritted teeth.

Then, a big-haired woman with a puffy, reddish face came up behind her father and put her arm around his shoulders. "Here you are, Rem. You left the tavern before I finished paying the tab. I figured you were trying to make off with the wine, and I was right." The woman chuckled.

Theo's father grinned toothily at the woman and also chuckled. "I jus' needed some air, darlin'. Then, I seen my daughter come out of this here building. I wanted to introduce you two." When he looked back at Theo, though, instead of a familial connection, suspicion colored his gaze.

Theo looked the woman over and said, "Why? She's no different from the others."

She always seemed to run into Rem at the worst times, sometimes with a woman and sometimes not. It never went well. His sudden need to introduce her to this woman was a mystery to her, however. She was just the same as the dozen or so other women her father bounced between, some while her mother was still alive. With a quick glance, Theo judged this one to be a little better heeled than Rem's average. The woman's clothes were unstained and well-cut, the opposite of Rem's. Theo guessed this woman was the reason he was in Middle City.

Her attention on the woman, she failed to see Rem's swing until his hand backhanded her in the face. She stumbled back from the blow, but recovered and fixated a glare on him.

"You need to mind yer manners 'round your elders and your betters. Don' think I don' know what yer doing here," he growled. "Bad enough Brien's been doin' that kind o' thing. I won' have you doin' it, too."

Theo swiped a hand across her bleeding lip and shot back, "At least he knows how to take care of me, Rem, and it ain't none of your business what I do."

Rem's girlfriend tittered nervously. "Oh, Rem," she interjected. "Must you fight so?"

Rem ignored her. "It's my business if I say it is, girl. I think it's time you came home with me."

He reached for her again, but Theo danced away from him.

"So you can do to me like you did my mother? Not a chance," she sneered. She looked at the red-faced woman and told her, "He liked to beat her 'til it killed her one day."

The girlfriend's mouth dropped open, and she withdrew from

Rem.

Theo spat at her father's feet and cursed at him. "You're dead to me," she told him.

Before he could react, Theo sprinted across the street and off in the direction of the temple to Morghell again, praying she might still catch Aeryn there.

17

Sevnor leaned forward in his throne and stared at Tynan. "Look into my eyes and concentrate on letting your inhibitions go. Let me into your mind."

Tynan did as he was told, and Sevnor's face tensed with concentration. The tiny ruby eyes of the skull carving atop Sevnor's bone staff began to glow. Tynan imagined he could feel Sevnor rooting around in his mind, picking at his past life. Sweat beaded on the priest's forehead, and he shook his head slowly from side to side. His mouth moved as if speaking, but no sound came out. A small drop of blood appeared below Sevnor's nose and trickled down his pale upper lip.

When the priest opened his eyes, he reached up and touched his hand to his nose. He frowned at the blood on his fingers. He took a dark blue cloth from a hidden pocket in his robes and dabbed at the blood.

"Does that happen often?" Tynan asked.

"Sometimes," Sevnor replied.

Tynan nodded. "Do you have an answer for me?" Impatience crept into his voice.

A half-smile crossed the priest's face as he gazed down at the cloth. "You carry a great many secrets with you." He tucked the cloth back into the hidden pocket and regarded Tynan with smug eyes.

"That is your answer? I hope you do not expect payment for it," Tynan sniped.

Sevnor leaned his back against the back of the throne and rested his elbows on its arms, pressing his fingers together. "I believe the secrets you continue to hold to you, as well as your desire to keep hold of your mortal goods, are partially responsible for your continued existence in this world.

"When you died, you were very focused on your possessions, your accomplishments, and you wished to continue your adventures. When a person dies thus, with unfulfilled desires, their spirit lingers until they let go of their desires. However, I sense something darker behind your current state, too."

It was as Tynan feared. "Will you tell Aeryn and others?"

The half-smile returned. Sevnor asked, "What do I gain by that? Surely, you cannot still worry about your reputation."

"Her father seemed to have felt a connection to my stories. I do not wish to ruin her view of me. I am sure there are others who must feel the same way. I was rather famous in my time."

The priest shrugged. "I have heard your name, Tynan Selvantyr, but your legend has faded much since 'your time'. You are not much more than a note in history tomes and the fascination of adventurers seeking to break the caverns' secrets for their own monetary reward."

Tynan stood up from the stone bench. "How dare you dismiss me so. Do you not know to whom you speak?"

"Did I not just say your name?" Sevnor asked him in an even tone. "Have I not just told you what you already suspected? It cannot be any more of a shock, then, for me to tell you that your lies and deceptions have put not just Aeryn, but all of us, in danger, and you would do well to tell her the truth soon so that she may have a chance at stopping what is to come."

"You do not know what is coming any more than I do, and I will not have you telling Aeryn anything in my stead," Tynan said.

Suddenly, the priest looked uneasy, and he held up a hand to calm Tynan while his other hand slipped back toward his staff. "Calm yourself."

Tynan brought his hands up, fingers spread, and barked out a spell. Bright light shot from his hands and struck Sevnor, who froze in place without even the time to ward off Tynan's strike. He admired the handiwork of his petrification spell for a moment and then turned away from Sevnor. The spell would last for several hours, he anticipated, if not several days. That was plenty of time for him to find a way to break the truth to Aeryn while preserving his own dignity and reputation.

Tynan descended to the lowest level of the temple and walked across the worship hall toward where Aeryn leaned against a stone pillar. She looked at him as he approached.

"Where is Sevnor?" she asked.

Tynan said, "He said he had other matters to attend to and could not see me out. Why?"

"I was hoping to leave something in honor of my father."

"I am sorry. Perhaps another time? I feel we should not linger here."

Aeryn said nothing for a moment, eyeing the stairs up to Sevnor's chambers. To Tynan's relief, Aeryn finally nodded and turned to leave the temple. Tynan followed her without a look back.

18

Theo took to the back streets and alleys to avoid pursuit should her father decide to come after her. Her brother taught her all of the best ways to get around Valis quickly and secretly that were not known to many of its citizens. This was Brien's best survival tip, which he taught her when they started living on the streets, after their mother died.

She kept running until she was less than a block from the temple, then she stopped to wipe a lingering bit of blood from her lip and ran her hands through her dark-blond her. She refused to show up at the temple looking like something dragged out of the gutter. She did not want Aeryn to give her the sword out of pity.

Before she started off again, Theo looked up at the still gray sky. The wind had picked up again while she was arguing with her father and the poor sap he was with. She was grateful her cloak dried overnight. She guessed she would need it to keep the rain off soon enough.

Theo darted down another pair of alleys until she was across the street from the temple. She saw no one outside of it. She crossed the street to the temple, glancing up at the three faces of Morghell before she laid a hand on the heavy temple door's handle and tugged. The door did not budge. It was locked.

"No, please," Theo whispered.

She grabbed hold of the brass knocker set in the middle of the door and used it to bang on the door. She got no response. She banged on the door again, but still nothing. Aeryn and Tynan were not there.

Theo turned away from the temple door. She ran her hands through her hair again and stifled the urge to cry. She had no idea how to find the sell-sword again. She and the ghost could be anywhere now.

Thunder rumbled overhead. Theo looked up at the sky and

decided she could not just stand around. There was one person she turned to for advice, and seeing as how time was running out, Theo decided this was the time to seek her out.

She pulled the hood of her cloak over her head and slipped into a nearby alleyway. She crossed through three more alleys until she came to one with a long series of doors facing into the alleyway. Theo passed eight of these doors, ignoring the stench that permeated the alleyway, and stopped at the ninth door. She knocked.

When the door opened, Theo shot past the overweight cook before he could shut the door on her. He shouted after her, but she ignored him and headed to the front of The Thirsty Noble's cluttered kitchen, where many of the serving girls collected during the slow hours. Three of the Noble's five serving girls were clustered there, wiping out mugs and stacking them, preparing for the rush that would start soon as night fell.

Theo pushed her hood back and walked up to the group. She asked them, "Where's Willa?"

One of the girls, Jilly, told her, "She's out front with Daphne and Mykel, hon."

Theo thanked her and started to head for the common room, but then Jilly asked about her brother.

"I haven't seen him here in a good while," Jilly explained.

Theo plastered a smile on her face and turned back to Jilly. She replied, "He's around. You know Brien. He's always up to something. I'm sure he'll be by again soon. You know he can't stay away for long."

Jilly giggled. Theo knew Jilly had a crush on her brother, the same as all of the serving girls.

"That's good. You tell him to get himself back here soon when you see him. I never met a thief with a bigger heart under all his attitude as your brother. Besides you, of course," Jilly winked at her.

Theo flushed pink and nodded. "I'll tell him, but don't let it get around about the big heart thing. You'll ruin our reputations."

71

"No problem, sugar. Your secret's safe with me."

Theo turned away again and stepped through the kitchen door into the common room, peering through the midday dimness in the room for Willa among the many wooden tables and chairs. Come nightfall, the common room would be ablaze with welcoming candle and lantern light. During the day, however, most of the lanterns were unlit to save on lantern oil. She spotted Willa leaning against the stone-topped bar, talking to another serving girl, Daphne, and the bartender Mykel, just as Jilly said.

She plastered another smile onto her face as she walked up to the trio and greeted them. They returned the greeting, and Willa nudged her with her elbow.

"So how did everything go?"

Only Willa knew where she had been, though she had cautioned Theo that she thought it was a bad idea.

Theo shrugged. "Oh, you know how these things go—sometimes well, sometimes not."

Willa nodded and said, "I have tables to wipe. Why don't you come with me and tell me about it?"

Theo followed after Willa, who stopped at a table near the back of the tavern room.

"Tell me what happened," Willa told her, her hands on her hips.

Theo hung her head to hide the quiver in her lip. "I screwed up. There was this giant spider that attacked me and broke my bracelet. The sell-sword caught me before we even got near the sword, and Pythun didn't go for the gold and jewels I managed to pick up either."

"Is she the one who gave you that cut on your lip, or did Pythun?"

Theo shook her head. "I ran into my father outside the Thieves' Guild."

Willa's face tightened, and she yanked a damp rag out of the pocket of her apron. "Why doesn't that man just die already?"

She watched Willa make furious circles on the table with the cloth. "Out of spite, I think."

Willa replied, "If I was the violent type, I'd have done to him what my mum did to my da, after yours killed your mum. She was a good woman, and my friend. She didn't deserve to have that happen to you, nor you and Brien to be left alone like you were."

"You said they almost hung your mother for what she did."

"Aye. But Mum always said being hung for killing him would've been a blessed gift next to dying by his hands. She did it for the sake of me and my sisters as much as herself. I'd do the same for you if I could. I'm just not that kind of person."

Theo said nothing for a moment and then she told Willa, "There's another problem I've got right now. Pythun's given me 'til the morn to find Aeryn and get the sword from her, and I've got no idea where I'm going to find her. I looked for her and the ghost at the temple to Morghell, but they weren't there."

Willa gave Theo a sideways look and raised an eyebrow. "Did you say 'ghost'?"

Theo waved a dismissive hand. "It's a long story."

Willa stopped wiping the table and straightened up again. "Is that her name—Aeryn? You're on a first name basis now?"

Theo frowned and then shrugged. "I guess so. I owe her my life, to be honest. A giant spider tried to make me a snack, and something bad happened when we left the caverns. Something came out of them—I don't know what. Some kind of black cloud. I think it killed Pythun's henchmen. I heard screaming." She shook her head to clear the sound from her mind.

"Theo, what in the hells have you and Brien got yourselves into?"

"I don't know. I just need to get us out of it as soon as I can." She frowned again, staring off. "I should have stayed with her longer, waited for an opening, instead of going to Pythun."

73

"I'm sure you'll think of something, as you always do."

Tears stung her eyes and she shook her head. "No, Brien always thinks of something, but he's not here now. Just me. And, I was never good at planning anything. Look how bad I've messed up so far. Brien is the smart one, not me. Now, Pythun's goin' to kill him, because of my screw up."

Willa pulled out the chair next to Theo and sat down. "Stop that," Willa told her. "You're just as smart as Brien. You're going to think of something. You have to believe that or else you might as well give up now. If you give up, though, Brien will die for sure. You aren't the giving up kind. You're just tired."

Theo swiped a hand across her eyes and rubbed at her dripping nose with her sleeve. "You're right. I'm just tired."

Willa sighed. "Alright, let's think about this. What *did* you find out about the sell-sword?"

"Not much," Theo said. "Her father was a soldier. He liked stories about Tynan and the Black Caverns. She left her horse at the Red Iron Smithery with Mulkin."

"What about that? Maybe you can wait for her there," Willa suggested.

"But, I've no idea when she's going to get him," Theo whined.

"You need to do something. Go there in the morning and see if she shows up to get her horse. If not, maybe you can find out from one of the stable hands where she's staying."

"Yeah," she agreed. "I can probably do that. I just have to avoid Mulkin. I don't think he recognized me when I was there with Aeryn, but I don't want to take any chances."

Willa nodded and stood. "Why don't you go up to my room for now? You've got a couple hours 'til the tavern gets busy, so it should be quiet enough. Just lie down and rest for a while."

Theo rose as well. "Yeah."

Willa hugged her and murmured, "It'll be alright. I know it will."

When Theo pulled away again, she went up the stairs to the second story of the inn, taking the stairs two at a time. Willa's door was at the end of the hallway. She unlocked it with the key she kept tucked away in her boot. The room was small and spare, but it had Willa's touch in the flowers stitched on the white cloth curtain over the window and the dried flowers tied to the headboard posts of her plainly-dressed bed.

Seeing an orange shape through the curtain, Theo went to the window and pulled the cloth back to reveal Willa's napping tomcat, Rillo. The tabby came smoothly awake and yawned and stretched, pinning his ears back as he did so. Deep-throated purrs emanated from him as he butted her hand with his big, orange-striped head. His tail twitched lazily as Theo scratched under his chin and behind his ears the way he liked.

"Caught any tasty mice today?" she asked the cat.

Rillo was a champion mouser if Theo ever saw one. Jonas, the tavern's ill-tempered proprietor and cook, said it was the only reason he let Willa keep Rillo, but Theo knew Jonas liked Rillo as much as everyone else at the inn. She saw him sneak the cat scraps from time to time.

Sighing, Theo picked Rillo up and pressed him to her. His purring comforted her as she stared out the window to the street below, watching the wind sweep debris from one side of the street to the next and slap at the cloaks of passersby.

"I've certainly got myself into a good one this time," Theo told the cat.

She set him on the bed and slipped off her boots. Then, she peeled back the coverlet on Willa's bed and slipped under it, resting her head on the pillow permeated with Willa's perfume. Rillo curled up next to her. As her tiredness forced her eyelids closed, Theo prayed she would find the sell-sword again and be able to save her brother.

19

The sounds of revelry woke Theo. For a moment, she did not know where she was, still caught in her dreams about her mother. The smell of Willa's dried flowers, combined with boiling meats and vegetables from below, reminded her that she was in Willa's room. A lantern, its wick turned low, glowed next to the bedside. Willa must have come up to check on her, Theo decided. Rillo stepped on her legs and his tail swished by the tip of her nose. She smiled and petted the cat.

Her stomach growled, reminding her she had not eaten since the morning. She decided to go down to the common room to get some food. Willa always made sure Theo was fed when she came to The Thirsty Noble.

Theo set the cat on the floor and then pulled on her boots again. She left the room, making sure Rillo stayed behind, and descended the steps into the common below, which was alight with candles and lanterns as usual. The multitude of open flames made the large room quite warm, but considering the way the wind still moaned outside, Theo counted it as a blessing.

The common room was busy, but not overly crowded, so Theo suspected that the night was still young. She slid through the room toward the bar, resisting the temptation to feel through pockets along the way. When Mykel saw her standing by the bar, he asked one of the patrons if he would let Theo sit down. The man grumbled but got up and moved away from the bar.

Theo climbed onto the vacated high stool and leaned forward to be heard over the other patrons, asking Mykel, "How long did I sleep?"

"Couple o' hours, probably."

"Willa should've woken me."

His answer was predictable enough. "She thought it best you sleep. Why? Somewhere you needed to be?"

She shook her head, unwilling to explain her situation all over again to Mykel. It was best to keep him out of it. She asked for a drink instead.

Mykel took a small mug from below the bar and poured her a few fingers worth of watered-down cider from a jug on the shelf behind the bar. He asked her if she would like something to eat. She nodded and then asked where Willa was.

He pointed to a table near the entrance. "She went to help the warrior woman and her, um, friend who walked in just now."

Theo's gaze slid in the direction Mykel indicated. Her eyes widen when she saw Aeryn and Tynan seated at the table at which Willa now stood. She could not believe her good fortune. Mykel addressed another question to her, but she ignored him. She focused on the sword Aeryn still carried.

Theo drew her dagger. She slid off her stool and stalked through the sea of people between her and the sell-sword's table, her pulse and her feet picking up speed as she went. She bolted past Willa and jumped onto the table. She heard Willa scream her name like a curse, but it was too late for Willa to stop her.

Theo dove across the table and collided into Aeryn. With a ferocity even she did not know she possessed, she growled, "Give me that damn sword!"

20

In Aeryn's mind, time slowed down and the tavern went silent when Theo dove onto the table and leapt at her, dagger drawn. She had no time to think, only react. With one hand, she grabbed the front of Theo's shirt, while with the other she grabbed hold of the hand that held the dagger headed for her throat. As the two of them fell backward, Aeryn twisted her body so that she landed on top of the girl. When they hit the floor, Theo's dagger skittered away, and the girl went limp under her.

Suddenly, the room came alive again. People shouted all around her, one of them the woman who came to serve her table. She was yelling, "What did you do?"

Aeryn sat back on her heels. "What did *I* do? She attacked me."

The woman knelt next to Theo's unconscious form and brushed the girl's hair away from her face. "You knocked her senseless." She said the girl's name and shook her arm.

Now that the scuffle was over, the other patrons lost interest and went back to their drinks. Tynan bent over Theo as well. Surprisingly few of the inn's occupants paid him much attention.

"The lady does have a point, Aeryn. You rendered the girl unconscious," Tynan said in an absent way.

Aeryn was incredulous. "Did you miss that she tried to slit my throat?"

"You could've found a different way to stop her," the serving woman retorted. By now the barkeep had joined them and looked anxious as he hovered. She addressed him. "Mykel, I'm going to take Theo up to my room."

Mykel nodded. "Do you need help?"

Willa looked to Aeryn. "I think you can help, since you're the one who knocked her senseless. I can only guess that you're the sellsword she was with. She's been looking for you."

"I gathered that from her reaction." Aeryn frowned.

"Please help me carry her upstairs."

Aeryn took offense at being pressed into ferrying the girl upstairs, but part of her did feel bad that the girl was hurt, despite her being the instigator. She picked Theo up and followed the woman through the crowd and upstairs. The girl weighed very little in her arms. Aeryn carried Theo into Willa's room and laid her on the bed.

Willa hovered over the girl and called her name again. "Theo, open your eyes."

The girl's eyes fluttered open. She looked at Willa and then at Aeryn and Tynan. "Great," she muttered. "You two. The bane of my life."

Aeryn glared. "What were you thinking, attacking me like that?"

Theo sat up, saying to Willa, "I guess you've met my companions from the caverns."

Willa sniped, "I can't say we've been formally introduced."

Tynan stepped forward and bowed. "I, my dear lady, am Tynan Selvantyr. My infamous companion is Aeryn Ravane."

Willa seemed to think a moment. "Tynan Selvantyr. Why does that name sound familiar?"

Tynan glowed. "I was an adventurer of great importance in my time." Just as quickly, his joy faded. "However, now I am but a shadow of my former self."

"Oh, yes, you lived in the Black Caverns, inside that accursed mountain. Didn't you die long ago?"

"Yes. Such is the reason for my current translucent existence."

Willa shrugged and started shooing Aeryn and Tynan toward the door. "I must get back to work and you two need to go now."

Simultaneously, Aeryn and Theo said, "No, I need to talk to

her."

Throwing her arms up in exasperation, Willa went to the door alone. "Fine, Theodora Weldon, but if she knocks you about some more, don't tell me I didn't warn you. You never listen." Turning on her heel, Willa stormed out.

Aeryn looked back at Theo and raised an eyebrow.

Theo shook her head. "Never mind her. I need your sword."

Aeryn looked at her blankly.

Theo sighed. "You know, Aric? The magikal sword or whatever it is. I need it."

Aeryn replied, "I know of which sword you speak, but I'm not very inclined to give the sword to you. Not only did you set me up for an ambush, you ran off without answering any questions and then you tried to slit my throat in the tavern downstairs."

Theo scowled. "I'm doing you a favor by asking nicely this time."

"Is that so?" Aeryn crossed her arms and stared back at the girl.

Theo paused and then her attitude took a sudden turn. "You don't understand. I need that sword. I'm in danger if I don't get it, and you are, too."

"Why? Explain."

For a moment, Theo's lip trembled. "I don't have time!"

Aeryn sighed, feeling like she was about to be conned. Tynan, however, gave her an uncertain look.

"I don't have the time or the patience for this," Aeryn said and turned away from the girl.

"They're going to kill him and then they're going to kill me," Theo sobbed.

Aeryn set her jaw but turned back to face Theo. Tears traced clean lines down Theo's otherwise dirt-smudged face, and Aeryn realized this might not be an act. The girl appeared genuinely upset.

Tynan saved her from having to respond. "Who, little one? Who has threatened you?"

Theo's small chest heaved. "They're going to kill my brother. Pythun and his goons are going to kill my brother."

Aeryn had no siblings, at least none that she remembered clearly, and yet she wondered what she might do for them if she had one still. "Someone will kill your brother for Aric? Why?"

Theo said, "I don't know, but Pythun wants it and will kill Brien to get it. Trust me; he won't hesitate to kill him."

Aeryn frowned. "Who is this Pythun character? Why were you and your brother singled out?"

"He's the head of the Thieves' Guild in Valis. My brother worked for him. My brother is a thief like me." Theo wiped away the last of her tears. "Brien's not been giving Pythun his cut lately. I told him to stop, because I knew Pythun would kill him if he found out what Brien was doing, but he wanted to get enough gold for us to leave Valis on one of the merchant trains. I told him leaving wouldn't do any good if Pythun sent people after us. He wouldn't listen.

"I went to Pythun after my brother disappeared. He admitted he had Brien and planned to kill him. I asked if we could make a deal. I told him I'd do anything he asked. He told me about you, an adventurer in the city looking for a sword he wanted. He told me to find you and follow you. He didn't think you were just another crazy adventurer like other people did. He never said why he wanted the dead adventurer's sword, but he said I should kill you if I had to. He's the one who gave me the Band of Invisibility to keep me hidden.

"Everything was going fine until Russin and his cronies followed me to the valley. Now, Russin is dead, and Pythun is even more pissed off. All I want is to give Pythun the damned sword and get Brien back. Then, I want to get the hell out of Valis."

Aeryn shook her head. "We are not going to give Aric over to Pythun, no matter his designs."

Tynan reproached her, "I do not like the idea of a child's life

81

being held in the balance because of Aric."

Theo stood up from the bed. "You killed his men. Add that to the fact that you have what he wants, it brings you to the top of his list of people to kill, second only to me and Brien. Pythun is smart, and tenacious. He will find you."

Aeryn replied, "Pythun's interest in Aric makes me wary. I will go to see Pythun myself."

"*You're* going to go see Pythun." A smug smile planted itself on Theo's face. "You and who else? He's no pushover."

Aeryn ignored her question. "After I help you, you are on your own."

"Deal," Theo said, rising from the bed. "But I'm going with you."

Aeryn exited the room, replying, "As you wish."

At the bottom of the stairs Theo stopped, saying, "I just need to tell Willa I'm leaving."

Aeryn nodded. "We'll wait by the door." She watched the girl head toward the bar, and wondered what she was getting herself into now.

21

Theo walked to the bar and asked Mykel, "Is Willa in the back?" He leaned against the wall, cleaning a pair of mugs; she wondered if she would ever see him again.

"That's where I saw her headed last. She's pretty mad." Mykel stepped closer to the bar. "You gave us all a scare, Theo."

Theo smiled at him. "That was just my careful ruse. I had everything under control."

Mykel tried to look stern but fell short. "Is that so?" he asked, a half-smile crossing his face. "All the same, be more careful, yeah? You'll live longer and give Willa and me less gray hairs."

Theo laughed. "Who wants to live to be old like you and Willa?" Then, she got serious again. "I want to tell Willa that I'm leaving again."

Mykel frowned. "She won't like it. She wanted you to rest after that tumble."

"I'm fine." Theo could tell by his hesitation that he did not believe her. "I can't stay. I've got some stuff to take care of."

"Is this about Brien?"

She nodded.

"Do you want me to tell Willa? Save you from the brunt of her fury? I know how she can get sometimes, 'specially with regards to you keeping safe."

Theo shook her head. "I'm alright with telling her myself." She added, "Willa and you have been really great to me."

Mykel's look of concern deepened, and he set aside the pair of mugs he was cleaning. He leaned over the bar. "I meant what I said, Theo. You be careful. If anything happened to you, you'd be sorely missed, and Willa would never forgive me or herself for letting you go.

So, do me a favor and come back safe, ok?"

Mykel smelled of ale and other liquors from the inevitable spills that occurred each night. It never bothered her, and it even comforted her, smelling it now. She nodded. "I swear I will."

He nodded and picked up one of the mugs again. "Well, I guess that's all that can be said. You'd better hurry and tell Willa—your friends are waiting for you."

Theo looked back at Aeryn and Tynan. "I don't know I'd call 'em friends. I'll see you around soon, Mykel."

Theo headed toward the kitchen. She found Willa near the back, filling a trencher with thick, greasy gravy and chunks of meat. Theo watched her for a moment, then said, "I have to go."

Willa stopped what she was doing. "Going where?"

"Willa, I just have to leave, ok? I can't go into it now."

"And I suppose you can't go into why or who with, though I think I can figure out both on my own." Willa blew out a breath in irritation. "She almost kills you, and now, you're leaving with her?"

Theo looked around. They were attracting attention, and Theo hated attracting attention. She lowered her voice. "Aeryn says she'll help me, so I have to go. I can't lose Brien."

Willa sighed and closed her eyes, but Theo could see the tears collecting on her lashes. "I know, I know. I just have a bad feeling about this, and you know it would kill me if anything happened to you."

Theo nodded and swallowed past the lump in her throat. "I just want you to know, just in case something bad happens, all you've done for me and Brien has meant a lot. All the times you let us stay in your room when we needed someplace dry to sleep. Well, I just wanted to say thanks."

Willa knelt in front of her, looked her in the eye, and grasped Theo's shoulders tightly. "Don't say these things. If you say these things, it'll bode ill." She pulled Theo into a tight embrace, whispering to her, "I wish to all the gods I could fix this for you."

"I know." Theo hugged her back, but only for a moment before she pulled away again. "I have to go. They're waiting for me. I'll be fine, I promise."

Nodding, Willa stood and ran a hand over Theo's blond hair. "You always come out on top." She slowly let out a shaky breath. "Go then, and hurry, so you can hurry back."

Theo gave Willa another brief hug, then broke away and jogged out to the common room again. She made her way to Aeryn and Tynan. "Let's go."

Aeryn pushed away from the wall her back rested against and opened the door, gesturing for Theo and Tynan to precede her. "You certainly took your time."

Theo wiped away the wetness around her eyes and did not look back at the sell-sword as she walked out of The Thirsty Noble. "I had some things to say. Give me a break."

"Fine. Lead us on to this Thieves' Guild," Aeryn said.

"Gladly," Theo replied.

She turned in the direction of the guild again and set off at a clipped pace. Time was not on her side.

22

"Master, tell me your bidding. I obey your will alone," Pythun chanted in the darkness.

He knelt on a dirt floor, encircled by a ring of candles whose meager light seemed absorbed by the room's black stone walls. His black hair and pale skin glistened with sweat, and his robes clung to his body. Yet, the room was not warm; in fact, the exact opposite was true. Pythun repeated his request and clouds of cold mist followed his words.

"Master . . ."

The color of Pythun's eyes suddenly shifted from their usual blazing green to a sickly yellow hue, and a voice no longer his own emerged from his mouth as his god spoke through him.

"I hear you, slave. You are a failure. Your promises have gone unfulfilled."

The tendons in Pythun's neck stood out in stark relief. Blood trickled from the corners of his eyes. Pythun whimpered in his own voice, "I have not yet failed, Master. I am going to get what you demanded. I promise."

He screamed incoherently and bent forward.

His voice changed again. "Silence! You are incapable of completing even a simple task. I will find one who is."

An unseen force threw Pythun backward. He knocked over several of the burning candles, plunging part of the room into darkness. He felt his god's presence withdrawing from his mind. He pleaded, "Wait, Master."

Pythun picked himself up and scuttled back into the remainder of the circle. Again he knelt, blood still trickling from one eye. He repeated, "I will finish the task, I promise you. I will get the sword you want, and I will kill the girl and the sell-sword."

A whisper came to him on the air. "Do not fail me again, or I shall dispose of you along with the rest of the unworthy." Then, only silence remained.

Nearly collapsing from his ordeal, Pythun rested his burning forehead on the dirt floor. His chest heaved. Once he caught his breath, he sat upright and wiped the blood and dirt from his face with the sleeves of his robes. Then, he stood and kicked over the remaining candles, plunging the entire room into darkness. In the darkness, he seethed.

No one was going to inhibit him from becoming his god's avatar, he told himself. Especially not a common thief and some sell-sword bitch. He would have them both and break their bodies on the stones of his master's altar. His network of thieves had served him well, but now it was time to show his true ambition.

Though his god's presence had receded from his body, Pythun could still feel it. His god's presence was constant now, and it gained strength and power. Feeding made the god's essence stronger, and that essence was on the move, drawing ever closer to Valis. Soon, Pythun would have the power he coveted and had waited for far too long. But first, he needed to rebuild his strength. Communing with his god always exhausted him.

Pythun rearranged his robes into a semblance of order. Tremulous fingers combed through his hair before he hid his hands in his voluminous sleeves. Pythun called to his bodyguards waiting outside. The wooden door opened, and light spilled into the pitch-black room through the doorway. Pythun squinted in the sudden bright light. Bartok appeared. He came as far as the door's threshold and no further. The guard's nervousness was thick and palpable like fog after the rain.

"Yes, Master Pythun?"

Pythun did not smile. "Come in, Bartok, and bring a few of the others. Close the door behind you."

Bartok hesitated only a moment before he did as he was told, beckoning to the other guards standing in the passage behind him. When the door closed behind them, the room turned full dark once again, and the fear of the men, now blind, became a thing Pythun could smell and taste on the air.

Pythun allowed himself to smile. *Soon, Master, soon.*

23

The night had grown even colder while they were inside The Thirsty Noble, and a steady breeze had picked up. Theo shivered despite the fast pace of her walk and pulled her cloak tighter around her. The weather was not treating her well this autumn. She would have to find warmer clothes soon, before the cold weather got worse.

Theo paused to let Aeryn and Tynan catch up and to unroll the sleeves of her shirt. She bunched the excess cloth of the too-long sleeves up in her small fists and then crossed her arms. "Hurry up," she whined at them.

When she turned to continue down the street, however, Aeryn laid a hand on her shoulder. "Wait just a minute," the sell-sword said.

"We don't have a minute," Theo huffed.

Aeryn replied, "There's somewhere else I want to stop first, on Sturgis."

Theo frowned at the mention of the street on which Mulkin's stable yards and smithery sat. Even though Sturgis was on the way, she squinted with suspicion at Aeryn as she asked, "Why?"

"We need to stop at Mulkin's stables."

"What? Why?" Theo demanded. She needed to keep a distance from the blacksmith.

Aeryn said, "Pythun's interest in the sword makes me uneasy. I want insurance that he won't get it."

Tynan gave a small grunt of agreement and then said, "That is not a bad idea, Aeryn. I admit his interest worries me as well."

"How do you plan to get this insurance?" she asked.

"By asking for a favor." With that, Aeryn turned and walked off in the direction of the stables.

Theo frowned more deeply. Giving the sword to Mulkin was going to complicate matters, but she also knew she had no choice but to agree. Aeryn was unlikely to go with her to the guild otherwise. Pythun was going to be pissed that he would have to get it from the blacksmith when she told him.

Glaring in the dark, Theo jogged after Aeryn. The ghost followed as well. Other than agreeing with Aeryn, he had been strangely silent. Theo assumed that the priest he had seen gave him bad news. Too bad for him, she decided, but his fate was of little concern to her right now. She was more worried about what Pythun would do if he could not have Tynan's old sword.

When they arrived at the stable yard, Aeryn headed behind the stables to the blacksmith's forge and the small dwelling beside it. All of the windows were dark, including the ones above the stables, where Theo guessed the stable hands slept. The only sound was the rustle of grass blades and hay in the breeze. Aeryn knocked softly on Mulkin's door. They did not have long to wait before a light sprang up inside. A moment later, Mulkin opened the door.

The oversize blacksmith blinked at them sleepily before rumbling, "Lady Ravane, have you come to collect Rowan already?"

The sell-sword shook her head. "I have come to ask a favor of you, if you are willing."

The big man frowned and glanced into the black night behind them. Then, he stepped aside and gestured them inside. "Come in, away from prying eyes."

Theo cursed silently but followed the others inside. The ghost passed Mulkin without eliciting so much as a raised eyebrow, but when Theo went to enter, head ducked down, the blacksmith stopped her. Theo's heart leapt into her throat.

"We didn't formally meet before you ran off earlier today, little one," Mulkin said to her and bent down slightly, but when she involuntarily looked up at him, he hissed, "You!"

Theo swallowed and backed up. "It was an accident," she stammered. "I swear!"

Aeryn came back to the door. "What's going on?"

Mulkin looked at her angrily. "*She's* with you, too?"

"Against my better judgment, yes. What is the problem?"

Straightening to his full height, Mulkin stared down at Aeryn. "She's a horse thief. Or at the least she tried to be. She tried to steal a horse from a team left by a Ciran trader, but she ended up releasing the whole lot of 'em. They panicked, and I had to put a bunch of them down because of injuries they took trying to stampede out of the corral. I lost a good-paying customer that day, and I got no compensation for the loss from this one, because she took off running when those horses did."

Aeryn glared at Theo. Theo considered making a break for it again, but the look in Aeryn's eyes told her if she was not careful, she would lose the sell-sword's aid in getting her brother back from Pythun.

"Tell him it won't ever happen again," Aeryn ordered her.

"I swear, on my life, it will never happen again." She meant it, too. She felt bad about the horses—she had not known some had to be put down. It was her one and only attempt at horse thievery, a dare from her brother.

"You're damn right it'll never happen again, because you'll not get near my horses again, girl." With a speed that surprised Theo, Mulkin grabbed the front of her shirt and pulled her off her feet and into the cottage. He nudged the cottage door shut with his foot and then set her in a chair near the door. He ordered, "Sit there and don't move."

Theo did as she was told without question or complaint. Aeryn took her coin pouch off of her belt and extended it to the blacksmith. Mulkin settled himself into a chair opposite Theo and waved a dismissive hand at Aeryn.

"I won't take your money for something she did." He took a deep breath and gradually relaxed his dark brows, which were hunched over his brown eyes like storm clouds. "Now, what is it you wanted to

91

ask of me?"

Aeryn drew Aric from its sheath and laid it out on the table in front of Mulkin. The blacksmith's eyes lit up as he stared down at the sword. He passed a gentle hand over the metalwork.

Aeryn explained, "A man I've never met is looking for this. I know not why, but I intend to find out. I need a safe place to keep Aric for now. Will you hide it?"

"This is a beautiful piece of craftsmanship," Mulkin replied, tearing his gaze from Aric. "Who was the swordsmith, may I ask?"

"Vortenthas," Tynan spoke up.

Mulkin's eyes widened. "The dwarven god?"

"The very same," Tynan replied. "You can see its importance, of course, and why it should not fall into the hands of the wrong person."

"Indeed, sir." Mulkin rose. "Yes, I will do this favor for you, Lady Ravane."

"Thank you, Mulkin," Aeryn replied, also rising. "I owe you a debt for your help. We'll take our leave and entrust Aric to your care. As soon as I can, I'll return for the sword."

The stable master nodded and shook her hand. Then, he walked them back to the door, where they exited out into the cold and breezy night.

"Lead the way, little one," Tynan said.

Theo nodded, drawing her arms and her cloak close to her again. "We have to hurry."

24

It did not take long for the three to reach the Thieves' Guild. The wind continued blowing, picking up speed as they walked, and it blew Theo's blond hair into her eyes time and again. Thunder rumbled in the distance and added tension to the knots already tightening in Theo's gut. Even though she knew she had to bring Aeryn to Pythun for the sake of her brother, a sense of foreboding lurked in the corners of Theo's mind. She tried to push her doubts aside, unsuccessfully.

At the guild house door, Theo glanced first at Aeryn and then at Tynan. Tynan nodded her on, so she reached for the knocker, but before she could lay her hand on it, the door swung slowly open on its own, revealing the guild house's interior, completely shrouded in blackness but for a glowing gray orb that floated in front of them, just above Theo's eye level.

Theo pulled her hand back, thrown off guard. She hesitated, unsure what to do next. She finally spoke to the ball, knowing she should feel silly doing so, and feeling anything but. "We're here to see Pythun? I brought the sell-sword, and her, uh, companion."

The wind moaned and whistled through the open door, between the hinges. The sound made the hair on the back of Theo's neck stand up, and she wondered if the glowing ball would pursue them if they just turned tail and ran. As if it knew what she was thinking, the orb darted in front of Aeryn and hovered for a moment and then darted in front of Tynan. Then, it drifted away from the ghost and back into the guild house where it stopped again, waiting.

Lightning flashed behind them, followed by a crack of thunder that made Theo jump. The sky broke open. Being soaked by the pouring rain helped Theo make up her mind. She entered the guild house, and

Aeryn and Tynan followed her. As soon as all three cleared the threshold, the door swung shut behind them, and Theo heard a lock click into place. She turned back, the knot in her stomach becoming a hard stone. Aeryn whirled to face the closed door as well, her hands landing on the daggers strapped to her hips. She spun back to face the glowing orb when the ball's glow grew brighter.

"I don't like this," the sell-sword said.

Theo only nodded. This was the exact opposite of the reception she had expected. Big, ugly guards grabbing them as soon as they came in, yes. Weird glowing balls, no. Tynan was the only one who appeared unfazed by the situation.

He addressed the gray ball. "Take us to Pythun."

Finally, the sphere moved forward, leading them. It was impossible to tell where, however—the sphere's glow never grew strong enough to see beyond a three-foot radius. Theo's teeth clattered lightly. The inside of the guild house was colder than it should have been, and a foul smell emanated from somewhere beyond the orb's glow. Theo knew what the smell was, having had the misfortune to smell it a time or two before. She looked back at Aeryn, and judging from the grim look on the sell-sword's face, Aeryn knew what it was, too—the smell of death.

The gray ball paused and glowed a little brighter still, illuminating a stone staircase and a passageway at the bottom. Theo and Aeryn glanced at each other again as the ball began to descend the stairway; Tynan again took the lead.

"Where are we going?" Aeryn whispered as they followed Tynan and the gray orb.

"I don't know," Theo replied.

Cold sweat dampened the back of her neck. She had absolutely no idea where the sphere was leading them. She had never been to this part of the Thieves' Guild, and she had a feeling that wherever the passage led, she was not going to like it there.

When they reached the bottom of the staircase, the orb led them into the passageway. The walls were black stone, like that inside the Black Caverns. Theo wondered if Pythun had brought it here from the Black Mountains, and if so, why? The stone possessed an almost living, throbbing quality. A headache worked its way into Theo's skull. She rubbed her forehead and looked back at Aeryn again. The sell-sword's eyes were wide, and her hands did not leave the hilts of her daggers. Her knuckles were white from the force of her grip on them.

A light suddenly flared into existence at the end of the passage. The glowing orb led them toward it, and they entered a large, circular room also made of black stone. At the far end of the room, a huge throne appeared to grow out of the black stone floor. Pythun sat upon this throne, resplendent in a crimson silk robe, as straight and rigid as a king about to cast a death sentence on a trio of prisoners.

Theo walked ahead of Aeryn and Tynan. She exclaimed in a voice as confident as she could manage, "I was beginning to think we had the wrong place."

Pythun held up a hand and shouted, "Silence!"

Theo froze in midstep, held by an unseen force. She groaned with the effort of trying to dislodge herself from it.

"Theo?" Aeryn called out behind her.

"I can't move!"

Pythun laughed at her. "Foolish little girl." He called out to someone behind her, "Take them."

Theo heard Aeryn pull her sword loose from its sheath. Out of the corner of her eye, she saw creatures that looked like they had once been living men lurch into the room, and she recognized one as Bartok. She whimpered as the dead men surrounded the sell-sword.

Aeryn struck out at them with her sword, but there were too many, and they quickly overpowered her. Other guards grabbed Theo and dragged her toward Pythun. Their dead hands were impossibly cold, and the cold seemed to spread throughout her body.

"Tynan, do something!" Aeryn cried out, but the ghost just

looked at her helplessly.

Staring down at his outstretched hands, he said, "My magik. It's . . . it's gone."

25

Pythun addressed the dead adventurer in a smug tone. "Of course it is, Lord Tynan. Only my master's magik works here."

Aeryn tried to struggle against her captors, but their cold grips stole her strength from her. They dragged her closer to Theo and the man she assumed was Pythun. As she was brought before him, he stood and slid away from the throne. His smug look deepened.

"You all belong to my master now."

"We had a deal," Theo hissed at him. "You said Aeryn and the sword for my brother."

Pythun leaned over to pat her cheek. "Deals were made to be broken. As for your brother?" His shoulders shook with silent laughter. "He's dead. He has been dead for quite a long time now, and you did not even know it."

"No . . . *No!*" Theo wailed, tears streaming down her face.

The sorcerer laughed harder. "You did not honestly think I would allow him to live, did you? He cheated me. No one does that to me and lives. No one."

Aeryn felt badly for Theo and her loss, but she also knew she did not want to share the same fate as the girl's brother. She demanded, "What do you want with me? I don't have the sword."

Pythun stopped laughing and frowned at her. "Yes, I can see that. Know this: I will kill you all, but before you die you will tell me where you have hidden it."

It was Aeryn's turn to laugh. "I won't."

Tynan strode forward and proclaimed, "You may have taken my powers, but you will not take my sword."

"Oh, shut up," Pythun snarled, waving a hand in Tynan's

direction.

The gray orb that had led them to the chamber darted forward, expanding until it was a huge bubble. Tynan turned as it shot toward him. Instead of striking him, however, the gray bubble wrapped itself around him. The ghost pushed on the bubble's walls, but he could not penetrate it.

Pythun smirked. "That is much better." He turned back to Aeryn. "Worry not. I will not harm your beloved hero just yet. Yes, I know much about you, all of you. My master has told me so much," Pythun said.

"You won't be finding out anything more from me," Aeryn growled back.

"My master will make you tell him what he needs to know."

Pythun turned away from her and returned to his throne, standing in front of it. He raised his hands over his head and turned his face upward. "Master, please come to me now and lend me your power."

For a moment, nothing happened, and all was silent. Then, a breeze passed through the room, and in an instant, quickened into a full gale. The wind whipped around the circular chamber until it became a whirlwind. Aeryn put her head down as the wind blew her dark hair into her eyes. Dirt and other debris pelted her.

She could no longer see Pythun but heard him shout, "Yes! Yes!" again and again. But suddenly, his exulted ravings were cut off by a cry of pain. The sound of a body falling to the floor followed, and the whirlwind ceased.

"No, Master, wait," Pythun moaned, and then Aeryn heard a gurgling sound.

Tossing her hair out of her eyes, Aeryn looked around; Theo met her gaze, but neither of them spoke. Pythun lay on the floor in a writhing heap in front of the black throne, seeming to struggle against a sickly yellow light that surrounded him. His mouth hung open in a silent scream. His body arched upright suddenly.

Pythun's face become more sallow and gaunt, and two lumps formed on the sides of his head, throbbing as if something there fought to get out. The skin broke open, and two horns emerged and curled down the sides of his head. Blood ran down the sides of his face, but Pythun did not seem to notice. He fell onto his hands and knees, with his heavy horned head resting on the ground. His fingernails dug at the dirt floor and changed into black claws. Then, Pythun stopped his writhing.

The creature formerly known as Pythun rose to its feet and opened its eyes, displaying bright yellow eyes with slits at their center, like the eyes of a serpent. The creature grinned at them, displaying two rows of thin, black, pointed teeth unlike any teeth Aeryn had ever seen before. When the creature laughed, its voice was nothing like Pythun's.

"No," Tynan whispered. "It cannot be."

The thing laughed again. "It can and it is. You thought you could wish me away, but you could not, Tynan Selvantyr."

"What are you?" Aeryn asked.

"The Harbinger," Tynan replied. The ghost's voice sounded hollow, defeated.

The creature Tynan called The Harbinger stretched its neck and shoulders, the joints audibly popping. Yellow energy bursts crawled over its body. The creature came toward her. Aeryn was unable to pull back from it, and it grabbed her chin with its clawed fingers.

"This world no longer knows my name. Too long has it been absent from this world. Once, the very mention of my name made you mortals tremble in terror. Those days will come again now, for I am The Harbinger. *The Bringer.*"

"Bringer of what? All I see is a whole lot of ugly," Aeryn sneered at him.

A smile curled the corners of The Harbinger's mouth. Darkness, thick and cruel, entered her mind and slithered around in it. Despair filled her heart at the same time as a stabbing pain behind her eyes brought tears to them.

"I am the Harbinger of Death," the creature told her. "I am the Harbinger of everlasting Darkness and untold Suffering. You have never known torment like I will show you. Tynan knows these things, for he knows me well, as I know him well. There is much in his past that would shock you, and it's a pity you will know none of them. Right now, you have something I want, and once I get it, your soul shall sate my hunger."

Aeryn's jaw tightened. "I will not tell you."

He grinned and stroked her face with his other hand. Yellow energy crackled along his fingers and touched her face, bringing with it sharp pain in her head and behind her eyes. Aeryn's eyes squeezed shut as she grimaced.

"Aeryn, fight him," Tynan told her. "You cannot let him have Aric."

The Harbinger snarled and let go of her. The dead men holding her kept her upright. She felt blood trickling from her nose and ears, but she forced her eyes open and saw the creature turn toward Tynan. The ghost's arms flew wide and his back arched. Then, he screamed with a pain Aeryn knew he should not be able to feel.

"I do not need Aric. I can use you just as easily. If I do not get the sword, this is exactly what I will do. Do not toy with me."

The Harbinger grabbed Aeryn again. "Do you understand this? I will use Tynan's energies in place of the sword, unless you tell me where it is hidden."

"Go to hell," Aeryn hissed.

The Harbinger growled and closed his clawed fingers around her throat. More of the creature's dark energies poured into her. Aeryn fought against it, but cried out with the pain it caused her. She felt the creature digging into her mind, searching for the information it needed.

Theo shouted, "Leave her alone!"

The Harbinger ignored her, and Aeryn continued to fight the creature. The struggle seemed to weaken it. Soon, The Harbinger grunted

100

with exertion and then let go of her.

Pythun's voice separated itself from The Harbinger's. "Master, perhaps the child can tell us."

The Harbinger made a sound of agreement and moved away from Aeryn to Theo. Aeryn wanted to protest, stop the creature, but she could only hang limp from the dead guards' grasp. The Harbinger told Theo, "It is your turn."

"Go ahead, puss bucket," she hissed.

He laughed. "That is no way to talk to a god. The only god this pitiful world will know, soon enough. Your brother knew this before he died."

A sob escaped Theo. "You bastard."

The Harbinger chuckled as he stared deep into her eyes.

Aeryn heard the girl cry out and then The Harbinger laughed.

"No, she has nothing to do with this! " Theo howled.

"We shall see. I think she would be the perfect person to hide the sword with."

Aeryn raised her head finally and saw the creature turn away from the girl, who sagged in the grip of the dead guards. The Harbinger ran a hand over the surface of the sphere holding Tynan. "Now, you will give me what I want, too. You know you have no choice," The Harbinger told him.

Tynan stood tall. "You can take what you will from me, but you will be stopped."

"Not likely. I tire of listening to you, Tynan Selvantyr." The creature's clawed fingers traced intricate patterns that turned into sigils on the swirling surface of the sphere. They glowed with shifting hues of red. "I once offered you the chance to aid me in my return from my banishment, but you refused me. If you had done so, you may have achieved the everlasting fame you so craved."

"You did not want aid from me. You wanted a willing slave, like Pythun."

"Pythun will be hailed through the ages as the one who sacrificed himself so I may once again rule. His name will be remembered, while yours will not."

"Such hubris," Tynan sneered at the creature.

The creature laughed at him. "You dare accuse me of hubris? That is a lot coming from the likes of you. Your pride was your greatest downfall. Always wanting to be the greatest, most daring hero of them all, and all the while pretending to be the purest, too. We both know that is a lie. In the end, your pride killed Rimen."

The ghost's face quivered with rage. "It was you who killed Rimen. I knew it was your hand that guided me that day, in retribution for my refusal of your proposal. *You* made me take my company into that valley that day, and *you* guided that arrow. You wanted to feed on my pain."

The Harbinger chuckled. "I had no hand in that affair, though I loathe to confess as such. Your pride drove you that day. You started something you could not finish, but you refused to admit it. You killed him. Be sure to tell him that when you see him in the underworld."

The creature finished drawing symbols on the sphere's surface and raised his arms above his head. He murmured words in a guttural language that sounded vile and evil to Aeryn's ears. The crimson sleeves of the silken robes he wore slid down, revealing emaciated arms traced up and down by crackling arcane energies. A new wind stirred in the circular chamber. Aeryn braced herself as the wind picked up. She wished to stop whatever The Harbinger was attempting, but though she struggled against the undead guards, they continued to hold her fast.

The Harbinger's voice rose. Lightning snapped in the air, followed by a roll of thunder through the room. The sigils on Tynan's prison flared brighter. His form floated to the center of the sphere, his arms coming away from his sides and his head tilting back. Tendrils of yellow light snaked around and between both him and The Harbinger.

The tendrils coalesced into a bright light that engulfed both their

102

forms. Thunder rolled through the room again, deafening in the close quarters. The wind became a fury, and Aeryn felt herself being pushed toward the walls of the chamber. Even the guards holding her and Theo were unable to keep their footing. Only The Harbinger and Tynan remained in the center of the room.

A blinding light burst forth from Tynan's prison, and Aeryn collided with the stone wall. Before her world went black, she heard The Harbinger say, "And now, all will suffer."

26

Not for the first time that night, Willa's thoughts turned to Theo. A full day had passed since Theo left the inn with the sell-sword and that strange ghost. Mykel assured her several times that Theo was fine, but Willa could not help feel like something must have gone terribly wrong if Theo had not returned to tell her everything went fine. Theo would not make her wait and wonder, and she felt an odd energy in the air. It seemed she was not the only one who sensed it either.

Even before evening set in, patrons came pouring in. Some complained of the rain that had begun the night before and still feel, and others complained of headaches. Willa found this latter complaint the most disconcerting, since she herself spent most of the day lying down with a painful headache of her own, much to Jonas's annoyance. It started in the afternoon, working its way from the back of her skull to the front until her entire head throbbed. She told herself the headache was just a symptom of worry for Theo, but hearing the complaints of the other patrons, she wondered if this was actually true.

Now, at nearly midnight, the common room was so filled with customers that making her way through the crowd to deliver drinks and food grew increasingly difficult. This was so not only because of the amount of people crowded into the common room, but also due to the level of their intoxication. They kept stumbling into her path, cajoling her to join in on songs or listen to a bawdy joke, or just plain grabbing her.

Willa was just about to beckon one of the inn's bouncers to save her from the grasp of yet another over-drunk patron, when the inn's front door thundered open, knocking patrons out of the way and banging into the wall behind it. A blast of frigid air, much colder than the season warranted, ripped through the common room. Everyone fell silent, including the man who was groping her just a moment before. All eyes turned to the door.

Willa, too, looked toward the open door. A gasp died in her throat. In marched a group of men, no, dead men—walking corpses, gaunt and ashen faced, with white eyes that did not blink. At their center walked a tall demon dressed in crimson robes. Curled horns, thick and heavy, grew out of either side of its head from a shock of black hair. Something about the creature felt ancient, and Willa sensed the profound evil of it pouring off in waves.

The men and women in the inn parted in silence to allow the entourage to pass. The group marched through the center of the common room until they reached the bar and halted without word or signal from their master. The creature looked over the silent common room, scanning the terrified faces of the patrons.

"Which of you is Willa?" it asked.

Willa was partially hidden by the patron who had been groping her, and who now stared dumbfounded at the newcomer. Were it not for Mykel and his close proximity to the demon, she may have fled the inn right then, but she stayed for him. She started forward, driven by some force she could not explain.

"I am," she told the creature as she stepped out from behind the patron obscuring her.

The creature's lips peeled back in the approximation of a grin, revealing black teeth as thin and sharp as razors. Before it could speak, however, Mykel jumped over the bar and placed himself between her and the demon.

"Leave her be," Mykel growled. He brandished a club at the creature, but although the creature was quite thin, its height alone—well over seven feet, Willa guessed—made Mykel and his club look insignificant.

Without a word, the demon grabbed Mykel by the throat and for a moment held him in midair. Then, it tossed Mykel back over the bar. He hit the wall behind the bar with a crunch of breaking wood and bones, and slid senseless to the floor. Willa heard Daphne nearby shriek with fear, and she herself quietly sobbed Mykel's name.

"Stop your blubbering, mortal," the demon commanded.

She did not. "What are you? What do you want?" she asked of it.

"I am The Harbinger. I seek the sword of Tynan Selvantyr, and I will slaughter everyone here until I get it."

27

Pain woke Aeryn, letting her know she was still alive. Other sensations, wetness being the most predominant, followed suit. Nearby, someone sobbed. Then came the stench of stagnant water, moldering wood, and decaying things. As full sensation returned to her, Aeryn realized that the lower half of her body rested in water, while her upper half lay against something mossy but hard.

Aeryn's eyes fluttered open. She faced a wall of stone blocks. Groaning, she shifted herself and saw her shoulders rested on a moss-covered stone, which stuck out of the shallow pool of water in which her lower half rested. Looking around, Aeryn saw bodies—at least a dozen—chained to the walls of the room, all in different stages of putrefaction. To her surprise, she found she was not chained, nor was Theo, who was nearby.

The girl huddled in the opposite corner of the room, sobbing quietly next to one of the bodies. The body was little more than a skeleton with clothes still hanging from it. Aeryn pushed herself upright into a sitting position, ignoring the ache that permeated every bone in her body. She called the girl's name. Theo did not answer, but she stopped crying and swiped her hands over her eyes.

Aeryn slicked back her wet hair and struggled to her feet, which were now bare. Her boots, cloak, and all of her weapons were gone. She slogged through the fetid water to where Theo knelt, careful where she stepped, and crouched down beside the girl.

"What's wrong?"

The girl wiped her face again, using the wet sleeves of her oversized shirt. She gestured at the grimy cell. "Besides the obvious?"

"Where are we?" Aeryn asked. She looked around the room

again and saw no door until she looked up. There, a round hole with an iron grate served as the only way in or out of the cell. "Is this the Valis dungeons?"

Theo shook her head. "This is my brother's body. This was Brien." She laid a hand on a silver chain that hung around the skeleton's neck bone. "This was his. He told me he took it right out of the pocket of a nobleman at a carnival. He said the mark didn't even know he'd been robbed until Brien had it around his own neck. Brien said the mark chased him for two blocks before he gave up. Brien was one of the fastest runners around, which is why Pythun used him so much."

She wiped away more tears, not looking at Aeryn. "He made a big mistake, alright, stealing from Pythun. But all Brien wanted was to collect enough for us to leave this dump and go to Cira, or maybe Lyre—any place that wasn't here. I couldn't save him, and Pythun or The Harbinger or whoever left Brien's body here for me to find. Sadistic bastard."

"Why not kill us, too?" Aeryn wondered aloud.

Theo shrugged. "I've got no idea. I heard something about everyone suffering before I blacked out."

Aeryn nodded. "I heard that, too."

"I think Tynan's gone. I saw a burst of light, like he was blasted out of existence."

Aeryn's brow knitted as a number of different emotions flooded her, but she shoved them aside, aware that they did her no good now. "It doesn't matter right now. What matters is our getting out of here."

She got up and positioned herself under the iron grate, looking for anything to grab onto to pull herself up to its level.

"Why bother?" Theo asked from behind her. "What's to say there's anything left out there? That thing seemed bent on taking its revenge out on everything."

Aeryn glanced over her shoulder at the girl. "I'm not going to sit here waiting to die. I'm getting out of here."

Theo rose and came to stand next to Aeryn. "But *then* what are you going to do?"

Aeryn sighed and went back to studying the only way out of the underground cell. "As far as we know, Aric is still safe. But that thing wants it, and he seems pretty adamant about getting it."

Theo crossed her arms over her chest. "You don't even know what he wanted it for, though."

"I'm figuring things out as I go," Aeryn muttered and then looked down at the girl. "Why must you always argue? What of your friends? Don't you want to make sure they're safe?"

"I don't have any—" Theo's eyes widened. Running both hands through her damp hair, she murmured, "Oh, no."

"What? What is it?"

"You're right. We have to get out of here. Now."

Aeryn did not question the sudden shift in the girl's attitude. Best to take advantage while it lasted. "I cannot reach the grate, but you can, if I give you a hand up. Can you pick the lock?"

Theo nodded. "Probably. I can pick most."

Aeryn knelt down and laced her fingers so that Theo could use them as a foothold. The girl put one foot in Aeryn's hands and a hand on Aeryn's shoulder to steady herself. Aeryn stood and raised her arms higher to allow Theo to better reach the hole, but looking up, she saw the girl's fingers barely reached the edges of the grate. Aeryn raised her arms higher. Perspiration stood out on her forehead. She could not push Theo up any higher or hold her for much longer.

"Step onto my shoulders to get higher. I can't hold you like this."

"I can't."

Aeryn closed her eyes. Her arms started shaking. "Don't argue," she hissed.

"Just drop me!"

Aeryn dropped her hands, and the girl jumped down into the water. Aeryn crouched down and rubbed her shaking arms.

109

"This isn't going to work," Theo told her.

"It will, if you just try. You have a choice to make an effort and make this work, so we can get out of here, or you can give up and die next to your brother."

Theo's lip quivered a moment then stopped. "Alright." She went over to Brien's skeleton and unclasped the chain around the corpse's neck and then put it around her own. "For luck," she said.

Theo returned to Aeryn, but as Aeryn stood up, Theo shook her head. "No, crouch down again. I'll sit on your shoulders and then stand up."

Aeryn crouched down again as instructed, and Theo climbed onto her shoulders. Aeryn stood up.

"Put up your hands, so I have something to hold onto," Theo told her next. "And lean forward."

Aeryn raised her hands, and Theo grabbed onto them and then placed one foot and then the other on Aeryn's shoulders. She crouched on Aeryn's shoulders, using Aeryn's hands for support. Slowly, the girl stood until she was high enough to reach the grate. Aeryn was thankful that the girl was lighter on her shoulders than in her hands.

"Okay, I can reach the lock," Theo said. "I can't see anything above the grate, though. Everything is dark up here."

"How are you going to pick the lock?" Aeryn asked her.

"The charm on Brien's necklace. It doubles as a pick."

Aeryn heard scraping sounds and then a dull click when the lock opened. The grate slid loose with a squeal of metal and swung downward, nearly knocking both of them off-balance.

"Whoa," Theo breathed when she caught it.

"I'll move back. Hold on," Aeryn told her.

She backed away from the falling grate, holding on to the girl. Theo let the grate swing open the rest of the way.

"Can you climb up?"

"I think so," Theo replied.

She grabbed on to the grate and stepped off of Aeryn's shoulders. Then, she scrambled through the opening into the chamber above. Aeryn waited for Theo to reappear, but several moments passed without her returning. She wondered if there was someone guarding the hole, even though she heard no sounds of a struggle. She was about to call up to the girl when a rope ladder spilled over the edge of the hole into the cell below.

Theo's face appeared at the edge of the hole. "You've got to get up here."

Even from far below, Aeryn could see the pallor of Theo's face. Aeryn climbed the ladder as quickly as she was able. What she found when she pulled herself over the edge of the hole and into the room above shocked her.

Only one torch still guttered in the room above the cell, but it lit the room well enough for Aeryn to see the pile of their belongings on one side of the room. On the other side, however, were ten or so corpses lying against the walls. It was the bodies that Theo stared at. Their skin looked stretched over their skulls, and their eyes sunken and grayish-white. It looked to Aeryn as though something had sucked the life straight out of them.

"I knew some of them," Theo murmured. "He killed everyone. Why did he do this?"

Aeryn did not have an answer for her. She wondered how her life turned so quickly from fulfilling her father's quest to facing something that did this to people. She grabbed up her boots and tugged them on. Then, she pulled on her cloak and her baldric, while Theo continued to stare at the corpses. Aeryn gathered up Theo's belongings as well and handed them to the girl.

Aeryn placed a hand on Theo's arm. "We can't stay here. We need to leave. Come on." She did not wait for an answer as she headed out the only other door in the room, bracing herself for what else they might find.

28

It seemed to Aeryn that an interminable amount of time passed between their escape from the underground cell and the moment they found their way out of the guild house to the street outside. From one room to the next, they passed dozens more corpses, all thankfully inanimate, but all in states similar to those they had found in the room above the cell. Theo said she recognized more of them. No child should have to see people she knew that way. The girl's face was a mask of sick horror as they made their way through the guild house.

When they finally exited the horror house, it was into a raging storm. Rain poured down on them and blew in sheets whipped up by the wind. Sharp forks of lightning lanced the sky, followed by furious cracks of thunder. It was night still, but the sky's eastern edge appeared to be getting lighter, indicating that dawn was near. Aeryn wondered just how long they were trapped inside the guild house. She looked up and down the street, but saw no other soul out in the storm.

Then, Aeryn noticed a strange sound on the air—no, more of a sensation than a sound—a thrumming vibration like the string of a musical instrument being struck again and again, but without any music. She tilted her head, trying to find where it was coming from, only it hurt her head the longer she concentrated on it.

Theo asked, "Where is everyone?"

"I don't know," Aeryn replied, shouting over the pounding of the rain. "Do you feel that?"

"Yeah," Theo shouted back. She slicked her dark blond hair back. "I don't know what it is, but I think we better get away from here."

Aeryn nodded but did not move. "It's familiar."

Theo moved closer and grabbed her arm. "We have to go," the

112

girl insisted.

Aeryn nodded again and pulled herself from her contemplation of the vibration in the air. They started off in a jog through the rain toward the city's main road. Most of the streetlamps had been extinguished by the storm, but the approaching dawn and lightning lit their way well enough. At the main road, Aeryn turned in the direction of Mulkin's smithery and then realized Theo was no longer beside her. Skidding to a stop, she turned around to look for her. Theo was headed in the opposite direction.

Aeryn called after her, "Where are you going?"

Theo stopped as well. "We have to get back to The Thirsty Noble."

She jogged over to Theo. "Why there? We need the sword."

"You get the sword. I have to find Willa."

The young thief started to turn away, but Aeryn put a hand on her shoulder, stopping her. "We shouldn't split up."

"I know." Theo frowned, and her brow furrowed as if she was trying to remember something. "I think Willa is in danger. The Harbinger—just go get the sword and meet me back at the inn."

"No. It is too dangerous for you to go on your own. We have no idea where that creature—The Harbinger—is now. We get the sword first and then we'll check on your friend."

Still, Theo hesitated. "I don't want you to end up like those people at the Thieves' Guild," Aeryn said.

Theo finally nodded. "Alright, but we need to hurry."

Aeryn turned back toward Mulkin's stables. The scene there was much the same as it was everywhere: the stable yard was eerily quiet aside from the sounds of the rain and thunder. No people came out to greet them. As they approached the blacksmith's forge and the cottage, the neighing of horses, high-pitched with nervousness, reached Aeryn's ears. The absence of people here was wrong, Aeryn knew—Mulkin always rose by first light. He told her so the first time she left Rowan

113

with him.

Aeryn drew her longsword and rounded the forge to Mulkin's cottage behind it. She rapped on the cottage door, softly at first and then harder. No one answered. Theo glanced at Aeryn, unease plain on her face. Aeryn tried the door handle; it was unlocked. She pushed gently on the door. It opened with a soft creak. The cottage was dark inside. A sick feeling of familiarity wormed its way into Aeryn's gut.

"Mulkin?" she called into the dark cottage.

Still, no answer.

She pushed the door open further and laid a hand on Theo's shoulder to indicate she should wait there. She stepped inside the cottage, both hands on her sword.

In the cottage's main room, she found several candles spent down to mere nubs, as though they simply burned until they extinguished themselves, and embers still glowed in the hearth. Mulkin *was* there, but where? A platter with half a loaf of coarse bread and a wedge of cheese sat on a tall round table, both half-eaten. Aeryn's stomach growled at the sight of the food, and she realized she could not remember when she ate last.

"Where is he?" Theo asked behind her, causing Aeryn to start.

Aeryn collected herself and chided the girl, "You should have waited outside."

"I didn't want to be alone out there."

"Where do you think he hid the sword?"

That was a good question. Aeryn glanced around the room. She had only been inside the cottage once, but she looked for anything that seemed out of place. Nothing stood out until she noticed a trunk near the doorway to the cottage's back room was slightly askew. Knowing Mulkin's penchant for precision, Aeryn knew it was not accidental. She sheathed her sword and went to the heavy trunk. She tugged on it. It barely moved.

"Help me," she requested.

Theo came over, and together they pulled the heavy trunk away from the wall. Underneath, a trapdoor with a recessed lock was cut into the floor.

"Can you do something about this?" she asked Theo, indicating the lock.

Theo nodded and took out her picks. Aeryn watched the girl open the lock with a swiftness that made Aeryn wonder how long the girl had been doing such things. When Theo removed the picked lock, Aeryn pulled up the trapdoor and found a stash of items atop a long blanket-wrapped object. She reached down and pulled the other items out of the hideaway and then pulled out the blanket-wrapped object. She left out a sigh of relief when she slid back the blanket and found the object was indeed Aric. Her relief was short-lived, however, when she placed her hand on the sword's hilt. The sword hummed in her hand with a soft vibration. She frowned.

"What is it?" Theo asked. "The sword's safe, so let's go to the inn."

Aeryn slid Aric back into the second sheath slung over her back. "First, we should try to find Mulkin so that he knows we're taking the sword back."

She stood and went into the only other room in the cottage. By the dim light coming through a crack in the cloth covering the single window in the room, she saw an empty bed. The bed was made and appeared not to have been slept in at all. She glanced down at the writing desk that sat under the window. An open book caught her eye. To better see, she pulled back the cloth, letting in a little more dawn light.

It was a journal. Elegant handwriting, surprising for a blacksmith, filled the pages. Aeryn leaned closer to read the last entry.

Fifth day of Ives
It has been more than a day since the sell-sword came to me to ask her favor. As promised, I hid it, but since then, there is something

115

odd in the air. People are acting strange. Everyone has shorter tempers than usual, and I've witnessed fights break out over nothing. Customers keep complaining of headaches.

I smell smoke in the air now. Something burns, and the smoke is thick and foul. The winds will be feeding it for certain.

I don't know what is happening to us, and I don't think I can fight the thoughts in my head anymore. I don't want to wait and see what will happen next. I must protect my boys. People are becoming monsters. I don't recognize myself. It can't continue. I hear thunder. I should hurry.

May the gods forgive me for what I know I must do now.

A chill ran down Aeryn's spine, and the sickness in the pit of her stomach grew. She reached down to touch the writing on the page. The ink was still wet. She reread the last line and then bolted for the cottage door, heading for the stables. Theo called after her, but Aeryn did not stop.

The constant rain had turned the stable yard into a thick swamp, and she slipped several times as she ran. When she reached the stable doors, she lost her footing again as she struggled to pull the doors open. She wrestled them open far enough to fit through. She passed several agitated horse that neighed at her. At the back of the stables, a ladder went up to the loft bunks. Aeryn scurried up the ladder.

At the top of the ladder was a hay loft and a wall with a door that she assumed led to the stable boys' bunks. She tried the handle. It was locked. Aeryn shouted Mulkin's name, but she received no answer from Mulkin or anyone else. She stepped back and kicked the door. It took her several tries, but finally, the door gave way. A single lantern illuminated the scene inside the bunkroom. She clapped a hand over her mouth at the sight of the horror before her, bile rising in her throat. She fought it back.

In the stables below, she heard Theo come to the bottom of the ladder and call her name.

116

"Don't come up here!" Aeryn shouted at her.

She stared at the bodies in front of her, Mulkin's included, and a wave of anger passed over her. She wondered first how Mulkin could do this, but then she realized this was not really him, this was whatever The Harbinger had unleashed once he was resurrected by Pythun. This was not Mulkin's doing. It was The Harbinger's.

Once Aeryn descended the ladder to the stables below, Theo asked, "What's up there?"

Aeryn shook her head. "We need to get to the inn and check on your friend."

Part of her knew what they would find there, but she prayed she was wrong.

29

The journey back to The Thirsty Noble was made in silence. Theo did not know what the sell-sword had found in the stable boys' bunkroom, nor did she think she wanted to know, based on the woman's pallor when she descended the loft ladder. Whatever she saw up there had rendered the normally reserved sell-sword even more so. Part of Theo missed Tynan's pompous chatter. That at least provided a distraction, which she desperately needed the closer they got to The Thirsty Noble.

The sun had now risen, though it remained behind a thick curtain of storm clouds. It lit the city better now. The absence of people, birds, and even animals became all the more stark. The rain stopped, but the wind continued, whipping at their hair and clothes, and pushing the smell of burning wood and something more pungent in their direction.

The smell thickened the farther they went. Fear clenched itself into a tight stone in the pit of Theo's stomach, making her feel sick. The sight of what was left of the inn stopped her heart. Theo let out a strangled sob.

Before Aeryn could bring Rowan to a stop, Theo threw herself down from the saddle. She skidded in the mud, but caught herself and ran toward the ruins of the inn. Most of the second story was gone, and smoke still curled from the charred remains. The lower floor did not look any better.

All of the windows and door were blown out, as if some great explosion took place inside. She ran through the remains of the front doors, crunching through the broken glass from the windows without heed. Before she got very far, though, arms wrapped around her middle and lifted her off her feet. She fought them, but Aeryn turned her away,

away from the scene inside the common room. Not before she spotted the piles of charred bodies, however.

Aeryn let her down, but held onto her, blocking her view of what was inside. "Stop! I don't think you want to see this," the sell-sword told her.

Theo continued to fight her, but with less conviction now. She knew Aeryn was right. Tears streamed down her face, but she said, "I know, but I need to find Willa, no matter what."

The sell-sword's mouth was a thin line as she looked at Theo. After a moment, though, she nodded and let Theo go.

Everything inside was black. Bodies lay one on top of another. They lined the walls, some burnt beyond recognition, and others like the bodies they found in the guild house. If she had any doubt before, Theo knew now that The Harbinger had been there, and it was her fault. Her shoulders shook as new tears came, but she steeled herself. She needed to find Willa, if Willa was here.

Aeryn stepped in front of her again and reached into a pouch on her belt, from which she extracted a flat white stone. She shook three times, and it started to glow. The sell-sword held the lightstone up, so they could see.

Black dust and ash rose up in small clouds with each step they took through the bodies and the rubble. Theo bit her lip as she identified the bodies of some of the inn's regulars and some of the staff by uncharred clothes and other identifiable items. Perhaps Willa made it out, Theo thought. This hope died when she reached the area of the common room where the bar was.

She spotted Mykel's remains first, identifiable by the woven leather bracelet he always wore, now a sooty black instead of red. Next to him lay Willa, her arms still wrapped around him. Theo knew it was her by the flower pin on her apron. Theo had given it to her. A sound, caught between a sigh and a sob, escaped her as she sank down beside her only friend. She reached out a hand to touch a piece of Willa's brown hair, the only part of her untouched by whatever destroyed the inn. It was no longer the beautiful chestnut color it once was. Now, it was dry and brittle, and strands of it broke off when she stroked it. Startled, Theo jerked her hand back.

After a time, Aeryn crouched next to her and spoke softly. "We should go. There's nothing you can do for her now."

Theo looked at the sell-sword. "I should've gotten here sooner."

"I think it would have been too late, even if we came straight here," Aeryn said. "We were in that cell for two days."

"Two days?"

"Mulkin's journal was open on his desk. The last entry was dated the fifth of Ives, today. We went to the guild on the night of the third. Even if we had come straight here, it wouldn't have mattered. I think The Harbinger came here first, after we were locked up in the cell."

Theo's angrily wiped her tears away. "This is my fault."

"Don't say that."

"It is," Theo insisted. "When The Harbinger questioned me about Aric, I tried to fight him, but I couldn't, and then Willa's face popped into my head. I think The Harbinger thought the sword was with her. I couldn't make him believe it wasn't. I couldn't stop him."

"I'm sorry," Aeryn said and tried to put a hand on Theo's shoulder.

Theo pushed it away and shook her head. "Don't. I just need to be alone."

"I understand, but I don't think that's the best course of action right now. We don't know where The Harbinger is. We should stick together and find him."

The last thing Theo wanted to do was find The Harbinger. In fact, staying far away from him seemed like a great idea. Yet, she also could not let what he did to Willa go unanswered. "Find him how?"

Aeryn frowned. "I don't know yet. I need to think." The sell-sword paused. "We should return to Mulkin's."

120

"Why there?"

"Because we know for sure The Harbinger *isn't* there."

Theo sighed but nodded. "Fine. Let's just get out of here." Without waiting for Aeryn, Theo exited the ruins of the inn. She did not want to remember it this way.

Aeryn remounted her stallion and offered Theo a hand up, but Theo shook her head. "If you don't mind, I'd rather walk."

The sell-sword nodded and nudged her horse into a slow walk next to Theo. If this was the farthest she could get from the sell-sword, she would take it. While Aeryn was being nice enough to her, Theo knew this forced partnership was not what either of them wanted. Yet, a part of her feared being without the sell-sword.

When she had woken in the cell below the guild house, she had found the sell-sword lying almost completely underwater. It was Theo who saved her for once and pulled Aeryn up onto the rock so that she would not drown. This did not make her feel any great kinship with Aeryn, though. Theo just wanted her life to go back to the way it was, with Brien and Willa both safe, and her never having heard of Aeryn or Tynan or The Harbinger.

Brien and Willa were among the few people Theo trusted in life, an attitude born out of necessity, and one influenced heavily by the lessons taught to her by Brien. He always said there were few people you could rely on other than yourself. This was the motto he lived by and taught her to live by. Theo was not ready to include Aeryn in the list of those she trusted implicitly. From her standpoint, she was officially alone in this world.

30

"I'll start a fire once we get inside. I just want to get the saddle off Rowan first," Aeryn said, removing his harness.

Theo nodded and glanced around at the dirt stretch behind Mulkin's property. She still felt the weird thrumming in the air. It was very faint, but it made her teeth ache. Strangely, the sensation seemed to fade whenever she was inside a building. Many strange things were happening now. She wondered why this should seem any stranger.

Aeryn finished placing the last of her gear in a neat pile against the cottage wall. She turned to the cottage door and unsheathed her sword before opening the door again. The sell-sword told Theo to stay outside while she checked for anyone who may have entered the cottage while they were at the inn. She returned only a moment later, telling Theo it was all clear.

While Aeryn busied herself with building a fresh fire in the hearth, Theo went through Mulkin's cupboards, looking for something to eat. Mulkin kept himself well-stocked with food, it seemed, but although there were plenty of things in his pantry that she would normally enjoy, she realized that for once she was not the least bit hungry. Theo sighed and closed the pantry doors.

Aeryn had a fire blazing in the hearth and stood watching it. She turned back to Theo. "Are you alright?"

Theo shrugged. "I'm not hungry."

"I'm not either. I'm going to look out in the shed I saw for something I can use to rinse out my clothes and wash up a little. The stench of that cell still hangs on me, and I would like to be rid of it. Stay and get warmed up while I do that."

Theo nodded and settled herself in an overstuffed chair near the hearth. She curled up in it when she heard the door close softly behind Aeryn. Her gaze went to the flames dancing in the hearth, and she thought back to when she and Brien sat by the hearth in the common room of The Thirsty Noble, three times the size of this cottage hearth, and drank spiced cider on cold nights. They would listen to the stories the drovers told of battling storms in the mountain passes and the adventurers' tales of frightening beasts they slew in the hills. Some talked of the rare beauty of the elven Forever Wood. Theo dared to imagine a different life for herself back then, one filled with hidden treasures Brien stumbled upon and used to take her away from the slums of Valis, but in the end, she was always just a dumb kid dreaming by the fire.

Theo started to drift off from the warmth of the fire in the cottage's hearth. Suddenly, a shout from outside and a metallic thud brought her fully awake again. Her eyes flew open, and she darted for the cottage door, wondering if somehow the dead stable boys had risen again and were attacking Aeryn.

She nearly ran into Aeryn, who was backpedaling toward the door Theo had just thrown open, her sword drawn again. Theo laid a hand on Aeryn's back to let her know she was behind her and then she peered around the sell-sword to see what spooked her. In the middle of the cottage yard stood a creature no taller than herself, with leathery gray skin and black eyes. It looked comical in a wicked sort of way. It wore no clothes other than some dirty rags fashioned about it here and there. Its bare skin appeared too big for it and hung in wrinkles. Perhaps the creature was very old, Theo thought.

The little creature shuffled toward them, one foot dragging slightly in the dirt. "The master. The master has been risen. He has. He has," the thing cackled, gesturing with one clawed hand. The creature held its other hand close to its chest. Paired with the dragging foot, Theo decided the creature looked more like an ugly broken toy than anything else.

"What is it?" Theo asked. She imagined it could be a goblin, if this was what goblins looked like, and if they smelled like rotting cheese, as this thing did.

Aeryn did not reply. She continued to shift backward while the creature moved forward. "Stop," she commanded the creature.

The creature did stop. It tilted its head as it stared at them with its black eyes, hard and blank like coal. "The master," it repeated. "You feel his power. All in the air." It moved toward them again, raising its good arm above its head and waving it in the air.

Aeryn stood her ground and shouted at it again, "Stop!"

It did not this time. "You will *die*. Like all the others. All dead. Fed the master." It giggled, childlike. The sound made Theo's flesh crawl. "You are nothing. Feed me. *Feed*!" It grinned, displaying rows of wickedly sharp teeth. The creature reached for them.

Aeryn lopped the creature's head clean off of its shoulders. Black blood spurted from its headless neck, but even without its head, the creature's body shuffled forward, clawing blindly at the air in front of it. Theo shrieked. Aeryn kicked the creature's feet out from under it and then plunged her sword down into its body as it fell. The headless body finally stopped moving.

"What the hell was that?" Theo asked as Aeryn yanked her sword out of the creature's chest.

"I don't know, but it was hiding under that tub in the shed." Aeryn gestured at the large copper basin lying a few feet away. "It surprised me when I picked up the tub. It looks a bit like a goblin or something, but smellier and more . . . talkative."

Shivering, Theo added, "And twisted."

"I don't want the body attract anything else," Aeryn said.

She wiped her sword clean and resheathed it and then grabbed the creature's ankles. She dragged it behind the shed, leaving a trail of congealing black blood. Theo heard her mutter, "Damn. It smells worse dead than alive." Then, she came back and kicked its head behind the shed as well. She cursed again as some of its blood sprayed onto her boot.

"Can we go back inside now?" Theo asked when Aeryn came

back again.

Aeryn nodded and grabbed the copper tub. Before she went inside, Theo glanced around the cottage yard bathed in the overcast gloom and wondered what other awful surprises they were going to encounter before the day was done.

31

Aeryn dragged the copper tub into Mulkin's sleeping quarters, having a wish for privacy while she bathed and washed her clothes, and then she went back outside to draw water out of the stable yard well. The stable yard was quiet still. No one passed by the gates, nor anywhere else she could see. Aeryn wondered if it was possible she and Theo were the only survivors in all of Valis. The thought chilled her to the bone. It took Aeryn several trips back to the well before she had enough water to fill the large kettle Mulkin kept by the hearth, and each trip unnerved her a little more when she failed to see anyone at all on the streets. Above, the skies stayed gray, but silent now, like the city itself.

Inside Mulkin's former cottage, the atmosphere was equally quiet. While Aeryn waited for the water she drew to heat, Theo sat in the chair on the opposite side of the fire, staring into the flames. Neither she nor Aeryn broke the silence.

When the water was finally hot enough, Aeryn carried the kettle into Mulkin's sleeping quarters and poured the water into the copper tub. The room had no door for her to close, but the wall provided enough separation for her mind. She wasted no time before stripping off her dirty clothes and stepping into the tub of hot water. Aeryn sank down into the water and let the heat ease the aches in her muscles. Her eyelids drifted closed as she contemplated what their next move should be.

Occasionally, the rain returned to slap against the cottage windows, but Aeryn barely noticed, lost in thoughts of Tynan and The Harbinger. Tynan had known who The Harbinger was. How? In all the texts she read on Tynan while trying to find a clue to breaking the curse, nowhere did she come across a reference to The Harbinger. Her father had never mentioned any such creature either. The same was true of

Trion Orinthwend. Why was this?

A far more ominous possibility rose in her mind next: what if The Harbinger was not something Tynan fought, but something he was in league with at one time?

Days ago, she might never have entertained such an idea. However, the things she saw in the caverns suggested to her there was more to Tynan Selvantyr than she ever thought. The murals, the carvings, all held a dark and sinister air to them. They were nothing like what she thought Tynan would have created, in caverns he supposedly built with his own magiks.

Sighing, Aeryn wished Tynan was here so she could get the answers she needed. She felt lost in her own ignorance. Her thoughts slipped back to her father and her true purpose for taking on his quest. She had Aric now, and she had accomplished something all on her own, as her father had wanted her to. No longer was she living only in his shadow. And yet, she still felt incomplete.

Why didn't you come?

Her eyes shot open, and she sat up with the realization that she had almost fallen asleep in the warm water. Leaning over the side of the copper tub, she picked up the cake of soap she had found among Mulkin's things and dunked it into the water. Idly, she rubbed the soap between her hands and lathered soap over her lean muscles.

Long had she heard her father's voice in her mind, his tone close to harassing. His haunting voice spurred her during her darkest hours after his death. His voice kept her focused when she decided to take up his quest. She thought the completion of his quest, the completion of a feat all her own, would cause his voice to fade, but that did not seem to be the case. There was more he wanted from her.

Since the clothes she wore previously remained wet and dirty, after Aeryn finished bathing, she pulled extra clothes from her sack, a spare set of leathers, and a long-sleeved shirt in a shade of gray that matched her eyes. She left Mulkin's room and asked Theo if she wanted to wash up as well. The girl shook her head, but when Aeryn came back from drawing more water in which to clean her clothes, Theo said she changed her mind and asked Aeryn to heat the water for her. Although mildly irritated, Aeryn repeated the task of heating it over the fire. She carried it to the tub for the girl.

Theo went into Mulkin's room, and Aeryn went to the hearth to clean her clothes. A moment later, Theo's clothes flew out of Mulkin's room, landing in a wet heap near the hearth. Aeryn heard the young thief splash into the tub. She stared at the small pile of clothes. Rising, she picked up the threadbare clothes and added them to her pile. Aeryn rolled up her sleeves and set to scrubbing the clothes in a pail she had found, removing every trace of the stagnant, death-filled water of the cell underneath the Thieves' Guild.

When finished, Aeryn hung the clean cloth and leather on a length of twine that was strung in front of the hearth opening. She sat in the chair by the fire to watch it crackle and burn. Not long afterward, Theo emerged from Mulkin's bedroom, cleaner than Aeryn thought possible. The girl had wrapped herself in a huge brown robe that obviously belonged to Mulkin. Most of it dragged on the floorboards. Aeryn might have laughed at the sight were it not for the somber look on the girl's face. She watched Theo come to stand by the fire.

Theo checked her clothes on the line, though they were obviously still wet, then sat next to the stone hearth, watching the fire again. She glanced over her shoulder and caught Aeryn quietly watching her. "Thanks for washing my clothes, but you don't have to feel sorry for me, you know." She turned her gaze away.

Aeryn said nothing at first. She did not blame the girl for being upset. Theo had lost so much in such a short time. "I don't pity you. I just remember a time when I was where you're at now."

The look Theo gave her was one of pure distrust. She scoffed, "Why? You've had everyone you ever cared about die all at once?"

"Yes."

Theo paused. "When?"

Aeryn settled into the soft padding of the chair and pulled her legs up, wrapping her arms around her knees. "I was about seven years old, I think. There was a dispute between the town my family lived in and the one neighboring it. I don't know what started it or how it ended, but I remember that my father and mother were farmers who resisted joining the dispute."

"I thought you said you father was a soldier," Theo interrupted.

Aeryn nodded. "My foster father was a soldier. My birth father was a farmer."

Theo squinted at her from over her shoulder but said, "Go on."

"Eventually, the fighting encroached on our family's land, and my parents and my four older brothers and sisters were slaughtered while defending our home. I was found by people searching for wounded. I don't remember much from before I was taken away from the remains of our home, but I remember my mother telling me to hide until she came to get me, and I remember the screaming, the sounds of fighting, and the smell of our burning fields."

Theo turned around to face her. "What happened after the people found you?"

"I was taken to a hospice with some wounded fighters. Seeing as I had no family or anyone else to care for me, I was told I would remain at the hospice and live there as a ward." She ran a hand over the gooseflesh that cropped up on her arm as she thought about those days.

"The hospice was run by a group of strict women, religious to the point of being zealots. They had two faces, the one they showed to the sick and injured, and the one they showed to a child like me. They expected me to clean the hospice and generally stay out of their way. But, I was so angry. I felt like I was abandoned by my family, like maybe if we had just left our land, everything would have turned out fine, but we stayed behind, and I was left to live with these cruel strangers. When I acted out, they punished me in the ways dictated by their beliefs. I hated it there, and I hated the women I considered to be my captors."

"What did you do?"

"I ran." She frowned. "After a few years, I couldn't stand their ways any longer, so I ran. I would have kept running until I couldn't run anymore, had I not been caught by a soldier while trying to steal food from a camp of Morghallan troops."

Theo gaped at her. "Isn't Morghall part of The Fang?"

Aeryn could not help but smile at the girl's shock. "Yes. I was born outside Belhaun."

"But, The Fang is . . ."

"A rough place to be an orphan," Aeryn finished for her. "You're right. We're taught from a young age to be strong and often stoic. A long time ago, The Fang was nearly scoured clean by barbarians from the Wasteland. They enslaved, tortured, and killed many of our people. After a time, a resistance emerged. They banded the people together and pushed the invaders out. The survivors decided the only way to keep the same thing from happening again was to be stronger and rougher than everyone else. It is a lesson passed down from generation to generation."

Theo nodded. "Well, if that's what you were used to, those nuns must have been demons."

"Not exactly, but close enough." Aeryn shifted in her chair. "My family was not a group of cutthroats, though. I remember enough of my childhood to know that we were happy together."

After a pause, Theo asked, "What happened when the soldier caught you stealing?"

"He threatened me at first, but then he saw how hungry I was. He offered to take me on as his aide and train me, so I began traveling with his battalion. He taught me to use a sword and to ride, and to appreciate the old stories of heroism and adventure."

The sword she carried was his. Rowan was his. So much of what was now hers was once his.

"He was your foster father?"

"Yes." Aeryn walked over to where her pack was. She removed a brush from it. Sitting in the chair once again, she took the brush to the few tangles in her long hair. "We spent almost every waking hour together and grew close. Eventually, he asked me to be part of his family. I accepted and took his name."

Theo gestured at the brush in Aeryn's hands, now idle, and asked, "Can I use that?"

Aeryn handed the brush to her, surprised that Theo asked. The first attempt she made was valiant, but the girl's hair was more tangled than not. Finally, Aeryn asked if she could help. Theo hesitated, but then nodded. Aeryn sat next to her on the hearth and began the task of untangling the girl's blond hair.

"You don't do this often, do you?" Aeryn asked.

Theo paused again, then she said, "Willa brushed it for me sometimes."

Aeryn nodded, understanding Theo's hesitance. Nothing more was said between them until Theo's hair was untangled and brushed to a shine. While Aeryn put the brush back into her bag, though, Theo asked what their next action was to be.

"We get some rest," Aeryn responded.

"Why? I think we rested enough in that cell." Theo's voice changed to a whisper when she added, "I don't want to sit here anymore. I want to *do* something." Theo gave Aeryn an appraising look. "Do you even have a plan yet?"

Aeryn sighed and closed her eyes. She did not want to have another argument with the girl, but she felt one brewing. She replied, "I have an idea or two, but I'm too tired to think any longer. I am going to lay down for a couple of hours. You may do as you please."

The girl pressed her lips together in a brief look of defiance, and then she said, "Fine. We'll have it your way, but I'm not sleeping in the dead blacksmith's bed."

Aeryn nodded. That, at least, was something they could both agree on.

32

When Aeryn woke again, tangled in the blankets she had laid out for herself near the hearth, she had no way to know how long she slept, but it was still light out, and she felt rested enough. The disarray of the blankets told her that her dreams had been restless, but she remembered none of them. Theo, on the side of the hearth, seemed to be sleeping soundly. Aeryn was glad. She felt the girl at least deserved that much for what she had been through, for which Aeryn knew she might be partly responsible.

She waited a few more moments before she rose, went to where Theo slept, and lightly shook the girl awake. Theo looked up at her, blinked several times, and then groaned and turned over again. Aeryn rolled her eyes and walked over to her saddlebags, rummaging through them.

"Come, it is time to get up," she told Theo.

After a dramatic show of groaning a couple more times, Theo finally kicked the blankets out of her way and got up. She asked, "What are you doing?"

"Checking my food supplies." Seeing she had very little left in her packs now, Aeryn went into Mulkin's pantry and began taking what she found to restock her pack. "You should eat something before we leave, if you're coming with me. I don't know when we'll be able to stop."

Theo rubbed her stomach. "You don't have to tell me twice. I feel like I haven't eaten in a month."

The girl stretched to reach the back of a shelf at her eye level. She took out a cloth-wrapped wedge of cheese, which she promptly unwrapped and then took the half-loaf of dark bread that Aeryn handed her. She took several bites from each before she paused long enough to ask, "What do you mean, 'if' I come with you?"

Aeryn replied, "You said you wanted to be alone, remember? I'm not going to force you to come with me. It's your choice."

"I can't stay here. Anywhere but here is fine by me. And, I need to get a little payback against The Harbinger for what he did to my friends. How will we find him?"

"I don't know, but I have an idea." She waited until Theo grabbed a few apples and tucked them under an arm before she closed the pantry door. "Before we do that, however, there is something else I need to do."

"What's that?"

Aeryn took the apples from the girl and put them in her pack. She asked Theo to gather up the blankets and then she went into Mulkin's sleeping quarters. She took his journal from his desk. This, she placed in her pack as well.

When all of their things were gathered up, she told Theo, "I don't want anyone who comes here after us to know what Mulkin did. He was a good man. What he did was not of his own choice. I am going to set the horses free and then burn the stables."

Theo's eyes widened, but she said nothing in opposition to Aeryn's plan.

Outside, clouds still covered most of the sky, and the temperature had dropped lower still. Theo shivered in her worn boots and her freshly laundered shirt and pants, both too large for her. Her cloak seemed to be the only thing that fit her right. Aeryn went to Rowan, whom she had left behind the cottage rather than putting him back inside the stables. She put her saddle and packs into place on his back and led him to the front of the stable yard. She left the girl with him.

Aeryn reentered the stables and unlocked the doors on each of the horse stalls. The horses only needed a little encouragement before they fled the stables, now as quiet as a tomb. When the last horse was freed, she climbed up to the loft. She did her best not to look at the corpses all around her. Fortunately, the cold kept the smell and the flies away. She rifled through the boys' clothing hanging on hooks near the door to their loft room. She grabbed a few items she thought might fit Theo. Near the loft ladder, Aeryn spotted an unlit lantern. She took this off the nail on which it hung.

When Aeryn returned to Theo, she handed her the bundle of clothes. "I found a couple of shirts. I think these boots will fit you, too. They will be better than the ones you have now. Sorry, but all the pants I found seemed too short or too long."

"It's okay," Theo muttered as she pulled one of the extra shirts on over her own shirt. She tried on the boots and said they fit well enough. Looking down at herself, she said, "This is kinda creepy."

"But better than freezing out here," Aeryn said. "I'll be right back."

Lantern in hand, Aeryn returned to the stables one last time. She lit the lantern and tossed it into a bale of hay lying below the loft. It caught immediately. Satisfied that the fire would spread to the rest of the stables, Aeryn went back outside. A distant rumble told her more rain was close by, and she felt thankful she was able to set the stables alight before the rain came again. Aeryn doubted the rain would arrive in time to extinguish the fire before the bunkroom was burnt beyond recognition.

Aeryn took Rowan's reins from Theo and started toward the road. It remained deserted.

The girl caught up to her. "So, this idea you had."

Aeryn replied, "Something that creature said stuck in my head."

"All I heard was gibberish."

"Gibberish about 'the master', and it said it could feel the master's power in the air. We both felt a weird vibration in the air when we came out of the guild house. I think that vibration is from The Harbinger."

"It's faded since then, I think." Theo looked around as it was something visible to find. "I don't feel it like before."

"It's lessened considerably, true, but it's still there." At the road, Aeryn pulled Aric from its sheath and extended the sword in front of her. She turned slowly, with the sword still in front of her. "Aric is humming, too."

"Aric is humming." Theo echoed.

Aeryn nodded. "Yes. I think it's humming in tune to The Harbinger's . . . rhythm. I know not what else to call it. However, Aric's hum feels different level than The Harbinger's. I don't think Aric is harmful."

"What do you mean?"

"I think the vibration is something The Harbinger emits. It drove everyone inside, but not before it made them angry and violent."

"Creepy," the girl said. "Why would he do that?"

Aeryn shrugged. "Perhaps to aid his escape. If everyone was inside the buildings, there was no one to see him pass through the city streets. No doubt he enjoyed the pain he inflicted in the process."

"Can I feel it?" Theo asked. Without waiting for a response, she put a hand on Aric's hilt. "I feel it."

Aeryn gently nudged the girl's hand away. Still holding the sword, she turned again. There. She found what she was looking for. "The humming is stronger when the sword is pointed in this direction. I think Aric is tracking The Harbinger's path." She slid the sword back into its sheath.

Theo's brow furrowed in confusion. "How'd you figure that out?"

"I felt a weird vibration in Aric as soon as we retrieved it from the hole in the cottage floor. I didn't know what it meant at the time, but when the creature started ranting about feeling the power in the air, I wondered if the two occurrences were connected."

"Alright. Where to now?"

"Westward to Cira, I think." Aeryn looked down at her. "Are

you sure you want to come? I can't imagine this will be a pleasant journey, nor can I promise it will end well."

Theo looked back at her evenly. "What am I going to stay here for? We both know everyone in the city is probably dead, killed by The Harbinger or each other. I told you I have a debt to settle with The Harbinger, and I mean it."

Aeryn nodded and mounted Rowan. "Then, let us be on our way."

Extending her hand down, she helped Theo up to a place behind her. Once Theo was settled, Aeryn turned Rowan in the direction of the city gates and kicked him into a gallop. She planned to reach Cira by nightfall.

33

The rain returned by the time they were on the open road, in the form of a light mist that damped not only the road but Theo's mood. When she had awoken earlier, she felt a sense of purpose over going after The Harbinger, but the continued lack of even a peek of sunshine dulled her mood again. After all of the death and destruction hovering around them, was it too much for her to ask for a little sunlight to lighten things again?

And yet, despite her sadness, Theo found herself captivated by the vividness of the world outside of Valis's walls. She noticed the difference when Aeryn stopped to give Rowan time to rest. The road was turned a rich chocolate brown by the rain. The grasses and other plants around the roadside showed their appreciation of the rain by turning a deep vivid green, dotted here and there by leaves turned red and yellow by the season. They were such a sharp contrast to the dull browns and grays that made up most of Valis.

It only occurred to Theo then, as she finally took in everything around her, that she was free now. She could not help but grin at the realization. Her face flushed bright pink in the cold air, and a laugh escaped her. Her laugh made Aeryn turn to look at her.

A slow smile curved a corner of her mouth. "What is it?" she asked Theo.

Theo laughed again. "I'm finally free. I'm finally free from Valis."

Aeryn nodded, smiling too.

Theo took a deep breath of air filled with the scent of the plants and earth. She wandered in the direction of a tree whose branches hung low to the ground. The grass whispered as her feet passed through the thick blades. She delighted at the sound, so unlike the dusty gravel of Valis's roads. Tiny red apples lay scattered at the tree's base. Theo picked one up, but decided it would be a bad idea to taste it. She lightly tossed it away.

She reached up and grabbed the tree's lowest branch, pulling herself up. She used the other branches to steady herself as she stood up to peer through the tree's golden leaves at the long length of road still ahead of them. The distance they had to travel still did not frighten her. The farther she got from Valis, the happier she would be. She bounced a little on the branch.

In Outer and Middle City, trees were mostly absent, as was grass. Theo heard of expansive gardens existing in Inner City filled with fragrant flowers, and that mammoth trees surrounded the governor's estate at the center of it all. Part of her wondered if it were true, and if so, were they better than this? She wished again that Brien could see what she was seeing now. Maybe he was.

The jingle of bridle and the creak of stirrups tugged Theo away from her thoughts, and she looked over to see Aeryn watching her from atop Rowan. The sell-sword guided the red-brown stallion under the trees branches to where Theo stood.

Aeryn extended a hand to her. "We must push on."

Theo took Aeryn's hand and stepped off the branch onto the horse's back. He snorted in protest of being stepped on, so she sat down quickly. "I'm ready," she told Aeryn.

Aeryn kicked Rowan into a gallop again, down the road to Cira.

For the remainder of the day, into the dusk, they rode hard in the direction of Cira. When they reached the low grassy hills that Aeryn said were close to Cira, Aeryn turned Rowan off the road and kept him at a walking pace. Theo began to feel a nervous churn in her stomach about what they would find once they arrived in Cira, but when Rowan crested the last hillock, lights twinkled in the distance. The sight put Theo more at ease, and she noticed Aeryn seemed to relax as well.

Theo laughed with her relief. "Well, at least someone's alive here."

"It seems so," Aeryn said in a noncommittal tone. She guided Rowan down the hillside, toward the road again.

When they reached the gates of Cira, they found the guards preparing to close the gates for the night. The guards spun around when they heard Rowan's hoofs on the road and scrambled to ready their weapons.

One of the three guards called out to them. "Halt! Who approaches?" His voice had a quaver to it.

Aeryn replied to him, "Two weary travelers. We wish to take refuge in your fair city for the night." She pulled back on the reins to stop Rowan.

"Come forward," another guard told them.

Aeryn guided Rowan into the circle of light provided by the gate's high torches. The three of them lowered their weapons. "Ye're lucky you got here when ye did," said the first guard. "We're closing the gates for the night. Strange days are upon us, and the gates open for no man but the lord of our city after darkness falls."

The other guards nodded.

"Understood, sir. May we take refuge for the night?" Aeryn replied. She said nothing of where they came from or the dark circumstances for their travel.

"Aye. A silver gets ye admittance. There's rooms in few of our inns left. I trust ye can manage to find something."

The sell-sword paid their fee, and at the guard's nod of acceptance, nudged Rowan on, through the open city gates.

What lay beyond the outer wall of the city was nothing like Valis. There was no filthy track of mud between an inner and outer wall, only a stretch of gravel along the wall that gave way to the city proper. Lanterns hung high on poles at the end of each block of buildings lighted their way much better as well. Although crowded together, the closeness of the buildings did not strike Theo as overcrowd, perhaps due in part to their brightly painted exteriors.

They had to go several blocks into Cira before finding an inn with a vacancy sign. Aeryn tied Rowan to a post out front at The Silver Pegasus and took her packs off Rowan's back, handing some of them to Theo. Bright candlelight spilt out through the windows of the inn, and its interior reminded Theo of The Thirsty Noble. Her heart ached at the similarities.

A large, smiling woman in a green dress and a starched apron bustled between the few tables, before approaching them.

"Looking for a room or a meal?" the woman asked Aeryn.

"Both," the sell-sword replied. "Also, boarding for the roan stallion out front."

The woman nodded and quoted a price to Aeryn that sounded high to Theo, but did not seem so to the sell-sword, who paid it promptly. The woman told Aeryn which room would be theirs and then handed her a small key. "Take any open table," the woman told them and then bustled off again to attend to the other patrons.

Aeryn pointed to a small empty table near the fire and told Theo to wait there for her. Then, the sell-sword headed off in the direction of the common room's bar. Theo went to the table and shoved the packs Aeryn had given her under it. She sat in the chair next to the fire, leaving the chair with its back to the wall and a better view of the door for Aeryn, guessing this would be preferred. She had watched enough types like Aeryn pick such a seat at The Thirsty Noble.

She glanced over at Aeryn. The sell-sword was talking to a pair of men at the bar. Theo saw her interrupt her conversation to stop the woman in the green dress and ask something. The woman nodded and then glanced over at Theo. Theo quickly looked away, uncomfortable knowing she was being talked about. She busied herself with counting the rings on the wooden table, her chin propped on her hand.

A few minutes later, the serving woman brought over a large tray and set it in the middle of the table. It held trenchers of meat, potatoes, and other vegetables smothered in greasy brown gravy. Also, a loaf of coarse bread, still warm from baking, and a mug of cider.

"Your friend asked me to bring you two some food. Go on and dig in, honey. Give a wave if you want anything else."

Theo waited only until the woman left her alone again before she started on the food. She had not realized how hungry she was until the food was in front of her. Aeryn returned with a mug in her hand soon after. She took the chair Theo thought she would and set the mug aside. Theo smelled spice ale from the mug.

Aeryn broke off some of the bread and dipped it into the gravy. She nodded in satisfaction at the food and then said in a low voice, "I wanted to see what I could learn in the way of the local gossip. It seems the one we're looking for has not passed through the city—I doubt he could have passed through unnoticed—but some say strange creatures have been seen walking outside the city walls. It started two nights ago. Clearly, he was nearby, but did not stop here."

Theo's brow furrowed as she considered this. "Why not?"

Aeryn chewed another mouthful and swallowed before answering. "I know not. I don't understand what his plan is any more than you do."

Theo glanced at the patrons around them again. She again noticed the similarities between the clientele of The Silver Pegasus and The Thirsty Noble. She said to Aeryn, "I wonder if anyone here, um, feels the same as the people of the last city."

Aeryn shrugged. "Perhaps. I don't think we have to worry about them turning violent, if that's what you mean."

Theo nodded, and Aeryn continued, "One of the men I talked to mentioned that no merchants or travelers have come from Valis in the last couple of days, as they should have. They don't know why, though all agreed they feel a darkness in the air."

Theo frowned. She assumed that Aeryn wanted to keep what

happened in Valis a secret, but that would be hard once people started to ask questions. She knew sooner or later someone would go to Valis to investigate the city's silence. And then what? "That could be bad," she remarked to the sell-sword.

Aeryn shrugged, seeming to catch what she meant. "I don't see the point in concerning ourselves with whether anyone goes to Valis to investigate. It's better we focus on our own plans."

Theo nodded, falling silent again. She made a valiant attempt at helping Aeryn finish most of the tray of food, but her appetite faded the longer she watched the comings and goings of the patrons and the serving women. Finally, she put the piece of bread in her hand back on the table.

"Thinking about your friend?" Aeryn asked, looking at her.

"This place is so much like The Thirsty Noble. It's not, clearly, but it feels similar. I don't know if that makes sense."

Aeryn glanced around the room. "A lot of inns are similar, but I get what you mean."

Theo picked up her cup and watched the water swirl around in it a few times. Then, she looked back at Aeryn and leaned forward. "Can I tell you something?"

Aeryn nodded, so Theo said, "I think there's something wrong with me. I miss Willa more than my brother right now."

The sell-sword set her own food down and leaned forward as well, her elbows on the table. "She was your friend."

"But, he was my own flesh and blood. Somehow, though, I don't miss him as much."

"Perhaps it's the surroundings," Aeryn suggested, "being in a place that reminds you of her makes you think about her more."

"Maybe." Theo sighed and then said, "Or, maybe I went so long without Brien that I got used to it. There were a lot of times he wasn't around, because he wanted to be on his own, and I'd just stay with Willa for a while. So, I didn't even think something was wrong until he didn't come back to the inn for more than a week. Another week went by before Pythun would finally see me and then two more weeks of following you around."

Aeryn said nothing in return. So, Theo continued talking, feeling the need to say the things in her head out loud rather than let them continue to fester inside her. "I was with Brien almost all the time when I was really little, after our mother died, but when he started getting older, he didn't want to be strapped to me all the time. I saw Willa more than I saw him, depending on his mood, and she was like a sister to me in a lot of ways. Maybe a little like my mother, too. They knew each other, you know."

Her fingers traced the lines in the wooden tabletop. She did not look at Aeryn. "My mother died five years ago. My father was a violent drunk and he beat her to death one night. He just wouldn't stop hitting her. I don't remember why he was so angry; I just remember that Brien dragged me out of our shack before we were next. After that we were pretty much orphans. My father couldn't have cared less about us, and after he murdered our mother, there wasn't much we had to say to him either.

"I've run into him a couple of times. He always acts like he doesn't remember what he did, like Mother just left one day. She should have."

A corner of her mouth twitched. Theo cleared her throat. "She worked at The Thirsty Noble with Willa, that's how I met Willa in the first place. When our mother died, Willa started to look after Brien and me however she could. Brien never took to that too much. He was seven years older than me. He taught me how to take care of myself on the streets and how to steal. Willa let me stay in her room and patched me up whenever I got hurt. She gave me advice when I needed it, even if I didn't know I needed it."

Theo glanced at Aeryn again and then away. "I should have listened to her and stayed at the inn that night instead of going with you

144

to the Thieves' Guild. Maybe she'd still be alive now."

Aeryn stirred in her chair. "Perhaps," she replied quietly. She leaned forward and gave Theo's hand a brief squeeze before folding her hands on the table. "I understand how you feel, and I think it is sad what happened to Willa. At the same time, maybe something good has come out of it. You said yourself that you are free now. Perhaps losing Willa was the sacrifice that had to be made in order for you to do that."

"Yeah, but why is it I don't really feel all that free anymore? I just feel alone." She swiped at the tears that stung her eyes.

"It's late," Aeryn said. She pushed back her chair and rose, setting some coins on the table for their meal. "I think sleep will do us both good and give us a better perspective in the morning."

Nodding, Theo rose as well and followed Aeryn through the common room. They went up the stairs to a room near the staircase, tucked under the building's eaves. The small room contained a squat wood stove in one corner and two narrow beds draped with brightly colored knit blankets. A nightstand stood between the beds, with a pitcher and basin on top. Behind the stove's door, a tiny fire struggled to stay alive.

Aeryn went to the hearth and fed the fire with some kindling. It sputtered and popped as it grew by degrees until it lent more light and heat to the room. Theo sat on the bed farthest from the door. The batting-covered straw mattress crunched beneath her. She pulled her new boots off and let them flop onto the floor. Her cloak and the extra shirt Aeryn gave her, which she wore over her own, once her brother's, followed her boots.

She watched the sell-sword stash her saddlebags, packs, and armor under the other bed. Aeryn's various sheaths and her longsword went next. Aric, however, went under the covers, close to the wall.

"Isn't that going to be uncomfortable to sleep next to?" Theo asked.

Aeryn sat down on her bed and pulled off her own boots, tossing them aside. She stifled a yawn. "Comfort isn't really a concern in this case. I want it close at hand."

"Do you think we'll have trouble?"

"Best to always be prepared. I think you have that covered, though. I saw you put that dagger under your pillow."

Theo flushed pink; she did not think Aeryn was watching. "An old habit."

Aeryn lay down on her side, her back to Theo, and pulled the coverlet over her. "Get some sleep. We leave early in the morning."

"For where?"

"Wherever Aric tells us."

Theo sighed quietly. She looked up at the ceiling beams, watching the way the orange glow from the stove created shadows that slipped across the ceiling. She turned her head to look at Aeryn again, but all she heard was rhythmic breathing. Aeryn was asleep already. Theo turned to face the wall on her side and wondered how Aeryn could just fall asleep like that. She squirmed between the sheets, trying to get comfortable. Then, something that sounded like claws scratched against the side of the inn.

Her eyes wide in the orange half-light, Theo told herself it was just a tree branch. A slow and painful moan followed the scratching sound. Theo squeezed her eyes shut and prayed that the moan was just the wind passing through the tree branch that scraped the side of the inn. She pulled the covers up higher, over her ears, knowing it was going to be a long night.

34

Morning dawned bright and fresh, all signs of the rain that had plagued them dried up by the time Aeryn woke. The clouds were few but white, and the sky brilliant sapphire. Aeryn noticed a change in the people of Cira as soon as she stepped outside to retrieve Rowan; many of them smiled as they passed her. Although heartened that these people were no longer plague by The Harbinger's darkness, she knew it likely meant The Harbinger was far ahead of them now.

The newfound cheerfulness affecting Cira's citizens did not extend to Theo. When Aeryn roused her, the girl peered up at her with irate, bloodshot eyes. This was followed by muttered curses as she poured out of bed and dressed. When Aeryn asked why she looked so tired, Theo looked at her with disbelief and asked Aeryn how she had missed all the raucous sounds the night before. The girl then went on about monsters scratching at the inn roof. Aeryn was unsure whether to take what the girl told her at face value or chalk it up to youthful imagination run wild.

After a quick meal to get them started for the day, they exited the city again. Aeryn saw no need to linger in Cira. She had gathered all of the information she felt she could without raising any suspicions. As they left Cira, she walked while Theo rode atop Rowan. Neither of them wore their cloaks, as the sun was warm enough to make extra layers unnecessary.

Sunlight reflected off of her shoulder plates and the narrow bracers she had donned. Beyond the city gates, Aeryn made her way to a stand of trees far enough from the city walls that she would not be easily observed. Theo slid down from the saddle when Aeryn pulled Aric from its sheath. She pointed the sword in a westward direction and then turned slowly to her right and left, a half circle in each direction. She frowned. Aric still indicated they should go west. Aeryn wondered if it was truly leading them or if she merely imagined it was. What could The Harbinger want in the west?

Aeryn resheathed the sword and turned back to Rowan, opening one of her saddlebags. She rooted through it until she found the map tube she sought. Map tube in hand, Aeryn knelt in the sparse grass between the trees, took the cap off the length of hollowed wood, and withdrew a thick roll of parchment. She unrolled the map and spread it on the ground before her. It displayed all of Cathell, parts of the Wastelands to the north, and Decathea to the south. Putting her finger on Cira, Aeryn looked at what else was to the west of them. Her frown deepened.

Theo knelt across from her. "Nice map."

"West," she muttered to herself.

"What's wrong?"

"If this sword *is* guiding us, then The Harbinger seems headed in the direction of the elven Forever Wood. But why? What would he want there?"

The girl looked up from the map at her. "Maybe something's hidden there?"

"Perhaps." Aeryn's brow furrowed as she looked down at the map again. "Beyond that is The Fang, and I can't imagine what he would want there, besides trouble."

Aeryn stood, rolled the map up again, and inserted it back into the tube. She sighed. "I wish I knew what he was up to." With no answers forthcoming, she knew they had no choice but to ride on. She climbed into the saddle and helped Theo up behind her.

"Why? I wish I'd never heard of him in the first place."

" 'To defeat your enemy, you must first know your enemy.' My father's words," Aeryn replied as she guided Rowan out of the stand of trees and onto the road again.

"If you say so," Theo shouted over the pounding of Rowan's

hooves on the dirt road.

The weather was perfect and calm, and by afternoon, Aeryn wondered if they would ever catch up to The Harbinger. Theo fell asleep behind her, with her hands clamped onto Aeryn's belt. Her head bumped gently against Aeryn's back. Although their start had been rocky, Aeryn felt a stirring of affection for the young thief. When all her defiance and sarcasm faded, a likeable person was left behind, one that Aeryn found herself able to relate to more and more. She remembered a time when she was just as angry and alone as Theo felt. It gave Aeryn a strange feeling of kinship toward her.

Her foster father was the one who taught her how to get past the anger she directed at the world, although not before she learned many hard lessons. Her hand rose and her fingers brushed over her left eyebrow and the thin white scar that cut through it. If he had not gotten through to her as he had, she knew she might not have survived her teenage years.

In her youth, after the death of her family and her confinement in the hospice, anger was the only thing left for her to feel, and it boiled to the surface often. Fights with the boys in the camp were commonplace for her. They enjoyed picking on her because she was one of the only girls. She never understood how the other girls kept the boys from getting to them the way they got to her. Eventually, though, her father taught her to channel her anger into other places than her fists.

Perhaps Theo had never had anyone to teach her such lessons, she thought to herself. Aeryn was unsure she wanted to volunteer for that task. She had no wish to replace Willa for her. In Aeryn's opinion, that would be disrespectful, as well as silly. She knew nothing about caring for a child.

So deep in thought was she that Aeryn almost missed the change in the scenery around them. The sudden fading of light caught her attention first. Aeryn looked up and saw that flat gray clouds had swallowed up the sky again. Then she noticed the color of the trees and plants on either side of the road looked washed out and tired, as though their very existence exhausted them. The birds and animals fell silent, and the air grew heavy. Rowan snorted and shook his head. He felt the change, too.

Aeryn guessed they were not far from the Forever Wood's eastern edge now. It was never clear how far or near the elven Wood was. It often appeared suddenly, always seeming to be far in the distance, and then it was directly ahead, as if it moved on its own. When Aeryn got her first glimpse of the forest ahead this time, however, its appearance shocked her for other reasons, and she had no doubt The Harbinger had been there.

She hauled Rowan to an abrupt stop before they could get any closer. He neighed in protest, and Aeryn put a hand on his dark mane as both an apology and calming gesture.

Theo was jolted awake by the sudden stop. "Hey, what's the . . ." Her words trailed off as she looked around.

"Gods above," Aeryn whispered.

"Is *this* the Forever Wood?"

Aeryn shook her head. This could not be the Forever Wood.

The Forever Wood's trees were renowned for their beauty, and their branches seem to rise up and out forever. It was said their leaves brushed the very sky. What stood before them was nothing like the tranquil Forever Wood Aeryn had passed through only weeks ago. What stood before them was a place of darkness.

The tall grasses that once flowed to the edge of the forest were now brown, straw-like stalks that rose from the ground at odd angles, littered with fallen branches, black and twisted. The trees, formerly straight and proud, were misshapen, contorted things that seemed to shrink from the light of the sun. They were black and leafless, hulking forms that rose high above the forest floor. The twisted forest looked like what a mad, sadistic mind might conjure up as dark parody of the elven forest.

Theo shifted behind her. "Did we get turned around?"

"No," Aeryn replied. She winced. Even her own voice sounded foreign to her in this perverse place. "This is where the Forever Wood should be."

"Did The Harbinger do this? I heard the elves protect the Wood."

"They do." A tremor passed through her. For the first time since their journey to find The Harbinger began, Aeryn felt the touch of doubt. If The Harbinger could reshape an elven forest . . .

"Aeryn?"

"We have to keep going," she replied numbly.

She urged Rowan forward. Fog, thick like smoke, floated out of the forest and hovered just above the ground. Tendrils curled at its edges, as though the fog beckoned them to enter. Gooseflesh rose on her arms when they passed between the first set of trees. Aeryn turned Rowan close to one of the trees and stopped him so that she could look closer at the tree's black bark.

"It looks like it was set on fire," Theo said.

Aeryn shook her head. "It isn't charred. It's like something stole their souls."

She reached out her hand, hesitated a moment, and then laid her hand on the bark. Deep sadness filled her. A low moan came from somewhere above them, little more than a whisper on the still air. Her hand jerked back. She swore the sound came from the tree.

Theo shuddered violently behind her. "This place is wrong. Must we go this way?"

Aeryn considered this and just as quickly rejected the idea of going around. "You saw the map. The Forever Wood covers much of the western edge of Cathell. We've no way to know how far The Harbinger's influence extends, and I am not willing to lag further behind while we look for a way around. We'll take our chances."

Without waiting for a response, Aeryn turned Rowan away from the tree and into the center of the narrow road through the Wood. She

151

doubted the trees were capable of coming to life and attacking them, but in her opinion, it was better to expect the unexpected these days.

"How long will it take us to get through the Forever Wood?" Theo asked.

Aeryn's gray eyes looked from one side of the trail to the other. "I'm not sure. At a hard pace, a little more than a day. I don't think we have that luxury now." She was thankful the trail at least was still intact.

Looking up through the twisted branches, Aeryn was able to make out the sun through the haze of gray that hovered above the trees. She guessed it to be about midday. A wave of anger passed through her. "This was once a beautiful place, and that thing killed it," she cursed.

"I doubt he much cared," Theo replied.

Aeryn shook her head, although she agreed with Theo's assessment. She sighed. "We will continue on until nightfall and then rest until dawn. I don't think we should try to travel after the dark comes."

"Fine by me," the girl said. "Hopefully, we won't get eaten in the middle of the night."

No birds or animals made a sound as they crept through the Wood, but low moans and sighs came from somewhere above them. Again, Aeryn wondered if the sound came from the trees themselves. Only debris in the trail slowed their progress. From time to time, however, Aeryn glimpsed a shape stalking them several paces off the trail, but it disappeared again whenever she looked in its direction. The unsettling sensation that they were being watched never abated. Eventually, Aeryn risked nudging Rowan into a fast trot and then a gallop, since it was obvious whatever was stalking them had no intention of coming forward just yet.

They only stopped once prior to dusk falling, when the chill in the twisted forest became too much to bear, and Aeryn and Theo needed to don their cloaks again. But, now, full dark was coming on, and Aeryn knew they needed to stop for the night. She slowed Rowan to a walk again and searched for a spot to leave the trail, but then decided it was a better idea to camp directly next to the trail. If the smoky fog that still floated above the forest floor thickened any more overnight, she did not want to have to worry about finding the trail again.

She brought Rowan to a stop. Something crashed to the forest floor somewhere in the dark, startling her. No sounds followed.

"What was that?" Theo hissed.

Aeryn only shook her head. She was unable to see more than fifteen paces on any side of the trail now. Without the glow the trees once naturally emitted, the coming darkness was black and thick as tar.

When whatever made that sound did not appear, Aeryn helped Theo dismount and then swung down from the saddle after her. Even in the growing dark, Aeryn could see the girl's eyes were huge and darted this way and that. Aeryn unrolled the blankets while Theo crouched down on the fog-covered trail and watched her.

"Could you hurry up and make a fire?" Theo asked.

Aeryn went into her saddlebags and took out food. "No fire tonight."

"What do you mean, no fire?"

"I don't want to draw any more attention to ourselves." She did, however, take out her lightstone and lit it so that they could at least see what they were eating. "Come sit down."

"I don't like it here," Theo pouted as she sat across from Aeryn. "I heard stories about the Wood. It always sounded like a nice place. This isn't a nice place."

Aeryn glanced sharply to her right as something moaned about twenty or so paces away from them. Only her eyes moved in that direction. Her hands busied themselves with cracking open the shells of some nuts. In the dark, it was hard to tell which moans were made by the trees and which were not. She saw nothing so she turned her eyes back to look at Theo.

"Why does it have to be so dark?" Theo whispered. She looked close to terrified.

"It gets dark like this all the time when there are no stars or moon in the sky," Aeryn lied. It was much darker than it should be. "Here, hold my lightstone if it will make you feel better."

She handed it to Theo. It cast a strange golden light over her face. Eerily enough, the fog seemed to shrink from the light cast by the stone.

"Do you think The Harbinger is here?" Theo asked her.

"I've seen no sign that he is or isn't."

"Could he be hiding?"

"Perhaps."

Theo shuddered and reached for another slice of bread. "Tell me a story."

Caught off guard, Aeryn did not respond at first. "A story?" she finally said.

"Yeah. Like how you ended up looking for Tynan's sword in the first place."

"That's not much of a story," Aeryn replied. "My father enjoyed the old stories, collected some of them. Tynan's stories were his favorite, and in his youth, he wanted to find a way to break the curse on the Black Caverns. He didn't get very far, but he always said that when he retired from his service, he would try again so that he could say he did something important in his life. He wanted to create his own adventure story, I guess. He was killed before his service ended, though, so after his death I decided to do it for him."

"How long did it take you to find out how to break the curse?"

"I read all of my father's collections about Tynan first and then I started traveling through the areas Tynan traveled, trying to gather more information and working as a caravan guard for money. Eventually, I looked up the father of Tynan's best friend, Rimen."

"He was still alive?"

"Elves live much longer than humans." She frowned at the

memory of the encounter. "Trion told me of the key."

Theo jumped when a long moan cut the night. Again, they waited, but nothing appeared.

"Tell me another story. Anything," Theo begged.

Aeryn floundered until a story finally came to mind. "How about a story about the Tynan's adventuring group, that my father told to me?"

Theo nodded.

"There was a three-headed dragon that lived in the crags of the Blood Ridge. It had jewels for eyes and scales of pure red gold. The Seven decided to travel into the Blood Ridge to find this dragon, because they were told it held the secrets to immortality. So, they went to the Blood Ridge and found the dragon's lair. Jewels glittered all around the dragon, and she sat upon a nest of spun gold. In the nest were three unhatched silver eggs.

"When Tynan approached her, with the rest of the Seven hidden, all three of the dragon's heads looked at him with disdain. 'How dare you disturb me while I care for my young, Tynan Selvantyr,' the dragon said to him. He was well known around the realm, even by dragons.

"Tynan replied, 'I only wish to know the secret of a long and fruitful life, and then I will leave you and your young in peace.'

" 'Is that so?' inquired the three-headed dragon, all smiles. 'There is no secret to immortality that I know of. The secret to living a longer life is certainly to leave in peace three-headed dragons such as I. Unfortunately, you've come upon that answer too late, for now you will make a tasty morsel for my children!'

"The dragon flew off her nest and charged at Tynan. A great fight ensued, which the rest of the Seven joined in. All except Rimen. He went for the dragon's nest while she was occupied with the rest of his companions. He notched three arrows in his bow, one for each of the dragon's eggs, and called to the dragon. Rimen told the dragon that if she let him and his companions leave safely, he would leave her eggs unharmed.

155

"The dragon was too far away to attack Rimen before he could spear her eggs with his elven arrows, so she was forced to agree to his terms. Tynan, however, did not trust the dragon to allow them to simply walk out of the lair unharmed. He turned himself and the rest of the Seven invisible, which enraged the three-headed dragon. The dragon blew fire across the lair, in an attempt to kill them, but accidentally set her own nest on fire. While she tried to save her unhatched young from the blaze, the Seven escaped, empty-handed but still alive."

Theo yawned when Aeryn finished the story, but smiled. "Not a bad story, but I kind of saw the end coming. I've heard enough dragon stories to know you never trust those things not to try to eat you by the end."

Aeryn laughed quietly. "That is true."

"So who set Tynan and the Seven up?"

She thought about this. "My father never told me that part of the story."

Theo shrugged and yawned again, so Aeryn suggested they go to sleep. The girl did not protest. The creatures in the forest seemed to have quieted finally. Aeryn and Theo put away the remainders of their meal and then laid down with their blankets within easy reach of each other. Aeryn extinguished the lightstone.

Theo fell asleep sooner than Aeryn expected, which left her alone to think. She stared up into the blackness and wondered again what The Harbinger's plans were. He seemed to be taunting them, leaving creatures to stalk them and frighten them, but never attack them. Did he want them to find him?

The longer she stared into the blackness overhead, the more questions came to her, and the more frustrated she felt over her lack of answers. Finally, Aeryn gave up. She turned over and prayed the answers she needed would come before it was too late.

35

Aeryn walked with Tynan through his caverns, but Theo was missing. She could not see Tynan's face. Every time she tried to look at him, he turned his face away from her gaze. She tried repeatedly to ask him what was happening, but he refused to answer any of her questions. He only replied in riddles. As they walked, she became ever more frustrated.

"Why won't you answer me?"

"Knowledge is not for those who seek it, only those who find it."

Aeryn shook her head. "What are you talking about?"

"How can you know of what I speak when you do not even know that which you ask?"

She tried to look at him again, but he turned away. He drifted down another passage. Aeryn was about to grab his arm, to make him stay still, when a high-pitched shriek cut the air.

Aeryn sat bolt upright, her blood feeling like ice in her veins. It was dawn. The blankets were tangled around her legs. Aeryn realized she had been dreaming. She looked around and saw the fog was indeed thicker. It engulfed the entire forest. Shaking the cobwebs from her mind, Aeryn looked for Theo and found her behind her. They looked at each other, and then started when another shriek cut through the air.

"What in the nine circles of hell was that?" Theo hissed.

"I don't know." Aeryn kicked the blankets off and grabbed Aric. She gestured for Theo to follow her. Where was Rowan?

Aeryn used one of the twisted trees as a shield and peered from behind it. Her eyes searched the fog-covered forest for the source of the horrific cries, but the trees beyond were little more than misty shadows. She turned her head to look at Theo, but then a firm hand clamped over her mouth and another clamped over Theo's. Someone dragged them backwards. Aeryn struggled against their assailant. The hand over her mouth felt abnormally soft and smelled strange. Then, a familiar voice hissed in her ear and stopped further struggles.

"Say nothing. Just back up, both of you. Do not take your eyes from directly ahead of us," Tynan whispered. The hands over their mouths withdrew.

Aeryn did as he told her, and he pulled them back behind another tree. Several tense moments passed. Finally, he pointed.

"There," Tynan said, his voice barely a whisper. "Do you see it?"

It took Aeryn a moment, but then she did see what he pointed at. A black shadow flitted between the trees, looping back and forth. The shadow was large and indistinct but seemed to suck in all of the light around it. Its path seemed aimless, but then it turned to face where they hid. Its face was ghastly. Aeryn's breath caught in her throat, and she felt cold all over. Theo clapped a hand over her mouth.

After what seemed like an eternity, the shadow turned again and drifted away from them.

They remained still until Tynan finally broke the silence. "A wraith. If it had found you, the encounter would have been a fatal one. I had to warn you. I apologize for the abrupt way in which I did."

Aeryn turned, about to spit a dozen different questions at him, but the words died in her throat when she looked at him. She could only stare at him, mouth open. Realizing it still hung open, she quickly shut her mouth and tried to think of something to say. Theo saved her the trouble.

"Oh, *shit*," the girl exclaimed.

"Theo!" Aeryn hissed, finding her voice again. She slapped the girl's shoulder. Theo slapped her back.

"Look at him," the girl muttered out of a corner of her mouth. "Don't tell me you don't see what I see."

Tynan gave them a weak smile and held up his hands. "No, it is alright. I understand your shock. I realize I am in quite a different state than when you saw me last."

That was an understatement. No longer was he a transparent ghost. He now stood in the flesh, but the flesh was not his own. Whomever the body had belonged to, they had looked very similar to Tynan, but there were enough differences that Aeryn knew Tynan had not simply regained his own flesh. The hair was a much lighter blond than Tynan's. It was shaggy and fell to his shoulders. Tynan's had been shorter. The eyes were a darker blue. Stubble shadowed the cheeks. Tynan had been clean shaven. The height and build, though, were almost identical.

"How . . ." Aeryn's question trailed to a stop. Her head tilted as she stared at him and her fingers went to the scar across her eyebrow. She rubbed the thin white scar while she thought about how she should word her question. Finally, she settled on, "How did this happen?"

Tynan shook his head. "We do not have time to discuss it right now." He looked over at Theo, who was walking around him and staring. "Gather your things. We must find the trail again. We cannot afford to lose any more time."

Theo stopped her scrutiny of the dead man. "What do you mean *find* the trail again? The trail is right there." She turned to where their blankets still lay. She frowned.

"The trail moved while you slept. The Harbinger has tainted this part of the Wood, and it is turning on those who travel through it. I passed a few unfortunate travelers brave and stupid enough to enter the tainted remains of the Wood, who are lost and have wandered for days trying to find their way back out. Do not worry, though, they are far enough from here that they will not hamper your progress."

Aeryn looked at Theo, then glanced sidelong at Tynan, more suspicious questions coming into her mind. She said nothing, though, and shifted her gaze back to Theo. "Come on, let's gather everything and

159

go, as Tynan suggested."

Theo looked unsure, but nodded and began picking her blankets up off the ground. Aeryn looked for Rowan again. She whistled, knowing he must have found his own cover when the wraith appeared. Sure enough, he trotted from behind a cluster of trees not too far away. Aeryn helped Theo roll the blankets up and tied them in front and behind the saddle. By unspoken agreement they forewent eating.

Before she mounted, Aeryn looked to Tynan and asked, "Will you be following us?"

"Yes. I have my own transportation." He looked over at a dark gray mare Aeryn had not noticed before, probably because it blended so well with its surroundings.

The mare did not so much as twitch her ears. She simply stood there and stared blankly ahead. Aeryn's unease grew.

Tynan must have sensed this, because he added, "I acquired her in Valis. She was so frightened of my current state that I could not control her by normal means. I put her under an enchantment to lessen her fear. She obeys me rather well now." Tynan made a clicking sound, and the mare came to him.

As Tynan climbed up into the saddle, Aeryn swung into Rowan's saddle and pulled Theo up behind her. Aeryn turned Rowan to face Tynan's horse and asked, "Any suggestions as to where we should look for the trail?"

He looked around them in every direction and frowned. "Perhaps it would be better if we simply head west toward Belhaun. I doubt, even if we did find the trail again, it would lead us in the correct direction."

Tynan pulled on a pair of suede riding gloves and glanced over at her. She looked back with a dubious expression. He told her, "As we ride, I will answer all your questions." Without waiting for an answer from her, he turned his mare and set off at a fast trot.

His words called her dream back to mind, and Aeryn shuddered as a chill crawled up her spine. Nonetheless, she turned Rowan to follow and kicked the stallion into a fast pace to catch up with Tynan.

36

Dozens of thoughts tumbled through Theo's mind as the three rode deeper into the tainted forest. So many, she found them difficult to sort. Tynan's reappearance was unexpected, to say the least, his new physical appearance even more so. It was obvious the body he had found to inhabit was that of a Valisian soldier—they were the only ones in the city that wore the type of green and gray leathers he now wore—but how did he take over someone else's body? And why?

Theo was reminded of Uvik, the old man who was always sitting on the corner by the marketplace in Middle City. He had full two-sided conversations while rocking back and forth. Sometimes he spoke in languages other than Common, languages that sounded twisted and foreign to Theo's ears. Brien said he was possessed by demons, and everyone gave him a wide berth so that the demons would not jump into them next.

She wondered if Tynan was like Uvik's demons, able to jump from one body to another at will. Would he jump into her next? Maybe he would grow tired of the body he was in, or maybe he would just do it for fun.

Theo peered around Aeryn's back to stare at Tynan and his hypnotized horse. There were grayish patches of skin around his temples; she wondered if the corpse was starting to go off. His horse gave her the creeps as much as his new body. The mare's blank stare was unnatural, and she never made a sound. Horses were not meant to be this way. Theo wondered why Aeryn allowed Tynan to lead the way in the first place. How did she know he had not used his magiks to transport them off the trail? Perhaps the trail had not moved at all, *they* had.

"Theo, stop staring at him," Aeryn ordered in a quiet but firm tone. It was like the sell-sword had eyes in the back of her head.

Theo jumped and straightened up again. "Well, it's not like you've asked him how in the hells he got that way," she said.

"I was planning to, eventually." Aeryn looked over her shoulder at Theo.

"You're taking too long."

Tynan stopped his horse and cleared his throat. "Ladies, if you continue in this manner, you will alert the entire forest that we are here."

Aeryn did not stop Rowan. "Where is The Harbinger?" she asked him.

"I know not. He is not here in the Wood."

"Then, where is he?"

"Again, I know not."

Aeryn glanced at him. "Then, what do you know?"

Sighing, Tynan slowed his horse so Rowan could come abreast. "I will tell you all, as promised, but to answer the young thief's question . . ."

The dead man looked at Aeryn, but Aeryn did not look at him, so he looked over at Theo. Her eyebrows rose, and she waited for him to speak already. He cleared his throat again.

"Where should I start?" Tynan muttered, as if to himself.

"How 'bout from the point where you popped out of existence?" Theo suggested.

Tynan nodded. "After The Harbinger used my magikal energies to regenerate, I am not sure what happened." His voice took on a theatrical tone as he proclaimed, "It was as though I ceased to exist for a time. Everything was dark, and I felt empty. After a time, my senses returned to me and I was aware, but I was unable to do much else but allow my consciousness to drift about the city. The Harbinger drained too much of my energy for me to take form again. I knew I had to find you both and help you."

Theo made a derisive noise, and he frowned but went on, "I did what I normally would consider unthinkable. However, under the circumstances—"

"You stole someone's body," Theo finished for him. She thought about Brien and how she would feel if someone had possessed and then walked off with his body. "I'm not the spiritual sort, but that's wrong on so many levels."

"I had no choice!" Tynan declared. "I needed to find you, and I needed to regain my powers quickly. I could do neither by floating aimlessly around Valis. So, yes, I stole this body, but the man who once inhabited it no longer needed it. He was already dead when I found him. I inhabited his body, found a horse to ride, and when I felt strong enough, I cast a teleportation spell that brought me here to the Forever Wood. When I arrived, I was as shocked as you no doubt were to find it in such a state."

Theo mocked him, "Did you shop around Valis a little, trying to find just the right look?"

"Of course not. I was lucky he was nearby when I came to my decision."

Aeryn stirred and glanced over at Tynan. "How did you find us? How do you know there are other travelers lost in the Wood?"

The sun broke free of the cloud cover suddenly. The hulking trees smoldered with thick green smoke where the sun touched them. Dejected moaning rose from the trees as they curled away from its rays. Theo's mouth fell open. When the sun was veiled by the clouds again, the trees stopped moving. Theo looked at the others, but neither of them seemed to have noticed anything other than their brewing argument.

"I still know many of my old tricks," Tynan said. "I enchanted some birds and used them as my eyes. It was much faster than searching for you on horseback."

"How long were you watching us before that wraith showed up this morning?" Theo asked him.

"I came upon you just before dawn, before the wraith appeared.

164

Yes, I was waiting for you to wake when the wraith appeared. I did not wish to disturb your rest before that."

"How kind of you," Aeryn said. Her voice dripped with a biting sarcasm that surprised Theo. Tynan looked both shocked and hurt when Aeryn looked over at him, flashes of anger in her gray eyes. Without warning, Aeryn brought Rowan around to face Tynan. "You lied to us," she all but growled.

The dead man brought his mare to a stop and opened his mouth to speak, but she cut him off. "Aric is not just some sword. It's hooked into The Harbinger in some way, but you didn't bother to mention that. You also knew there was something wrong when we mentioned the altar room, but would not tell us. Most important, you knew about The Harbinger, but didn't warn us. Now you say you didn't want to disturb our rest? That is bullshit, Tynan. You were afraid of how we'd react when we saw you again."

Tynan's mouth fell open, and it was several moments before he regained his composure. His mouth finally closed, and his chin rose with pompous pride. "My deception about the sword and altar room was my way of protecting you. I never thought those were things you would need to know."

"Protecting me." Aeryn laughed. "You're doing a damn fine job, too. I think you should try telling the truth for once, and do it now, before I leave you right here."

"The truth? What do you think is the truth? You seem so sure you know."

Aeryn's hands tightened, white knuckled, on Rowan's reins. The horse shifted nervously. "I don't know what the truth is because you keep dodging every question I ask. Stop speaking in riddles, dammit!"

Tynan leaned forward and hissed, "Keep your voice down. You'll have every creature in this wicked forest down on our heads."

"What creatures? All we have is your word there are any. For all we know, *you* conjured them all up. Maybe to delay us longer?" the sell-

165

sword asked.

The dead man stiffened as if he had been slapped. "You would accuse me of such treachery? Perhaps I have misjudged you."

"No, I think it is I who have misjudged you." Aeryn's gaze did not waver from his. "Are you working with The Harbinger?"

"What?"

Theo looked at Aeryn in disbelief. The thought had occurred to her as well, but she did not think that Aeryn would ask him in so outright a manner.

"You heard me."

"I am doing no such thing. If you knew what you were up against, you would not ask such a thing."

"Then tell me what I'm up against, dammit," Aeryn cursed at the dead man.

Tense minutes of silence passed. Neither of them moved. Birds cawed in the deformed branches overhead, making the only sounds in the forest. Everything else seemed to wait with bated breath as Theo did to see who would break first. Finally, Tynan looked away from Aeryn and up into the sky.

"Midday is near. Let us stop here for a while. Neither of you have eaten. We will talk more while you eat, if that will satisfy you, my lady."

"No more lies," was Aeryn's response.

He nodded. "No more lies."

Theo took Aeryn's calloused hand and slid down from Rowan's back. Aeryn fed Rowan and then the three of them sat down, with Theo and Aeryn alone breaking their fast. Tynan talked.

"Yes, perhaps you have misjudged me, but I believe the fault to be my own in that regard," he muttered. His words held no pretense this time. "In life, I tried to cultivate an air of flawlessness and glory. I am afraid I have continued the practice in death as well. Not everything you read in books is true, and that applies to me as well.

"I did not create the caverns. I stumbled upon them purely by luck, or so I thought at the time. It is true that I walked away from my company's camp and hiked partway up Nightstone, as it is that I fell through the cavern's ceiling. The part of my legend where I wandered a maze of naturally formed caverns and later made a proper home out of the caverns using my magiks is not. All that you saw was already there when I stumbled upon the caverns. I changed the existing runes, however, and I added traps to keep others out—and a desire to keep something in.

"The runes I found in the caverns were ancient, and I was only able to discern the meaning of some of them. They were not benevolent symbols, I knew, but what I did not know at the time was that they were containment wards. All I knew for certain was they originated from magiks I was not completely familiar with—some were actually dwarven. I assumed that the caverns were once used as the site of some dark rituals and the runes were intended to bring harm, but they were so old they simply lost their power. The murals and the carvings I discovered seemed to support this theory.

"I mutilated the carvings and the murals, with the intent to destroy any lasting powers they may have possessed. I created the amulet you discovered for Rimen. He also believed the story I told him, which was passed down to your time, but only he was allowed into the caverns on a regular basis, the only one I trusted. Strangely enough, he saw the same things you did in the caverns, but he never questioned me. His loyalty as my companion was true all the way to his death." Tynan's smile was bitter.

"What about the rest of your friends?" Theo asked.

Tynan cleared his throat, picking at a piece of skin on his hand that had begun to peel off. "Do not misunderstand, the members of the Company of Seven were my companions and fellow adventurers, and for the most part I trusted them with my life. We were not friends as you think of friends. We started out that way, maybe, but my lust for fame

167

turned them against me eventually. We had many harsh arguments after Rimen died and were barely on speaking terms by the time I met my demise. The idea of splitting the group was mentioned right before I left Valis for the last time. It was the reason I was headed to the caverns in the first place—to think and to figure out a way to recover my reputation after my own adventuring company decided they did not need me anymore. I am frankly surprised they tried to avenge my death after the Black Order ambushed me. Perhaps it was out of some foolish sense of honor. Whatever it was, it got them all killed."

He sighed and returned to his previous story. "Nothing immediate happened after I changed the runes that covered the interior of the caverns. When I was away from the Company of Seven and Rimen was not with me, I spent my time familiarizing myself with the labyrinth of tunnels and chambers. Even I did not know every square inch of them until after my death, when I had eternity to learn. There was a strange outcropping of rock in the altar room that is not there now. It always gave me a strange sensation when I was near it, and then the dreams started. They were not outright frightening at first, just sinister.

"I saw in them ancient peoples and places. Night after night, a story soon unfolded in these dark dreams. I saw a coven of spell-casters called the Pillars of Ki. According to my dreams, they were the highest power in Cathell at one time, protected and served by an elite group of knights called the Maerinus Order. These Pillars of Ki were a proud and arrogant lot who believed that they alone controlled the light of the world. An evil god calling himself The Harbinger tempted them into darkness with the promise of untold power and omnipotence. They were either unable to see his true purpose or did not care. He coerced them into creating the caverns for their blood rituals in his name, which lent him more power until he was able to take power over more than half of the continent's peoples. Terrible atrocities were committed in his name.

"Eventually, the other gods stepped in and freed the Maerinus Order from The Harbinger's spell so that they saw through his manipulations. At the behest of the gods, the knights slaughtered the Pillars of Ki, breaking The Harbinger's hold on the world and greatly weakening him. The gods and a handful of surviving Pillar members helped the Maerinus Order imprison The Harbinger's essence in Nightstone Peak, in the caverns. The runes on the walls were put there to keep The Harbinger sleeping until the end of time, with that outcropping serving as his tomb. The remaining Pillars of Ki and the Maerinus Order sealed themselves into the mountain after The Harbinger was imprisoned, forfeiting their lives in an attempt to keep The Harbinger's name from ever being known again, which would risk his revival.

"After these things became known to me, I built up the rock around The Harbinger's tomb and forbade Rimen from going into the altar room. I warded the altar room as heavily as I could and replaced many of the runes that originally decorated the caverns, as many as I could call to memory. I had hoped to stop the dreams and to keep him from ever fully waking. I can see now how foolish I was to think I could keep The Harbinger locked away on my own. I should have blasted those corridors into nothingness and never returned."

Tynan stopped talking and looked at Theo and Aeryn.

"You saw all this in your dreams?" Theo asked, unsure she believed such an explanation.

"Yes," he replied. "I know not whether The Harbinger expected me to feel pity for him, trapped in a stone tomb for however many hundreds of years then. Eventually, he tried to tempt me as he had the Pillars of Ki, with visions of the power he would give to me if I freed him. The Harbinger knew I was powerful enough to free him if I chose, and I believe he may have still possessed enough power to draw me to the caverns in the first place and cave in the ceiling so I would find his resting place. Looking back now, I think he was drawn to my greed and arrogance. The Harbinger feeds on those and other base emotions— anger, hatred, lust, greed—the rawer the better.

"When I did not accept his offer, I had terrible nightmares of

169

people being tortured and slaughtered by the thousands in ways you would find unimaginable. I do not know whether these were visions of the actual past or some kind of threat. I traveled to the great libraries of Pius at one point, but found little information on either the Pillars of Ki or the Maerinus Order. What I found was little more than a passing reference to their existence, and nothing at all about The Harbinger."

"How did Pythun know about The Harbinger?" Aeryn asked.

"I wish I knew the answer to that. It is a question I, too, have mulled over many times since the night he allowed himself to be taken over. I was wise to that which Pythun was not: The Harbinger did not want an ally, he wanted a slave to control and then inhabit."

Theo shivered at the thought of having The Harbinger inhabiting anyone's body. Just the brief contact she had with the god in Pythun's underground chamber made her not want to repeat the incident.

Tynan did not begin speaking again, and they sat in silence. After a time, Aeryn spoke up. "How did The Harbinger escape? And what is Aric's connection to him now? Why did he want the sword, and why is it vibrating now?"

The dead adventurer gestured vaguely. "Aric's power is strong, because it was created by the dwarven god Vortenthas. I drew on those powers, worked with them, and created extra safeguards through the sword to protect myself from falling under The Harbinger's spell as long as Aric was near me. The Harbinger undoubtedly wanted to drain the sword's power to strengthen himself. He took the power from me instead.

"I do not know what causes Aric's vibration. When I was alive, Aric vibrated all the time, stronger when it was pointed in the direction of the caverns or inside the caverns themselves. It was an unexpected side effect of the enchantments I added, I believe. The sword pulses in time to the subtle throbbing I always felt around The Harbinger's tomb. I assume this is why you have come the way you have to find The Harbinger—you discovered the pulse gets stronger when directed toward

170

The Harbinger's location."

"Yes," Aeryn replied. "I didn't notice a thrumming in Aric until after I retrieved it from Mulkin's."

Tynan's face turned thoughtful, and he rubbed his chin. "That is interesting. I know not what that could mean."

Aeryn stood, clearly finished with Tynan's explanations. "If you knew that Aric was an integral part of keeping The Harbinger imprisoned, why did you give the sword to me?"

Tynan paused before he answered. Theo saw him searching for the right answer to the question and frowned, wondering what it was he wanted to hide. Finally, he said, "When you told me about your experience in the altar room, I knew The Harbinger was trying to draw you in, and it was only a matter of time before The Harbinger broke free. I wanted the sword as far away from him as possible. I was afraid he might try to drain its power."

"So why not tell us after we witnessed that black cloud come out of the caverns?" Theo asked.

Again, Tynan paused. "I used some containment spells that I hoped in vain might have some retarding effect on him."

Theo wanted to laugh at the lunacy of this statement, but Aeryn headed her off by saying, "Thousands of people died as a result of your lies and your secrecy, Tynan."

Tynan bowed his head. "I only did what I felt was right. However, I have been honest with my answers to your questions now."

Theo wondered if this was really true.

Aeryn replied, "I don't know that that is enough. I cannot trust you as I may have before. You may continue to travel with us, because I believe we can use all the help we can get now, but if I think you are lying at any point, or are hampering our progress, I will leave you behind." With that she turned her back on him and went to Rowan.

Theo glanced from one of them to the other, then followed after

171

Aeryn. Behind them, Tynan said, "I am humbled by your honor, Aeryn, and I will work to regain your trust. I promise you."

Theo rolled her eyes. Aeryn said nothing at all.

37

Aeryn woke with a start, her father's accusations from her dream nothing more than half-remembered echoes in her head. She opened her eyes but shut them again when she saw it was daylight already. She sat up and combed her fingers through her long hair and rubbed her face. She felt as though she had gotten no sleep at all, and a sensation like a thousand wasps filled her head. When she opened her eyes again and saw Tynan across the camp extinguishing the remains of his fire, Aeryn rubbed her face again, feeling a headache coming on.

After Tynan's confession, the remainder of the previous day was spent riding in tense silence. Even the tainted forest seemed to hold its breath as they passed through it, although Aeryn could not help but wonder if the sudden change in their environment had more to do with Tynan's arrival that anything else. An overly suspicious thought, perhaps. Before the three of them lay down for the night, Theo suggested to her it was possible she was judging Tynan too harshly for his all-too-human failings.

Aeryn told her that finding the secret to breaking the caverns' curse came at a large cost, and the discovery of Tynan's vast shortcomings only added further injury to this. Though Theo clearly wondered what she meant by this, Aeryn decided to keep that story to herself. Frankly, she hoped to keep these failings of her own to herself as long as she could. The gods could judge her later. Theo's words forced her to examine herself, however, and she supposed that the young thief had a point.

Shaking her head to clear the sleep from it as much as to clear these thoughts, she finally rose from her tangled bedding and stretched her limbs. She was eager to be free of this twisted parody of what the

Forever Wood once was. She looked over at Theo sleeping nearby. Even with their close proximity, the girl was nothing more than a misty form under the blanket of fog skulking over the forest floor. Theo stirred without Aeryn's prodding her, so she left the girl to attend to Rowan. The stallion was sniffing at dry, brown stalks that Aeryn assumed used to be grass. When she approached him, he whickered softly. She patted his side and went into her saddlebags, which lay on the ground nearby. Aeryn took from them the small bag of feed she kept for those times when there was nothing suitable for Rowan. She held the bag out, and the stallion gratefully dug in.

Tynan's mare also stood near Rowan, but Aeryn made every effort to ignore it. This became difficult to do when Tynan walked over and began brushing the horse. He was gentle enough, but he did not speak to it and clearly felt no connection with it whatsoever. Tynan seemed just as emotionless toward his mount as the mare was toward him.

"Why don't you release the enchantment on her?" Aeryn asked.

"I have tried. I think, because she can sense my undead nature, it continues to make her skittish. This mare has no training for combat. I should have sought out a more suitable horse." He looked over at her, a deep sadness on his face. It surprised her. "Watching you with your horse makes me miss my own horse, Duraden. Yours does not flinch at my presence, indicative of good breeding and training, much like my Duraden. He died the same day I did."

Theo came over and asked if they were going to eat before they left. Aeryn told her to get herself food from her pack next to the saddlebags, then Aeryn asked her to gather up the camp, too. When she turned back to Tynan, his back was to her, and he was saddling his horse.

Aeryn asked him, "Why has The Harbinger not attacked us?"

Tynan did not turn around. "I think he sees us as insignificant. His focus is to the south."

Her brow furrowed. "I thought he was headed west, though I

174

know not why."

Tynan turned to her now, a surprised look on his face. "He means to use the North Gate so that he can get south; the West Gate is too heavily guarded by the elves in Alethia."

The North Gate to which Tynan referred was in Morghall, deep in the heart of The Fang. Aeryn replied, "Do you really think he can get past The Fang's army to reach the North Gate? Why?"

The strategic significance of the four Gates of Cathell meant they were heavily guarded within the regions in which they were located. Aeryn agreed that The Harbinger was unlikely to take on the elves in their seat of power in Alethia; the collective magiks were old and formidable, and such a battle could prove too costly. Aeryn wondered if The Harbinger thought the forces in charge of the North Gate would prove easy to break. He was in for a surprise if so.

"I believe he means to so that he has a pathway to the south and Pius, City of Gods."

Theo spoke up. "Wouldn't he want to stay away from other gods, 'cause they might want to stop him?"

"The old gods banded together to imprison The Harbinger once, when he grew too powerful and threatened the balance. The new gods are more arrogant than the old gods, and I doubt they see him as much of a threat to them yet," Tynan replied. "He, however, means to take vengeance for his usurping a thousand years ago by destroying Pius and delivering a blow to their hold over Cathell.

"Do the highest level clerics not still have their temples there, as they did in my own time? Imagine, if you will, what would happen if all of those temples were destroyed and the worshippers slaughtered. The gods need temples and the faith of worshippers to lend them power.

"If The Harbinger destroys those things for the other gods, he upsets the balance and can lay claim to the worshippers from the other dark gods, increasing his power and causing the gods who have fallen from favor to go into a deathlike slumber. If that happens, it will be much harder to wrest power from The Harbinger a second time."

"Do you honestly think The Harbinger has the power to destroy the City of Gods?" Theo asked.

Tynan's expression was grave. "The Harbinger stole almost all of my powers, which even in death were great. Coupled with Pythun's powers and the ancientness of the powers he still possessed even in dormancy, I believe he is strong enough and has likely drawn additional followers to himself. He will continue to draw in more faithful and use their power with each place he passes through. What he has done to the Forever Wood, overriding the elven influence, was no small feat. I fear we are seeing but a taste of what he is capable of accomplishing."

"The Fang will fight The Harbinger to the death before they allow him access to the North Gate," Aeryn said.

"Then, they will die," Tynan replied. "Their deaths fuel him, too."

Doubt scratched at Aeryn's mind. She turned away from Tynan and started saddling Rowan. "We are too far behind. The Harbinger will reach The Fang and the North Gate before us." She asked Tynan, "Can you teleport us to Morghall ahead of him?"

"Nay. I wish that I could, but I was lucky to be able to transport myself and this horse to the Forever Wood to meet you. Transporting the three of us plus two horses would be an impossible task for me now. However, do not despair, I charmed a raven and sent it out with a message for Pius as soon as I could, warning them. I pray they received it and heed its warning."

Aeryn nodded and swung herself into the saddle. She pulled Theo up. Nervousness churned in her stomach even as she kicked Rowan into as fast a pace as she dared push him with the unsure footing in the fog-covered forest. She could not allow The Fang to be left to fight The Harbinger alone. As well, she could not imagine what would be required to kill a god; never had she heard of a god being slayed by a mere human before. This was her fault, however, and Aeryn resigned herself to do whatever it took to stop him, even if it killed her, too.

At their fast pace, it was not long before the edge of the tainted Forever Wood became visible. Then, one of Tynan's mare's hooves caught on something, and she stopped abruptly, almost throwing Tynan from the saddle. Aeryn turned in the saddle to see what stopped the horse, but suddenly, Rowan reared up, surprising her and throwing her off balance. She grabbed hard onto his reins and managed to stay in the saddle. Theo, however, lost her grip on Aeryn and tumbled off Rowan's back with a scream. The girl hit the ground and rolled over, but had a stunned look on her face. Before she fully recovered, Rowan spun around and started to bring his front hooves down in the direction of Theo's prone form.

"Theo, *move*," Aeryn shouted, as Rowan's hooves descended on the girl.

38

Aeryn's heart jumped into her throat, but Theo rolled out of the way just before Rowan's front hooves thundered back onto the ground, kicking up clouds of black dirt. Aeryn saw the girl stand, unharmed, and open her mouth to say something, but she was cut off when something—vines, snaking out from the bases of the trees—wrapped around both of her arms and her midsection.

"Run, Rowan!" Aeryn dove out of her saddle. When she landed, she drew her longsword and ran toward Theo.

More vines wrapped around Theo's legs and dragged her away from Aeryn. Theo struggled, but it was a losing battle. A chorus of moaning filled the air, and other vines shot out from the direction of nearby trees. Aeryn tried to dodge them as she ran toward Theo, but the vines caught her and lashed around both of her legs, binding them together. A harsh curse escaped her lips as she was brought down, and the vines dragged her in the opposite direction from Theo. Aeryn flipped onto her back. She sliced at the vines wrapped around her ankles, but more took their place. She cried out in frustration.

Tynan shouted at her, "Use Aric!" His mare was dragged down by the vines, but he jumped from his saddle before she fell.

The dead adventurer rolled to a stop on the ground and was immediately seized around the ankles by vines shooting out from the bases of other trees. He snarled out a lightning spell, shocking the vines holding him. They receded for only a moment before coming at him again full force. Soon Tynan's hands were bound, preventing him from aiming more lightning bolts at the vines.

Aeryn tossed away her father's longsword and reached for Aric, only to find one of the vines snaking around Aric's pommel. She brought a dagger up with her other hand and snapped the vine. Just as she grabbed Aric, a new vine wrapped around her wrist and tried to pull her hand and the sword away from her. Aeryn gritted her teeth and used all of her strength to pull the sword and her hand back toward herself. She kept pulling until the vine was in reach of her mouth. She bit into the vine as hard as she could. Bitter sap filled her mouth, but she did not release the vine. Aeryn swore she heard the vine squeal in pain. It let go of her wrist. With her arm free again, she used Aric to hack off the other vines wrapped around her.

Aric cut through the vines like butter. Where struck, the vines smoldered as though the sword burned them. Once her legs were freed, Aeryn scrambled to her feet and searched for Theo. Theo, she discovered, could no longer scream, because of the vines wrapped over her mouth. Her eyes where wide with panic as she was steadily dragged toward a hole at the base of one of the trees that looked like a gaping maw. Green slime oozed out of its edges. Panic spurred Aeryn into a sprint after the girl.

Aeryn dove onto Theo to slow the vines down. She sliced through the vines before they succeeded in dragging both of them into that gaping maw. Before more vines could attack them, Aeryn scooped Theo up by her midsection and ran in the opposite direction of the tree. She set the girl on her feet where she thought Theo was out of danger and helped her remove the dying vines still wrapped around her.

"Can you run?"

Theo nodded, wincing as she rubbed her arms.

"Make a run for the edge of the forest and find Rowan," Aeryn told her and turned to aid Tynan, who was now muzzled as well, which prevented him from casting spells entirely.

Aeryn used Aric on the vines holding Tynan and his horse. Once he was freed, he took the reins of his horse and the three of them backed toward the edge of the Forever Wood. The horse was limping badly. Aeryn scooped up her father's sword again, and she and Tynan fended off further attacks from the vines as they went. Finally, the trees gave up their desperate attempts to keep them from leaving the Forever Wood. The moaning ceased and the vines withdrew into the bases of the trees. However, it was not until Aeryn and Tynan reached the green grass at the western edge of the tainted forest that Aeryn finally relaxed.

Theo ran to her, leading Rowan by his reins. "Gods be damned. What in the nine hells was that?"

Aeryn replied, "A trap, I believe. Are you alright?"

"Just some cuts and bruises, I think."

"And you?" Aeryn asked Tynan.

"Just bruised."

"Good. Let's get moving before we encounter any more surprises."

"Rowan was hurt," Theo told her.

Aeryn frowned, a spike of concern stabbing in her gut. "Where?" She laid her hands on his thick neck. Rowan did not move under her gentle touch.

Theo pointed out a long cut on his hindquarters.

Tynan knelt by his horse, checking her legs and hooves where the vines attacked her. "The mare was badly cut by the vines as well," he confirmed.

Rowan's injury was not deep, only superficial, but the mare's injuries needed more advanced care than she could provide. Aeryn knew then that they had no choice but to stop again. She told the others, "I can treat Rowan, and temporarily bandage the mare, but she needs someone else to attend to her before we go much further. We will stop in Belhaun only long enough to get her help and refill our supplies."

Tynan nodded. "Perhaps that would be best," he said.

Aeryn went into her saddlebags and retrieved her waterskin. She washed the lingering bitter taste of the vine sap from her mouth and then washed and treated Theo's cuts. She attended to Rowan's wounds after Theo, then Tynan's mare. When finally the horse was ready to travel again, Aeryn made haste to remount Rowan. She gave her hand to Theo, who looked nervous about getting back on Rowan, but she accepted Aeryn's hand and climbed up to her place behind Aeryn.

Without a word to the others, Aeryn turned Rowan toward the road to Belhaun, clearly visible not far from where they exited the tainted Forever Wood. She kicked Rowan into a gallop, the fate of her homeland on her mind.

39

With Belhaun's close proximity to the Forever Wood, the journey was short, and Aeryn spotted the high walls of the city long before the sun reached its highest point. Meadows gave way to farmland and cottages. To her relief, people tended their fields with any obvious signs that trouble had passed their way. Once they reached the high walls of Belhaun, Aeryn saw no signs of trouble there either, and they were allowed into the city without incident. It did not escape her notice that Tynan drew his hood up to cover his face when they passed the curtain wall guards.

Aeryn led the way over the drawbridge covering the city's moat, through the curtain wall gate and inner wall gate typical of all Fang cities since the time when the barbarians were pushed back. The area between the two walls offered not only protection to the city but refuge to citizens from outside the city, should the area come under siege. The Fang's coastal cities also used these barriers to provide shelter when storms battered the area in summer and winter. People pulled together to aid one another in The Fang, completely unlike Valis, where only the privileged and the elite received protection.

Right now, the outer area was occupied by children playing chase. They laughed and dodged out of Rowan's way. Aeryn glanced over her shoulder at Theo and caught her staring after them with a look half of contempt, half of longing. She could only imagine what the young thief was thinking. Aeryn knew what it was like to miss having a normal childhood.

At the inner gate, a pair of burly but polite guards stopped them and requested the usual admittance of two silvers each. Tynan paid the guards as Aeryn did, from a purse he likely found on the body he stole. A twinge of something close to revulsion passed through Aeryn, but she made no comment as they entered Belhaun.

The streets were wide, covered in gravel or cobblestone, and lampposts were prevalent. Everyone they passed openly carried a weapon of some kind. Though it had been well over a year since Aeryn returned home, it was just the same as Aeryn remembered.

They passed the city's outer rim of shops, the smells of baking bread and grilling meats dogging them as Aeryn took them deeper into the city to where the residential areas and governmental buildings were located. Fortunately, the streets were not too clogged with traffic that day, and they were able to navigate the streets without trouble.

Theo nudged her. "You know, we haven't had much to eat, and I'm kind of hungry."

Aeryn shook her head, saying nothing. Theo moaned a little.

When Aeryn turned in the direction of the residential streets and the size of the houses grew from cottages and row houses to manor houses, Tynan rode his mare up next to her. "Aeryn, where are we headed?" Tynan asked. His hood still hid his face.

Aeryn nodded her head at the manor house at the end of the lane. "There."

At the end of the lane stood a large, three-story manor house of puddingstone construction. Though nerves tickled at her, the house managed not to look ominous or foreboding. Brightly colored flowers lined the iron fence surrounding the property; it stood open for visitors. Aeryn turned down the tiled carriageway, at the center of which was a mural of a swooping raven—a symbol that matched the tattoo on her left shoulder.

Two boys ran out from the small stable at the back of the house. When Aeryn and Tynan brought their horses to a stop, one boy took Rowan's reins and the other took the reins of Tynan's mare. As Tynan dismounted and Aeryn helped Theo down, a thin man with ginger hair emerged from the portico off to the side of the house. He hurried toward them in as stately a manner as he could manage.

Aeryn swung down from the saddle after Theo and addressed the ginger-haired man. "Corinn, would you summon the lady of the house?"

Corinn stopped short of the group and bowed. He nodded. "Of course, Lady Aeryn." As quickly as he arrived, he turned and disappeared back into the house.

Theo gaped at her, but Aeryn ignored this. She turned to the two boys who stood stock still nearby and waited to be addressed. She smiled at them. "You know you don't have to wait for me." She handed each of them a ten-copper piece. "Please take Rowan and my friend's horse to the stable. Give them food and water, and ask Marta to attend to the mare's wounds, but ask that she do so quickly. We cannot linger."

The boys looked disappointed, but replied in unison, "Yes, ma'am." They led the horses away.

"Aeryn. Just Aeryn," Aeryn muttered to herself.

Glancing at Theo, Aeryn caught a look of confusion and hurt that crossed her young face before the girl turned away, feigning interest in the flowers lining the fence and driveway. Then, a woman emerged from the side of the house with Corinn and called her name.

"This is such a surprise! You should have sent word you were coming. We would have planned a better welcome," the woman said as she hugged Aeryn. She returned the hug with a little touch.

The woman was as tall as Aeryn and had jet-black hair tied in elaborate braids on top of her head. Her pale blue eyes illuminated her delicate face with the laugh lines that were becoming permanent. Her simple but iridescent blue dress complimented her eyes. When she pulled away from Aeryn, she turned to the others and smiled broadly.

Aeryn, however, said flatly, "We cannot stay long. Just long enough to restock our supplies and tend to our horses."

The woman rolled her eyes theatrically and waved a dismissive hand. "You are always on the run, my dear. I take these chances to spend time with you whenever I can."

To the others, she said, "Honestly, Aeryn's manners are atrocious sometimes. It is a pleasure to welcome you to the House of Ravane. I am Dahna, Aeryn's aunt."

40

Tynan stepped forward, still hooded, and took Dahna's hand in both of his gloved hands. "I am Darius, dear lady. I met Aeryn in Valis a short time ago and have been honored to make her acquaintance, as I am now honored to make your acquaintance."

Dahna blushed. "So charming, sir." She winked at Aeryn.

Aeryn rolled her eyes, both at his pretentiousness and his use of his middle name rather than his first. For the sake of anonymity? That was unlike him.

Dahna looked next at Theo. "And who is this young lady?"

"I'm not a lady. Just Theo," the young thief replied. An insolent look slipped easily into place.

Dahna glanced at Aeryn before she commented, "You're so young. Your parents don't mind you traveling with Aeryn, Theo?"

Theo shrugged. "My family's dead."

Aeryn opened her mouth to reprimand Theo, but Dahna cut her off first with a laugh. "Fair enough. Welcome to you both. Please, come in." She turned away and headed for the main house before Aeryn could protest.

She followed after Dahna and repeated, "We cannot stay long. We have urgent business in Morghall."

Dahna smiled at Aeryn, but she saw the hurt in her aunt's eyes as she led them into the high-ceiled receiving hall. "You have not been back here in nearly two years, and now, you are running off again?"

She opened her mouth to reply, but her aunt shook her head. "I heard you: urgent business. So much like Derrick." Looking to Tynan, Dahna asked him, "Can I have Corinn take your cloak, Darius?"

"No, thank you," the dead man replied politely. "I have been unwell and would rather keep it for the warmth, Lady Dahna. I hope you do not mind."

"Not at all," she replied. "There's been many illnesses going around of late. All the rain we've been having, I suppose. Well, what about you, Aeryn? Theo?"

Aeryn shook her head, but Theo nodded and slipped out of her cloak and handed it to the waiting butler. Both of them looked uncomfortable. Corinn took the dirt-spattered cloak without comment and then turned away and left the hall. Dahna then led them into a sitting room with bright rugs and ivory-colored furniture.

Tynan took a spot on a long couch near Dahna, while Aeryn stayed standing, but Theo looked afraid to sit on the furniture. Dahna said, "Oh, fear not. If the furniture gets soiled, we shall just upholster them again. I enjoy changing the colors every so often anyhow."

Once Theo chose a chair, Dahna asked Aeryn, "Since it is clearly not to visit with your family, to what do I owe this visit, my dear?"

"Like I said, we have a need to restock our supplies, if you don't mind sparing some food for our travels." Aeryn knew her aunt did not, but asked out of politeness. She was starting to wonder if it had been a bad idea to stop here, but she had to know her aunt was safe. "Also, I need some information. Have you noticed anything unusual around the city lately?"

"Of course, you can have whatever you need." Dahna's smile faded. "As to unusual things, yes, unusual things have been happening in the last few days. Soldiers passing through the city from the east and south have said something terrible has happened to much of the Forever Wood, from its border with the King's Wood to nearly the edges of Alethia.

"You know we Belhaans are not prone to panic, but people are very wary. Calm has held for the most part, as it always has, but I myself have noticed a marked undercurrent of tension in our neighbors of late. Guards have been placed on the outer wall where there were none, and more archers patrol both walls than I can ever remember seeing. Little has been heard from the east, and there is talk something may have happened that way. In your last letter, you said you were in that area. I am glad to see you are safe, because I have been terribly worried for you these past few days."

Aeryn frowned at her aunt's unspoken question, which she did not answer. "Does anyone know what may have happened or what changed the Forever Wood?"

"No, but I can tell you that not long after word of the change in the Wood reached Belhaun, there were rumors that a strange figure— very tall and shrouded in dark, hooded robes—passed through the farmlands outside the city, accompanied by a crowd of similarly dressed people."

"A group of robed men?" Tynan leaned forward in his seat.

Dahna nodded. "The governor sent some of his men to inquire of his intentions, so large was this entourage of his. His answer must have satisfied the men, because the governor's men left them alone. They did not remain near the city long, no more than a day and night, but I heard some Belhaans left with them. No one knows what the man's purpose was here. It was all very strange."

Aeryn pushed away from the display cabinet she was leaning against, knowing they could not stay any longer. They were close to The Harbinger, but not nearly enough. "I'm sorry, but we must ready to leave now. I am glad to see that you are safe as well."

Her aunt nodded, but was visibly upset. "Aeryn, what is going on? What has happened in the east and in the Forever Wood? Can you not tell me?"

Aeryn went to her aunt and took Dahna's hands in hers. "I wish I could stay and explain, but I cannot. Something very bad indeed has happened in the east, and it's not over. More horrors will come if we're too late to stop it. I hope you can understand."

Dahna nodded, squeezing Aeryn's hands. She stood as well.

"Yes, of course."

"Good. I must attend to Rowan before we go. Can Corinn gather food and fresh water for us?"

"Of course. Whatever you need is yours to have, you know that."

Aeryn nodded. She glanced at Theo. "And, Theo said she was hungry."

"I'm fine," Theo told her. "Don't have to do me any favors."

"Nonsense." Dahna smiled at the girl. "Aeryn and Darius can ready your horses, and you can come with me, Theo."

"To where?" Theo asked, hesitance in her voice.

"Well, we shall get you fed and do a little shopping in my boys' closets. I know we can find something better fitting for your travels." She took Theo's hand and led the girl away. "Theo. What an interesting name. Is that short for something?"

Aeryn did not stay to hear the rest. She headed outside with Tynan in tow. He was silent for once, but she could feel his eyes staring at the back of her head. "Why did The Harbinger pass through Belhaun without leaving it in ruins as it did Valis and the Forever Wood?"

Tynan caught up to her and agreed, "I wonder that as well, but I was also wondering about your family's home." Tynan gestured at the house and its gardens. "When you said your father was a simple soldier, I took it at face value."

"A lot of things have turned out to be the opposite of what they seem," Aeryn retorted and then she sighed. "My adoptive father was a cavalry man, but his father, my adoptive grandfather, rose to the rank of general, and when he retired, he became involved in the city's politics. He's a good man, but he doesn't live so simply."

"I see," was all Tynan said.

Aeryn found Dahna's oldest son, Greggry, in Rowan's stall. He was about Theo's age, and possessed the same black hair and blue eyes as his mother. He was busy brushing Rowan to an immaculate shine. His brother, Handell, was brushing Tynan's horse. She laid a gentle hand on

Rowan's nose and rubbed it. Rowan whickered and bumped her with his head. Aeryn smiled.

She asked him, "Think you can stand going with me a little farther? I can't promise what will happen from here on out."

"He's been fed, and I gave him water. I cleaned out his cut with Marta's help, too," Greggry told her. "Marta put healing salve and fresh bandages on your friend's horse, too. She is acting strangely, though. Marta wondered if she might be sick."

"Good job, Gregg, and thank you. Why don't you and Handell take a break? My friend and I will take over."

The boy nodded and handed Aeryn the brush. She ruffled his dark hair as he passed.

He called to his brother, "Come on, Handy; let's go see if Corinn for some sweets." He grabbed his younger brother around the neck, and they wrestled their way out of the stable.

"Don't call me that!" she heard Handell whine before the door closed behind them.

Aeryn brushed Rowan slowly, mindful of his injury. She glanced over her stallion's back at Tynan patting his unresponsive mount. "Did you want to borrow one of my aunt's horses?" she asked him.

"No," was his quick reply.

"Does where my father grew up bother you that much?" she asked him. "I spent most of my time traveling with him and his battalion."

Tynan took a deep breath and then replied, "I suppose not. I came from a wealthy family as well. It would be hypocritical of me to fault you for where you come from."

"I don't come from this family. I was adopted into it, but they've always treated me like their own flesh and blood. I would die for them."

He nodded. "I believe you, but this mare has served me well enough. I see no reason to change her out now. Believe me, I have no desire to ride a horse that must be enchanted before I can even go near it.

All of these horses sense what I am, and it makes them skittish. I would have to do the same with any of them."

Aeryn glanced across the aisle to the other stalls. He was right—most of the horses were shifting nervously in their stalls. Her reply was abrupt and blunt; she could hold it in no longer. "I pray you take care. If anyone in Belhaun found out you've possessed the dead body of a Valisian soldier . . ."

"Which is why I have kept myself hidden!" he hissed. "They would treat me as an abomination, I know. Perhaps I am an abomination, but I could not sit idly by and let The Harbinger slip away. What is happening now is as much my fault as anyone else's. Frankly, I believe the gods themselves did a half-assed job of ridding the world of him. It is up to us to finish what they started."

They fell silent for a time. Finally Aeryn returned to the original subject. "So, why pass through Belhaun as quietly as he did?"

Tynan took his saddle and bridle off the shelf and began to outfit his horse again. "The Harbinger knows what Pythun knows. The people of The Fang would be formidable enemies. Mayhap The Harbinger wanted to avoid excess conflict that could drain his resources, and instead settled for gathering more faithful as he passed on to Morghall. He may leave the people of Morghall alone as well. We have no way of predicting. Knowing that your family is here, however, I believe he may also have been trying to send you a message just by stopping here and gathering followers from Belhaun. He is taunting you."

Aeryn nodded. She felt it, too. The Harbinger was telling her that he knew where her family was, and he would come for them next, after he took care of her and Pius both. She would not let him, however. Whatever she needed to do, she would do it to stop him.

To Tynan, she said, "Come. We've lingered here too long. We need to get to Morghall now."

41

The anteroom outside the Council Hall buzzed with the muffled but excited talk of the waiting sceptors. Sceptor Allemar, standing near the head of the long, teardrop-shaped oak council table, could hear them even through the thick doors that separated the hall from the anteroom. His waist-length braids and normally resplendent white robes seemed to droop with the weight of why he had called the meeting of the Council of Sceptors. Only the human sceptors were in attendance, however. He had failed to convince his elven and dwarven counterparts to attend as well.

The elven clerics left Pius to help their people secure their borders in the wake of the tainting of the Forever Wood, and the dwarves deigned not to attend, simply because he, a human, called the meeting. In their expressed opinion, what was going on in the world now was a human problem.

The fact that only human sceptors would be in attendance disappointed him, but worse, he felt he had failed to live up to the High Father Aephis's expectations that he bring calmness and order to the collective mouthpieces of the gods. None of the other sceptors knew exactly what was going on, of course. Only he knew even part of the story of Kaliphesh prior to the missive he had received the previous night. It took communion with his god and much digging through dusty tomes, none of which had seen the light of day for many centuries, before he understood the full significance of that missive.

Bitterness touched him briefly as he reflected on how little of Kaliphesh's story was passed from one of Aephis's sceptors to another, and he wondered why. Why did it take the tiny scroll of parchment sitting on the table before him, claiming to be from the late Tynan Selvantyr, before the whole story came to light?

The Harbinger is coming. Prepare now.

Allemar had no reason to doubt the authenticity of the message, and Aephis did not seem surprised when Allemar mentioned his name. He pushed his bitter thoughts aside and told himself that the High Father had methods and reasons to which mortals were not privy.

Finally, he looked at the bearded young man standing at the other end of the oaken table, which matched the paneling on the walls. Allemar nodded. "Let them in, Ferrin."

The young man turned away and walked to the tall, wooden doors. He pulled them open. "Ladies. Gentlemen. Please enter."

Each of the sceptors came in, one by one. Noray, sceptor to the High Mother Cira, sat at his right hand, while Oren sat to his left, as befitted the sceptor of Aephis's eldest son, Symon, god of Madness and Chaos. Yulonda, representative of the goddess of Music and Revel, Lilleth, came in with Veria, representative to Aspin. As the sceptor to the goddess of Forest and Nature, Veria leaned heavily on Yulonda's arm. Allemar knew that Veria felt Aspin's tumult over the tainting of the Forever Wood—a downside to having such a close connection to one's goddess. Iaman, sceptor to Aspin's husband Cerapis, followed closely after and pulled out a chair for Veria before sitting down beside her. The two sceptors' gods were connected not only by their influence on the world but marriage, and the sceptors were similarly close. Iaman's concern for Veria was evident on his face.

When all of twenty of the other sceptors were seated, Allemar cleared his throat, and all of them fell silent. Usually, his was the face of kindness and humor, but today, it was grim. Today, he had a story to tell them. "Honored sceptors, thank you for coming on such short notice."

"What is this all about?" demanded Quion, sceptor to the god of Dark Magik, Xenophon.

Allemar paused as he considered where to start. "Ladies and gentlemen, we have a problem, and that problem is on its way here." The sceptors looked at each other, confused. "Undoubtedly, you are all aware of what has happened to the Forever Wood. I received word by raven this very morning that the darkness that committed that act is on its way here

193

as we speak."

All the sceptors began talking at once, shouting questions at him.
"How can you be sure this is true?"
"Who sent it?"
"Why Pius?"

Allemar held up his hands for silence. They quieted down after a few moments. "I must tell you a story that has been passed down from the highest sceptors of the Order of Aephis, one to the other, for the last thousand years. As you know, Aephis is one of the nine eldest gods worshipped at present, with Cira, Anora, Aspin, Heldanic, Tempes, Ireteah, and Fortesis also in his birth line. There was another. When Aephis's father, Yurevis, was the High Father, a son was born to him and his wife, Ietena, then High Mother not long after Aephis. He was named Kaliphesh."

Allemar looked at the sceptors seated around him. Their faces were filled with deepening confusion. He knew that they wondered why they had never heard of this son, but they seemed willing to let him continue uninterrupted.

"Since Aephis was the first male born to the High Father, he was to succeed Yurevis when he stepped down to go into the eternal sleep, but Kaliphesh was not satisfied to play second to Aephis, whom he considered to be inferior to him. He considered all other gods inferior to him. When he matured, Kaliphesh began calling himself 'The Harbinger', and preached to the other gods that the world had grown weak in its ways and needed to be reborn through destruction and death.

"Even the dark gods were taken aback by the fervor of his convictions. They recognized, as the other gods did, that the tenuous balance between the light and the dark must always remain in place. The scale tips to one side or the other from time to time, but it will always return to the middle. This is the way it must be. To tip the scales of balance completely to the side of darkness would leave the world in chaos, and all that the first High Father and Mother worked so hard to

194

create would be destroyed in the wake of the darkness. The Harbinger believed this destruction was necessary to create a perfect new world, one in his dark image.

"His hatred and lust for power twisted him into something hideous and unrecognizable to the other gods, and when he finally grew tired of being ignored and shouted down by them, he staged a coup. He corrupted an arrogant sect of sorcerers, known as the Pillars of Ki, who held sway over great magiks unlike those seen elsewhere in Cathell. The Harbinger promised them limitless power over the world he would create, and they accepted without question. He used their powers in combination with his own to usurp many of the other gods' powers.

"The Pillars of Ki grew drunk on the power granted them by The Harbinger and gladly betrayed their people for him. They overthrew the governing lords of Cathell. Their will was the only obeyed besides The Harbinger's. Cathell was swept under in a wave of terror and destruction that lasted many years. So many mortals were slaughtered in The Harbinger's name that whole rivers ran red with their blood.

"Although the other gods, kept in power only by the rebellion of select worshippers, pleaded with Yurevis to intervene for the sake of their followers, he tried to stay neutral, in the hopes someone would overthrow the Pillars of Ki. When The Harbinger almost succeeded in stealing Yurevis's own powers, however, the High Father knew it was time to stop his second eldest son. The High Father worked directly against Kaliphesh, the first time one god aided in the downfall of another. Such an act was considered a cardinal sin within the pantheon, but because of the atrocities The Harbinger committed against the mortal and immortal world, no one objected to Yurevis's intervention.

"There existed a group of elite knights called the Maerinus Order, former protectors of the Pillars of Ki. When the Pillars of Ki swore their allegiance to The Harbinger and overthrew Cathell's lords, the knights abandoned their posts. Yurevis sought out the Maerinus Order. With his aid, the knights slaughtered most of the Pillars. The remaining Pillars understood their time had come to an end and agreed to help bring The Harbinger down. They tricked their god, and the High Father and the other gods managed to finally strike him down. Yurevis could not kill his own son, however, so the Pillars created a prison for The Harbinger within Nightstone Peak.

"Yurevis and the heads of the other races' pantheons forbade anyone, god or mortal, to again speak of The Harbinger, in the hopes it would keep him from ever regaining his full strength. All records of Kaliphesh's existence and reign were destroyed—this is why none of you has heard of him. Although these precautions should have been enough to send Kaliphesh into the eternal sleep, the High Father discovered that his power was too great, and Kaliphesh remained wakeful and active even in his prison.

Allemar skirted the truth and told them, "Although Yurevis forbade speaking of Kaliphesh in his day, Aephis knew in his heart that Kaliphesh would try to break free of his confines someday. When he became High Father, he passed knowledge of Kaliphesh and his betrayal down to his highest sceptor and gave her the duty of teaching her successor, so when the time came, they could be prepared.

"He was right to be concerned, too. Hundreds of years after he was imprisoned, an adventurer by the name of Tynan Selvantyr 'accidentally' found the caverns left over from the time of the Pillars of Ki, buried deep inside Nightstone. Aephis knew then that The Harbinger had found the one he would try to use to escape.

"Tynan was like him in many ways, and The Harbinger no doubt assumed he would be as easy to corrupt as the Pillars of Ki. To keep this from happening, Aephis intervened by asking the dwarven smith god, Vortenthas, to craft a sword for Tynan capable of recharging the wards placed by the Pillars of Ki to keep The Harbinger trapped in the caverns. The sword, Aric, was given to Tynan as a gift, but he had no idea of its true purpose. When Tynan learned of The Harbinger, he added his own enchantments to the caverns and the sword for a similar purpose, but in

196

truth, his spells alone were not enough to hold The Harbinger. Aric would have continued to do it job, but according to Aephis, the sword was recently allowed to be removed from the caverns by none other than the ghost of Tynan Selvantyr. The Harbinger's essence escaped from the Black Caverns and has gathered enough strength to taint the Forever Wood, remold it into something dark and twisted to give us a taste of things to come."

A murmur of shock and irritation passed through the group of other sceptors.

Allemar told them, "Late this morning, a message arrived to my chambers. I wish Tynan's message was more detailed, because we do not know in what form The Harbinger will arrive. I assume whatever form he takes, he will not come alone. No doubt he has gathered followers for an army with which to invade our city. It is clear to me that The Harbinger intends to destroy Pius in order to secure his succession to power. We must prepare, as Tynan says." He handed the tiny scroll the raven brought him to Noray. She read it and passed it to Oren.

Oren frowned as he passed the message on. "And just how do you propose that we prepare a defense against this god?"

"It will be a difficult fight. On such short notice I do not know what we can do against him either," agreed Mana, sceptor to the Harvest goddess Oleandar.

Allemar shook his head at their hesitance. In order to defeat The Harbinger, all of them must be united. He saw it would be an uphill battle to get them to see that. "There is one who can help us defeat him. We simply need to hold The Harbinger's forces at bay until she reaches the city. We *must* be united in our efforts," he said.

The god of Murder's sceptor, Terryk, scoffed, "A mortal woman?" The sceptor to Raen's twin, Kayen, god of Hatred and Torment, nodded in agreement to his skepticism.

"Don't doubt the abilities of a woman, especially when given the right weapon," argued Danfar, sceptor for the god of War, Fortesis. "My god's female followers have struck down just as many cutthroats flying the banner of your fell gods as his men have. Perhaps you jeer at the idea because you secretly welcome the destruction this Harbinger will bring."

Terryk and Rodric took loud offense to Danfar's statement, considering his own god's proclivities. In an instant, the room dissolved into a shouting match between the sceptors. Allemar sank down into his chair, knowing they could accomplish nothing while arguing among themselves. His aide hovered near his shoulder. Allemar beckoned him to lean down. He spoke into the young man's ear. "Send for Caeleb and the brothers. I want to make sure this woman makes it here safely. Bid them to make haste."

Allemar feared for the curse breaker's safety. He prayed that Tynan also knew of her power and was bringing her to Pius straightaway. The Harbinger must at least suspect the power she held, though his reluctance to kill her outright spoke to his arrogance. Aephis told him that he had done what he could to keep her true power secret from The Harbinger, but Allemar knew it was a gamble all the same. She possessed secrets that were gnawing at her soul, and that would make The Harbinger's job so much easier, should he decide to kill her for the sword before she reached Pius. If that were to happen, they would all be lost.

42

"Theo is short for Theodora," she reluctantly told Dahna as she was led up to the second floor.

"Theodora," Dahna echoed. "What a pretty name. Although, I suppose at your young age, that's not very important to you, is it? Theo is lovely, too."

Theo gave Dahna a weak smile. She felt unsure how to act around the woman. Dahna seemed nice enough, but the shock of finding out where Aeryn's family lived made her feel off-balance. Dahna herself was something of a surprise. Theo expected someone rigid to live in a house like this one. Dahna Ravane seemed to be the exact opposite. She just hoped the woman did not try to put her in a dress. She would be forced to make a run for it.

Once they reached the top of the house's central staircase, Dahna turned left and led Theo down a long hall paneled in light-colored wood, with paintings hanging on either side. Theo noticed one of the paintings was a portrait with a brass label that read "Derrick Ellis Ravane."

Theo paused in front of this one. "You mentioned Aeryn being like someone you called Derrick. Is that Aeryn's foster father?"

Aeryn's aunt stopped as well and came back to the painting. She nodded. "Yes, this was Aeryn's adoptive father. They were so close. It was like they were born to be a part of each other's lives." Kissing her delicate fingers, she gently pressed them to the cheek of the man in the painting. "I miss him so much still."

Derrick had dark hair like his sister, and coincidentally, like Aeryn as well. His eyes were a very dark brown but kind looking, and something about his smile in the painting hinted at a mischievous nature in her mind. "He actually looks a little like Aeryn," Theo commented when they started to walk again. "Did he know Aeryn's birth family?"

"No, not directly, I do not think, but they were from a farm close to the city, so perhaps there is a passing connection between our families somewhere down the line."

Dahna led Theo into a bedroom. Another woman was already there, placing folded garments into a tall chest of drawers. Dahna addressed her, "Mari, could I trouble you to go down to the kitchen and bring Theo here something to eat? I believe some of those little sandwiches and the cookies you baked yesterday would do the trick. Oh, and a glass of fresh milk, too."

Theo could not recall anyone ever offering her milk to drink. "You don't have to go to any trouble for me, really," she said again, more politely than the first time, but Dahna just waved off her protest.

Mari smiled and nodded. "Yes, Lady Dahna."

Dahna thanked her. When Mari left the room, she urged Theo, "Please sit. This will be fun." Aeryn's aunt went to a set of wardrobes and thrust the doors open.

Theo sat in a chair. "Whose room is this?" she asked, watching Dahna sift through rows of garments. There were more clothes in the wardrobe than Theo had seen in her whole life. Aeryn's adoptive family lived a life so much different from the one she knew just days before. Theo wondered what Dahna thought when she looked at her. Her clothes were nowhere close to being as nice as the clothes Dahna looked through. For that matter, how did Aeryn see her, having come from all this?

"This is my son Greggry's room," Dahna replied as she took some items out and laid them on the bed. "You already met him. You are about the same age and built. He is always moving. We can never keep weight on him."

Mari returned with a plate of food and a glass of milk, and set them on the small table next to Theo. Dahna asked her if she could send her son up, and Mari left again while Theo tried one of the little sandwiches on the plate. She made a conscious effort not to stuff it into her mouth. It tasted wonderful, but she did not want Dahna to see how hungry she was.

"I met him?" Theo asked between mouthfuls.

"Yes, in the carriageway."

Theo stopped chewing. "Your kid's a stable boy?" When she realized how the question sounded, Theo turned bright red. She began to stutter an apology, but Dahna started laughing.

"That is alright. Both of them are my sons. Greggry and Handell tend to the horses in the afternoons. They enjoy it, and having jobs teaches them responsibility. We have a regular stable hand as well. She and the boys are the only ones who tend to the stable, though. We try to keep a minimum of people on staff. It was a tradition my father started. He climbed his way up the ranks in his military days, from the lowest rank to general, and he simply does not believe in a lot of servants. He feels we should do many things for ourselves rather than rely on others to wait on us for everything. My husband and I wholly agree, so we make sure Greggry and Handell have jobs to do."

Returning to the plate of food, Theo nodded her approval of the idea. "Where is he? Your father I mean."

"At the commerce building, likely. He stays away from the house as much as Mother will stand. Too many reminders of Derrick, he says."

Dahna took out a few more items and laid them on the bed, then she shut the doors of the wardrobe. She sat on the bed and watched Theo eat for a time. "When Derrick died, my father seemed to fade away from us. He could not bear that he had outlived one of his children."

"Your mother lives here, too?" Theo asked, trying one of the chocolate chip cookies. It was still soft, and she delighted in the way it melted in her mouth.

"Oh, yes. It is a big house, plenty of room for all of us. I imagine she's in town with some of her friends and her assistant, Samuel. She does not get around as well as she used to. She will be sad she missed Aeryn."

A boy entered the bedroom and looked at Theo and then at Dahna. Theo remembered him from when they arrived at the house. "Mari said you wanted to see me, Mother?" the boy asked.

Dahna stood. "Yes, come in. Greggry, you met Theo, did you not?" She gestured to Theo, who promptly set the cookie in her hand back down on the plate.

"Hi," she said.

The boy smiled at her. "Hello."

Theo suddenly realized she probably had chocolate on her face. In as nonchalant a manner as she could manage, she brought her hand up and wiped her fingers across her mouth. She was saved from further embarrassment when Dahna told Greggry she was looking through his closets for things to give Theo.

"I picked out a couple of items that do not fit as well anymore. I thought they would fit Theo, but I wanted to make sure there was nothing here you were particularly attached to first."

He looked over the items and shook his head. "Nope, these are fine. I hear she and Aeryn and that man are going again. They just got here. You must have some exciting things to tell," he said to Theo, a twinkle of hope in his eye.

Theo tucked a strand of her hair behind her ear as the heat of embarrassment returned to her face. "A few," she replied, shyly.

Dahna smiled at Greggry. "Dearest, you know how Aeryn is. She is very busy right now. Perhaps she will come back soon and be able to stay longer. Now, you run along, so Theo can try these things on."

"Alright." Turning, he smiled at Theo again. "Nice to have met you. I hope you like the clothes." He scurried out of the room and down the hall.

Dahna held up a shirt for her. "I'm sure Aeryn will be ready to leave soon. Why don't you try some of these things on, and decide which

202

ones you want to take with you? I will be right back."

"Sure," she replied, taking the shirt.

Dahna slipped out, and Theo tried the clothes on. They fit her well. She only selected a few shirts and two pairs of pants, knowing that Aeryn would want to continue to travel light. The pants were thicker suede, so they would not itch like Theo's wool pants. She kept one pair on, discarding her old pants, and folded the other pair to take with her. Theo also selected a black cloak made of boiled wool, wanting to trade in her old one, with its patched holes and mended seams. She wished for a moment that Greggry had a pair of boots for her, too, to replace the ones Aeryn took from the stables in Valis, but then felt greedy for having such a thought. What Greggry and Dahna were giving her already was more than generous.

After hard consideration, Theo took off not only the shirt Aeryn found her at Mulkin's, but also the one under it, Brien's. She pulled on two of Greggry's shirts in their place. The shirt that formerly belonged to one of Mulkin's stable hands, she left on the bed next to her old cloak and pants. The other shirt, she held up to herself for a moment before she folded it neatly and placed it atop of the other clothes she had decided to take with her.

There came a knock at the door, and Dahna asked if it was alright to come back in. Theo said that it was. "Did you find anything you liked?" the woman asked as she entered. She held a bundle of thick, dark gray wool in her arms.

"Yes, I quite like these shirts, the cloak, and the pants . . . if that's alright?"

Dahna set the bundle on the table and then stood in front of Theo. "Of course." Reaching out, she untucked Theo's long blond hair from inside the shirt's collar and smoothed out the shirt's shoulders. "The clothes look lovely on you."

Dahna noticed the shirt sitting on top of the clothes Theo planned to take and said, "That doesn't look like one of Gregg's."

"No," Theo said. "It was once my brother's. It doesn't really fit, but I'd like to hold on to it for a while longer I think, even if I don't wear it still."

The woman nodded and smiled at her. "Nothing like hand-me-downs to remind us of family. It is a shame I cannot give you Aeryn's old clothes, but as Derrick often said, if she did not wear holes in them within a month, she wore them until the stitches fell off."

"Does Aeryn have a room here?"

Dahna nodded. "Upstairs, but I think we should head downstairs before Aeryn thinks we got lost."

"What was she like when she was younger?" Theo asked as she slipped on Gregg's cloak.

"A lot like you," Dahna replied, picking up the woolen bundle from the desk. "Angry at the world, fighting with anyone she could, and as defiant as possible." Dahna smirked at her, though, letting her know she meant this in an affectionate way.

"Aeryn was always getting into fights with the boys in Derrick's camp. The boys who worked for the other soldiers used to poke fun at her because she was one of the few girls in camp."

"Really?" Theo laughed a little at this. She could definitely see Aeryn doing that.

Dahna's face became serious. "That's how she got that scar across her left eyebrow. Did you know that?" When Theo shook her head, the woman nodded. "During one of her scuffles, one of the boys drew a blade and tried to cut Aeryn's face open with it, Derrick told us. She was lucky it narrowly missed all but her eyebrow and forehead. She came out on top at the end of that fight, gave that boy a beating he likely still remembers. She was proud of that, but we could all tell she was scared, too. Aeryn almost lost her eye, and she knew it. After that, she started to straighten out and listen to what Derrick kept telling her about learning to focus that anger of hers."

"How do you know I'm like she was?"

Dahna smiled at her. "I can see that same fire in your eyes as I saw—and still see—in hers. The reasons behind it might be different, but I can guess the result is the same."

"Did she have many friends when she was younger?" Theo asked.

"No. She kept mostly to herself, unless Derrick was around. She stuck to him like glue."

As if on cue, Theo heard Aeryn calling for them from downstairs.

"Yes, Aeryn, we are coming down now," Dahna replied. To Theo she said, "Speak of the devil. Well, I suppose that ends our tour through the Ravane family memories. I do so hope you will come back with Aeryn again, Theo."

Theo nodded and realized that she hoped so as well. She liked Dahna and did not feel as though the woman thought less of her for growing up as she did, so different from how Aeryn had. She picked up the clothes from the bed and followed Dahna downstairs. Aeryn and Tynan were waiting for them in the receiving hall. Dahna called for Corinn to see if he was done preparing supplies for Aeryn. He entered the hall a moment later, carrying a satchel.

"Everything is ready, as requested, Lady Dahna." He handed the satchel to Aeryn, bowed, and then left again.

"A man of few words as always," Dahna said wryly.

Aeryn smiled at her aunt. To Theo's eyes, it looked forced. The sell-sword asked Dahna, "Will you see us out?"

"Of course," her aunt replied and followed the three of them outside.

Tynan swung up into his saddle and prattled on to Dahna about what an honor it was to meet her, and how he only wished he had more time to get to know her and the rest of Aeryn's family. It turned Theo's stomach. Aeryn seemed to ignore him while she tucked the satchel into one of her saddlebags. Theo gave her the extra clothes she was taking and those went into the saddlebags as well.

Dahna managed to disengage herself from Tynan finally and came to stand next to Aeryn, handing her the bundle she carried. "It was father's cloak. I know he would tell you to take it, if he was here. It kept him warm and gave him luck for all those years in the service." She tried to keep her voice light, but it was obvious she was concerned for her niece.

For a moment, Aeryn said nothing, but finally, she took the cloak. "Thank you, Aunt Dahna. I really appreciate everything." Slipping off her cloak, Aeryn unfurled the bundle and put it on over her shoulder plates. The chain clasp was adorned with a raven in flight.

Dahna nodded. "I know you do, dearest. Please be safe." Her smile was tight with apprehension. She turned to Theo and said, "It has been wonderful to meet you, and I meant what I said about you coming to visit us with Aeryn again. Maybe you can stay a little longer next time." She winked at Aeryn.

"Thanks for the extra shirts and stuff. And, tell Greggry I said thanks, too," she replied.

Aeryn hugged Dahna, who told her again to be careful. Aeryn said she would and stepped back, swinging up onto Rowan's back. His coat shone in the sunlight. Aeryn held out a hand for Theo and helped her up to the usual spot. They were off again with hardly a look back. The sell-sword seemed in a hurry to put distance between them and her family's house.

Once they left the residential part of the city, however, they encountered large groups of people shopping and working, everyone in a hurry. The three of them were forced to slow to a crawl to keep from trampling anyone. Finally, Aeryn stopped Rowan and told Theo to get off; they were going to walk to the city gate. Tynan dismounted as well, but followed at their rear.

As they walked ahead of Rowan, Theo commented "Your aunt seems nice."

206

"She is," Aeryn replied.

Theo wanted to be angry that Aeryn never mentioned her foster family was well off, but in truth, Aeryn did not talk much about her life at all. Theo felt like she hardly knew anything at all about the sell-sword, beyond that she was orphaned at a young age, her adoptive father took her in after she tried to steal from him, and now, that her adoptive family was rich. She kept coming back to that last fact. It was the one that irritated her the most, despite how much she liked Dahna and Greggry.

Theo wondered if the only reason Aeryn allowed her to come along was because Aeryn felt sorry for her. So what if Aeryn had been like her when she was Theo's age? She was adopted by a soldier with a rich family. How could Aeryn *not* think she was better? Theo was nothing more than a kid nobody cared about, who stole from people like Aeryn's aunt.

Theo started to lag behind between Rowan and Tynan. She considered running off, disappearing into the crowd. Belhaun might not be too bad of a place to start over, after all. If things got too rough, maybe Dahna would take her in, like Willa did. Aeryn sure did not seem to visit her aunt often, so that might work out. She would rarely ever see Aeryn. Right now, that sounded just fine to Theo.

"Keep up," Aeryn said to her, and Theo suddenly realized Aeryn was watching her over her shoulder.

Theo looked back at Tynan. He did not say anything, but he was watching her, too. It was creepy. Her head jerked back around when she realized Aeryn had said something else to her. "What?"

One of Aeryn's eyebrows quirked. "I said, you can ride Rowan, if you don't feel like walking."

"That's all I am to you, isn't it? Just a hassle." She glared at the sell-sword.

Aeryn looked confused. "Excuse me?"

"You just feel bad for me," she said.

"What are you talking about?"

Theo looked back at Tynan. He was still watching her. "Why do you keep looking at me like that?" she demanded.

The dead man tried to look innocent, but she knew otherwise. "I merely wondered if you are feeling well."

"I feel fine. I've figured it out, though. You don't care about me." She did not notice that Aeryn had stopped, and she walked right into the woman. Stumbling back a step, Theo growled, "Hey, what's the deal?"

"I could ask you the same. Why are you acting like this? You're acting childish."

"Really? Guess what, I *am* a child. This is how I act!" Theo snapped. People were beginning to stare, and she bit her lip to keep the quiver in it from showing.

Aeryn rubbed her forehead with the hand not holding Rowan's reins and took a deep breath. "Look, just walk with me instead of hanging behind."

Theo crossed her arms and her glare deepened. "What if I don't want to?" She could hardly see through the tears that were blurring her vision. She blinked them away.

"Do it anyhow," Aeryn growled back. The sell-sword gave her a small push to get her moving. "We're wasting time and attracting attention."

The three of them began to walk again, leading the two horses through the traffic. None of them said anything until Aeryn finally asked Theo, "What was that all that about?"

Theo did not reply for a time and then declared, "You look down on me and think I'm nothing but a burden to you."

"What?"

"You heard me."

Aeryn gave a short laugh that held little amusement in it.

"It's obvious." Theo said. "Look where we just left! I'm an orphaned thief. You acted like you were this poor orphan taken in by the kind soldier. You forgot to mention that the kind soldier grew up in a huge house. You probably had a whole lot handed to you after you got adopted."

Aeryn's face tightened. "I don't need to justify my childhood to you, but that is far from the truth. I don't look down on you for being an orphan or a thief. We all do what we must to survive in this world, Theo."

"But you think of me as a burden, don't you?" Theo broke off what else she wanted to say as emotions she did not want to voice rose to the surface.

Aeryn asked her, "What do you want to hear from me? I cannot replace Willa for you."

"Who said I wanted you to? Never mind, it's stupid anyhow," Theo said.

Another silence stretched between them. Aeryn reached over and touched Theo's shoulder. She shrugged the sell-sword's hand off, but when Aeryn took her arm and pulled her closer, Theo did not resist.

Aeryn told her, "If I thought you were a burden, I would have found someone to take you in, back in Cira. I like you, and I've liked having you with me." She sighed. "Does that make you feel better?"

Theo nodded almost imperceptibly. She felt foolish. A tear ran down her face, but she swiped it away with her sleeve before Aeryn could see it. She let her hurt feelings get the best of her, but the last thing she wanted was for Aeryn to see her as just a little kid who she had to take care of. Theo told herself she had to prove to Aeryn she could be of value. Then, the sell-sword would not decide to leave her behind. Theo never wanted to be the one left behind.

43

After they left Belhaun, Aeryn turned them northwest and left the road, kicking Rowan into a gallop across the countryside in the direction of Morghall. Theo trusted Aeryn knew the way. They passed many farms and plantations, but few of them interested Theo. The wildlife captured her attention on the sprawling meadows. Never before had she seen so many rabbits, deer, and birds. The birds flocked in large groups, settling in the branches of trees not as tall or massive as those in the Forever Wood, but whose branches were draped in autumn's colors.

Eventually, it occurred to Theo she had no idea what exactly the North Gate they were trying to reach was, so she asked Aeryn about it.

"It's a dimensional door at the center of the city that can transport a single person or small army to any of the other three gates in Cathell," Aeryn said over her shoulder. She had to shout to be heard over the sound of Rowan's hooves pounding on the grass and dirt.

Theo wondered which gate they would travel to from the North Gate, but figured she would ask once they arrived in Morghall. Shouting back and forth while they rode was too difficult. She felt relief when Aeryn finally pointed Rowan in the direction of the road again and slowed Rowan to a fast trot. Aeryn said they were almost to Morghall. The sun, now reddish orange, had begun its slow descent to the horizon.

Just when Theo was afraid they would not make it before nightfall, she caught sight of black walls ahead of them. Another flock of birds flew overhead, in the opposite direction from them. She watched them go, shielding her eyes with a hand. Her attention returned to Aeryn a moment later when the sell-sword suddenly brought Rowan to a complete stop.

"Why are we stopping?"

"By the road," was all Aeryn said.

Tynan pulled his horse up next to them and also looked. Theo peered around Aeryn's back to see what they were staring at. In the middle of the field ahead, near the road, were dozens upon dozens of birds. They were large and black, and feeding on something. She squinted to make out what had attracted so many of them but could not. She caught the profile of Aeryn's face. It was grim and tight.

"Are those blackbirds?" Theo asked.

"No."

Theo felt the sell-sword's body tense the moment before she kicked Rowan into a mad dash straight for the eye of the flock. Theo held on for her life as Aeryn let loose a distressed cry and drew Aric.

44

What Theo mistook for ordinary blackbirds was a flock of ravens. The ravens fed on several dozen corpses lying in the field, and the red fabric that still clung to the bodies told Aeryn they belonged to Fang soldiers. Their desecration sent rage coursing through her veins, and she kicked Rowan into a full charge, straight for the ravens. As Rowan plunged through the heart of the flock, most of the ravens took flight in a hurricane of black wings and feathers. Aeryn turned Rowan tightly around again to charge at those scavengers that remained at their festering meal. Theo swore behind her as they made a second pass. Her grip tightened further around Aeryn's middle, but Aeryn did not bring Rowan to a stop until all of the ravens were gone. Then, she swung one booted foot over the stallion's neck and jumped down. Sword in hand, she walked to the side of one of the bodies. It lay on its stomach.

Theo called after her.

"Stay with Rowan," Aeryn snapped, without so much as a glance back.

She knelt and turned the corpse over onto its back. The stench of flesh rotting in the sun was overpowering, and this close to it, she had to keep her stomach in check. The sight of it was not much better. The corpse's eyes were gone. Her teeth clenched, and she sucked a breath in through her mouth rather than her nose.

The corpse's face was unrecognizable due to burns that covered most of it, twisting the man's features, but for an instant she swore she looked into the face of her dead father. The empty sockets glared at her. *Why didn't you help me?*

Aeryn closed her eyes and forced herself to focus as her stomach knotted painfully. Fear she might be sick washed over her. She reminded herself that her father had not looked anything like this poor man when she found him. The sensation passed. When she reopened her eyes, the man's face no longer looked like her father's. It was just the face of an unfortunate stranger. Her gaze went to his uniform, and her fears were confirmed. Rising slowly, Aeryn went to another body and found it was wearing the same uniform as the first. They all were.

Tynan brought his mare to where Aeryn stood among the bodies, staring at the walls of Morghall in the distance. "What is it?" he asked.

Theo chose not to wait with Rowan as Aeryn had commanded her to and came to stand beside her as well, her hand over her nose, only to stumble back a step when she came close enough to get a better view of the bodies. "Gods above, not only do they smell awful, they've been pecked at."

"I told you to stay back," Aeryn replied.

Theo ignored her. "The Harbinger did this?"

"Likely."

Tynan asked, "Who are they?"

"Fang soldiers."

Her anger boiled over, and Aeryn turned on Tynan, pulling him from his horse. He landed on his back. Dry dirt flew up in his wake. Aeryn landed on top of him and punched him square in the mouth. It was like hitting soft dough stretched over bone. His lip split but did not bleed, which somehow made her angrier. Theo shouted at her, but Aeryn paid her no attention.

She grabbed the front of Tynan's shirt and pulled his face closer to hers. "*Did you even warn them?* You didn't, did you? Why?" Tynan only stared back at her, his hands around her wrists. Aeryn shouted in his face. "Damn you! These men and women didn't have to die this way. They were Fang soldiers, like my father. Tell me why you didn't warn them."

"Aeryn!" Theo tried to push her off of Tynan.

She held the girl off, but released Tynan and stood up.

"What are you doing?" Theo shouted at her.

"He didn't warn them," Aeryn repeated. Tynan began to rise from where he lay, but she pushed him down again with her boot.

Tynan pushed her foot away. "Enough." He glared back at her as he stood. "Warning them would have done nothing. They would have been slaughtered just the same. They would not have run from him. These people had no defense against The Harbinger at their disposable."

Aeryn combed her hair out of her face with her fingers, staring at the carnage that surrounded them. She knew he was right—the people of Morghall never ran. "So this is my fault then."

"No, it is not."

"If I hadn't stopped in Belhaun, we could have gotten here hours ago. We might have made it here before the battle was over."

"Aeryn . . ."

In her heart, she knew this battle was over long before they reached Belhaun, but her guilt pulled on every part of her. "You said these people had no defense against him. You said Aric can stop him, but the sword was with me, and I wasn't here. If I had been, I could have helped them."

"Not here."

"Why?"

"Because you are not ready yet. This was not the place for you to make your stand. Pius is."

Aeryn stared at him for a moment, then asked, "What makes you so certain I will be ready to face him once we reach Pius? How can I believe *anything* you say? All you've done is lie."

Without waiting for a response, she turned on her heel and whistled to her horse. Rowan came to her, and she swung up into the saddle. She collected Theo and did not bother to see if Tynan followed before she turned Rowan toward the gates of Morghall. It was only then that she noticed the smoke that rose up from somewhere in the black walled city. The Harbinger had taken his wrath out on the city, too. She urged Rowan into a gallop for the city gates. Twilight was coming.

Corpses lay on the ground all the way to the gates, like a foul offering to welcome her to the city. It solidified her resolve to find The Harbinger at any cost, but in the darkest regions of her mind, her doubt in her ability to stop him grew. She shifted her gaze away from the bodies to Morghall's gates and noticed a man standing by the gates. As they drew closer, she saw he held a crossbow in the crook of his arm. A small crowd of people, battered but well-armed men and women, stood nearby and also watched their approach.

Before they reached the gate, Aeryn stopped Rowan. She stared at the man while he stared back. Dried blood covered one side of his face, and patches of his short hair looked scorched. Bright slashes from sword strikes decorated his black chain mail. The man did not flinch under her scrutiny, and the people standing near him did not look away from her or Tynan. Aeryn kept her hands away from her weapons. The look in their eyes told her these people were wound tight.

"What business do you have here?" the man asked her in a calm baritone.

"We have come to use the North Gate, if we may," Aeryn replied, just as calm.

"Who are you?"

"I might ask you the same, sir," Aeryn replied. Theo's hands tightened on her belt, and the girl whispered to her about the crossbow, but Aeryn made no sign she heard.

"I am Lord Norestis, governor of this city, and I have no patience for your insolent tongue. I ask again, *who* are you?" He took a step forward, his grip on the crossbow no longer relaxed. The people behind him shifted forward as well.

Aeryn bowed her head in obeisance. "Aeryn Ravane, my lord. My companions are Theo and Tynan."

Norestis acknowledged her sign of respect. "Aeryn Ravane. He told us to expect you." The people grumbled angrily at his words. Some nodded, some flexed the hands in which their weapons were held.

"Who did?" A warning went off in her brain. Her grip on Rowan's reins tightened.

He did not answer her question. "You need to come with us."

Theo whispered something else that Aeryn did not understand, but Aeryn kept her attention on Norestis and his soldiers. "Nay, sir. I decline that invitation."

"Did I say it was an invitation? Do you know of our ways in The Fang, Aeryn Ravane?"

She nodded once. "I was born here."

"Then you know it is best not to argue with us." Without any signal from their lord, the others stepped closer and laid hands on their weapons. There were at least twenty of them. Norestis raised his crossbow.

Aeryn did not back down. "I won't allow you to take us anywhere without a fight."

"Mark my words, sell-sword, I will shoot you and your companions."

She felt Theo shift behind her and knew the girl meant to bolt. Reaching behind her, Aeryn grabbed Theo's arm and squeezed it. Theo stopped squirming, but pressed against her for protection. The people behind Norestis drew and raised their own weapons. Aeryn drew her sword with her other hand. Her eyes dared him to shoot her before she could cut him down.

Norestis's eyes met hers. Each held the other's gaze until a begrudging smile caught the corner of his mouth. "You have spine." He looked at his soldiers, silently telling them to stand down. "We heard about strange occurrences in the east, whisperings about some horror in Valis and a taint in the Wood, so we fortified our gates with extra men, but somehow a man I've never seen before got my men to open the gates for him. Before we knew what was happening, an army hidden by some fell illusion materialized behind him, and the man turned into a demon.

This I saw with my own eyes.

"His soldiers howled and snarled like dogs and swarmed through the open gates before my men could close them again. The demon's magiks and his army tore a bloody swath through our city as they went straight to the center where the North Gate stands. Even the North Gate's guards, good casters among them, were no match for him. The demon and his hellhounds disappeared into the portal. He left a barrier in place around the North Gate to keep us out and a creature to guard it. That thing he left behind has been taunting us ever since, with our city burning around us."

"The demon told you to expect us?"

"No. That thing left to guard the gate. It told us to expect a sell-sword named Aeryn Ravane and two companions, that you are following the demon, and you are to be brought to the North Gate when you arrive. The gate will be released for you." Norestis appraised her once more. "I take offense at being given orders in my own city, but so far nothing we've tried has broken that barrier. What connection do you have with this demon?"

"The Harbinger is no mere demon; he is a fallen god. He intends to destroy Pius, but we intend to destroy him first. We must use the North Gate to pursue him."

Norestis seemed to consider this before he nodded. "Come, my soldiers and I will escort you."

Turning, he went through Morghall's gates. Aeryn did not completely trust Norestis, but felt she had little alternative, so she urged Rowan forward to follow the lord into his ruined city.

All around them, parts of Morghall still burned and the corpses of citizens and soldiers alike littered the streets. Aeryn spotted the remains of undead soldiers among the corpses, like those they had seen in Valis, but the number was proportionately small. People gathering up the dead watched them as they passed. None of them looked frightened, only watchful and wary. Aeryn wished she could apologize to them for

217

letting The Harbinger do what he did.

"Why are the city walls black?" Theo asked her.

"After the barbarians were pushed back, the people of The Fang painted the walls of Morghall black to symbolize the pain and loss they endured during their struggle for freedom. They wanted an eternal reminder for future generations." She added, "Funny how history repeats itself."

On their way through the city, at Norestis's request, Aeryn related some of the events in Valis and the Forever Wood, but she gave him only the barest of details. Aeryn felt unable to refuse his request outright. If he decided they were working with The Harbinger instead of against, he would surely try to keep them from reaching the North Gate, and their pursuit might end at Morghall's gallows.

Norestis listened as they walked past the burned buildings and homes and the bodies, past the ruined statue of the city's patron god Morghell. He did not seem particularly surprised at anything she told him. Seeing the carnage around the city, she guessed that little could surprise him now.

Although she had never used or seen the North Gate, Aeryn knew it stood inside the city's council hall. It was considered to be the most secure building in the city. Such did not seem to be the case anymore. As the group filed through the high-arched carriageway cut into the center of the square building, several of Norestis's people snagged torches off the walls, lit them, and all of them drew weapons.

The sun behind them was close to setting, but something about the way the inky blankness inside the carriageway seemed to swallow the light caused the hairs on the back of Aeryn's neck to stand at attention. She drew Aric. A harsh throb pulsed through the sword and into her hand. She glanced over at Tynan. He rode beside her, but his hood masked his face.

"Do you have a weapon?" she asked in a low voice, reluctant to address him at all.

"I still have magik at my disposal," was his reply.

The group moved quickly down the tall, wide corridor toward the courtyard at the building's center. All of the torches hanging on the walls closest to the courtyard entrance were out. The light from the torches carried by Norestis's soldiers was the only guiding light available to them. It illuminated the corpses lining the carriageway, many dressed in the bright silk of courtiers, while others appeared to have been guards. When the group reached the open air courtyard at the center of the building, the descending sun was barely lighting anything at all in the courtyard, but it was impossible to miss the towering ivory arch at its center, no less than thirty paces across, encircled by a low stone wall. Arcane energies crackled up and down its sides.

Their escorts stopped and parted for Aeryn and Tynan's horses. Lord Norestis gestured at the North Gate at the center of the courtyard.

"Do you see it?"

It took a moment, but then she did see it: a thin yellow barrier surrounding the gate. When she nodded, what she at first took for another corpse lying next to the gate shifted and rose to its feet. Aeryn glanced at Lord Norestis, and he nodded.

"That demon god, or The Harbinger, as you called it, put the barrier in place just before he and his army entered the portal. He left *that* in its place. So far we've been unable to break through, and it's—"

"It's been laughing at you and your pitiful attempts to break the barrier," the creature on the other side of the barrier cackled. It lurched closer, and Aeryn saw it was one of The Harbinger's animated dead men. "Who have you brought me now, my dear Lord of Fools? All those stupid priests and spellcasters have had little effect."

The muscles in Norestis's jaw visibly flexed, and he glared poisonously back at the thing. "Aeryn Ravane."

The corpse grinned, displaying broken and rotted teeth. "Truly? Come closer then."

Aeryn dismounted and walked to the barrier. "Release the gate."

The corpse sneered but waved a hand and the barrier around the North Gate dissolved. "Bring your party forward."

"You will send us to where The Harbinger has gone?"

It nodded.

"How do we know it's not a trap?"

"You don't."

Aeryn looked back at Theo and Tynan. Theo looked at her with clear apprehension, and Tynan said, "We have little in the way of choices, Aeryn."

The corpse grinned again. "How true. Coming?"

Aeryn had a bad feeling about the whole thing, but Tynan was right. They had little choice other than to take the creature at its word.

Lord Norestis approached her. "I wish I could send some of my people to aid you, but as you can see, we have much work on our hands here. I hope you will think no less of us for it."

"Of course not. I understand. Besides, I believe the one-way pass to The Harbinger was intended for my companions and me, and no one else."

"I wish you luck then," he said, then gestured at the animate corpse standing by the North Gate. "We will take care of that thing for you, after you're safely through."

"I'm so frightened," it mocked him.

Aeryn nodded and returned to Rowan. Theo grabbed her arm when she took Rowan's reins to lead him to the gate. She assured the girl that everything would be fine and led Rowan to where The Harbinger's creature waited. It stopped her before she reached the portal.

"One last thing. The master told me to pass a message on to you," it said. "He hopes you enjoyed his gift on the road to the city. You are not long from ending up just like them." The corpse snickered.

Aeryn growled, "Just ready the gate."

"So pushy." The corpse laughed again. The stench of its fetid breath stung her nose. "The portal is already set. Enter, and you will be taken to your final destination."

Aeryn looked at the portal. A thick mist formed at its center. When the mist cleared, she could no longer see the wall on the other side of the North Gate. Instead, she saw a pair of deer grazing in an unfamiliar clearing. Her brow furrowed as she looked at the trees standing at the edges of the meadow. There was no road in sight. "What am I looking at?"

"Just get in there!"

Suddenly, The Harbinger's messenger grabbed her and pushed her toward the gate. Caught off guard, she let go of Rowan's reins and tumbled forward, sliding into the portal. She heard Theo scream her name right before everything went black.

45

The Harbinger stirred when the North Gate was activated. He had been dreaming of a time long ago, when he still walked the dark halls of Rillenvair, the palace of the human gods on the immortal plane of Iritor. Banished from the land of gods and left imprisoned among the mortals he once ruled, he knew he could not have fallen any lower. His teeth gnashed as he thought about the humiliation his banishment imposed upon him.

Mortals knew nothing of the pleasures offered by Iritor, both light and dark. No mortal had lain eyes on that place except in their most pleasurable dreams and tormented nightmares. When he returned to Iritor, it would be as Rillenvair's lord and master, the Dark Father.

The sell-sword was an obstacle to this.

Even so far away, he could feel the tremor of doubt and fear deep in her soul, and it delighted him and strengthened him, yet she continued to dog him. He should not have let her live, he knew now. This angered him. He placed the blame on Pythun for weakening his mind with his humanness. It had made him decide to torture the sell-sword and thief by forcing them to watch their world collapse around them before he ended their miserable lives, when in reality, he should have killed them outright.

A sadist's smiled touched The Harbinger's demonic face as he felt the former master of thieves and human garbage writhe and scream inside him. He planned to torture whatever remained of Pythun's craven soul as long as he was able, sipping at it until he had drunk every last drop of him. This would be Pythun's reward for his arrogance in thinking his god would *share* power with him. How stupid.

Still, Pythun's misery alone did not satisfy him.

A tremor of fear all his own hummed deep inside him at the thought of the sell-sword finding him too soon, Vortenthas's sword in hand, before he was ready. He should have razed the city until he found where she hid it, but he had not. He had decided instead to begin his conquest right away, assuming she would never find out the true purpose of the sword. He never anticipated that that posturing fool Tynan Darius Selvantyr would manage to make his way back to them so that he could guide them, or that the sell-sword possessed a well of untapped power capable of using the sword for its intended purpose. Her power had been hidden from him. But now, after having devoured many souls and having gathered more still to him, he was strong enough again to see through the deceptions Aephis used to cover her power—only the High Father himself was capable of this. His brother was wise to shield her true nature from him.

The apple did not fall far from the tree. Like Yurevis before him, Aephis was working against him. His hatred for Aephis, much deeper than what he felt for Pythun, curdled into a hard stone inside him. Aephis would not be successful, however. He would ensure that.

In the end, he would kill the sell-sword and drink her soul, as he did Pythun's. And then he would kill the thief and Tynan Selvantyr while she watched. Then, he would kill everyone in her beloved Belhaun, leaving her aunt and nephews for last.

In his mind's eye, he did this while he took pleasure in her despair.

46

For a moment Aeryn was paralyzed, held in space and time, and then she fell free and rolled to a stop on the meadow grass she had seen through the portal. Her abrupt arrival and loud cursing as she picked herself up caused the two grazing deer to dash for the tree line. Her skin tingled from the effects of the portal. She rubbed her hands over her arms, trying to massage the pinpricks away, and looked around. She was alone.

Aeryn picked off the grass blades that clung to her armor. She told herself not to panic as she looked around this totally unfamiliar place in the darkening twilight. Few clouds hung overhead and stars twinkled into being. The mostly clear sky might mean she would soon have bright moonlight to see by. But this was cold comfort, considering she might be forced to go ahead without Theo and Tynan, on foot, and try to determine where The Harbinger's wicked messenger had sent her.

The trees around her clearly did not belong to the Forever Wood, tainted or otherwise—they were too small and tightly packed. That meant she was probably nowhere near Alethia and the West Gate, and the air was too cool for these woods to be near Kings Town and the South Gate. The fact that she had not ended up in Alethia was the only thing that gave her comfort now, though small comfort at that. A shudder ran through her at the brief memory of her last visit to Alethia. She pushed it aside. That memory would do her no good now.

Before she could decide what her next move would be, Theo, Rowan, Tynan, and his mare appeared to walk out of thin air not far from where she stood. Rowan trotted straight to her, with Theo forced to go along for the ride. Though in the saddle, Theo's legs were not long enough for her feet to reach the stirrups. Under any other circumstances, the look on Theo's face as she held on to Rowan's dark mane might have been comical. When the stallion finally came to a stop in front of Aeryn, Theo vigorously rubbed her arms as Aeryn had.

"Kellen below," the young thief cursed. "I was sure we'd got separated from you forever. I thought I was going to be stuck with just him," the girl jabbed a thumb at Tynan as he pulled his mare up beside Rowan, "for the rest of the journey."

Aeryn patted Rowan's neck and scratched between his ears before she helped Theo down.

Theo went on. "When that corpse thing pushed you into the portal, Norestis's men rushed it. It started cackling like it'd gone completely insane, and they started punching and kicking it. Norestis told 'em to stop, all while Tynan's shouting at it to tell him where you went."

"Fools!" Tynan said as he climbed down from his horse. "They destroyed The Harbinger's messenger before I could get any answers from it."

"Like it would have told you anything." Theo shook her head, still rubbing her arms. "Why does my skin feel like it's crawling?"

"It's the effect of the portal," Aeryn told her.

She looked around at the dark trees and meadow again. It was hard to see anything now, and she found herself willing the moon to rise a little faster. She finally relented and took her lightstone from her pouch. The meager circle of light it cast around them did little to penetrate the night's darkness.

"Where are we?" Theo asked.

"I don't know. I'm going to use Aric to get a fix on The Harbinger's location again."

Concerned now that they had ended up too far from The Harbinger to ever catch up again, Aeryn found it difficult to control her anxious thoughts. She closed her eyes and shook her head, trying to wrestle her mind into order again. She held Aric in front of her as before and slowly turned in a circle. The vibrations in Aric were still strong, but something was wrong. She turned in the opposite direction and frowned. The vibration did not increase or decrease. There was no difference in it, no matter which way she turned.

She opened her eyes. "Something is wrong," she told the others. "Each way is the same. Aric pulsates equally in every direction I turn."

Theo suddenly backed into her. Aeryn asked her, "What are you doing?"

"Something crawled over my foot. A couple somethings."

Aeryn crouched and held out her lightstone to illuminate the ground. Her breath caught. At first, it looked as though the grass was moving on its own, but then, Aeryn saw that the grass was filled with spiders, beetles, centipedes, and the like, moving through it en mass. They all appeared to be headed in a single direction. Judging by the moon just now rising into view, the direction was roughly south.

"I don't like this," Theo said. "Let's hurry up and get out of here."

"That could be a problem," Aeryn said.

"What do you mean?" Theo asked.

"I can't tell what direction we need to go in, and I have no idea where we ended up." Aeryn tried to keep her apprehension out of her voice.

Tynan held up a hand and replied, "Let us be logical. These creatures are not here out of coincidence. Since they are headed south, we will follow their direction, and they may lead us to The Harbinger."

"But what if they're going the *opposite* direction as The Harbinger?" Theo asked.

Tynan thought about this and then suggested sending out another bird, as he had done when searching for them in the Forever Wood.

"Alright, send out your bird," Aeryn replied. "In the meantime, we'll head south and look for a road. Maybe that will give us a better idea of where we are."

They left the meadow clearing on horseback. The moon cast

226

enough light finally to guide them. While they rode, through whatever magiks he had at his disposal, Tynan called a gray owl to him. The majestic predator swooped down and landed on his outstretched leather gauntlet. Theo made a sound of awe at the sight of it. Tynan smiled a little and stroked the bird's head. The owl did not seem to mind, and even let Tynan stretch his arm out so that Theo could also touch the bird. Then, Tynan whispered a few words to the bird and tossed the owl back into the air. The bird took to its wings and disappeared into the treetops.

Aeryn prayed the bird could indeed bring them information about where they were. Above all things, she did not like the idea of being lost. It was how her father had died, lost in a sudden snowstorm. Aeryn felt all her fears crowd in on her, weaken her. She closed her eyes and breathed in the forest air, filled her lungs with it. She tried to relax but could not. Whether it was in a snowstorm, woods, or an open field, lost was lost. They were losing time in the race to find The Harbinger, and in certain regions, one could wander for days before reaching a settlement. All of the maps in her saddlebags were worthless unless she could determine where they were. Tension knotted in her shoulders.

Something cried out in the woods behind them, a low and keening call. Theo started at the sound. Tynan's owl returned a moment later. He stared intently at the bird for a time and then send it off again. He grunted quietly.

"The owl says there is a settlement of some kind nearby. We should run into it with the route we are taking. Also, something is following us," Tynan told them.

"A person?"

Tynan shook his head. "It did not say human, just something traveling through the trees."

"Through the trees?" Theo asked.

"Yes."

Aeryn's brow furrowed and pulled Rowan to a stop. "Where?"

Tynan pointed, "There, roughly twenty or so paces away."

227

Aeryn pressed her lips into a thin line and looked into the trees in the direction the owl had indicated. She saw nothing. Her irritation that she missed someone or something following them that closely goaded her into action. Tossing her reins to Tynan, she swung down from the saddle. She drew Aric and set off in the direction of their pursuer.

"Wait!" Theo hissed behind her, but Aeryn ignored her.

To her frustration, dead leaves crunched underfoot with each step she took, and the river of creatures crawled over her boots and legs whenever she paused. She tried to move faster. She did not have far to go before she heard the faintest rustle of branches. She stopped and looked up into the dark trees overhead. Whatever was up there hardly made a sound, which made tracking it all the more difficult.

Finally, Aeryn called up into the tree, "Too much of a coward to face us? Stand and show yourself now."

Another branch creaked. Squinting, Aeryn could just make out a dark shape standing on one of the branches. Dead leaves crunched behind her and she glanced back to see Tynan and Theo following after her, several paces behind. She put her focus back on their pursuer.

The silence stretched on and then a woman's voice called down to her, "Bold words for one so at the disadvantage."

To Aeryn's shock, she recognized the voice. She stood speechless as the dark shape dropped from the branch to land in a crouch a few feet from her. The figure rose to stand and face her.

"Now, what is the scholarly sell-sword doing riding through my woods?" the woman asked, amusement heavy in her tone. "I'm glad to see you again, Aeryn."

The woman's appearance filled Aeryn with sudden relief. With a laugh, Aeryn pulled the woman into an embrace. "Thystle! Trust me; not more than I am."

47

Near a crossroads south of Pius, three men sat around a tiny campfire that did little to hold off the uncommon chill in the night air. The first, whose face betrayed his youth, was dressed in clerical robes made dusty by travel. The second man was years older than the first and dressed in dark leathers and chainmail. The hardness of his face told the story of a man who had seen many years of travel and as many battles. The third man was not as young as the first, nor was he yet the age of the second. His leathers were as broken in as the older man's, but the eyes with which he stared into the fire were untroubled.

None of the three broke the night's silence with words. Each occupied themselves with their own thoughts. Soon, they would rejoin the road and ride through the night into the next day. Already they were much farther behind than any of them would have liked. For now, hunched behind a high cluster of stones, they waited while their horses rested. They themselves planned to rest only after their task was completed. They would avoid the main road as much as possible.

The dark one would come that way. They knew this, but also that they could offer him no interference. Their purpose was singular: find the one with the sword of Vortenthas.

The man who was neither young nor hardened looked at the other two and nodded. It was time. By silent agreement, the three rose and smothered their tiny fire. Walking to their horses, they mounted them just as silently and turned north.

48

Thystle grinned at Aeryn. "My, you did look worried. You flatter me. I didn't think I was that frightening," she said with a smirk.

Aeryn was saved from making a reply when Theo cleared her throat. She looked over at the girl and at Tynan. She apologized to them. "This is a friend of mine, Thystle Moran."

Thystle stood a bit taller than Aeryn. Her heavy boots were worn, and her gray-green eyes glinted with mischievousness when she looked back at Aeryn and nodded. She looked just the same as the last time Aeryn saw her, with her characteristic long dark coat, pale shirt left open at the throat, and dark leather leggings. For the two years Aeryn worked as a caravan guard with her, Thystle never rode without that coat, unless the heat was overwhelming.

"Great. Can you lead us out of here already?" Theo grumbled. "And, why were you following us?"

Thystle glanced from Theo to Aeryn again and said, "She's direct, isn't she?" She shrugged and replied, "I was out for walk, heard voices, and decided to eavesdrop. I recognized Aeryn and decided to just follow a bit. I wanted to see how long it would take Aeryn to discover someone was following her. Too long, I might add. You needed a *bird* to tell you. You're slacking, my friend."

Aeryn squinted at her. "How did you . . ." She left the question drop and shook her head. "Never mind. Theo is right; we cannot linger here."

"Why, what's wrong?"

Tynan cleared his throat and interrupted. "Since Aeryn will not make formal introductions, I will do so myself. I am Darius."

Aeryn rolled her eyes. "He is not. This is Tynan Selvantyr."

Thystle looked him over. "Not *the* Tynan Selvantyr! I heard a lot about you from Aeryn before she went running off on that quest of hers. You are remarkably well preserved for having been dead a couple hundred years. I'm going to guess that meat suit isn't yours."

Tynan looked surprised. Then the dead man's smile turned sheepish. "A pleasure to meet you all the same."

Aeryn gestured at the young thief. "And this is Theo."

Thystle nodded. "So tell me, what brings you here? And, what is going on in the Northlands? I've heard a lot of strange stories of late."

Aeryn took Rowan's reins from Tynan. "First, where is 'here'? We went through the North Gate in Morghall and ended up in some meadow. I don't know where we are or why we ended up in that meadow instead of another gate." She added, "No jokes about us getting lost."

"Now, why would I joke about that?" Thystle deadpanned. "You're south of Alethia, near a town called Haven. Perhaps you were supposed to end up at the West Gate, but the elves closed off their Gate, and you were diverted here instead? It wouldn't surprise me. The elves are protective of their borders even on a good day—sometimes they're worse than dwarves—but I've heard from travelers coming from the north that something happened to the Forever Wood."

Aeryn nodded. "We passed through it a day ago. Have you heard, is it like that all the way to Alethia?"

"I don't know."

Aeryn swung up into her saddle. "I will tell you what I know so far, but you need to lead us to the road. We must continue south."

Thystle nodded. "The road isn't far. Why don't you come to Haven for the night, instead of continuing on straightaway? There are rumors of more creatures stalking these woods at night that did not before. I don't know the reason for the change. I know you are more than capable, but I'd be remiss if I didn't warn you. A stop in Haven overnight won't take you too much out of your way, I would think, and it will give us time to get caught up."

"I could use a meal and a rest," Theo said.

Aeryn preferred to go on, but she did not want to press their luck for the moment. They could set off again at first light. "Alright. Lead us to Haven."

Tynan offered to let Thystle ride with him, but she shook her head. "No, I'm fine walking." She set off toward the road at a relaxed but brisk pace.

Aeryn watched her friend a moment. Thystle looked paler than Aeryn remembered, as though she had been unwell for a long time, but maybe that was a trick of the moonlight. She also picked up on Tynan's borrowed body instantly. And she was following Aeryn and the other through the tree branches. How was that possible? Aeryn had only ever heard of elves and certain magikal creatures possessing that ability, but Thystle was human. Nearly a year had passed since last she saw Thystle, but clearly, something had happened to her friend since then. Aeryn was not ready to ask what as yet.

Aeryn trusted Thystle well enough to tell her all of the events of the past several days, starting with the Black Caverns. Periodically, Theo interjected her own comments into the story. Tynan remained silent.

When Aeryn finished, Thystle looked back at them with a grim expression. "As I said, we've heard the rumors of dark happenings in the North. However, we've not had any such problems in Haven, nor have I heard of this Harbinger character. I suppose it's possible The Harbinger passed through the area without our knowing."

"I think you'd know if he was in town. He's not quiet about it," Theo replied.

Aeryn noticed lights up ahead.

Thystle went on, "Perhaps The Harbinger is to blame for more creatures than usual hunting in the woods at night. Someone said they spotted a wraith the other night. There have been stories of other beasts as well. The uptick has kept me busy." She explained to Tynan and Theo, "I do sell-sword work like Aeryn, but I also track and kill the nastier things that go bump in the night for bounties."

Theo asked her, "Is this how you learned to walk on tree branches?"

They had reached the town's edge, and Thystle evaded the question by telling them they could stay at the Fallen Rose Inn, where she had residence. This, too, surprised Aeryn. Thystle rarely stayed in one place or another for long.

She led them through the streets of Haven. Looking at the tidy shops and cottages they passed, Aeryn wondered what attracted Thystle to this place. It seemed more . . . wholesome than the other places she had stayed with Thystle. Many of the people they passed nodded or waved to Thystle. When she brought them to the two-story clapboard building that was the Fallen Rose Inn, a pair of drunken men on the inn's front steps raised their mugs and shouted out Thystle's name in greeting. That at least was in keeping with Thystle's style. Aeryn remembered she was always very popular with the drinking crowd.

Thystle waved to the men as she led Aeryn and Tynan to a set of stables behind the inn. No one came out to meet them, but she unlocked the stable doors and opened them wide. Aeryn swung down from Rowan's back after Theo. She led the stallion into an empty stall between several others that were occupied already. A few of the horses whickered softly at them.

Aeryn got Rowan settled in while Tynan did the same for his horse. Theo waited outside the stall, and Aeryn handed the girl one of the lighter packs to carry. The saddlebags she slung over her own shoulder before walking outside to join Thystle.

Thystle started to lead them toward the building's entrance, but Aeryn gently grabbed her arm, stopping her. "What is going on with you?"

"Things have changed since you last saw me," Thystle replied after a long pause, keeping her voice low. She started to walk away again.

233

"What things have changed?" Aeryn pressed her.

"Things. It's not important right now, is it?"

The night suddenly seemed darker to Aeryn. Something was very wrong with her friend, she could feel it. Thystle kept her gaze averted and would not look her in the eye.

"Thystle, look at me."

For a long stretch, none of them moved. The smell of the late roses that surrounded the inn seemed stark in the darkness, and the only sounds came from the crickets around them and the activity inside the inn's kitchen. Finally, Thystle turned back and looked at Aeryn. Aeryn almost gasped. Thystle's eyes glowed faintly green in the dark, obvious enough now that Thystle met her gaze straight on. She might not have noticed it at all inside a lighted room.

"By the gods, Thystle." Her voice was little more than a whisper as she let go of Thystle's arm.

"Let's not talk here." Thystle looked around as though afraid someone was watching. "We can talk inside."

Thystle walked away without waiting for an answer. This time, Aeryn let her go.

49

Inside the Fallen Rose Inn was a crowd not as loud as the ones she once sat among in The Thirsty Noble, but the noise comforted Theo all the same. It was a sign of normality that she missed. No one inside the Fallen Rose seemed unhappy or troubled in any way. It gave Theo hope that there would be something left for them to return to after everything with The Harbinger was finished. If they were successful and survived, that is. Theo did not want to entertain ideas of what the world might look like if they did not stop The Harbinger.

The Fallen Rose's common room was paneled with pine boards, and candelabras made from deer antlers tied together hung from the ceiling. On one side of the room stood a huge fireplace with mismatched couches and chairs around it, all of which were delightfully overstuffed and occupied. Opposite the fireplace was the bar and several tables of different shapes and sizes. Many of the tables were occupied, as were the stools at the bar.

Thystle led them across the common room and asked Aeryn, "Would you and Theo like to have my room for the night? I won't need it."

Aeryn hesitated for a moment and then agreed. Theo thought about what they had seen outside. She did not know what it meant, but it had seemed to give Aeryn pause. She felt tired enough to take any room that was offered to her, though. The idea of riding through the night made Theo's entire body groan.

Thystle asked Tynan if he wanted to rent a separate room or sleep on the floor of her room. The dead adventurer looked at her with nothing short of disdain from inside the shadow of his hood. He replied that he would rent a room of his own. Thystle went to the bar and spoke to the barkeep. She returned with a key, which she handed to Tynan.

"Let me show you upstairs, so you can drop you bags there," Thystle said.

She took the stairs two at a time and then led them down the hall to her door, number 9. Tynan kept going, saying he would remain in his room for the rest of the night. He asked Aeryn to knock on his door in the morning when she was ready to set off again. The sell-sword agreed. Theo wondered what Tynan was going to do in his room all night. Sleep? The idea struck her as odd, but she kept this to herself.

Thystle opened her door. There was a small fire burning in the hearth already, and the few lanterns in the room lit it well. Theo was surprised by the size of the room. It was large enough for a four-poster bed, a nightstand, a chest at the foot of the bed, a writing table, and a tall wardrobe. There were even a few books lined up on a shelf over the writing table. Next to the wardrobe was a door Thystle said went to a private washroom.

Theo marveled at this. "Those bounties you take on must pay really good."

Thystle looked uncomfortable for a moment and replied, "I get a reduced rate for helping the owner around the property."

Thystle told them she was going to head downstairs to get them a table and order food. "Take your time. I'll meet you downstairs." From the doorway, Thystle tossed Aeryn the room key and asked, "Still a drinker of Voran spiced rum?"

Theo raised an eyebrow—she knew this liquor to be particularly strong. She had seen it turn enough people into complete fools at The Thirsty Noble. Aeryn told Thystle yes, and Thystle said she would get them a bottle.

When Thystle had gone, Theo smirked. "Voran spiced rum?" She had trouble imagining the stoic sell-sword drunk.

Frowning, Aeryn looked around the room and laid her saddlebags on the bed. "I drink it on occasion."

She opened the door Thystle said led to the washroom and looked in. The small room was dimly lit with a single candle in a clay holder on the basin cabinet. In the corner sat a short tub.

Standing on her tiptoes to look into the mirror that hung in the bedroom, Theo ran a hand through her dark blond hair and noticed that her face was dirty again. The dirt on her nose in particular made her frown, because it made her look so much like a child. She thought to herself that if she could just look grown up and pretend to be grown up, she might convince herself that she actually was grown up. She might stop feeling so afraid of the world beyond the borders she knew in Valis. This world excited her and frightened her all at once. The idea of being left alone in it scared her most.

Her gaze slid to the doorway behind her, reflected in the mirror. She could see part of Aeryn's reflection. Although the sell-sword was not the most open or affectionate person, Theo knew that Aeryn was all she had now. When she was separated from Aeryn at the North Gate, she was more scared than she let on that she was going to be stuck with just Tynan. At least Aeryn was still alive. Tynan, though she understood he meant well in his own way, was so cold in many ways. And how long would it be before that body Tynan inhabited broke down? Then what?

Theo knew she needed Aeryn. She doubted that Aeryn needed her, however. Aeryn did not seem to need anyone at all. Theo turned away from the mirror.

She found Aeryn sitting on the bed, staring at the wall.

"What's wrong?" Theo asked her.

The sell-sword shook herself from her daze. "It's nothing." She stood and slid her saddlebags under the bed. "Do you mind if I take the side of the bed closest to the door?"

Theo shrugged.

Aeryn slipped off her cloak, taking it and Theo's and hanging them on hooks by the door. Then she went into the washroom and rinsed off her face with water in the pitcher on the basin cabinet. Theo sat on the bed as Aeryn had and watched her. After Aeryn toweled off her face, she stood and stared at her reflection in the mirror for several moments. Theo slid off the bed and went to the doorway.

She asked, "Are you worried about Thystle?"

Aeryn's gray eyes reflected in the mirror glanced in her direction. "What makes you ask that?"

"You seemed upset behind the inn."

Aeryn replaced the towel on its hook. She said nothing.

"What did happen? What's wrong with her?" Theo asked.

"I'm not totally sure, but I have an idea," Aeryn replied.

"What?" Theo pressed.

Aeryn turned to her. "Have you ever met a vampyre?"

The question caught her off guard, and she was quick to shake her head.

"I did," Aeryn said. "Only once. In Belhaun, the summer after I turned seventeen. It was a very warm night, the crowds were thick, and I got separated from my father and his companions as we were headed to a tavern near the warehouse district for supper. I knew where I was going, so I cut through the alleys between the warehouses and stumbled into a man bent over a woman, suckling at her neck. He dropped her when he saw me, but she didn't move. She was dead. He looked at me with eyes that glowed like Thystle's did outside, only his glowed bright red. I was certain he would kill me as well, but I couldn't move, not even to draw my dagger and defend myself. I was absolutely mesmerized by those eyes. But then he just turned and ran."

"Do vampyres always kill their victims?" Theo whispered.

"I don't know," Aeryn said.

Theo watched Aeryn shove her father's sword into the chest at the foot of the bed. She left Aric in its sheath on her back. Theo asked, "What if she is a vampyre, like that man you saw?"

"I confess I don't know very much about vampyres. Not all are evil, I know that much. I wonder how she got this way and what changes it has brought to her, how it has changed her. She was human when I traveled with her before."

Finally, Aeryn asked Theo if she was ready to go downstairs. Theo said she was, and they left Thystle's room. From the second-floor landing, Theo could see Thystle sitting at a table just large enough to accommodate all three of them. As she and Aeryn walked down to the common room, Theo wondered if she would have an appetite after Aeryn's story and its implications. However, once she sat down, and she looked at the tray piled high with food in the center of the table, next to the amber bottle of Voran rum Thystle had already started on, her stomach gave a great rumble. Theo served herself while Thystle poured more rum into her own mug and Aeryn a mug as well.

Aeryn eyed the liquid in the mug for a moment before she drank it. Neither she nor Thystle said anything. It was not long before this silence made Theo uncomfortable. She cleared her throat and ventured to ask, "How did you meet?"

Thystle said, "I was a caravan guard for some merchants based in Iro. When we passed through Belhaun, Aeryn approached the caravan boss, looking for work. We were already short a guard, food poisoning or some such thing, so the merchants hired her on. She was a little wet behind the ears, but I took her under my wing." Thystle tried to smile, but it faltered when she caught the look Aeryn gave her.

"That's bullshit." Aeryn laughed shortly. "I was plenty capable."

Thystle harrumphed at this. "You still had things to learn."

"My father taught me everything I needed to know." Aeryn took a long drink, glaring at Thystle over her mug.

So intent was she on the fight developing before her, Theo forgot to chew her food all the way before trying to swallow it, and ended up choking. Thystle and Aeryn looked over at her when she violently coughed. Thystle poured her some water and handed it to her while reaching over and patting her on the back. Theo smiled with gratitude once she choked her food the rest of the way down.

"See what you did?" Thystle said to Aeryn. "You upset your young friend. I don't know why you're picking a fight." She poured herself another drink.

The muscles in Aeryn's jaw tightened, but she asked Theo if she was alright. Theo nodded.

Aeryn said, "You're right, I apologize." She closed her eyes a moment and sighed. "I am worried about you."

Thystle glanced around the room, at everyone but them. Her eyes finally settled on the contents of her mug. "Not long after you left the caravan to go your own way and finish that quest of your father's, I left, too. It wasn't as much fun without you around, so I went back to traveling on my own. I ended up here in Haven.

"I just decided to have a little fun while I was here. You know, my kind of fun—drinking and getting into fights. I made more enemies than friends. One night things got really out of control. My friends walked out on me. As soon as they left, Eryc, this guy I'd had arguments with before, came up and started in on me. I'd heard he was a vampyre, an old one who was strong and flat crazy, too. That night, I was just drunk enough to let him goad me into a real fight. Eryc almost beat me to death, but this guy named Wiat stepped in.

"I knew Wiat well enough to know he was well-liked and well-connected. For the most part, I avoided his kind, but he saved my life, and for that, I felt like I owed him. We became friends, and I found myself sitting at a table with him more nights than not. Most of his crowd consists of vampyres. Eventually, curiosity got to me. I asked Wiat to tell me what it was like to be a vampyre. That's when he offered to show me first hand."

Theo looked over at Aeryn. The sell-sword had her eyes closed and was rubbing her forehead like she had a headache. "So, you let him," Aeryn said to Thystle when her eyes opened again.

"Not at first," Thystle replied, finally looking at them. "But Wiat can be very persuasive. He told me that I would be faster and stronger than ever before, and I liked that idea. Eryc humiliated me, and Wiat all but assured me that by becoming a vampyre, that wouldn't happen again."

"Does being a vampyre make you immortal or impervious to pain?" Aeryn asked. "Which kind of vampyre are you now: a Wiat or an Eryc?"

Thystle's face tightened. It was flushed from the liquor. "I'm neither. I'm the same person as I've always been. It may not have turned out as I expected, but the decision was mine. At least I'm not living in someone else's shadow like you."

Aeryn stood quickly, and her chair violently slid back. "Damn you to hell, Thystle. I've had enough of your judgments." She turned on her heel and stormed out of the inn.

Other patrons in the common room stared at them. Thystle let them stare for a moment and then told them to mind their own. Theo jumped at the outburst, but after a few moments, normal conversation resumed in the room.

Thystle poured herself the last of the Voran rum and sipped at it while staring off. Theo lost her appetite. The tension Aeryn left in her wake weighed on her. Thystle did not seem evil like the Eryc person she described, so she wondered why Aeryn asked what she did. Finally, Theo pushed her plate away.

"Why does she do that?" she asked Thystle.

Thystle blinked and set her mug down. "What?"

"Why does she shut people out like that?"

"I don't know. She's just like that. Although, she at least expressed how she feels pretty well for once."

Theo frowned and took one of the utensils off her plate, poking at the table's surface with it. "I just don't know how I'm supposed to do this."

"Do what?" Thystle asked. She reached across the table and gently took the utensil away from Theo.

She let Thystle take it without argument and said, "You know, travel with her. She's all I have now. My mother's dead, my brother's dead, my only friend in Valis is dead. Aeryn is the only person left that I have any kind of a connection to. Besides Tynan, but he's . . . you know." She shrugged.

Thystle asked her, "How old are you, Theo?"

"Almost eleven. I think. I didn't celebrate many birthdays, but I'm pretty sure."

Thystle nodded, looking sad for a moment.

"You're going to say I'm too young to get mixed up in this, aren't you?"

Thystle smiled slightly. "I was going to say that I should go make up with Aeryn."

Theo did not believe her, but let the subject drop. "I'm going to turn in."

The vampyre stood up. "Look, Aeryn doesn't like to talk about herself any more than I do, and she generally doesn't like anyone else talking about her either. She's been that way as long as I've known her."

"Why?" Theo asked, standing as well.

"She's insecure about parts of her past. I think she's always afraid she's being judged—by me, her dead father, people who don't matter at all. I really don't know why exactly, but I just know she's like that. I forget that sometimes. Just try not to let it bother you too much." Thystle smiled at her.

Theo smiled back, glad to have an actual conversation with someone that was more than three sentences in length and had nothing to do with The Harbinger. "By the way, what's with her and her dead father anyhow?" she asked Thystle, hoping to understand at least a piece of Aeryn.

"Guilt, mostly," Thystle said. "She blames herself for not being able to save him. I don't know what she told you, but he died in a snowstorm. Aeryn believes that if she had been with his group or gone

242

looking for them, she could have saved him. She's never listened when I've tried to tell her it wasn't her fault."

They parted ways, and Theo went up to Thystle's room. Since Aeryn took the room key with her, however, Theo had to pick the lock. It only took her a second to get the door open. Before she went into Thystle's room, she glanced at Tynan's door and again wondered what he was doing inside. She heard nothing from inside his room and decided that was for the best. She just wanted to sleep.

50

It was cold enough outside that Aeryn saw a faint cloud of mist when she let her breath out in a deep sigh. When she first came outside, she had not noticed the chill; the heat of her anger and the rum had kept her warm enough. Now that her initial anger was gone, Aeryn found herself wishing she still had her cloak or a warmer shirt on. She rubbed her arms, unwilling to go inside just yet. She wondered if Theo and Thystle were talking about her. Probably, she decided.

Aeryn picked a small stone off the step on which she was sitting and turned it over and over in her fingers as she turned the argument with Thystle over in her mind. She wondered if her anger was truly because of the judgment she received from Thystle. Or, was it a case that she knew Thystle was right, and she had lived too long in her father's shadow, doing what she thought *he* would want her to do rather than pursuing what she wanted in life. Her quest to find Tynan's sword in the caverns was a selfish goal, for certain, but it was her father's quest to break the curse that had brought her to the Black Caverns in the first place.

Being alone to think at least gave her comfort. She thought about how long it had been since she was alone like and was shocked to discover that nearly a fortnight had passed since she set off for the Valley of Death with Phineas. Sometimes it felt like no more than a moment ago to her.

Aeryn realized she also had not thought about Phineas since the Black Caverns. She wondered if her father's old friend made it out of Valis before The Harbinger's influence took hold. She hoped he did.

The inn's door opened behind her, and someone stepped out onto the porch with her. Aeryn looked over her shoulder and saw Thystle by the door. She said nothing, waiting for Thystle to speak. Thystle said nothing, though, and did not come to sit beside her. Instead, she walked to the more shadowy corner of the porch and leaned against the railing. When Aeryn heard something crunch from that direction, she allowed herself another glance Thystle's way. Thystle had a piece of what looked like a peppermint stick in her hand. She offered it to Aeryn, but Aeryn shook her head.

It seemed that some things never did change. Thystle always had something with her to chew on—peppermint, slivers of wood, jerky, once even an iron nail. When Aeryn asked her why, Thystle just said it was a habit she picked up in her adolescence. It was calming. As Aeryn got to know her better and found out that Thystle left her family and village at a young age, she wondered what it was that Thystle was leaving out of that story.

"I thought vampyres just stick to blood," Aeryn commented finally.

"Depends on the vampyre," Thystle replied. "I feel like there's more to life than just blood."

Aeryn sighed. "So what does this 'new life' of yours mean? Are you dead, like Tynan?"

Thystle laughed quietly. "Gods, no. It's a parasite that causes vampyrism, passed through the blood from a vampyre to a human. The parasite gives us powers and longer life, but forces us to feed it blood."

"Do you kill for it?"

"It's not necessary, and I prefer not to."

"And, this Wiat?"

Again, Thystle laughed, but there was no humor in the sound. "My Maker was not the best of teachers. He left for a few months and no one, his wife included, would tell me where he'd gone off to. He made sure I was set up with a room here at the Fallen Rose, and left a note saying that I know the basics and I'm on my own now. When he returned, he claimed it was a test for me to prove that I can survive as a vampyre without his help. I don't speak to him much anymore."

Aeryn only nodded, feeling a little sorry for Thystle that she made this choice for herself and then was promptly abandoned.

"Why are you so angry at me?" Thystle asked.

"I'm not, exactly. It's just that you're the best friend I've ever had, and I just want the best for you. Choosing to let Wiat turn you seems like something very silly that you did on a whim."

"It isn't silly, and it wasn't a whim. I thought long and hard about it."

"But you did it anyhow."

"Yes. I want the best for myself, too. I wanted to *be* the best."

"This has always been your problem, Thystle. You always had something to prove."

"If only you knew how hypocritical that sounds."

Aeryn could not help but smile a little. "I suppose you have me there."

Thystle finally sat next to her. "After Wiat saved my life, I felt like I saw the world with new eyes, and the other vampyres fascinated me. They are strong, and though they don't always get along, being vampyres is a tie that binds. Wiat offered me more than just new powers. He offered me a new family and a place where I belonged. I wanted all of those things. It turned out to be a false vision he sold me, so I've made a new way for myself. Things are better now than they were then."

"I'm sorry things didn't work out the way you hoped," Aeryn said.

She studied Thystle's profile as Thystle looked out into the night. They were so much alike, Aeryn thought to herself. When she first met Thystle, it was during a time when she lacked confidence in whether she could make it on her own, without her father beside her, and Thystle seemed so self-assured to her. She wanted that. Now, Aeryn wondered if Thystle's brash nature covered her own self-doubt. Aeryn also felt herself doubting her choices again.

"I feel like I don't know what I'm doing now," Aeryn told her.

"I'm chasing after a dead god I helped free when I completed my father's quest. The idea makes me ill, and I don't know if I can stop him."

"You're always putting a world of expectations on yourself."

"What do you mean?"

"You took on what your father never had the chance to finish. Why? So you could make him proud? Although I never knew the man, I feel sure he was plenty proud of you. Now, you're chasing after this god, trying to stop it, even though no one asked you to."

"I refuse to let this go without a fight."

"Then you know exactly what you're doing. Your purpose is clear. You just need a little help to get this job done. That's why I'm going with you tomorrow."

Aeryn knew she could not talk Thystle out of the idea, even if she wanted. She did not want to talk her out of coming, however. She liked the idea of Thystle joining them. Aeryn agreed without question. Then, she rose from her place on the porch step, knowing she needed sleep.

"Where's Theo?" she asked.

"Theo turned in a little while after you left. Speaking of her, I think you should cut her a break."

"What do you mean?"

"Seems like the kid's gone through a lot and doesn't understand why you're shutting her out."

"I'm not shutting her out. I just don't think I can be her caretaker, though she needs one."

"Just be her friend, Aeryn. That's what she needs right now."

Aeryn nodded. "I'll try. What are you going to do now?"

Thystle's smile was mysterious. "I have some things to take care of."

Aeryn shook her head, also smiling. "We're leaving early, don't forget."

Thystle walked down the porch steps and waved a hand over her shoulder. "I'll be awake."

Aeryn went back inside and returned to Thystle's room. Theo was fast asleep with an open book over her face. She did not stir when Aeryn gingerly removed it, wondering if the girl was actually reading it when she fell asleep. It occurred to her then that there was so much she still did not know about the young thief. Aeryn hoped she would get the chance to find these things out some day. For now, she focused on The Harbinger and what the morrow might bring. She prayed that they were not too far behind.

51

Tynan sat in the middle of the bed in the spare but clean room, his legs crossed and folded close to him. No fire heated the room, nor did any candle light the space. The only light in the room came from the ball of energy floating in Tynan's hand. Gently he tossed it from one hand to the other. The ball paused in midair when Tynan heard Aeryn's footsteps come down the hall toward his room and Thystle's. Unlike Theo, however, she did not pause before entering Thystle's room. He knew Theo was curious, but she was wise enough to leave him alone. He wanted to be undisturbed.

The ball of energy floated back into his left hand when he heard the door close behind Aeryn. Tynan sighed. She was still angry with him over the incident in Morghall; he knew this. As if it was his duty and his alone to warn the entire land of The Harbinger's plans. She could have sent word herself when they were in Belhaun, he told himself, although he knew it was far too late by then. Tynan only hoped she would get over her anger. He did not like being held to blame for everything, though she seemed bent upon doing so.

He tossed the energy ball to his right hand and twisted it slightly, staring at its surface. It was brilliant purple and then it shifted to lilac and to violet. It was not gray or sickly yellow like The Harbinger's energy. Instead of cold, it was warm, majestic and noble like he once was.

Sighing again, Tynan tossed the ball up into the air and uncrossed his legs. He lay on his back to watch the purple energy project swirling colors over the ceiling for a time, then he spoke the word to dissipate the energy ball. It quickly dissolved, shrinking by layers until it disappeared altogether. Tynan was satisfied that his magiks were still up to par. They were far from what they once were, but they were enough.

They had to be. He could not afford to be useless, Tynan told himself. No doubt Aeryn would leave him behind if he was no longer useful to her, and he desperately wanted to see their journey to the end.

That's why you're still stuck in the mortal world, the Rimen that lived in his mind told him. *You could never let these things go.*

From the day Rimen died, Tynan had kept a piece of Rimen alive inside of himself. Sometimes, Tynan wondered if he would see his friend when he finally did pass over into the underworld.

Tynan turned onto his side and stared at the wall. This night happened to be the anniversary of his greatest failure in life. Fitting, that it would fall in the middle of their pursuit of The Harbinger, he thought. Closing his eyes, he saw the wind on the hillside ripple through Rimen's pitch-black hair. The elf smiled as the orcs sent another volley of arrows over their heads.

His indigo-colored eyes danced as he shouted, "Come on, Tynan, let's give them one last run for their money!"

Grinning, Rimen leapt from the rocky embankment they hid behind and charged forward. The other six of the Company of Seven were less enthusiastic about charging into the midst of the remaining orcs, but Tynan saw Rimen reach a ruined stone pillar halfway between their retreat point and the cave entrance. Just inside the cave entrance, the scattered band of orcs were launching their desperate offensive.

Rimen fired arrows at the cave entrance and looked delighted when he picked off two more orcs, leaving only five o dispatch. Then, he made his fatal mistake when he turned to look back at the rest of the Seven and wave them forward. As he turned back to assault the orcs again, three arrows were fired at him. The second struck its intended target, striking Rimen in the leg, but as he fell, Tynan witnessed something that for the rest of his life convinced him a supernatural force was at play that day. The third arrow, seconds behind the first two, missed Rimen completely, but struck the ruined pillar and ricocheted off, only to imbed itself in Rimen's chest.

"We should never have been there," Rafin grumbled, days later, as Tynan and the others watched Trion Orinthwend ride away with his son's body, wrapped in blankets and lashed down on a sled pulled by his horse.

Tynan did not miss the accusing looks the rest of the Seven gave him when they turned away from Trion's departing figure. Trion had given him no such look, but Tynan did not doubt the man held him responsible for Rimen's death all the same. How could he not? Everyone else did, including Tynan himself.

Why didn't you tell her about the sword? his mental version of Rimen asked. Tynan replied that he had already told her about the sword.

Not everything, was Rimen's reply.

Tynan said nothing in return.

She deserves to know.

Tynan closed his eyes again. She would know everything in time.

52

Dawn was close. Normally, the coming of the sunrise lifted Colin's spirits, but Caeleb knew there was no chance of that this morning. When they again stopped to rest their horses, the young cleric suddenly let out a wail of dismay and fell to the ground weeping. When they calmed him enough that he could speak, he told them that the caravan they passed in the night was slaughtered. The Harbinger had found them.

The evil god's entourage had passed Caeleb's group first, though Colin sensed his approach in time so that they could get off the road and find cover before they were seen. They would have otherwise suffered the same fate as the caravan.

Caeleb had expected Colin to have trouble during their journey. Seeing the young man hunched over his saddle as he was now, praying softly for the souls of the slaughtered, Caeleb wished he could do something to ease Colin's suffering. At the same time, Caeleb knew Colin needed to work through his suffering on his own.

The young cleric was still overwhelmed by the strong emotions of others. The sleepless night and the stress of their journey left him wide open to the emotional wave of terror and agony from the caravan, broadcasted into the area as they were killed. He was unprepared for the onslaught.

By the time the sun breached the horizon, Colin's constant praying for the souls of the dead while they rode had worn his brother Loric to the breaking point. The ranger looked around Caeleb and hissed, "Enough. For Aephis's sake, Colin! They are in the High Father's hands now. It is time to move on."

The two brothers could not have been more different from each other, Caeleb thought, not for the first time. Neither looked like the other, save for their pale eyes. Loric was tall and broad-shouldered with hair that came to his shoulders. The beginnings of gray streaked his beard. Colin, on the other hand, was fifteen years younger, the youngest of his siblings, and husky where Loric was well-built. His blond locks were trimmed short. He was also paler, but his smooth cheeks had a constant flush to them, adding to his boyish look.

"Loric, relax. Let him be." Caeleb looked from brother to brother. "We are nearly there. This will be over soon enough."

"For good or ill," Loric added with characteristic cynicism.

Caeleb frowned slightly as he turned back to watch the road. Loric was right, but he preferred not to think that way.

53

Aeryn woke to Tynan gently shaking her shoulder. Opening her eyes, she looked into the face that did not rightfully belong to him. She then glanced over at the other side of the bed. Theo was not there. Aeryn asked him where she was, and he told her that the girl was already downstairs with Thystle. He had allowed Aeryn to sleep a little longer, because Theo told him that she had been up late.

"You shouldn't have done that," Aeryn said, irritation slipping into her voice again as she threw the covers back and swung her feet to the floor. She felt tired still. Troubling dreams had kept her busy all night. "We've lost time by you letting me sleep. What time is it?"

He stepped back to give her room. "It is still early."

The door opened, and Theo walked in, carrying a plate of sausages, eggs, and thick biscuits. "I knew you'd be upset for us letting you sleep in, so I brought breakfast up to you to save time."

Aeryn thanked her and snatched up a sausage link as she yanked open the chest at the bottom of the bed. She readied herself to leave as fast as she could, grabbing food off the plate as she went. Theo pulled the saddlebags and packs out from under the bed. She left them in a pile on the floor and then started to tidy the room.

"Where is Thystle?" Aeryn asked when the plate and Thystle's room were both cleaned. She ushered them out into the hall.

"Readying the horses," Theo replied.

Aeryn headed down the stairs and outside. She found Thystle waiting for them outside, casually leaned against the short fence around the inn's lawn. She held the reins of her black charger, as well as those of Aeryn's and Tynan's mounts. When she saw them exit the inn, Thystle straightened up and tossed away the rest of whatever it was she was chewing on now.

She threw Tynan the reins to his mare and asked him, "What's wrong with your horse? She didn't make a sound or even budge a muscle while I saddled her."

"He had to enchant her to make her less skittish," Aeryn replied for him as she secured her packs behind Rowan's saddle.

"Oh," Thystle said, and only half covered a snicker. Tynan did not look amused.

While Aeryn readied Rowan, Theo petted Thystle's horse. "What do you call him?"

"Devil," the vampyre said. She smirked, looking at Theo through a pair of oval-shaped spectacles. When asked, Thystle told the girl that the glasses were specially made to protect her eyes from the daylight.

"Vampyres can see at night as well as if it were day, so the sun hurts our eyes," Thystle said. "Being a fan of daylight, I found a way around that little problem."

Theo nodded her approval, her admiration for Thystle plain on her young face. Aeryn felt a twinge of jealousy.

She tightened and buckled the last strap on her saddlebags and swung herself onto Rowan's back. When Theo was settled behind her, she let Thystle lead the way out of town and south. As soon as they passed out of the farmland immediately outside of Haven and met the open road, though, Aeryn could tell something had changed overnight.

The farmland and pastures far beyond Haven was strangely empty and quiet. She knew she should see people working their fields, but she saw no one, and no animals grazed in the pastures. Nothing stirred.

By late morning, the quiet had Aeryn's nerves on edge. Miles south of Haven, and still no birds, no animals, no people. Thystle nodded when Aeryn asked if she had noticed this, too.

"I have. You're right; there should be animals in the pastures, people working their fields, travelers on the road." Thystle frowned as she looked around them. "The woods shouldn't be this quiet either."

"The Harbinger was here," Tynan said.

By early afternoon, clouds thickened in the sky, and the sun fought its way through them less and less. Then, Aeryn spotted scavenger birds in the distance. She glanced at Thystle, who nodded and urged her charger into a faster gallop. Aeryn and Tynan matched her pace until they reached the crossroads between the road south to Pius and the road west to Kess and Masser. Aeryn caught a foul stench on the wind and pulled Rowan to a stop. Thystle pulled up as well, as did Tynan.

"You smell it also?" she asked Aeryn.

Aeryn nodded. "Let's go slow."

It did not take long before they spotted the dead on the roadside ahead of them. A pair of wagons were pulled off the road. The foul smell came from the burnt bodies lying near the wagons. Aeryn stopped Rowan near the wagons and dismounted, hoping to find someone alive nearby. Theo followed Aeryn as she moved toward the ruined wagons. Aeryn drew Aric. The sword rhythmically pulsated in her sweating hand. Aeryn knelt beside two bodies she found near one of the wagons and saw that they were not only burnt but partially dismembered as well. Their skin still smoldered.

Rising again, she passed her free hand over her forehead and wiped away moisture. Aeryn realized she was sweating all over. Her sweating palms made her grip on Aric slippery, so Aeryn sheathed the sword again and wiped her hands on her cloak. Taking a deep breath, she turned to Theo, who was pale and wide-eyed. Aeryn wished she told the girl to stay with Rowan.

She checked the wagon bed next, but it was empty. Its contents appeared to be scattered over the ground. If this was the work of The Harbinger, Aeryn asked herself, why rifle through the wagons?

When it was obvious there were no survivors, Aeryn led the way back to the horses. Tynan returned next, followed by Thystle. Altogether, they counted five bodies. Aeryn suggested they continue past the crossroads, to get downwind of the stench from the dead, and then stop.

"The horses could use a short rest, and I think we could as well," she said.

"Shouldn't we bury them?" Theo asked quietly.

Aeryn looked at the bodies strewn across the side of the road. "We don't have time," she replied with reluctance.

A few miles south of the crossroads, they pulled off the road. The area they picked was open, affording them a visual advantage. They left the horses to graze and settled down on the grass next to the road. It was clipped short from the grazing of other animals that passed along the road, even bare in some spots. Only Theo did not sit. She paced in a circle, agitated by the scene they had just left.

Suddenly, Rowan whickered, and Aeryn glanced over at him. Next to him, Devil's head came up and his ears flicked back. Tynan's horse continued to graze and remained typically silent. From the behavior of the other two horses, however, Aeryn knew something was wrong. She glanced around, but saw nothing that might bother them. There was nothing around them but open field and a small copse of trees farther up the road.

Thystle stopped chewing the piece of bread in her mouth and looked around as well. "Do you hear that?"

Aeryn was about to shake her head when she felt a faint vibration in the ground. It quickly grew in intensity. Theo and Tynan stopped what they were doing as well and stood up. Thystle and Aeryn followed suit.

"What's going on?" Theo asked as Rowan and Devil shifted nervously.

Aeryn gripped Aric and pulled the sword from its sheath, only to find it throbbing wildly. Cursing, she looked around them again. Thystle drew her longsword, and Tynan began muttering words under his breath. His words were cut short when something burst from the ground less than a dozen paces to their left. Dirt and clods of grass struck them, and the group stumbled back, shielding their faces.

A giant serpent streamed forth from the ground, its anemically pale head rising high above them. It stopped with part of its body still buried in the earth. The serpent turned and peered down at them with sickly yellow eyes. The serpent made a hissing sound that sounded to Aeryn like laughter. Then, it spoke in The Harbinger's voice.

"Aeryn Ravane, do you remain steadfast on your quest to find me? So be it." He laughed again. "Come. See what I have done and witness the rebirth!"

She shouted back, "We *will* stop you!"

"We're gonna kill you, you bastard!" Theo added.

"There is no stopping The Harbinger."

"You talk too damn much," Thystle growled and ran up to the serpent, lunging at its belly.

She slashed The Harbinger twice and two ragged tears opened in its pale belly. The Harbinger hissed with agitation, but the gouges from her sword closed almost as soon as they were made. He laughed again as Thystle snarled and hacked at him again. Her attacks remained ineffectual. Tynan threw a pair of magik bolts at the serpent, but both bounced cleanly off The Harbinger's pale scales and reflected back toward Aeryn and Theo. They scattered to avoid being hit by the ricocheting missiles.

"Watch where you're throwing those things!" Theo shouted at Tynan from where she landed near the horses.

The Harbinger laughed harder. "Fools!"

Aeryn ran forward, leading with Aric. She swung the sword at The Harbinger. Aric cut deep into his belly and then Aeryn buried the blade almost to the hilt in the serpent's hide. She yanked the blade free to strike again, but The Harbinger roared in pain and reared back. The cut she made did not close as Thystle's had. The Harbinger rose farther out of the ground with a lightning speed and then plunged toward the ground, straight at the horses and at Theo.

"Theo!" Aeryn ran toward her and knocked her out of the way as The Harbinger descended, fangs bared.

Devil and Rowan dashed away from the diving serpent. Tynan's mare, however, stood stock still where it was. The serpent's jaw opened wide and came down on the horse's front half, dragging the silent horse into the hole it made. The rest of the serpent flowed into the new hole like rushing water. Its tail whipped around to slap Aeryn before it disappeared underground. She hit the ground with bone-jarring force and slid several feet on her side. Still, she held onto Aric until The Harbinger was gone and the ground was still again.

Thystle came over to her and reached down a hand to help her up and asking Aeryn if she was hurt. Aeryn accepted her help. Looking over at Theo, she saw the girl was on her feet again and was brushing herself off.

"I'm fine," Aeryn muttered as she stood and resheathed Aric.

She rubbed her arm where the serpent's tail struck her and slowly rotated her shoulder to make sure nothing was broken. Nothing was. She was fortunate that she only received a glancing blow. If not, Aeryn guessed she would have been knocked unconscious from the force.

"Are you alright?" she asked Theo.

"Yeah, I'm okay. Thanks for pushing me out of the way."

Aeryn nodded. "I've had more than enough of this," she said.

She whistled to Rowan. When he came to her, Aeryn made sure he was unhurt, too, and then turned to the others. "No more stopping. No rest until we reach Pius. We ride through the night."

259

54

Hidden in the copse of trees farther up the road, the three riders watched the group and the attack by The Harbinger in serpent form. Though Caeleb wanted to aid them, he knew they had to fight this particular battle on their own.

Though one of their horses did not live through the encounter, the four fought well. The woman, whom he assumed to be the one he sought, wounded The Harbinger thoroughly. Once the battle was over, Caeleb knew it was time.

"Let's join them," he told the brothers.

Loric and Colin looked at each other. Loric's eyebrows rose, but neither he nor Colin questioned Caeleb. After all, they were sent to find the woman and her companions. To continue to follow them still, without alerting the group to their presence, was not part of the plan, not to mention dishonest, beyond what the situation warranted. Caeleb had a feeling it was going to prove difficult enough to gain their trust.

The riders urged their horses forward and left the cover of the trees, riding down the road toward the group.

55

Theo and Tynan gathered up what was left of their brief camp. Far down the road, Thystle argued with Aeryn, and with good cause. The idea of riding straight through the night was not pleasing to Theo's ears either. She also understood Aeryn's point: with The Harbinger coming for them directly, could they afford to rest now?

Theo kept seeing the serpent's open jaws descending upon her and the horses. It was good that Aeryn pushed her out of the way in time, because her own legs refused to move for her. The only thought that went through her mind was that she hoped she did not wet herself before The Harbinger swallowed her whole. The thief who wet herself on her way out was not how she wanted to be remembered.

Aeryn and Thystle continued shouting at each other, but Theo could not make out what they were saying. They were too far down the road from where she and Tynan were. Theo could tell Tynan wanted to be part of the discussion, but Aeryn had made it clear she did not want Tynan's input on much of anything anymore. Theo did not have such hang ups, though, and asked him for his opinion on the situation.

"Aeryn seems unusually agitated," was Tynan's simplistic reply.

"No kidding." Theo rolled her eyes as she walked over to Rowan and tried to put Aeryn's pack into its proper place. Unfortunately, she was too short. After several failed attempts, she gave up and turned back to Tynan.

"Do you think The Harbinger is making Aeryn go crazy, too? What if by the time we catch up to him, we're all so tired that The Harbinger kills us without any trouble?"

The dead adventurer walked over and buckled the pack into

place for her. "No, I do not think that. I think she is determined not to let The Harbinger have the upper hand any longer."

"I think it's too late for that," Theo muttered as she took another glance at Aeryn and Thystle from around Rowan's backside, avoiding his tail as it swished by her face.

The argument appeared to be over. Aeryn and Thystle were walking toward her and Tynan. Thystle was frowning, and Aeryn looked downright livid. Theo had little time to wonder what was said between them before Aeryn began barking orders.

"Tynan, you ride with Thystle. Theo, gather up our things."

"I already did. We're ready to go."

Aeryn curtly replied, "Fine. Let's go then."

Something up the road caught Theo's eye. Three riders were approaching. "Maybe we should find out what those riders want first," she said as she pointed to the riders.

The others turned and stared for a moment before both Aeryn and Thystle drew their swords and Tynan began muttering another of his spells. Theo took a step back behind Aeryn and drew her dagger. She wondered if the men were bandits, but the middle rider did not seem to be holding a weapon. In fact, he raised his hands and smiled. The other two did not. The man to his right had a crossbow laying across his lap, and the man on his left, although dressed in cleric's robes, carried an oak staff.

When they were close enough to shout, the rider in the middle called out, "We aren't here to fight you."

"Stop there. Who are you?" Aeryn shouted back.

The riders stopped as ordered, and the middle rider said, "I am Caeleb Wallace. I've been sent to find you." His voice held a hint of an accent whose origins Theo could not place.

"Sent by whom?"

"Well, that requires a bit of explaining." Caeleb smiled in a casual way, apparently trying to lighten the mood. It had no effect on

262

Aeryn whatsoever, and he cleared his throat. "We mean you no harm."

He looked at his two companions and urged them to put away their weapons. The one with the staff tucked it into a special holster on his saddle, but the one with the crossbow waited several moments before he slung it over his back. Theo could tell by the look in his pale eyes that he was definitely not the trusting sort. He reminded her of Aeryn.

Aeryn and Thystle slowly lowered their swords in kind, but did not sheath them. Aeryn repeated, "Sent by whom?"

"Sceptor Allemar in Pius. He sent us to make sure you reached the city safely."

"How?"

Caeleb repeated, "How?" He shook his head.

"How did he know about us?"

"Tynan's raven, of course, and a little information from the High Father."

Aeryn squinted at him. "If you were sent by a sceptor in Pius, then why are you coming from the north?"

Caeleb's eyes shifted. Clearly he had hoped she would not ask that question. "We actually came from the south, but we allowed your party to pass us sometime back. We have been following you."

Aeryn's mouth formed a hard line. She asked, "How long?"

"Only a few hours. We were waiting for the right moment to approach."

"Did you see the giant serpent attack us?" Thystle asked him.

"Yes."

The vampyre let out a mirthless laugh. "And, you didn't think *that* was the right moment to show yourselves? We could have died."

"Not to be callous, but we felt it would be better to let you deal with The Harbinger on your own."

"You wanted to see if we could fight him alone, without your help. A test, is that it?" Aeryn squinted at him.

"Yes."

"Your honesty is refreshing, Master Wallace—"

"Caeleb."

"—but if you don't mind, I'm not in the mood for these games," Aeryn said.

"I wasn't playing one. If you would let us explain . . ."

Aeryn gave him a tight smile. "I thought that's what you were doing."

Caeleb took a deep breath and let it out slowly. Clearly, this was not how he expected the conversation to go, and now, his companions looked ill at ease. The young-looking one dressed in red clerics' robes kept darting his eyes from Caeleb to Aeryn, while the older one seemed to be trying to drill a hole into Thystle's face with his eyes. She was doing the same to him from her end.

Caeleb's smile fell back into place. "Perhaps we can start over again. My name is Caeleb Wallace. I am a paladin sent to find you by Sceptor Allemar in Pius, as I said. The young cleric on my left is Colin Fane, and the angry ranger on my right is Loric Fane. My apologies for our secrecy. Frankly, we were unsure how best to approach you." His smile turned sheepish. "Although, in retrospect, an introduction such as this would probably have served us just as well a few hours ago."

Aeryn acknowledged all this with a tip of her head. After a long period of silence, she said, "I accept your story for now. You may join us, but I warn you, we are traveling through the night. We are not stopping until we reach Pius."

The three riders seemed surprised to hear this. The one called Loric said, "Facing our enemy unrested strikes me as ill advised."

"You may do as you like, sir. *We* are riding through the night." Aeryn turned away from them and remounted.

Caeleb nodded. "We will ride with you through the night. We've been charged with seeing you to your destination, and that is what we will do."

Aeryn gave Theo a hand up and then looked at Caeleb again.

"We've gotten this far on our own. I'm allowing you to join us as a courtesy, nothing more."

With that, Aeryn kicked Rowan into a gallop south again.

56

Night fell, but still Aeryn pushed them on. Though they had to repeatedly slow to a walking pace for the sake of the horses, Aeryn did not let them stop. Their breakneck pace south was taking its toll everyone. It surprised Theo that Aeryn seemed so callous about pushing the group and the horses. Suddenly, Thystle and Devil shot past them, and then Thystle turned him in the road ahead to face them. Aeryn quickly pulled up to avoid a collision and asked Thystle what she was doing.

"We're stopping here," the vampyre stated as she nudged Devil forward so that he was almost nose to nose with Rowan.

"We're more than halfway to the city now," Aeryn argued. "We can be there by morning."

"No. Everyone is exhausted. Tynan and I may be able to go without much sleep, but the rest of you cannot."

"I've gone without sleep many times before," Aeryn angrily retorted.

"Stop being stupid. If we keep pushing the horses, they will not be able to carry us at all. We will have to walk to Pius."

"I agree, Aeryn. We need to rest the horses, and you need to rest yourself as well," Tynan said from behind Colin as the others gathered around them. The young cleric was roped into carrying the dead adventurer and looked worse for wear because of it. Theo suspected he had been talking Colin's ear off for the last several hours.

Aeryn looked away from them but then nodded. "Fine. We rest here until first light."

Thystle looked relieved as she slid down from Devil's back and led the horse off into the patchy grass on the side of the road. The others followed after her. Theo did not move for a minute. Aeryn glanced back at her.

"Do you need help down?" Aeryn asked, agitation heavy in her tone.

"No," Theo replied before sliding to the ground. "Are you okay?" she asked in turn when Aeryn descended from Rowan's back. Aeryn seemed unsteady.

"I'm fine."

"I could have kept going," Theo told her.

The sell-sword's face softened, and she squeezed Theo's shoulder. Aeryn smiled briefly. "I know you could have gone on."

Theo followed Aeryn as she led Rowan to where Thystle had hobbled Devil on a long lead. Caeleb and his two companions were taking some of their horses' gear off not far from them. Aeryn began taking her gear off of Rowan, and that was when Theo noticed the woman's hands were shaking.

"Aeryn?" Theo asked, concerned.

The sell-sword made no reply. When Aeryn took the last of the packs off of Rowan, she picked them up and turned to walk away. She got as far as a pair of nearby rocks and then let the packs drop from her hands. She sat heavily on one of the rocks and leaned forward, her elbows on her knees. Theo went to her side, putting a hand on her shoulder.

"I can get the others."

Aeryn shook her head. She was sweating. "No, I'm fine. Thystle was right, I'm just tired." She straightened up enough to take off her sword sheaths with trembling hands. The swords were dropped next to the packs.

"You're not," Theo said. She turned in the direction of the others. "Tynan!"

Thystle and Tynan appeared to be in the midst of building a fire. When Theo called for Tynan, both of them stopped what they were doing and hurried to Aeryn's side. Caeleb and his companions came over as well and asked if everything was alright.

"I think Aeryn's sick," Theo told everyone.

"I'm fine," Aeryn repeated, but she was hunched forward again with her head in her hands.

Tynan frowned and knelt in front of her, but when he tried to put his hands on her, she pushed him away. "You are not fine, Aeryn. Stop resisting. You have a fever. Theo, can you get Aeryn's waterskin?"

Theo went into Aeryn's saddlebags and found it for him. He poured some of the water onto a piece of cloth and pressed it to her forehead. Then he told Aeryn, "Come, you need to lie down by the fire we started."

Thystle knelt down next to Aeryn and put the sell-sword's arm around her shoulder. "Lean on me." She helped Aeryn to where they had been making a fire. The others followed.

Aeryn sank down next to the ring of stones. "We shouldn't have a fire," she told Thystle.

"It's cold out tonight, and it isn't like The Harbinger doesn't know where we are already." Thystle struck flint against steel, and the sparks caught on the dried leaves she had gathered already.

"Here, drink this," Tynan said and handed her the waterskin.

She did as she was told and then said, "We are too close for me to be ill now."

Tynan frowned. "I believe this may be Aric's influence."

"How?" Caeleb asked.

"I imbued Aric with the ability to temper The Harbinger's influence and keep him trapped in the caverns. However, in order to do this, the sword took energy from me when I was alive. In the caverns, The Harbinger was easier to control, since he was mostly dormant. It also did not affect me much, because I was resistant to being drained by magikal items.

"Undoubtedly, after I died, Aric's power stores became depleted, and it weakened. When the sword chose its new wielder, it also chose its new power source: you. I believe Aric has been taking small bits of energy from you since you took it from the caverns. You did not notice, because it was subtle. As The Harbinger has gotten stronger, however, I believe Aric is drawing extra energy from you while it struggles to exact some kind of control over the god's powers. The confrontation earlier today would have taken a particular toll on the sword and you."

"Did you not know this would happen?" Caeleb asked.

Tynan paused. "I did not know for certain. I was afraid it might, but I did not tell Aeryn, because I saw no reason to cause her undue alarm."

"Dammit, Tynan. I told you to stop lying to me," Aeryn said.

"I omitted. I did not lie. You had enough on your mind already without my adding to it."

"Can't anyone do anything?" Theo asked.

"I believe I can," Caeleb replied.

He knelt next to Aeryn and placed his hands on her. Closing his eyes, he murmured some words. A pale blue glow surrounded his hands and spread over Aeryn's body. The crease in the sell-sword's brow relaxed, and she stopped sweating. The glow faded.

Caeleb opened his eyes again. "Better?"

Aeryn nodded.

"Rest still," he told her.

"What was that?" Theo asked him.

"I was asking the High Father to grant her strength." He smiled at her. The peace in his smile made her feel better, too.

"Is that what paladins do? You ask for stuff, and Aephis gives it to you?"

Caeleb laughed a little, though she could tell he was not laughing at her. "It's a little more complicated than that. I pledge to fight in my god's name and to give him my undying faith, and in turn, he grants me certain powers."

Theo nodded. It sounded noble to her.

Before she could ask him more, Thystle touched her shoulder. "I think we should let Aeryn rest."

"Yes, that would be for the best," Tynan agreed and rose to his feet.

The others did as well. Aeryn touched Caeleb's hand, though, and said, "Please stay for just a while."

He nodded and knelt down next to her again. Theo felt a twinge of jealousy for the way Caeleb looked at Aeryn.

Thystle tugged at Theo's sleeve. "Let's go gather up Aeryn's saddlebags," the vampyre said gently. "Then, I'll let you sharpen my longsword."

Theo looked up at her and nodded when Thystle gave her a knowing smile. She allowed herself to be led away and let Aeryn have Caeleb. At least for now.

57

Colin brought over a bundle of blankets, smiling shyly before he scurried away again. Aeryn watched him go and then pushed herself up onto her elbows. Caeleb reached for her to help her up, but she waved him away.

"I'm not an invalid," she told him.

"I didn't say you were."

Caeleb grabbed the blankets that Colin brought over to them and bunched one up. He put the bundle behind her shoulders and looked about to drape the other over her, but the look Aeryn gave him seemed to make him rethink this. He handed it her instead. She took it from him and spread it over her legs. The night was so cold.

"What do you know already about The Harbinger?" she asked.

"Not as much as Allemar, clearly, but as I understand everything from him, he was a very bad god a very long time ago. The other gods overthrew him and banished him to caverns in the Northlands."

This was a watered-down version of things, but Aeryn accepted he knew enough. "How does this Allemar know of The Harbinger? I thought it was forbidden to speak his name by the other gods, too."

"Allemar said that Aephis told the story of his brother to his sceptor, in case The Harbinger ever broke free. The story was passed down through the ages from one sceptor to another. Allemar fills that role now."

Aeryn studied his face by the firelight. "Did Allemar also tell you how The Harbinger broke free?"

Caeleb shook his head. "He did not discuss that with us. Time was something of the essence."

"It was my fault. I broke the curse and took the sword from the caverns."

He nodded. "I am not a cleric, if you are worried I'll judge you."

She shook her head. "I thought you should know."

"I see. Why did you? Take the sword, I mean."

Aeryn told him of her father and his quest.

"Taking on his quest was for him. If he were here now, I don't know if he would even care that I broke the curse for him. I think he'd care that I was selfish enough to want Tynan's sword for myself. If I hadn't taken it, none of this would be happening now. The dead left in The Harbinger's wake are on my head." She left out telling him that Tynan gave her the sword.

Caeleb considered what she said for a moment and then said, "I think it was only a matter of time before he broke free. Curses don't last forever. Once the curse on the Black Caverns broke, someone else would have taken the sword. Perhaps they would not be able to wield it and stop The Harbinger. Things happen as they are meant to happen. It's doubtful that someone else could do as well as you have done."

She scoffed at this. "I hardly think 'well' is how everything has gone so far."

"You're still alive, are you not?"

Aeryn asked him, "How long ago did The Harbinger pass your party?"

"Last night. We were only a day behind him, but The Harbinger's army does not rest as we must," Caeleb told her.

She frowned. He stirred and told her to rest, then he rose and stretched his long limbs.

Aeryn watched him walk to the campfire his companions had set up several paces from Thystle's. His words gave her comfort. She fell back against the blanket bundle he made for her. The Harbinger would reach Pius long before they did, and he would lay waste to the city while he waited for them. How could she hope to defeat him now?

58

It was a beautiful night for their ritual, Baris Getling thought to himself as he led his group to the clearing he chose three nights before, not far from the walls of Pius. He and his people, followers of Oleander, walked the miles barefoot in order to fully experience the miracles Oleander provided for them. In past years, followers walked to the chosen place for the harvest prayer in the nude, but that practice had ended before Baris's time. Considering the unseasonably cool weather, Baris decided this was fortunate. Bare feet were enough.

The sky remained clear and stars shone down upon them. Baris imagined them to be signs that the goddess smiled down on them from above. As soon as they reached the clearing, Baris's people built a roaring fire to stave off the chill. Then, they gathered around the blaze, singing a hymn to Oleander. Baris led their voices with his strong tenor. The cleric felt the love and goodwill flowing among the men and women around him.

When the hymn was finished, Baris raised his arms over his head and chanted, an exulted smile on his broad face. "Dearest Oleander, we, your faithful flock, humbly ask that you bring us yet another bountiful harvest so that we may last all winter until the spring, when we can again glorify your name. Let not the winter see us into famine, sickness, and despair. Protect us as you always have."

Baris looked around at his fellow worshippers as they murmured words of encouragement and bliss. A cold breeze ruffled his hair. Gooseflesh rose on his arms, and he let them fall to his sides so the sleeves of his sun-yellow robes covered them again. It suddenly seemed much colder than before.

He ignored the cold and continued, "Dearest Oleander, we have come to pay you tribute so that you may aid us in our time of need. We ask you to bring us the fruits of your divine influence. We ask—"

"So pathetic," a voice called out from somewhere beyond the circle of light cast by the bonfire.

Baris faltered. His followers glanced about to see who had spoken. He would have thought that the goddess herself had spoken to him, if the voice had not been so masculine and malevolent in tone.

Baris began again. "We ask . . ." His words dropped off once more when an icy breeze struck him. The flames of the bonfire shifted crazily in response.

Faint laughter floated to them from the edges of the clearing. Baris saw ominous clouds racing in to block the clear light of the moon and stars. He looked around his circle of worshippers and found their faces reflecting the same worry he knew his own face cast.

He forced his lips into a smile and told his people, "Let us sing another hymn together. Everyone hold hands."

Their collective voices rose again. The wind and the laughter rose in kind.

"Sing louder!" Baris cried out.

They sang louder, but a moment later their voices fell off as a figure in black robes stepped into the clearing into the light cast by their fire. The plants it passed withered and died. The figure had a hideous face and towered over all of them, surpassing the height of normal men by several hands. Two thick horns curled around either side of the demon's face. The demon stared at them with yellow eyes, and a grin spread across its sallow face.

"Do you think Oleander has time to listen to your pathetic prattling?" the demon asked them. "The gods have more important things to concern them these days. Like me."

"W-Who . . . *What* are you?" Baris stammered.

"I am The Harbinger. Mine is the last name you will ever know."

Baris's followers started screaming. The bonfire's flames twisted and caught on Baris's robes before he could back away. His hands beat uselessly at the burning fabric as the flames spread up and over his body.

Within seconds, he was engulfed. He fell to the ground, screaming in agony. His followers broke and ran, heading back in the direction of Pius. They did not get far before they again halted in their tracks. Several pairs of red eyes stared at them from the darkness of the woods, beyond where the firelight reached.

The Harbinger's army stepped forth into the light. Their red eyes glowed with bloodlust. The Harbinger's followers threw their heads back and let out a collective howl, like wolves. As one, they fell on Baris's people, striking them again and again.

"Welcome to the rebirth," The Harbinger said as basked in the blood of the followers of Oleander.

59

The stirring of Colin and Loric woke Caeleb, and he opened his eyes the predawn dark. The farthest edge of the eastern horizon was lightening, but nothing else. He looked to his left and saw Colin turned to the east, his arms and his face stretched to the sky to receive the first rays of the sun when it rose. His eyes were closed, and his lips silently moved to the words of his predawn prayers. Caeleb wondered where Colin found the energy for such things so early in the morning. His own hand rose to his mouth to stifle a yawn as he sat up. He froze mid-yawn when he saw Loric watching him from the other side of the campfire.

"I always knew you had a thing for me, Loric," Caeleb said, a broad grin on his face.

He was rewarded by a glare from the ranger.

"I wondered how long you were going to sleep," Loric grumbled.

"Cheerful this morning, aren't you?" Caeleb said as he fetched some food from his pack and began to put together a morning meal for the three of them. The others, he assumed, would make their own preparations. "I was surprised you were asleep when I came back to the campfire last night. I thought you would want to discuss plans for when we reach Pius again."

"I did not see the point in waiting up while you chatted with the sell-sword."

Caeleb's knife paused in its circuit around the potato he was in the process of peeling. He looked at Loric inquisitively. "What are you implying?"

Loric said nothing.

"We only talked," Caeleb said.

"Did I say otherwise?"

Caeleb's brow wrinkled. "Then, what is the problem?"

"I want to make sure you keep your eye on the target. We all need clear minds for the battles ahead of us," the ranger replied.

"I think you are getting ahead of yourself. We talked for mere moments."

"Really?"

Caeleb frowned and returned to peeling the potato in his hand. He could not help but glance over at Aeryn. She appeared to be just waking. Her sleep had been restless; he had heard her talking in her sleep before he turned in. His gaze trailed back to Loric. The ranger was still staring at him. He raised an eyebrow.

"Oh, stop it," Caeleb told him. "*She* asked me to stay." Even to him the distinction sounded petty. The knife stopped again. "I don't think it is wrong to want to get to know them better, rather than just keeping it to 'Hello, we've come to help you kill a god.' That doesn't leave a very good impression."

Loric replied, "I did not know leaving a good impression with them was the priority."

"Not the priority, no."

"I understand she is attractive, but you might well remember that we are likely walking to our deaths. The Harbinger does not care what impression we make. I simply do not think you should get too close to the sell-sword or her friends."

Caeleb looked around to see if any of the others were listening to them. To his relief, they were not, but he leaned forward and lowered his voice all the same. "Gods above, Loric! That is the most cynical statement I've ever heard. Do not get close to them, because they might be dead by tomorrow?"

"We all could be."

Caeleb frowned. He began to peel the potato in his hand with a vengeance. Then, he stopped again. "I disagree. How can we expect to have any kind of cohesion as a group without having spoken more than three words to each other?"

"How much cohesion do you think we will need, Caeleb? Likely this will all be over by the time the sun sets this eve. We have unity of purpose. That is enough for me."

Caeleb knew this was the way Loric protected himself, but it was not Caeleb's way. He wanted to know more about the person he fought next to than just their name. Finally, he asked, "Do you think of our chances of survival as so grim?"

"I honestly know not. I reserve my judgment on our chances until we reach the city. I simply prefer to expect the worst. It's easier than receiving a nasty surprise." Loric glanced at Aeryn as she gathered up her things and scattered the remains of her campfire. He looked at Caeleb again. "My advice for you, my friend, is to guard your heart on this venture of ours. Do not get too attached."

Caeleb glanced Aeryn's way as well. He hoped that Loric was being overly pessimistic as usual. While he watched Aeryn and the others, however, the sun behind them turned the eastern sky bright red. At the same time, the knife in his hand slipped, and the blade bit deep into his thumb. He jerked his hand back and watched the blood run down the palm of his hand.

His eyes went to Loric again. Their gazes met and held each other over the dying fire between them. Loric looked away first. Caeleb knew these things were signs he should heed, but he did not want to see them. It was too early in the morning to think about death.

60

Theo rolled over and sat up when Aeryn touched her shoulder. She had been awake for some time, listening to the others stir. She chose to feign sleep to keep from being bothered as long as she could. The night had treated her unkindly. A rock jabbed her in the side every time she tried to turn to the right, until she finally removed it, and then nightmares broke into her sleep. When the sun rose, Theo felt starkly aware that it could be the last time she witnessed this event. Pius, and The Harbinger, were only half a day away. She wanted to enjoy as much of the life she had left.

Looking around, she saw Thystle was with the horses, grooming Devil. Colin appeared to be performing some ritual not far from where Caeleb and Loric were talking across their campfire. Tynan was on the opposite side of the fire from her, his eyes closed and his shoulders relaxed. Aeryn stayed crouched near her, staring at Tynan.

Now, Aeryn's stormy gray eyes shifted from Tynan to her.

"What is he doing?" she asked Aeryn, nodding in Tynan's direction.

"I don't know," the sell-sword replied. "Memorizing spells maybe." She stared at Tynan for another few moments before she asked, "Did you sleep well?"

Theo shook her head. "Did you?"

"I slept," Aeryn replied and stood up.

"Are you okay?"

Aeryn looked toward the road, her eyes distant. "I'm fine."

The sell-sword scooped up some dirt and threw it onto the small fire in front of them, dousing the majority of the flames. She stamped on the remainder with a booted foot until only smoking wood was left, then she turned away, walking toward the collection of horses.

Theo took this to mean they would be leaving soon. She saw that Aeryn had already collected her own things. Rising, Theo gathered up her blankets. As she folded and rolled them, Theo saw Tynan was looking at her. "I guess we're skipping breakfast this morning," she said to him.

Tynan shrugged as he picked up a book she had not seen before and stood. "I would assume such, yes."

"What is that?" Theo asked him, pointing to the book in his hands.

"A spell book I acquired in Valis. I wanted to see if it contained any spells that I had not seen before." He smiled slightly and started to walk toward the horses. He said over his shoulder, "It did not."

Theo watched him go and then rolled her eyes. She wondered why none of the people in their group were normal, except for Caeleb. He seemed normal enough. Aeryn called her name. The others were already grouped around the horses. Theo jogged to them and handed her things to Aeryn.

"There are four roads into Pius," Caeleb was saying. "I don't know what things will look like once we get to Pius, but I assume that The Harbinger and his army have already reached the city."

The deep frown on Aeryn's face told Theo that she did not like hearing such news. "I want to reach the city before midday," Aeryn said as she mounted Rowan.

The others nodded and mounted their horses. Theo grabbed Aeryn's hand and climbed up to her usual spot behind her. Tynan rode with Colin again. A light rain began to fall as the group rejoined the road at a gallop. Theo looked up and cursed the clouds that had moved in at some point during the night. She pulled the hood of her cloak up and leaned against Aeryn. She felt Aric vibrating in its sheath and pulled away again.

It seemed to her that the sword must be vibrating very hard for her to be able to feel it through the sheath. Theo wondered if Aeryn was able to feel it, too, but refrained from asking. Aeryn seemed more tense this morning than she had the night before. Perhaps it had something to do with whatever she and Caeleb had talked about, Theo thought.

Butterflies filled her stomach. She was glad they had skipped breakfast. Eventually Theo closed her eyes and leaned against Aeryn again, praying that the road to Pius was short. If they were going to be slaughtered, she wanted to get it over with. The waiting was killing her.

Caeleb called a halt late in the morning and the group dismounted to water the horses and eat a quick meal. The tension in the air around them was as thick as a fog bank off the Black Mountains. No words were exchanged among them. The prospects of what might be waiting for them curbed even Thystle's odd habit of constantly chewing on something.

While they ate, Theo noticed the bandage around Caeleb's thumb and asked about it. Caeleb smiled and said, "My knife decided that I would taste better than the potato I was peeling."

In the halo of his smile, Theo felt better. She asked him, "What does being a paladin mean?"

"We should get moving again," Aeryn said, and Loric seconded her statement.

Theo frowned at the interruption, but rose with the others. They were not on the road again for long before she noticed a change in the air. Suddenly, it felt like the Forever Wood had—sounds were muted, and the colors of everything around them looked dull and washed out. Then, Theo caught sight of the City of Gods.

Pius began as a dot on the horizon and then grew slowly into an immense form spread across the landscape. Many domes and spires towered above the level of the other buildings, but did not seem to dominate them. Only a low wall encircled the city. The black smoke that rose from inside the city told Theo that Pius should have had a higher wall.

Aeryn and the others brought their horses to a halt near the woodlands not far from the city wall. Loric suggested he scout ahead to see if the main gates were being watched. Thystle said she would go with him. Tynan suggested casting a mirage spell over them before they went, to give them better protection.

Aeryn rubbed her forehead. "Just do it quickly," she said.

Tynan's blue eyes narrowed in concentration as he muttered the words to his spell. His hands took on an orange hue, and he placed them first on Thystle's shoulders and then Loric's. The orange glow spread from Tynan's hands over their bodies. When he let go, the glow lingered for a moment, but shifted from orange to green. Their bodies suddenly appeared to be covered in grass blades. Slowly the glow faded but the camouflage stayed.

"That is really neat," Theo breathed as she reached out to touch Thystle's clothes. They did not feel any different.

"It feels funny to me," Thystle replied, looking down at herself.

"Come on," the ranger growled and jogged toward the city wall.

Thystle rolled her eyes and jogged after Loric.

While they waited for Thystle and Loric to return, Theo and Aeryn dismounted. Aeryn sat in the grass near Rowan. Caeleb came over. His concern for Aeryn was clear on his face.

"Do you feel sick again?"

Aeryn shook her head. "Just tired, and my head hurts."

Colin searched around in one of his pouches and pulled out a gangly-looking root. He held it out to Aeryn. "This will help with your headache at least."

Aeryn took the root, looking at it quizzically.

"Oh, uh, you chew it," Colin told her. He smiled shyly.

The sell-sword smiled back at him. Theo was wondering what the root might taste like, but the pinched look that came over Aeryn's face when she put the root in her mouth and started chewing told Theo it was not something she would enjoy.

"It is probably a little bitter," the cleric said.

Aeryn nodded, but said, "That's okay. I've had worse."

"What's going on?" Thystle asked from behind Theo.

Theo jumped and spun around. She had not heard the vampyre's footsteps behind her. "Could you *never* do that again?" Theo asked her.

Thystle just grinned and ran a hand through her sun-streaked brown hair. The camouflage spell was fading from both her and Loric. Their skin looked less and less green. Thystle asked again what was going on, and Colin quietly filled her and his brother in.

"Can she go on?" Loric asked Caeleb.

Aeryn answered for him. "*Yes*. I'm feeling better, thanks the root Colin gave me. What did you find?" She stood up.

Thystle told her, "We checked out the main gate on this side. There don't seem to be any guards, either of Pius's or The Harbinger's. No one at all is on the streets as far as we could see."

"Pius's gates are well guarded as a general rule," Loric said. "There was never any need. Pius has never been attacked. Allemar said he planned to organize a resistance if he could. What disturbs me most is that we didn't see any bodies." He looked at Caeleb.

"This isn't good," Colin said. The young cleric looked like he wanted to be sick.

"We should enter the city now, while we can," Tynan said.

Aeryn held a hand up. "Tynan, surely you must know how we can use the sword to defeat The Harbinger. We should discuss that before we do anything more."

The dead man told her, "I believe we should ascertain what is happening inside the city and where The Harbinger is. That will best facilitate any plan of action we have."

Aeryn's eyes narrowed as she looked at him. "No. I think you need to tell me what I need to do with the sword first, beyond just hacking at The Harbinger with it. If there is another power that Aric possesses, now would be the time to share that."

Tynan pressed his lips into a thin line and then said, "I believe you must call upon the gods represented by the seven sigils on Aric's blade: Aephis and Cira are one, and the rest represent Heldanic, Tempes, Fortesis, Ireteah, Aspen, and Anora." He paused. "However, I am ignorant as to whether the order in which the gods are called or the wording used to call upon those gods must be specific. I believe this Sceptor Allemar that Caeleb says sent him and his companions can better answer that question."

The sell-sword stared at Tynan for a time. No one else said anything. Only the wind stirred.

The look on Tynan's face spoke volumes to Theo about how much finally telling the truth pained him.

Eventually, Aeryn asked, "If Caeleb and the others hadn't found us, how might we have known what we needed to do with the sword?"

Tynan looked down at the dirt road. "I have no good answer to give you, Lady Ravane."

Aeryn nodded and then stood. There was nothing else to be said to him. She went to Rowan and climbed into the saddle. The rest of the group remounted and rode the rest of the way into the city. Thunder rumbled in the distance.

The damage to the city was not immediately apparent. Only when they passed through the courtyard between the wall and the outer rim of buildings did they see The Harbinger's handiwork. Storefronts were destroyed, and the smell of smoke grew thicker the farther into the city they went. Blood streaked the cobblestones, but there were no bodies. Somehow, this scared Theo worse than if the streets had been filled with them. A shudder passed through her.

Caeleb said to them, "We need to seek out Allemar. I just hope he's still in the temple."

Aeryn nodded. "Lead the way."

Caeleb urged his horse forward. Loric let the rest of the group pass him and took up a position at the back of the group. As they proceeded deeper into the city, things felt more and more wrong to Theo. She had expected to see a scene like the one in Morghall, where the bodies were everywhere.

"Where are the bodies?" she whispered to Aeryn.

Aeryn shook her head.

Suddenly, Thystle called their attention to a figure up the road from them. The person had their back to them and was bent over another figure lying in front of a small tavern. As they got closer, Theo saw the person was dressed in black leathers and chainmail.

"Don't—" Caeleb said, but too late.

Thystle called out to the person. The figure stopped what they were doing and stood to face them. It was a woman. She stared at them and chewed on something that half hung out of her mouth. It was someone's finger. The blank look on the woman's face quickly changed to one of snarling hatred. Her fingers curled like claws when she raised her hands. Theo was about to tell Aeryn they should run when the woman threw her head back and howled like a dog. Then the woman launched herself at them at a full sprint.

"My big mouth," Thystle muttered and drew her sword from the sheath slung across her back.

The woman's attack was cut short by one of Loric's crossbow bolts. It caught her square in the throat, knocking her backward. The woman fell to the ground and did not rise again.

"Let's get out of here before someone else notices us," Caeleb said.

"Agreed." Aeryn spurred her horse after his.

The group only got as far as the next street. They stopped short when they rounded the corner and saw half a dozen soldiers coming toward them. They turned their horses to go back the way they came, but that way was blocked as well. More people came out of the alleys around the buildings on either side of them. Unlike the woman Loric killed, these people were armed. They grinned as they advanced on the group.

"Shit," Thystle muttered, backing Devil toward Rowan.

"Dammit, Thystle," Aeryn hissed as she drew her sword.

"Don't blame this on me," Thystle said, pulling off her glasses and tucking them into a pocket of her long coat. The cloud cover was completely blocking the sun now. "You wanted to know where The Harbinger is, maybe one of these creatures could tell you."

"Why don't you just climb down and ask one of them?" Aeryn retorted.

The numbers kept growing.

"This isn't good," Theo breathed.

She watched in sick horror as the crowd started to stalk toward them. A low droning sound started up all around them. Chills ran up the length of her spine when Theo realized the sound was being made by the crowd moving in to surround them.

"Get in a circle and stay together," Caeleb shouted to them over the droning crowd.

Loric got tired of waiting for them to attack. He notched another bolt into his crossbow and fired into the crowd. It felled one, but the rest kept coming. Theo's heart felt like it was about to pound out of her chest. Then, The Harbinger's followers stopped.

It seemed like the air stood still.

In the next breath, the soldiers let out a keening howl and rushed forward, barking like wild dogs. Colin's horse reared up and dislodged the startled cleric and Tynan. Colin cried out as the crowd surged hungrily toward them. His horse tried to bolt, but was soon surrounded by the masses. They clawed, hacked, and bit the horse as it screamed. Theo clapped her hands over her ears to block out the disturbingly human sound.

"Gabby, no!" Colin got his feet back under him and tried to save his horse, battering at the crowd with his staff, but the crowd pressed in on him, too.

Loric shouted his brother's name and tried to make his way to him, but the crowd was too thick for him to get through. People grabbed Loric's legs and tried to pull him off his horse. He fought himself free from their grasp, but he could not reach Colin. Soon, the crowd reached the rest of the group, and they could not reach the cleric either. Theo heard Colin scream in pain and turned her head, not wanting to see his last minutes.

"Flaridos!"

Theo's head jerked around again. The shout came from Tynan, wedged somewhere between Rowan and the barking mob. Flames shot out from his hands in a stream, setting several people in the crowd aflame. They reeled away from him, into the rest of the crowd, and set others on fire as they went. This created enough of an opening in the crowd that Tynan was able to grab Colin and pull him back. Colin was bleeding from a deep cut on the side of his face, but otherwise, he seemed to have all his limbs, and fingers, intact.

Thystle spurred Devil in front of Colin and Tynan to shield them. This left a gap on Aeryn's left side, which the soldiers quickly took advantage of. They swarmed in, snarling like rabid animals. Aeryn cursed Thystle again. She tried to turn Rowan but could not in time. Theo screamed when someone grabbed her ankle and yanked her off Rowan's back.

Aeryn let loose a cry of her own and leapt from Rowan onto the man who had grabbed Theo, and managed to drag another pair of men with her. Freed, Theo staggered back into one of Rowan's hind legs. She saw Aeryn slash and disembowel the men she dragged down. Somewhere on the other side of the battle, Thystle cried out.

"We need to get out here!" Theo shouted at Aeryn.

Aeryn fended off the blows of two more of The Harbinger's people and then shouted back, "Can you get back on Rowan without my help?"

Theo was shaking. She looked up at Rowan's saddle. It looked miles above her. "No."

"Stay behind me until I can find us a way out of here. Don't get in my way." Aeryn shifted Aric to her left hand and drew her father's sword with her right.

At first, Aeryn cut the howling soldiers down with ease, but then her strength seemed to flag, and people crowded in on her. It was not long before they pressed in hard enough that Aeryn was forced to give them ground or be taken down. Theo drew her dagger and dove forward to help her, swinging wildly at anything and everything. Aeryn shouted at her to get back, but something hit Theo in the head before she could acknowledge the sell-sword. Everything went gray, and she stumbled. Theo felt someone's hot breath on her face.

Aeryn cursed, and then Theo heard another body fall. Someone grabbed her and pulled her back. Her vision cleared as Aeryn said, "I told you to stay behind me."

Theo could see the sell-sword's fatigue on her face. The fighting was taking its toll on her. "I want to help," she protested.

"No." Aeryn shoved a pair of soldiers back into the ones behind them and turned again. "Reach for Rowan's saddle, and I'll help you up. Hurry."

Theo did as she was told. Aeryn sheathed her father's sword to help Theo up into the saddle. Theo clambered up onto Rowan's back. When she was settled in on Rowan's saddle, she turned and saw a pair of soldiers dive in Aeryn's direction.

"Behind you!" she cried out.

Aeryn turned in time to deflect the strike from one but not the other. His dagger stabbed her in the thigh. With a cry of pain, the sell-sword fell to one knee. Someone else's club smacked into Aeryn's side. The soldiers pressed their advantage, knocking Aeryn to the ground. As another one raised his sword, he was impaled by one of Loric's crossbow bolts. Caeleb came charging through the crowd next, shouting Aeryn's name.

"Shield your eyes," he commanded. He raised his sword high

288

over his head. "Light of Aephis!"

Theo covered her eyes just in time to keep from being blinded by an intense white light that shot out of Caeleb's sword. The remaining soldiers screamed as they were blinded.

"Be quick, I don't know how long their blindness will last," Caeleb told them all.

Theo opened her eyes. Tiny spots danced before her eyes, but she saw clearly enough The Harbinger's soldiers staggering around, blindly swinging at whatever they bumped into, mostly each other. She would have thought the scene worth laughing at, had the circumstances been different. Theo saw that Colin was with Loric. Thystle was on the ground now, but Tynan was helping her up again. They made their way to Devil, and Tynan helped Thystle onto the black charger before he climbed up behind her. Aeryn limped over to Rowan and told Theo to slide forward. Aeryn swung up onto Rowan with her uninjured leg and settled in behind her.

"Caeleb, lead us out of here," Aeryn said to the paladin.

"Gladly." He turned his horse and spurred it forward, battering his way through those soldiers who stumbled into his path.

The others followed closely behind him. Renewed howling from behind them told Theo that Caeleb's spell was losing its potency. A dagger went flying past them. Ahead of them, more soldiers poured into the street, creating a human wall.

"Don't stop!" Aeryn shouted at the others.

Theo was about to ask what she planned to do when she saw Caeleb's horse hurtle over The Harbinger's people. "Oh, no."

"Hold on," Aeryn said in her ear.

Her stomach dropped as Rowan's hooves left the ground. Rowan soared over the heads of the soldiers. When Rowan landed, Aeryn spurred Rowan into a sprint after Caeleb's horse, leaving Theo no time to catch her breath.

61

When they finally escaped the mobs, Caeleb led them onto a street dominated by a rectangular temple constructed of white stone. A statue portraying the High Father Aephis, made of polished gold, stood outside the temple, next to the white marble steps that rose to the temple entrance. Aephis's Staff of Wisdom rested in one hand and a sphere to represent the sun rested in his other. He stood in judgment of them as Aeryn and the others stopped their horses at his feet and dismounted.

Aeryn heard Tynan call out, "We need some help over here!"

She looked back to see Thystle partially hunched over Devil's neck. She could not tell if Thystle was conscious or not. Caeleb and Loric went to aid Tynan, easing the vampyre down off of Devil's back. Aeryn let Theo down and then swung down from Rowan's back, limping to Thystle's side as Caeleb and Loric set her on the ground.

"I'm alright," Thystle muttered as she slumped to the ground.

"Just be still," Aeryn said.

Colin joined them and knelt by Thystle's side. "Let me see the wounds," Colin said as he gently peeled Thystle's coat back.

"It's nothing," Thystle said. "I just looked left when I should have looked right."

Caeleb said, "You still held that mob back well so that we could get to Colin. He probably owes you his life."

"I do," Colin agreed.

He pulled Thystle's coat away to reveal multiple puncture wounds in her shoulder and side. The bleeding had already slowed considerably, though.

"Amazing," Colin breathed. "Your wounds have already begun to heal."

"It's a vampyre thing," Thystle said as she pulled her coat back into place and slowly sat up.

The cleric sat back quickly. "Oh, I'm so sorry. I did not know."

Thystle smirked. "It's fine. I'll feel better again after I rest a bit."

Colin only nodded and stood. He looked worried that Thystle might suddenly get hungry.

Aeryn backed up to give Thystle more room and winced. Pain stabbed her in her wounded thigh. Caeleb caught her look of pain and took her arm.

"I'm alright," she told him.

He gave her a wry look. "So I keep hearing from you. Colin?"

Colin came over and knelt down so that he could look at her wound. He frowned a little at it. "This is bad," he said and then went into his pouch. He took a bundle of herbs out and pulled sections of it off. Then, he said, "This is going to hurt, I'm afraid."

Aeryn nodded. He pressed the herbs into her open wound with his thumb. She cried out through gritted teeth.

"Sorry!" Colin whispered and then closed his eyes. He then brought his hands together and started muttering a prayer.

Within moments, Aeryn's leg started to feel better. She looked down and saw that the herbs he had pressed into her wound were glowing bright green. The green glow spread, and the edges of the wound started to mesh together and heal. When Colin stopped muttering and opened his eyes again, her injury felt much better, and she could flex her leg again. She thanked Colin for what he did.

"Of course," he said, smiling.

"We should get inside," Caeleb told them and nodded to the temple entrance at the top of the marble steps. "Can you walk?" he asked Aeryn.

She nodded. "Thystle?"

The vampyre nodded as well and rose to her feet.

Before they could ascend the temple steps, the doors of the

291

temple opened and a complement of five guards dressed in white-enameled breastplates thundered to the edge of the steps, spears at the ready. Their breastplates bore the sun insignia of Aephis.

Caeleb called up to one of them. "Kuma, where is Allemar?"

The guards relaxed at seeing Caeleb and put their spears up again. The one named Kuma replied, "He awaits you within the temple."

"Understood. Can you and your men attend to our horses so that we may speak with Allemar straight away?"

Kuma nodded and his men descended from the temple entrance to take charge of their horses. Aeryn patted Rowan before she turned his reins over to one of the temple guards. Then, she followed Caeleb up the steps of the temple with the rest of the group.

Aeryn remained cautious about meeting this Allemar that Caeleb spoke of. Many high-ranking officials, connected to a god or otherwise, made her uncomfortable with their self-absorbed nature. She hoped that Allemar had information that would prove valuable in the fight ahead, but she was not optimistic about it.

Inside the temple entrance was an expansive room with soaring ceilings and walls also made of white marble. Huge gold candelabras cast light into every corner and illuminated the faces of the men, women, and children huddled within. A quick glance told Aeryn there were more than a hundred of them gathered there. Most of the high-backed worship benches had been moved out of the way and were stacked along one wall. Others served as cots for the wounded.

Caeleb led them toward the altar. Eyes filled with fear followed them as they passed, and a quiet murmuring went through the crowd. Caeleb took the group up to the altar area, where a man dressed in white linen robes knelt before another towering statue of Aephis. Caeleb went to the man alone.

"Sceptor Allemar, they're here," he said quietly to the kneeling man.

The man rose and made his hands into the shape of a circle,

kissed the top of this circle, and then raised his hands to his forehead. His hands dropped back to his sides, and he turned to greet them, a wide smile on his face. Aeryn's breath caught.

"He looks like Pythun," Theo gasped.

His hair and robes were different, and he was taller, but the man's features were too similar for him to be kin to anyone else. Aeryn drew Aric, and Tynan threw back his cloak to free up his hands for casting. Thystle drew her sword as well. Behind her, Aeryn heard Loric cock his crossbow and then someone in the crowd of refugees started screaming.

62

Aeryn ignored the pandemonium behind her. The man at the altar, however, looked bewildered. Suddenly, a young man with almost carrot-orange hair and beard jumped in front of the sceptor. He drew his sword. Before anyone could make the first move, though, Caeleb rushed between her and the young man.

"Whoa! Whoa. Everyone stop." He looked at each member of the tense group. "Please lower your weapons. Aeryn, no one here will harm you."

No one moved or backed down.

Finally, the man standing at the altar addressed them in a voice that was not overly loud but that commanded attention. "I do not know what is going on here, but please, everyone, lower your weapons. Blood shall *not* be spilt in this holy sanctum. Neither the High Father nor I tolerate violence here."

Loric uncocked his crossbow, but did not move from behind her. Colin went to the man at the altar and stood slightly behind him, his eyes darting nervously from one person to the other. The red-haired young man hesitated, but finally lowered and sheathed his sword. Aeryn lowered her sword, too, and gestured for her companions to do the same.

"Who are you?" she demanded.

"I am Sceptor Allemar. The girl mentioned someone named Pythun."

"Yes. We met a man named Pythun in Valis. You bear a striking resemblance to him, sir."

The man claiming to be Allemar sighed and nodded his head. "That explains much."

Aeryn frowned. "Elaborate, please. I didn't come here to be

toyed with."

"I believe much explanation is in order, yes," he said. "Let us repair to somewhere we may all speak more freely. Come with me." Allemar looked over the crowd of refugees huddled in the worship area. They seemed to have calmed down, but the sceptor obviously did not want to speak in front of them.

He turned and walked toward the statue. Aeryn and the others followed him. There was a hidden door behind it, which the young man with red hair opened and gestured for them to go through. Allemar went first, followed by Colin and Caeleb. Despite her reservations, Aeryn followed them too. Loric and the red-haired young man were the last to pass through the door, and the young man closed and locked the door behind himself.

The hidden door opened into a wide anteroom, and beyond the anteroom, Allemar led them into another chamber with a teardrop-shaped table and enough chairs for everyone.

"Colin, would you mind getting us some refreshments?" Allemar asked. "No doubt you could all use something to eat and drink after your difficult journey here."

Colin rose and left the room, Allemar bade them all sit. Allemar sat at the head of the table and the young man sat at his right hand, then Caeleb and Loric sat on the opposite side from Aeryn and her companions. Aeryn sat across from Caeleb and stared, wondering if he had somehow known how she would react to Allemar. Was he again testing her? If so, why?

The sceptor cleared his throat and spread his hands on the table. He looked at Aeryn and her companions. "Perhaps we can begin with you telling me how you came to be associated with The Harbinger."

Aeryn took immediate offense. "None of us are *associated* with The Harbinger."

"I apologize for my wording. I am very tired these days. I meant only to ask how you first came to know of The Harbinger."

"Before I do, why don't you explain your connection to Pythun, The Harbinger's avatar?"

Allemar took a deep breath and leaned again the back of his chair. "Pythun is related to me. The fact that you say he is The Harbinger's avatar tells me much."

"Such as?"

"When I received Tynan Selvantyr's message, I was mystified. For one, because Tynan Selvantyr died long ago, and for another, no one outside the select circle of sceptors has heard The Harbinger's name spoken in nearly a thousand years. Since you say Pythun is The Harbinger's avatar, I understand how The Harbinger's resurrection came to be."

Allemar paused when the door opened, and Colin entered with a woman carrying a tray of breads and cheeses and nine glasses. Colin held two bottles of wine. The woman set the tray on the table and handed a glass to each of them, then she took the wine from Colin and filled everyone's glass. Even Theo received a small amount of wine. The woman exited again without a word.

"Please, help yourselves to the food," Sceptor Allemar said.

Aeryn, Thystle, and Tynan passed, but Theo helped herself. The red-haired young man did not eat either, nor did he move a muscle in his chair. Aeryn began to wonder if he was mute or even human.

Allemar went on. "I was thirteen winters old when my family sent me away from our farmstead near King's Town to begin my studies at this very temple. I was tutored by the clerics of Aephis here, and since I had a great aptitude for my studies, I became a cleric as well when I was old enough and rose quickly through the order's ranks. My connection to the High Father was so strong that Aephis took me on as his sceptor when I was only twenty.

"That same year, I received word from my father that my younger sister was to be married. I wished to attend the ceremony and journeyed home, but during the trip, I fell ill. I was able to hold on until we reached my family's home, before I collapsed fully. There, I remained for several weeks with a raging fever. My family feared I would die, and many family members took turns watching over me and caring for me. My cousin Pythun was one of them. He was just fifteen then.

"When my fever broke, and I was making my way back to health, I found my cousin to be much changed from how I had known him, bright and cheerful. My aunt confided in me that while Pythun had cared for me, she noticed a strange shift in his mood and behavior. His moods became dark, and he brooded often. The family assumed that it was seeing someone close to him so near death, that it had somehow made him fear his own mortality.

"I came to know this was not the case when Pythun took me aside one night and told me that during my feverish nights, I raved about 'the great darkness' and 'the bringer of death'. He wanted to know what I had been talking of. He suddenly seemed transfixed by the subject. To this day, I do not understand why my ravings affected him so, but I warned him to never ask me this again. I returned to Pius a month later without the subject ever coming up between us again.

"Some years later, through correspondence with my aunt, I learned that Pythun left King's Town. She thought he meant to go north, but where she did not know. By then, he had grown so distant that he hardly ever spoke to anyone in the family anymore. They said he had picked up many strange and frightening habits, such as locking himself in his room at night, from which they heard chanting late into the night. My aunt said that a part of her was relieved to see him go. I was concerned for my cousin, but that was the last I heard about Pythun, and to be honest I have thought of him little since then, until his name was mentioned today."

"Seems he busied himself with a lot more than just chanting when he went north," Thystle said when Allemar was finished.

Aeryn proceeded to tell Allemar their story from the beginning.

297

He listened in silence, nodding here and there. When she was finished, he related the story of how Kaliphesh became The Harbinger.

Allemar said to Tynan, "When you 'accidentally' found the caverns, the ones that were once used by the Pillars of Ki, Aephis knew The Harbinger had found the one he would use. You were as prideful as Kaliphesh, and no doubt he assumed it would be easy to corrupt you. To keep this from happening, Aephis secretly aided the dwarven god Vortenthas in creating the sword Aric. You further helped them when you added your own enchantments to the caverns and to Aric. Your enchantments alone would never have been enough to hold him."

Tynan looked somewhat crestfallen at this revelation, but Allemar went on. "The one flaw in Aephis's plan, the flaw he has acknowledged himself, was he did not consider that the sword might ever be removed from the caverns permanently. He did not consider that anyone could break the curse that Tynan left and be able to take the sword."

Allemar looked straight at Aeryn, and his eyes seemed to see right through her, into the very center of her, and she knew what his next words would be. "It is interesting to me that one so young and inexperienced as an adventurer was able to find the amulet that would allow you to break the curse on the caverns so easily."

Aeryn frowned. "I learn fast."

"And someone just gave this to you? It seems like it could be considered a valuable instrument," Allemar said.

"We should stay on the subject of defeating The Harbinger," Aeryn replied.

"I believe this *is* on the subject. How did the amulet come into your possession?" Allemar asked, still staring at her.

Tynan said, "You told me Trion gave it to you. I gave it to him after Rimen died, because I knew he had no use for it and would protect it. He was an honorable man."

Aeryn's throat felt dry. "Honorable." She laughed a little under her breath.

"How did it pass from Trion to you?" Tynan asked.

Aeryn could feel all eyes on her. She closed her eyes a moment and then looked at Tynan. "Did you really think that he was going to honor your request forever? In his eyes, you were responsible for the death of his only son. No, he was holding on to it for a special day, but he did not give the amulet up easily. There was a price."

She hung her head, unable to look Theo, Caeleb, and the others in the eye. "I killed him. I did what I had to do in order to get that amulet; I killed Trion for it."

The room was silent until Allemar said, "I do not think that is the whole story."

"No, it's not," she replied. "When I was searching for the key to breaking the curse, I realized that the only way Rimen could have passed through the caverns unharmed was with some magikal aid. If it was an object, since no one had ever discovered it, the only place it could be was with Rimen's body. So I headed to Alethia to see what I could find out.

"When I arrived, I discovered that his father, Trion, still lived, in self-imposed isolation outside the city. I went to see him. He knew all along what the amulet was, though Tynan didn't tell him, and that someone would eventually come looking for the key to Tynan's caverns. Trion agreed to give it to me if I agreed to do something for him. I said yes without hearing his full terms first.

"Trion required that I best him in a fight. He claimed another had asked for the amulet, some years after Tynan's death, but that challenger failed. He had waited a century for someone else to come looking for it.

"Trion's hatred of Tynan for his part in Rimen's death warped him. He hated all things connected to Tynan, and he wouldn't give up the amulet willingly. His ferocity when he attacked me made it obvious he meant to kill me and had probably killed the previous challenger, too.

"I didn't want to kill Trion, but his attacks were relentless. I was finally able to strike him down, but when I refused to deal the final blow,

Trion delivered a fatal injury to himself. I don't know what changed his mind, but before he died, he told me where he hid the amulet. I retrieved it and fled Alethia."

Aeryn stopped speaking and the silence in the room seemed as loud to her as any shouted recrimination. Then, Tynan's gloved hand reached over to cover her hand. When she looked up, Aeryn saw that everyone was staring at her, but none of them looked at her with disgust or loathing as she had expected.

"My quest to fulfill my father's unrealized dream has turned me into something I never wanted to be—I was willing to rob someone's grave if I had to. I antagonized a man who had already suffered greatly. As far as I'm concerned, his blood is on my hands," Aeryn told them.

The last person she expected to offer her comfort was the first to speak. Loric said, "Many a man has experienced great loss, but rarely does one let it twist him as this Trion allowed his suffering to twist him." The others murmured their agreements.

"Your guilt over these things is a heavy burden you have carried with you to this place," Allemar said from the head of the table. "The High Father told me you carried a secret that is poisoning your soul. It was evident to me as soon as you walked through my temple's doors, and it is crucial to the success of your mission that you release your guilt here, before you continue on. The final part will be more difficult than any other has been for you.

"I will not belittle your guilt for the things you have done, but you are no murderer. Aephis considers Trion's injuries a matter of self-defense and his death the suicide of a desperate man. Hearing your story, I concur. If you can begin to accept this, I believe you are finally ready to face The Harbinger. Do you believe this as well?"

Aeryn could not say for sure whether she accepted that Trion's death was not her fault, but something felt different inside of her. She no longer had something to hide. "I do feel better now that I've told my story." She wiped a stray tear from her face.

Allemar smiled. "Confessions are like that: freeing."

"What is next?" Aeryn asked, uncomfortable with being the center of attention still.

"Where are all the other people in the city? Other than the ones hiding inside the temple, we've seen no one other than The Harbinger's soldiers," Theo said.

The red-haired man answered, heavy derision in his tone, "In hiding, cowering like door mice in the other temples around the city. They pray that the gods will save them, but the gods will not."

Allemar explained, "Kaliphesh is one of the old gods, totally unknown to the newer gods. They have no idea the kind of darkness he is capable of bringing about and mistakenly believe that if they ignore him, he will fade away. The Harbinger will do no such thing. He has regained much of his former powers. It is only a matter of time before he regains all of it, and then he will be much harder to stop. He has followers once more and sacrifices have already been committed in his name. He will go after the other gods next.

"Aephis spoke to the older gods and told them they must unite against The Harbinger, but they are hesitant. The old gods remember what Yurevis did to save them, but feel it is not their place to interfere." Allemar sighed with great sadness. "The new gods are too frightened, and feel bound by the immortal laws prohibiting a revolt against any other god. It will be their downfall. After The Harbinger begins killing gods and taking their powers, their faithful will see no other choice than to follow The Harbinger or die in the bloodbath. More gods will fall as a result."

"What about the resistance?" Caeleb asked him.

"It was not large enough. I met with the other sceptors and warned them of what was to come, but the discussion of what action should be taken dissolved into petty bickering among the sects. The sceptors for the gods of light refused to unite with the sceptors for the dark gods, and vice versa. The sceptors for the neutral ones were too like

301

their gods, unsure that we should act at all."

Again the red-haired man spoke. "What resistance was formed was quickly squashed by The Harbinger's soldiers. Such a great howling I have never heard. There were rumors that the living fought beside the dead. When the battle was over, the resistance was gone, literally. Few bodies were left in the street, only blood. I don't know what happened to them or what evil purpose The Harbinger could have for taking the bodies."

"Will Aephis not do anything on his own, as Yurevis did?" Caeleb asked Allemar.

"Yes." Allemar paused. "By immortal law, gods cannot do harm against other gods, but as I told you all, Yurevis once broke that law and aided mortals in the uprising against Kaliphesh. In that same way, Aephis will help you now. With this," the sceptor produced a small, black orb from his robes, "you will imprison Kaliphesh permanently. You have been chosen to do this, Aeryn."

"I don't know how."

Allemar replied, "I will show you. Tynan, you have some knowledge of how to make the sword work against The Harbinger, do you not?"

Tynan nodded. "Some."

Thystle leaned forward. "What about the rest of us? I'm not letting Aeryn do this alone."

"No, of course you are not," the sceptor assured her. "The other six of you will go as well. It will take all seven of you for success in this."

Aeryn let this tumble through her head before she repeated, "The other six."

"There will be no others?" Loric asked, clearly displeased at such a low number.

"No. It will only be the seven of you, including my son, Ferrin." He laid a hand on the shoulder of the young man sitting next to him.

302

"Seven has great significance in the universe. It has power. Therefore, it can be no more and no less than seven of you. You have all been chosen."

"What about Tynan?" Aeryn asked.

There was a period of silence, then Tynan said, "I am not coming."

"What?" Aeryn breathed. Suddenly, the idea of him not being by her side through the rest of the journey was unacceptable. Something in his tone told her that he had known this for some time. As usual, for his own reasons, he had not seen fit to tell her.

"I cannot go," Tynan said. "The Harbinger will sense me before you can get close enough, and the battle will be lost. You must go without me."

Before she had a chance to respond, the ground under them shook violently. They all grabbed onto the thick table and looked up as small pieces of the richly ornamented ceiling fell onto the table from the force of the quake. The tremor lasted for several tense moments, then stopped as abruptly as it had started.

Suddenly, Allemar stood and cried out, grabbing his head.

"Father!" Ferrin jumped out of his chair to grab Allemar as the sceptor's knees buckled.

Allemar's face pinched with pain, and he remained this way, supported by his son. Finally, the spell seemed to pass. He patted his son's arm, standing again on his own. "I am alright, Ferrin," he assured the young man in a whisper, but when Allemar looked at them all again, his eyes shone with tears. "It has begun. The Harbinger has seized Symon's powers. Symon has been taken first." Allemar named the oft mischievous, sometimes cruel god of Luck, Chaos, and Madness.

He told them, "He will start with the neutral gods, who will not oppose him, and then the gods of light and darkness will fall, before he sets his sights on the High Father and High Mother. We do not have much time. Kaliphesh will need to rest to regain his strength, and you

303

must strike before he can regain himself." Standing, he stretched a hand out to Aeryn. "Come. You and Tynan both. We must prepare you for the ritual now. Then, you must go."

Her fear of her own limitations thickened in every fiber of herself, but Aeryn rose and followed the sceptor out of the room. As soon as she and Tynan were back in the anteroom, she stopped him. "You knew all along you weren't coming with us to face The Harbinger, didn't you?"

"I suspected I would not be with you at the final confrontation, but until now I did not know for certain."

"I don't want to do this without you," she whispered. She had not realized until this moment that he was her fallback. When she did not know what was happening around them, even if he hid it from them, she felt that Tynan did understand what was happening. If he was not with them at the end, she had no one to fall back on.

Tynan touched her shoulder. "I will be there with you in spirit. You are strong enough to do this. You must believe that."

Allemar opened the hidden door behind the altar and waited for them. Tynan went through the door. Only Aeryn hesitated. She went to the doorway and looked out into the temple's worship hall.

Standing by the door still, Allemar asked her, "Are you ready?"

She stepped through the door, but replied, "I don't know if I am."

He smiled at her. "I have much faith in you."

Aeryn wished she could say the same. Tynan spoke of believing just as Allemar spoke of faith, but a thousand questions pitched through her mind. What if she could do not believe in herself as they did? Would she still be able to end the tyranny of a god? She had vowed to give her life to stop The Harbinger, but what if sacrificing her own life was not enough? Would their mission fail if she found neither belief nor faith inside of herself?

Her breath caught when Allemar said, "Let us begin . . ."

63

After Aeryn, Tynan, and Allemar left, the rest stayed put. Theo continued trying to process all of the information she had been fed in the last hour. Perhaps the most stunning was Aeryn's confession. She agreed that the sell-sword probably did the best she could have, and it seemed like Trion was bent on dying no matter what. Theo looked around at the others, wondering what they thought of all that just happened.

Ferrin sat in his seat, unmoving like a statue. Theo guessed him to be younger than even Colin, more than a boy, but not yet a man either. She wondered if he felt he was there to make sure they stayed in line. He looked at each of them as though they might suddenly decide to pillage the temple. When his eyes met hers during his sweep around the table, he glared briefly before moving on to stare at Thystle.

Caeleb stared thoughtfully at the table while Colin helped himself to more of the bread and cheese still on the table. Per usual, Thystle chewed on something, this time her thumbnail. Loric had one of his long daggers out and seemed absorbed with checking the edges of it.

Loric reminded her of a wolf, constantly aware and waiting. She imagined that, should a troll crash through the door this very minute, Loric would have no trouble abandoning his study to dispatch the creature and then sit down again just as calmly as if nothing had happened.

Theo quickly grew bored with her study of the others and inhaled and exhaled deeply in a loud sigh. She wondered how long Aeryn and Tynan were going to be. The wait, added to the silence in the room, grated on her nerves. She hated to just sit, and wait, and not speak.

Finally, she blurted out, "What if one of us doesn't want to face The Harbinger?"

All eyes turned to her.

Ferrin was indignant when he declared, "You should feel honored to have been chosen for Aephis's plan, little girl."

Most of those in the room rolled their eyes. In addition to his youth, Ferrin might actually be more pompous than Tynan, Theo decided.

She replied, "I will face The Harbinger for the sake of my brother and for my friends who died. But I did not ask to be chosen for this. I should feel honored? What's wrong with you? The Harbinger, or Kaliphesh, or whatever his gods-damned name is, will likely kill us. It doesn't make me feel honored to die that way."

"I love your optimism," Thystle told her.

"I'm just a kid."

"Don't worry, we'll look out for you." Thystle ruffled Theo's hair in a playful manner, but Theo was in no mood for playing around, and pulled away.

"Thystle is right. We shall do whatever we can to make sure you have a long life ahead of you when this is over," Caeleb told her.

Colin put aside the hunk of bread he had half-devoured and said, "Oftentimes we don't see why we have been chosen to suffer or benefit from the circumstances in our life, because we don't see the larger picture that the High Father sees. In time, you may understand it. Perhaps for now it should suffice to know that you have been chosen for something special."

Theo had something snide to say in response, but she bit it back. She could tell Colin was trying to be helpful, in a cleric kind of way, and she tried not to fault him for it. Instead, she sat back in her chair and crossed her arms over her chest. Everyone fell silent again.

Caeleb said, "Rather than sniping at each other, our time would be better spent readying the horses. When Aeryn returns, we will leave directly."

Ferrin shook his head. "Father did not say we could leave here."

306

"Have it your way. Be warned, we won't wait if you're not ready to go when we are."

Caeleb led them out a rear exit of a temple. As they headed to the stable, Theo asked him, "What's with Ferrin?"

Caeleb shrugged. "He's been that way as long as I have known him. He thinks because his father is a sceptor and leads the council, he has a leg up on the rest of us in the eyes of the gods."

"Personally, I believe it takes more than just that," Colin said.

"I hope so," Thystle muttered as she pulled her dark glasses out and put them on. The sun was thoroughly hidden behind an ever-thickening layer of clouds, but she wrinkled her nose as she looked up at the sky.

"Looks like more rain is ahead," Theo said as they entered the cover of the stables.

The horses were lined up in neat little stalls, everyone's gear stacked on shelves nearby. She went into Rowan's stall and was nearly knocked over by the huge stallion when he gave her a nudge with his head. She blushed at the show of affection and laughed a little as she patted his side. She did not know much about horses, but as Theo looked him over, she guessed he was alright after the battles on Pius's streets. He had a few cuts and scrapes, but it looked like they had been cleaned and treated by someone, although she saw no stable hands about. She looked around, wondering if the stable hands at Aephis's temple were invisible or godly in some way. The idea sent an eerie chill up her spine.

Theo wished she could ready Rowan for Aeryn but knew that she would probably do something the wrong way and just irritate Aeryn. Instead she went to help Thystle. They were checking Devil's hooves when Ferrin walked in.

No one stopped what they were doing, but Loric asked him, "Afraid you were going to miss your destiny, Ferrin?"

Ferrin replied, "Aephis says that too much idleness leads to chronic laziness. It is a better use of my time to prepare myself and my

307

mount for the battle ahead than to sit alone, since the rest of you abandoned your posts."

Theo rolled her eyes and asked Thystle, "Can we leave him behind? Things won't change too much if we're one short, will they?"

Thystle laughed, which sparked a fierce glare from Ferrin. He said nothing to them as he walked past to a stall near the end of the stable. There, he began brushing a piebald mare and kept his back to them. Theo got the distinct impression that her comment had somehow wounded his pride.

Caeleb cleared his throat and nodded toward the open stable doors. Aeryn was walking down the path toward them. She came alone.

Aeryn entered the stables and went down the center aisle without looking at the rest of them. She headed straight to Rowan's stall and began checking him over, running a hand down each of his legs and then over his neck, back, and belly. Theo and Thystle looked at each other and left Devil's stall.

"So?" Thystle asked her, leaning on Rowan's stall door.

On the outside, Aeryn did not look any different, but something was different about her below the surface. "I think he's okay," Theo said as she went into the stall. "Someone cleaned him up when they put him in here."

When Aeryn still said nothing, Theo asked, "Are you okay?"

Aeryn finished her inspection and gave Rowan a vigorous brushing for several moments before she said, "I'm fine."

"No, you're not," Thystle replied. "I know you better than that, Aeryn. What's wrong?"

"I wish Tynan was coming with us."

"Why?" Theo asked, confused now. "You've been angry at him since before we left the Northlands, and how many times has he lied to us?"

"I know." Aeryn continued brushing Rowan. Then, she stopped and turned to them. "I feel like he has known more about what's going on than any of us."

Ferrin stepped out of his horse's stall and came down the aisle toward them. "I believe my father explained well enough what is going on. Perhaps you weren't listening as well as you should have been."

"Shut up, Ferrin," Thystle hissed at him. "No one needs to hear from you right now."

"I will do no such thing, demon." Ferrin narrowed his eyes. "Do you think I do not know what you are, vampyre? I do. Aephis told my father, and he told me. You are a cursed thing as far as I'm concerned, and I will not listen to you. It's bad enough that you've been chosen to join our quest, though I have no idea why."

Thystle's eyes flashed bright green in the dim light of the stable. "Perhaps Aephis needed someone to kick your ass, you little weasel," she growled. Thystle took a step toward him.

Ferrin did not flinch as he backed up a step and his hand dropped to the hilt of his sword. "You are welcome to try."

"Thystle, stop it," Aeryn said.

"Get him," Theo muttered gleefully. If anyone needed slapping around, it was Ferrin.

"Both of you, stop it," Caeleb commanded. "We're not going to get anywhere if you don't stop squabbling like children."

"They have no faith!" Ferrin protested. He jabbed a finger at Thystle. "Her least of all."

"My faith lies with the blood god Saerifis and his minions," Thystle told him. Even though her face did not show it, Theo knew Thystle was mocking Ferrin, trying to goad him into making the first move.

Ferrin obliged by flinging himself at her. "Evil one!"

Loric intercepted him and shoved Ferrin back. "Enough! You and your aberrant ideas need to leave."

Loric continued to shove Ferrin until he was outside the stable doors. Ferrin looked angry enough to try to take Loric on as well, but the ranger gave him a warning look. Ferrin finally turned and stormed off.

Loric said to Colin, "Get his horse saddled and out of here, too, and pick a horse for yourself. It's time we were all on our way." He gave the rest of them a stern look and then led his own horse out of the stables.

Colin nodded and did as Loric told him. He led Ferrin's horse and a chestnut bay out of the stables. Caeleb watched him leave and then came out of his horse's stall.

"Forget about them. What troubles you?" he asked Aeryn, standing outside Rowan's stall with Theo and Thystle.

"Tynan is the only one of us with any prior experience with The Harbinger. He knew The Harbinger's story before any of us, and he knows what The Harbinger is capable of firsthand." Aeryn returned to brushing Rowan.

Theo thought that if Aeryn brushed Rowan any more, they would never be able to sneak up on The Harbinger, because of the reflection coming off the horse's coat. Caeleb seemed to read her mind.

He said to Aeryn, "He's been brushed enough. You're going to rub him bald."

A corner of Caeleb's mouth twitched in a half-smile as he took the brush from her. Aeryn let him take it, but she moved right into putting Rowan's gear on.

Caeleb told her, "It's obvious you have doubts about facing The Harbinger."

"Tynan and Allemar kept telling me to have faith that I have power to defeat The Harbinger, but I'm unsure." Aeryn tightened the buckle on her saddle and checked the stirrups. "Allemar said that I need to forget my past regrets and fears, or else The Harbinger will use them against me. I couldn't help thinking about my father again. The Harbinger may not know about what happened with Trion, but he knows about my father. He made that rather obvious in Morghall. I fear he will use my father against me."

"Explain what you mean," Caeleb said.

"My father and the soldiers he led were attacked one night when out on patrol—we never discovered by whom. My father and another man were wounded. The group must have turned back to return to our camp, but then lost their bearings in the snowstorm that buried us overnight. In the morning, after the storm passed, I went with the group sent out to look for them. We found them not more than a hundred yards from camp, frozen to death."

"And, you believe you could have done something to change that?" Caeleb asked.

"I promised that I would go with him that night, but I injured myself while riding the previous afternoon, and my father told me to stay behind to rest. I should have insisted on going. Having another fighter among them may have changed the tide of the attack. They wouldn't have had to turn back."

Thystle said to her, "As I've told you before, the storm would still have come. Who's to say you could have found shelter? You might have died, too."

Theo felt that Thystle was right, but she felt bad for Aeryn. So much about her was coming to light now, and Aeryn was nothing like who Theo thought the she was. Aeryn felt scared and alone sometimes, just like her.

"I could have gone to search for them sooner, when they didn't return as they should have. I cannot escape the feeling I let him down."

"Your father's death was an accident, Aeryn," Caeleb told her. "You should not hold back because of something that wasn't your fault. You cannot go on blaming yourself for a storm. His death was a tragic accident."

Aeryn shook her head. "I have made one bad choice after another, and more people die each time. First my father, then the people The Harbinger killed, and now maybe you and your friends, and mine as well. The Harbinger will use these things against me, and I don't know if I will be able to resist him. We may fail because of me."

311

"You aren't in this alone," Thystle said.

"The past must remain in the past today," Caeleb told Aeryn. "Our past can teach us important lessons, but it can get in our way as well. You must decide if you can leave the past behind for today. If you cannot and feel you cannot go forward with this battle, we may well fail for your inaction. I won't lie to you about that. However, none of us can make you go forward. You must decide to do this." He walked away and gathered up his things. "I will leave you to make your choice. I'll stand by you no matter what you decide, but you must make a decision before we go any further."

When he left them, Thystle added, "I agree. I think it's time you let your grief and pain go, for your own sake. Forget about how it may affect the outcome of our battle against The Harbinger. It's killing you. You need to stop letting your grief eat you alive."

Thystle led Devil out of his stall and said to Theo, "Let's go out with the others and leave Aeryn to think."

"You go ahead," Theo said. She waited until Thystle was outside before she told Aeryn, "This thing with The Harbinger isn't just your fault. I won't let you take all the blame. I thought that I had to handle Pythun on my own, and as a result, we gave him just what he wanted. If I had reached out to you sooner than I did, told you what was going on, things might have turned out differently. Or, we might still be here, no matter what either of us did back then.

"When Willa died, you told me there was nothing I could have done to save her and still be alive myself, and you were probably right. The same applies to you. There wasn't anything you could've done to save your father, or save Trion, or those people in Morghall. If your father was anything like your aunt told me he was, I think he'd be upset now that you're beating yourself up over his death." She paused. "Besides that . . . I need you to help me."

Aeryn looked startled by this.

Theo looked quickly away. "I'm afraid to, but I'm going to fight

312

The Harbinger, whether you come or not. I have to do it for Willa. I believe she died because of me, so if I die, too, it would be fitting. I need you to help me try to kill The Harbinger, for Willa and Brien, and all the rest. I need the strength I know you have in you, that I don't have in me."

Theo then jogged out of the stables before Aeryn could say anything. Outside, Caeleb and Loric were talking, but stopped when they saw Theo come out of the stables alone. They looked at her, silently inquiring about Aeryn. Thystle, standing off to the side, stopped polishing her sword blade as well. Theo could only shrug. She had no idea what Aeryn would decide to do.

Thunder rumbled from the dark clouds overhead.

Tynan was there now, as was Allemar. Theo walked to where Tynan stood. He seemed to be watching Ferrin whine and complain to his father, who stood on the steps of the temple. Allemar had a look of vexation on his face as he listened to his son. Colin stood near his mentor, looking equally annoyed, but he remained silent.

Theo looked up at Tynan. "So you're really not coming, huh?"

The dead adventurer shook his head. "No, I am not. I do not enjoy remaining here, but it is as it must be."

"Aeryn's still unsure."

Tynan nodded. "I know she is."

"What is it that Aeryn has to do when we find The Harbinger?" Theo asked. "I mean, if she decides not to go, can someone else do it in her place?"

Tynan shook his head. "No. Aric has bonded its energies with her. She has to be the one." His eyes focused on something behind her. "I do not think you need to worry about her, however."

Theo turned to see Aeryn ride Rowan out of the stables. A bolt of lightning flashed and thunder rolled in its wake above her, as if to put a mark on her decision. She pulled Rowan up next to Theo and reached down to her.

"Thank you for what you said," Aeryn told her.

Theo took her hand without hesitation and took her place behind Aeryn on Rowan's back.

Aeryn looked down at Tynan and nodded. "Lord Tynan."

"Luck be with you, Aeryn," he said.

Guiding Rowan between Thystle and Caeleb, both of whom were now atop their horses, Aeryn said, "And, my thanks to you as well."

Caeleb smiled and nodded, and Thystle patted Aeryn's shoulder.

Colin scrambled to mount his new chestnut bay. Theo wondered if Colin had named this horse something as equally cute-sounding as he had his last horse, while the butterflies in her stomach returned and grew into the size of blackbirds. Only Ferrin seemed to take his leisure getting to his horse.

"Come, Ferrin," Loric said as he swung up onto his horse. Thunder rumbled again, sounding closer this time. "Fate waits for no man."

"You must go to Symon's largest temple, near the center of the city. The Harbinger will be there," Allemar shouted over the thunder. He held his white robes close to him as the wind gusted. "All the blessings of Aephis and Cira be with you."

To Caeleb, Aeryn said, "Show us the way."

Caeleb grinned and strapped a shining steel helm onto his head as a fine mist began to fall from the sky. "Gladly," he said. The paladin kicked his horse into a gallop, leading them toward the center of Pius and The Harbinger.

64

The ominous sky let loose its burden as Caeleb led them to the center of the city. Despite Allemar's blessing, lightning split the sky and thunder rolled in a distinct sound of menace, while the rain poured down, turning the blood in the streets into pale red rivers. No soldiers came to stop them as before, but Aeryn's tension did not ease. Worse, it only grew stronger. The thunder, rain, and gusting wind reminded her too much of the morning after the first encounter with The Harbinger. Things had now come full circle.

The words Caeleb, Thystle, and Theo said to her made her realize that by continuing to doubt herself and wondering if she would be the cause of their failure, she was playing right into The Harbinger's hands. She really was losing herself. She also realized that she had spent so much time trying to earn her father's forgiveness that she lost sight of the man he had been. Her guilt had turned him into a bitter man in death, a false memory bent on torturing her for the rest of her days.

In reality, Derrick Ravane had been one of the kindest men she had ever known, strong-willed and strict in many ways, but forgiving. She had never once felt doubt over calling him Father. He taught her everything she knew, including how to give her best to every effort. To do that, she had to see the battle with The Harbinger to the end.

Caeleb slowed his horse and then stopped, and the rest of them followed his lead. He pointed to the pillared, red stone temple ahead of them. Symon's temple was smaller than Aephis' temple, square instead of rectangular. The most notable difference, however, was the immense hole blown into the front of it, where once was an ordinary entrance, or so she assumed. Even from several yards away, she could see straight through into the courtyard at the center of the temple. At the courtyard's center stood a tall monument.

"Do you see anyone?" Aeryn said over the pounding of the wind and rain.

Caeleb squinted, but shook his head "No. He's still here, though. I sense his evil all over this place. I can't pinpoint its exact origin."

"Let's take a look," Aeryn said and nudged Rowan forward until they reached the tying posts in front of the damaged temple.

She let Theo dismount and then swung down after her. Aeryn kept her eye on the temple, looking for any movement in or around it, but she saw none as she tied Rowan to one of the posts. She walked toward the hole in the temple's face. At the edge of it, Aeryn stopped and waited for the others.

Thystle slipped a pair of slim daggers from their sheaths, checked their blades, and hid them again. Loric recinched his thick leather bracers. Caeleb checked the buckles on his leather armor. Ferrin took a small shield from its place beside his saddle and strapped it to his right arm. Colin gripped his oaken staff as if it was his life, and Theo tucked the dagger she normally kept in her boot into her belt.

Aeryn watched them, knowing they would need more than just their weapons and armor against The Harbinger's darkness.

Caeleb seemed to have trouble with one of the straps on his side, so she walked back to him and pulled the strap tighter. "Better?"

Rainwater ran from his helm and down his handsome features. He smiled at her. "Yes, thank you."

Aeryn looked away from him, embarrassed at the way she felt when he looked at her. She went to Theo. She was much too young to be mixed up in such business, but Aeryn vowed to do everything should could to make it up to her when everything was over.

She touched the girl's shoulder and said, "Do me a favor and stay behind me."

Theo agreed.

Aeryn looked around at the others. Loric settled an iron half-helm onto Colin's head. The short spike on its top looked almost comical on the young cleric. Loric stared into his brother's eyes a moment, nodded to him and clapped Colin on the back before he turned away to remove a second quiver of crossbow bolts from his horse's pack, which he settled his shoulder.

Caeleb stepped close to Aeryn and said, "Let's go before the storm washes us away."

She nodded and drew Aric. To her relief, the sword was not throbbing wildly, as it had before whenever they were close to The Harbinger. A tight grip on the sword's hilt, Aeryn led the way through the gap in the temple's wall and walked across what looked to be the temple's former entry hall. The gray stone floor was streaked with red. The rain blowing in through the ruined walls had not washed it away yet. Just beyond the reach of the daylight, Aeryn could make out the shapes of bodies sprawled in the dark interior of the temple.

Aeryn continued into the courtyard as another peal of thunder rolled across the sky. A garden once occupied the courtyard of Symon's temple. The withered and brittle-brown state of the plants and flowers now left no doubt in Aeryn's mind that they were on the right track to finding The Harbinger. Her eyes swept over the courtyard, watching for signs of an ambush, but she still saw no signs of an ambush or guard of any kind. The Harbinger, it seemed, was either very confident, or very foolish.

A sense of dread and darkness drew Aeryn to the monument at the center of the courtyard. Lightning flashed as she approached it. The remains of a statue, probably Symon, were covered by the monument's wide circular roof. High columns supported the roof, some of which was visibly cracked or missing altogether, and all that remained of the statue was the lower half of its legs and its feet. The monument's roof was damaged as well, allowing rainwater to pour down onto the monument's floor through several cracks in the ceiling.

"Aephis above," Colin breathed, when they walked up the three steps into the monument.

It was obvious now where The Harbinger went. A large opening existed in the monument's floor. Everyone stopped. Loric took the lead and crouched down, shuffling slowly toward the hole with a long dagger in his hand. When he was close enough, he probed the hole's edge with the dagger's tip. The formerly solid marble squished when Loric poked it, and blackish liquid oozed up from where he poked it.

"It's soft," Loric said, repulsion in his voice.

Then, the wind shifted and blew a stench toward them like none Aeryn had ever smelled. Everyone fell back from the hole and covered their noses. Thystle turned away, gagging. Her nose was probably more sensitive because of her vampyre nature, Aeryn thought.

When the wind shifted away again, Caeleb groaned, "It smells like a poorly sealed tomb down there."

"Are there crypts under the city?" Aeryn asked. Her eyes watered from the stench.

"Yes," Colin replied, "but not under Symon's temple, as far as I know."

Aeryn nodded. "We need to get down there."

Loric said he had a coil of rope tied to his saddle and jogged off to get it.

"One of us should go to the edge and look inside," Caeleb said while they waited.

Their gazes settled on Theo. The girl stared back at them. "Why me?"

Thystle replied, "You're the lightest, kiddo."

Theo moaned, "Something might grab me from inside."

"We'll hold your feet if you'd like," Colin suggested.

She frowned. "Thanks."

"Take my lightstone," Aeryn said, lighting it and handing it to her.

Theo reluctantly took it and crawled toward the hole. When she

318

was close to the edge, she got down on her stomach and slid the rest of the way. Theo held the lightstone over the edge and looked in. Aeryn prayed the girl did not drop the stone by accident. Theo lay there staring into the hole for several moments and then quickly backed away from it.

Aeryn helped the girl up. "What's the matter?" she asked her.

Loric rejoined them with the rope.

Theo thrust the lightstone back at Aeryn and wiped her hands on her cloak. The black ooze had turned the front of her shirt dark gray. "It stinks in there."

"We know that already. What did you see?"

"Not much. The walls of the hole absorb the light. But, it looks . . . slimy in there."

Aeryn nodded. The absorption of the light was in keeping with other places they encountered The Harbinger's influence. It could present a problem once they went down there.

Loric volunteered, "I'll go down first."

Aeryn tied quick knots in the rope to give him something to hold onto, while he secured one end of the rope on the nearest column. Then, Aeryn tossed the rest of the rope into the hole. Loric leaned on the rope with all his weight to make sure it could hold him. Satisfied with its stability, he took a large lightstone tied to a leather thong from one of his belt pouches and settled it around his neck. Aeryn and Caeleb held on to the rope to steady it for Loric. He then descended into the hole.

The ranger disappeared from her view as soon as his head cleared the edge of the hole. If Aeryn did not know better, she would have thought the hole was carnivorous. They waited for several tense minutes before Loric reappeared, climbing up the rope. Caeleb gave him a hand with climbing the rest of the way out.

Once he was on solid ground again, Loric told them, "The girl was right, the walls absorb the light, making it difficult to see. The walls and floor are very slippery, but the hole widens and levels off into a tunnel of some sort."

319

Caeleb looked at the others. "If no one has any objections, then in we go."

Aeryn nodded. It was time to see this to the end.

65

Caeleb took the lead and descended into the hole as Loric had. Aeryn went in after him, followed by Theo. Water from the storm above poured into the opening and made the footing even more precarious. As she and Theo descended, she could hear Thystle and Loric arguing with Ferrin above them. She silently cursed all three of them.

"You go next. I don't want you at my back," Thystle told Ferrin.

"I don't want you at my back either, vampyre," the red-haired young man hissed.

"Both of you, be quiet!" Loric growled. "Ferrin, go in now before I kick you in. Thystle follows you. *I* will be at the rear."

Aeryn saw the sceptor's son take the rope and descend into the hole.

As the group descended, they slipped often, but managed to keep their grip on the rope. Aeryn was relieved when the tunnel finally started to level out. By the rope's end, the tunnel's slope was at a manageable angle. When the entire group reached the end of the rope, they all stopped and stared down the tunnel. Aeryn could see nothing but blackness beyond the circle of their lightstones.

The charnel house air was heavier and more pronounced inside the tunnel, and Aeryn heard Theo behind her muffle a cough. Aeryn drew Aric, and Caeleb drew his sword. It gave off a soft glow, but even so, she found it hard to see more than a few feet down the tunnel.

"I don't dare make the sword's light brighter. We don't know who else is down here," Caeleb said, his voice barely more than a whisper.

Aeryn nodded in agreement.

"It looks as though the tunnel's been *chewed* straight out of the rock," Loric said.

He ran a hand over the wall before he turned away. It came up coated in black slime. He raised his hand and sniffed at it. His nose wrinkled. He muttered a curse about goblin dung as he shook his hand to fling the slime off. Only some of it came off. He had to suffice with wiping the rest on his pants leg.

Beside her, Theo shivered and wrapped her arms around herself.

Aeryn frowned. "Let's get moving. Time is not on our side. If The Harbinger is sleeping like Allemar said, I don't want him waking before I can start the binding ritual."

She and Caeleb took the lead. The tunnel grew ever wider as they continued down. She tried not to choke on the stench with every step. The sound of the rainwater flowing into the tunnel echoed around them. It was the only sound around them. None of them spoke until Thystle tripped over something.

"What in the hells was that?" she muttered.

Aeryn aimed the light from her stone down at Thystle's feet and discovered a human hand, torn from whatever body it had once belonged to. She grimaced as she looked around. It was not the only body part scattered across the floor of the tunnel. She spotted many of them.

Something wet dropped onto her shoulder. She looked up but could see nothing but blackness above her. Raising her arm, Aeryn tried to stretch the glow of her lightstone up to the ceiling of the tunnel. Loric noticed what she was doing and took the lightstone from around his neck, holding his stone up in kind. Still the light did not stretch far enough. By now the rest of the group had stopped and come to stand around them.

"What's wrong?" Caeleb asked.

"There's something dripping from the ceiling," Aeryn told him.

"We shouldn't stop," Ferrin said.

"Just hold on, Ferrin," Caeleb said. He made his sword glow brighter.

With the combined lights, they could see the ceiling of the tunnel. Aeryn gasped.

Heads. Dozens of them stuck to pikes hanging from the ceiling. It reminded her of a twisted version of the ceiling in the temple to Morghell in Valis, much like the tainted Forever Wood was a twisted version of the elven forest.

"What the hell is this?" she asked aloud.

"The inside of madness," Caeleb said. Aeryn could not think of a more accurate statement as she watched blood drip down from the ceiling in globs.

He went on, "This must be the result of Symon's powers melded with The Harbinger's perversion. We must be very careful from here on in, because things will only get worse."

Colin groaned. "Oh, no." His face paled as he stared up at the heads.

"What is it?" Loric asked him.

"I recognize some of the . . . heads. They belonged to clerics of Symon. These were the people from the temple above."

Theo's hand went to her stomach. "I don't feel so good," she whispered.

Aeryn knelt down to her. "Look at me. Just keep your eyes on me, and we'll get through this, I promise." She told the others to get walking again.

Farther down the tunnel, their light revealed a head on the wall set apart from the others. Ferrin walked up and leaned his face close to it. Before they could warn him away from it, he poked the head's cheek with the point of his sword. Its eyes opened and looked right at him. Ferrin turned as white as a sheet and jumped back, running into Loric at the same time as the head let out a bloodcurdling shriek. It was an alarm.

Caeleb moved forward to stop it and buried his sword blade between the head's eyes. This succeeded both in cutting off the sound and in pulling the head from the wall. The head stared at him from the end of his sword, the light from his sword blade lighting up the head's eyes and mouth, making it an even more ghastly sight. Theo covered her eyes and backed toward Aeryn.

Aeryn and Loric together hissed at Caeleb to get rid of it. In a panic, Caeleb flung it from his sword. The head flew off and landed at Ferrin's feet.

"Aephis save me!" Ferrin whimpered.

The sceptor's son turned tail and ran back the way they had come, but Loric chased after him, caught him by his collar, and roughly pulled him back. Loric was rewarded by Ferrin doubling over in front of him and vomiting, almost on Loric's boots.

"*Gods damn you,*" Loric cursed, jumping back from the emesis at the same time as he shoved the smaller man away from him.

Ferrin fell to the ground sobbing. Then, they heard a sucking sound come from above them. The blood dripping onto the floor stopped and then began dripping *up*. Then, everything went dark. The lightstones and the light from Caeleb's sword quit. Suddenly sightless, Aeryn crouched down and pulled Theo to her, wrapping her arms around the girl and keeping Aric pointed ahead. She felt the girl's breath coming fast and hard.

Aeryn heard feet shuffling around her as the others tried to keep their bearings. Muttered curses came to her through the inky blackness. She hissed at everyone to be still and silent—there was whispering coming down the passage, too. Ferrin, however, would not stop his sobbing. She heard a quick scuffle from the direction she thought he and Loric were in. Loric growled something. Everyone fell silent again, all but whatever whispered further down the tunnel. It started coming closer.

Aeryn shuffled in the direction where she thought the tunnel wall was, pulling Theo with her. They waited.

Something shuffled up the tunnel toward them. It drew closer, until Aeryn thought she could reach out and touch it. Theo held her breath. Whatever stood near them smelled stale, and its breath rasped in and out. Theo's hands found her hand and squeezed it tightly. Her palms were damp. Aeryn held her tighter.

After what felt like an eternity, the thing in the tunnel sniffed at the air twice, then turned and shambled away. The whispering came back in the wake of the shuffle steps' departure. Aeryn relaxed her grip on Theo and listened to the sound. She tried to make out the words. Then, her father appeared in the darkness beside her. His eyes were cold and sightless, his face luminous and death white. She gasped, the sound sharp and loud.

He glared. "Why didn't you come to save me? You left me there to die. You failed me."

He looked solid enough to touch, if she were to just reach her hand out, but she did not. Aeryn managed to choke out, "You are not real."

The phantom's face pinched. He raised his fist.

Light flared in her eyes, and she squeezed her eyes shut, raising her hand to shield them.

A hand fell on her shoulder. She jumped and opened her eyes again. Caeleb stood beside her, his sword alight again. So was the lightstone in her hand and the one Loric held. She looked around, but the phantom was gone.

Loric helped Colin up from where he knelt on the floor. Colin looked as though he had been praying there. No one helped Ferrin rise from the tunnel floor where he was huddled.

Caeleb squeezed her shoulder. He cautioned, "Don't listen to the voices. They will have nothing good to tell you here."

To Colin, Caeleb said, "Do what you can to shield our presence from The Harbinger's notice. I don't want him to know we're coming until it's too late." He started back down the tunnel, taking the lead again.

66

Farther down the tunnel, a light from the other end became visible. The group extinguished their lights as they continued forward. The tunnel ended in a steep gravel slide that dropped to the floor of a cavernous room lit by glowing gray stones buried in the walls. The stones bathed the room in a cold blue-gray light. When she looked into this light, Aeryn thought of death and wondered if the afterlife looked like those lights.

From the top of the slide, Aeryn could see that the room below was filled with hundreds, if not thousands, of bodies, stacked one on top of the other, explaining where the Pius's dead had disappeared to.

"I don't see The Harbinger here. He must be farther in," Caeleb said. "We have to get to that doorway on the other side of the chamber."

The stacks of dead, however, created a maze of corpses that the seven of them would need to pass through to reach the opening Caeleb point to on the other side of the chamber. Further complicating Caeleb's plan, creatures like the one Aeryn had killed behind Mulkin's cottage moved among the dead. Some appeared to be stripping bodies that lay upon stone slabs, while others loaded the dead onto wheeled litters. Those bodies missing limbs appeared to be discarded into a tangled pile.

"What are they doing?" Theo asked.

Aeryn knew from their first encounter with The Harbinger. "Preparing them for recruitment into an army of the dead."

Loric notched a bolt into his crossbow and said he would cover the group until everyone reached the bottom. Caeleb went down the slide first and the rest followed, one at a time, making as little noise as they could. Each time one of them reached the bottom, they pressed themselves against the first wall of corpses and waited for Loric to send the next person.

To Aeryn, the blue-gray light in the chamber made the bodies next to her look like they had drowned or frozen to death. They reminded her of how her father looked when they found him and the others frozen in the storm. She pushed this thought aside, telling herself it did her no good now.

Aeryn's breath caught when Theo slipped on her way down and slid the rest of the way on her side. Fortunately, the girl kept from crying out. Caeleb caught Theo when she reached the bottom and kept her from tumbling into view of the body gatherers. Theo pressed herself against the body wall next to Aeryn and offered her a sheepish smile. Aeryn brushed gravel off of the girl. She was bleeding from several scratches on her hands and face. Aeryn got Colin's attention and waved him over to tend to Theo's wounds.

"I'm fine," Theo whispered as Colin attended to her.

Colin smiled at her, but cleaned out her wounds with a sharp-smelling salve anyhow.

When Loric reached the bottom, the group made their way single file through each segment of the maze, freezing in place each time one of the body gatherers passed by an opening in front of them. At the end of the maze, as one, they left the cover of the body walls and ran to the passageway out of the chamber. The Harbinger's body gatherers seemed so engrossed in their task that they did not appear to notice them. Safely inside the next tunnel, Aeryn silently thanked the High Father for their safe passage to this point.

It was even colder in this new passage than in the tunnel above, and a sickly yellow glow came from the next chamber at the end of it. Aeryn knew it must be The Harbinger's lair beyond. She took the lead and shuffled to the end of the short passage and to the opening into the next chamber.

There were no gray stones in the chamber beyond. Sludge that covered the walls gave off its own glow. Its light was not great, but enough for her to see by and to illuminate the fire pit at the center of the chamber. Hot coals still smoldered inside it, and ringing the pit stood twelve wooden posts, with a body chained to each.

Beyond the sacrificial pit, against the far side of the chamber, The Harbinger sat upon a throne constructed of stone and bones. Her pulse quickened as she stared at her target. No longer the size of the man he had possessed, The Harbinger was now more than twelve feet tall. She wondered if all gods were giants. The Harbinger's eyes were closed. Aeryn was thankful, hoping they still had plenty of time before he woke again.

She turned back to the others and whispered, "I will draw a half circle around The Harbinger and then begin the binding. If he wakes, he will try to stop me. Whatever happens, he must not leave the circle."

The others nodded.

Aeryn turned back and entered the chamber, Aric stretched out before her. Crumpled forms that appeared to be more of The Harbinger's soldiers lined the edges of the round chamber. None of them moved, however, when she walked through the chamber, and they looked like they might even be dead.

She kept looking at The Harbinger, making sure his eyes remained closed as she made her way to the center of the room with the others following close behind her. Yards of black silk, tattered in places, draped the fallen god's disease-thin body. A necklace of human bones, still glistening with gore, hung about his neck. The bones of The Harbinger's face protruded grotesquely; his skin was stretched over his skull like parchment. His lips were peeled back, no longer covering his pointed teeth, making The Harbinger look like he was grinning wide enough to split his head in two. It was the true face of evil, Aeryn thought.

Aeryn was mindful of traps set to warn The Harbinger of intruders, but she saw no evidence of any. Did The Harbinger think she could not reach him here, or was the lack of traps a trap in of itself?

She kept going until she reached the sacrificial pit. She avoided looking too closely at the twisted, mutilated faces of the sacrifices as she then made her way around the pit and its tormented audience. She could see some had been burned, though, and others flayed. A gentle breeze blew at the loose straps of skin remaining on the sacrifices, creating quiet flapping sounds. Aeryn swallowed back the bile that rose in her throat.

She held up a hand when she reached a place she thought was close enough to The Harbinger that she could begin the binding spell. The others formed in a protective half-circle behind her. She removed the black orb Allemar gave her from one of her belt pouches. Taking a length of leather thong, she bound the orb into the place where Aric's blade met the crossguard, at the bottom of the seven descending runes etched into the blade's center. *"One for the union of the High Father and Mother, and six others to represent the remaining old gods,"* Tynan had told her when they were in Allemar's study.

Her palms were damp, and her fingers fumbled with the knot. The knowledge of how deep they were, and that there was only one way out of the chamber, started to get to her. Aeryn struggled for control and tried to knot the leather faster.

When the orb was affixed tightly to the blade, Aeryn closed her eyes and gathered her thoughts, bringing to mind the instructions given to her. Before she could begin, though, she heard a rasp from the passageway behind the group. All seven of them turned. A small figure tottered into the yellow light of the chamber. It was another of The Harbinger's dead gatherers. The thing opened its mouth, but it never had the chance to utter a sound. Loric's crossbow twanged, and a bolt buried itself between the creature's eyes, killing it.

Loric notched another bolt into his crossbow as Caeleb softly said, "Begin. We'll watch your back."

Aeryn nodded and turned back to The Harbinger. She closed her eyes again.

"I have no knowledge of magik," she had told Tynan.

He shook his head and said, *"Aric will do most of the work. You must say the words and believe in their power."*

Believe, she told herself. *Believe.*

She opened her eyes again and then walked closer to The Harbinger. As quietly as she could, she drew a half circle in the dirt with Aric, ringing The Harbinger on his throne. When this was done, she walked back to the center of the half circle, in front of The Harbinger, and raised Aric over her head. Speaking quietly, she began the ritual.

"In the first days, the High Father and Mother created a world of balance. The Light, the Dark, the Neutral. Since those days the rule of this world has been passed down and divided among the other gods. The eight eldest gods, whose strength overpowers all other gods of Man, invoke their will against you."

A low chuckle echoed through the chamber. The Harbinger's eyes opened, and Aeryn's heart sank.

"I am pleased you finally made it. Welcome to your nightmare," The Harbinger said as he laughed at them. He rose to his feet, but did not advance. "Rise, my army. Smite them and bring me the sword of Vortenthas!"

Aeryn turned to see the huddled shapes at the edges of the chamber twitch to life and rise to their feet. There were dozens of them, each with glowing red eyes and a weapon at the ready. Theo groaned. The soldiers lurched in their direction.

Aeryn remembered Allemar's words and tore her eyes from the awakening soldiers. *"If you stop for any reason, The Harbinger will take advantage of your lapse. No matter what happens, you must stay focused,"* he had told her.

She shook herself and called to mind the next part. "I call upon Heldanic, Lord of Water, to drown your hatred."

She drew wavy lines in the cavern floor with Aric. Heldanic's symbol on the sword's blade glowed to life. Rain suddenly poured down from the ceiling, turning the dirt floor into mud, slowing down The

Harbinger's soldiers. They snarled and tried to quicken their pace.

Caeleb said to the others, "Get between them and Aeryn."

The others spread out, creating a barrier between Aeryn and The Harbinger's soldiers. Emerald light filled the room as one of Loric's bolts, burning with green fire, flew through the air and impaled one of the soldiers. The man screamed as he dropped. It was a thin sound that echoed back and forth over the walls. Aeryn looked over to see Colin holding a green fire between his hands. Loric lit another bolt on this fire and sent it into the crowd of soldiers surrounding them.

The soldiers broke into a charge and fell on her companions with fanatical energy. Steel rang against steel. Thystle shouted at Theo to get behind her. The girl did as she was told, her dagger at the ready. Aeryn hesitated, wanting to protect the girl herself. She told herself the best way to protect Theo was to end this as fast as she could.

She turned away from the others and focused again. "I call upon Tempes, Lady of Fate and Time, to slow the spread of your influence and turn the tides of Fate against you. You were never meant to return to this world, Kaliphesh."

She drew three straight lines in the mud—past, present, and future—and Tempes's symbol glowed on Aric. She looked up. The Harbinger's eyes were focused on her. They narrowed. A strange sensation came over her, but she ignored it.

Before she could say the next part of the ritual, Tynan and Allemar appeared on either side of her.

"I lied," the figure of Allemar told her. *"You were never chosen to do anything but fail."*

"I never liked you, and I think your father was a coward to die in a snowstorm," the figure of Tynan told her. *"You cannot succeed. I knew this all along, but I lied to you."*

Aeryn faltered. "You're not real," she said to the apparitions.

She drew a shield on the ground. "I call on Fortesis, Lord of War and Strength, to give me strength against you. You are *weak*, Kaliphesh."

331

Fortesis's symbol glowed on Aric's blade. She felt her resolve hardening again. The apparitions faded away. The Harbinger stood up from his throne and snarled wordlessly at her. He raised his hands. Suddenly, something struck her in the side of her head.

Aeryn was knocked backward and slid in the dirt. The mud was gone. In fact, the entire cavern was gone. She rolled onto her hands and knees and looked back to see who had struck her. Her mouth fell open. Trion Orinthwend stood only a few paces from her, a look of pure hatred on his elven face and his fighting staff at the ready to strike her again. She was outside his home again.

"Tynan was a self-centered and petty man who cared only for his own glory. I despise him and all things associated with him. If you want that accursed amulet, you will have to get it across my lifeless body."

Aeryn shook her head, desperate to shake away this memory and its apparition, too. It did not work. Trion charged at her. Instinctively, she raised Aric and was met with a solid blow from Trion's staff. She grunted from the unexpected force and then pushed herself upright, knocking him back. He recovered quickly and swung the staff at her two-handed like a club, forcing her to flip herself backward to avoid the blow.

When she landed, something struck her in the back. She again rolled in the dirt. Springing to her feet, she turned to see her father on the dirt tract on the opposite side of her from Rimen. That was not right, she told herself; he was not in Alethia that day. This was all an illusion, created by The Harbinger, but her mind could not fight its way out.

Her father's skin was blue-gray, like the bodies in the maze, stacked up by The Harbinger's gatherers. He was a member of The Harbinger's army now, just like Trion. He laughed at her, a high pitched sound very unlike his laughter in life.

Aeryn closed her eyes. "None of this is real!" she shouted.

"Failure. Failure. Failure," her father chanted at her. *"Worthless*

failure. Were you afraid of the snow? Were you afraid of facing it to save me? You knew I would die when I didn't return, but you left me out there anyhow."

"No," Aeryn sobbed.

She gripped Aric like it was her lifeline. "Strife!" She drew a pitchfork in the dirt. "I call Ireteah, Lady of Hardship, and smite thy hordes with pestilence."

Ireteah's symbol on Aric's blade glowed, but her father shouted at her more loudly, and neither he nor Trion faded out of existence.

"You wanted me to die, so you could be free of me and find your glory away from my shadow. Coward!"

Aric suddenly burned like an inferno in her hands. Aeryn cried out in pain and dropped the sword. Rimen and her father and The Harbinger all laughed at her. The sound became a cacophony. She fell to her knees, clapping her hands over her ears. She closed her eyes as Rimen and her father advanced on her.

"This isn't real!" she shouted again.

Rimen's staff cracked her over the back, and she fell to the ground, gasping in pain.

"Now you are mine!" The Harbinger laughed in her ears.

67

The Harbinger's laughter echoed through the chamber, a horrid sound, filled with gloating and wicked amusement. Theo would have given anything to shut him up in that moment. Caeleb, Ferrin, Loric, and Colin were rapidly losing ground to The Harbinger's soldiers. Whenever one of them gripped her companions, their touch seemed to have a numbing effect, slowing down all but Thystle.

The vampyre was a fiend in battle, hacking through The Harbinger's minions one after another. Her eyes glowed bright red as she fought with all the fury of a wild animal, taking on multiple attackers at once and ripping out throats at every chance she got. Despite her efforts, however, Thystle was still only one fighter. The rest of them would be dead long before she managed to finish off The Harbinger's army. So Theo decided it was up to her to help the rest of them.

She made the most terrifying battle cry she could manage and leaped at the soldier attacking Caeleb. She sliced into its leg with her dagger. It let go of Caeleb and turned on her. Backpedaling, she swung her dagger at the soldier, trying to fend it off. Released from the soldier's grip, Caeleb shook his head like a man waking from a long nap and beheaded the soldier as it grabbed for Theo.

He nodded when she thanked him and then turned away to aid the others. The tide turned back in her companions' favor again. But then, Aeryn faltered and fell silent.

A sudden rumble came from overhead. Theo looked up to see the ceiling of the chamber shaking. *"Look out!"* she cried as huge rocks tumbled from the ceiling. She flung herself to the side but was clipped in the shoulder by one of the rock. She cried out in pain.

Thystle grabbed her up and covered her as more rocks fell. The others scattered around them to avoid the falling rocks. Several of The Harbinger's soldiers were also felled. Loric was struck in the back and rolled to the ground. Colin shouted his name and then raised his staff over his head.

"Domri rez!" A shimmering dome appeared above his staff and spread out to cover the seven companions. The falling rocks bounced off the shimmering shield, then stopped falling.

Dots of sweat appeared on Colin's forehead. Loric rose and went to his brother. "Don't exhaust yourself. Save your strength." The protective dome collapsed.

"Keep going!" Caeleb called to Aeryn.

Theo heard Aeryn call Ireteah and pestilence against The Harbinger's soldiers. Many of them grabbed their throats and tumbled to the cavern floor. They did not move again. Theo laughed out loud.

The Harbinger shouted in a rage, "Rise, my evil ones!"

A hand burst free from the dirt, followed by an arm. Dozens of dead men clawed their way upward out of the ground. A hand grabbed Theo's ankle and pulled her foot into the dirt. She screamed in terror. Thystle growled and chopped the hand off, pulling Theo away.

The dead men let out a collective howl. The other remaining soldiers took up their battle cry and amplified it. The sound filled the chamber. The Harbinger started laughing as the renewed forces fell on her companions again. It was then that Theo realized she could no longer hear Aeryn. She looked back and saw the sell-sword doubled over on the ground. Aric lay in the mud next to her.

"Aeryn!"

Thystle turned to look. "Go, help her," she shouted above the howling of the soldiers and The Harbinger's laughter.

Theo ran to Aeryn's side, calling her name.

Suddenly, Aeryn's hand shot out and grabbed her, pulling Theo roughly to her by her collar. She cried out, "Aeryn, stop! You're hurting me."

Aeryn grinned in her face and did not let go. Her storm-gray eyes had turned to red. When Aeryn spoke, Brien's voice came out of her mouth. *"Hello, sister."*

"Oh, gods," Theo sobbed.

Brien voice laughed at her. *"Don't bother weeping. Did you think you'd never see me again? Lucky you. I've come to ask you why you let me die. Willa, too. It's your fault we're dead and part of The Harbinger now."*

"No. No, that's not true!" Her hands shook as they grabbed hold of Aeryn's wrist. The sell-sword's grip on her was like iron.

"Of course it is, little sister. So, as repayment for your betrayal, you're going to know the same suffering I did before I died." Aeryn raised her dagger to Theo's throat.

Theo tried to pull away, but she could not. The things with Aeryn's face and her brother's voice grinned more broadly as Theo felt the blade cut into her flesh with painstaking slowness. The creature that possessed Aeryn meant to slit her throat, and do so in a way that she would feel her own flesh tearing away. Was this how Pythun had killed her brother? Tears spilled down Theo's face as she begged Aeryn to wake up.

Suddenly, the pommel of a sword came down on Aeryn's wrist, breaking her grip on Theo's collar. Caeleb shouted at Aeryn and kicked her in the ribs, away from Theo. Aeryn rolled away from her, and Theo fell to her knees, sobbing. She grabbed at the wound on her neck. It was not too long and did not bleed too heavily. Her whole body shook with the understanding that Caeleb had reached her just in time.

The sell-sword recovered and knelt with her back to Theo and Caeleb. The paladin shouted at Aeryn to wake up. Aeryn shook her head and turned and then charged him. Caeleb grabbed her when she collided with him. They fell to the ground, each wrestling for control of the other. Caeleb managed to get an arm free and punched Aeryn in the side of her head, at the same time shouting, *"Purify!"*

Blood poured from a cut caused by a ring on Caeleb's hand, but this time, when Aeryn shook her head, the spell she was under seemed to break. Caeleb let go of her.

"I'm alright," Aeryn whispered.

She rolled over and looked at Theo and the trickle of blood that ran down her neck. She grabbed Theo again and held her in a tight embrace. "I'm sorry," Aeryn told her in her own voice, thick with emotion. "I'm so sorry."

Theo buried her face in the sell-sword's shoulder, just relieved Aeryn was Aeryn again.

Then, Aeryn let go of her and grabbed Aric from the cavern floor. It seemed to pain her to do this, but she gripped the sword tightly. She choked out, "I call Anora, Lady of Hearts, and purify your evil with *love*." She drew a heart in the mud and another symbol glowed on Aric's blade.

The Harbinger roared in unmistakable pain. His soldiers joined him.

"Keep it up!" Caeleb shouted at her.

"Now, you will die." Raising his arms again, The Harbinger said, "I call Chaos!"

The Harbinger threw a burst of yellow energy at his remaining soldiers. Theo spun around to see each of them double and then triple. She cried out in disbelief as The Harbinger's forces returned to their original numbers. The soldier's faces shifted and twisted until they became the faces of hideous demons. They closed ranks.

Aeryn cried out, "I call Aspen, Lady of Nature and the Forest, to bind your minions." She drew a tree in the mud. Almost all of the symbols on Aric's blade glowed now.

Roots burst forth from the ground and snagged the ankles of the soldiers fighting Caeleb and the others. The soldiers howled with fury, but their cries were cut off as the others started to cut them down. The Harbinger called upon Chaos again, but then Aeryn shouted him down.

"In the name of Cira, controller of the Stars and High Mother to all mortals and gods, I take back Symon's powers from you. I reclaim that which you stole from the Lord of Madness, Keeper of Chaos and Luck. I restore his power and restore Symon to the pantheon that rejected you before, Kaliphesh, and does so again now!" She drew stars in the mud.

The Harbinger cursed her. Suddenly, the number of soldiers in the chamber was cut to just a handful. The extra soldiers The Harbinger created were nothing more than illusions. Thystle and the others made short work of the remaining soldiers.

The Harbinger took a lumbering step forward.

"Keep him in the circle!" Aeryn shouted at the others.

Theo saw the fallen god's hideous face tighten with a purpose. His clawed hands curled into massive fists as he charged toward her and Aeryn. Theo flashed back to The Harbinger's serpent maw bearing down on her, but this time she did not freeze. She pushed Aeryn out of the way.

Caeleb, Thystle, and Loric ran to intercept The Harbinger, but Ferrin arrived first. Swinging his sword mightily, the red-haired man sliced open The Harbinger's legs in two places. The Harbinger stumbled but kept his feet. The wounds closed, though slowly.

Ferrin's face twisted with dissatisfaction, and he swung again, but his blow was struck aside. The Harbinger seized Ferrin by his arms.

The Harbinger raised him high enough to look Ferrin in the eye and then he ripped Ferrin's arms off. They separated from his body with a wet pop, like that of drumsticks being pulled from a roasted chicken. Theo turned away, hands clapped over her ears. Still, she heard Ferrin's body land. The Harbinger laughed.

The others screamed in fury. Theo turned back to see them attack The Harbinger as one. The fallen god was forced backward again by their attacks. Colin ran forward and dragged the sceptor's son back from the fighting, toward her and Aeryn. She did not want to look at him, but she heard him whimpering and felt compelled to go to him as his life

338

drained away.

She knelt down next to Colin. The young cleric sobbed as he prayed over Ferrin's dying body. Blood ran down his face from a deep cut on his forehead, but he did not seem to notice.

"What do I do?" she whispered to no one in particular.

Ferrin looked at her, blood trickling from the corner of his mouth. "Did I do well, Father?"

Theo choked on a sudden lump in her throat. She nodded. "You did great."

Ferrin smiled faintly, and then he was gone.

"Aephis has an honored place for you in his great hall. Go in peace," Colin told him.

The Harbinger expressed no pity for Ferrin's passing. He bellowed, "You cannot stop me! I am eternal."

He struck Thystle aside and swung at Caeleb. Caeleb managed to dodge the blow in time. Thystle rolled with the force of The Harbinger's strike but got up slowly, stunned. Caeleb and Loric rushed The Harbinger, shoving him back into the binding circle.

As soon as The Harbinger crossed the line of the half-circle, Aeryn said, "I call Aephis, controller of the Sun and Heavens, High Father to Mortals and Gods, and ruler over all. I bind you." She drew a circle below the stars she had already drawn in the mud.

The last symbol on Aric's blade glowed, making seven in total. The half-circle Aeryn drew around The Harbinger's throne flared bright white, and Caeleb and Loric jumped back. Just as they did, a wall of energy rose up from the ground, sealing The Harbinger behind it.

"You cannot stop Terror," The Harbinger growled.

Aeryn fell to her knees in obvious pain. Still, she raised Aric over her head, with the black orb facing The Harbinger. The sword's blade started to glow now.

"You are a false god with false ways. By the power of the eight eldest gods known by Man, I steal your life," the sell-sword said through gritted teeth.

"No."

A black mist poured out of The Harbinger's mouth and flowed into the black orb. The Harbinger's legs buckled, and his horned head drooped, then his entire body tipped to the side and fell. The chamber shook with the weight of his fall.

The others backed toward where Theo and Colin stood, behind Aeryn.

"May the light push back the darkness you've brought to this land once and for all," Aeryn said.

A beam of white light shot out from Aric and struck The Harbinger's body. The light spread out until it encompassed the god's entire form. The intensity of the light grew until it was too much for Theo to look at. She shielded her eyes. Someone grabbed her and began pulling her back as a warm wind picked up in the cavern.

Theo called Aeryn's name as she was dragged back toward the passageway into the cavern. Aric became a hot white dot. Through her fingers, Theo could just make out a dark shape still standing with Aric.

Over the roar of the hot wind, she heard Aeryn shout, "That which was unbound is bound once more!"

Then, a burst of light, wind, and heat came from where Aeryn and Aric had been. Theo and the others were thrown the rest of the way to the passage, where they landed on their backs. Debris pelted Theo's face and arms. She tried to scream Aeryn's name again, but dust and acrid smoke choked her.

The burst of energy faded away, and the chamber fell quiet once more. She heard Aric clatter to the ground a moment later, a stark and hollow sound, as though the entire sword was now spent. Theo ventured to open her eyes. The others stirred as well. They were all scratched, cut, and dirty, but seemed otherwise unharmed by the explosion.

The wooden posts around the sacrificial pit had been knocked over and scattered, and the remains still chained to them looked all the more piteous, lying on their sides on the dirt floor. Theo looked for Aeryn and saw her lying near where The Harbinger's body had been. Aric lay beside her.

Theo jumped to her feet and ran to the sell-sword's side. She gently turned her onto her back. Somehow, the blast had not burned her, but she was covered in deep cuts from the explosion wherever her armor pieces did not cover her. She seemed to be bleeding from everywhere at once. The sell-sword's blood coated Theo's hands. Its metallic smell filled her nostrils.

Aeryn stirred in Theo's hands, and Theo was relieved that she was still alive at least. She brushed stands of Aeryn's dark hair away from her face and spoke her name. Caeleb and the others came over to her side.

Thystle picked up Aric. The black orb Allemar had given Aeryn was gone, but a round scorch pattern on Aric's blade marked where it had been. Thystle wrapped Aeryn's fingers around its hilt, perhaps believing the sword might heal her. It did not.

"You have to help her," Theo whispered to the others.

Loric tore strips of cloth from his own shirt and began wrapping Aeryn's wounds while Colin closed his eyes and whispered the words to a prayer or a healing spell, Theo could not tell which.

Aeryn's eyes fluttered open. Her storm-gray eyes looked up at Theo but seemed not to see. "I can hardly see you," she said.

"It was the light," Caeleb said, his voice catching as he spoke. "It will pass. You'll be just fine."

Theo saw the tears in Caeleb's eyes. She knew his words were full of lies. He thought Aeryn was going to die, like Ferrin had. Theo looked at Aeryn again, stricken. "You have to help her," she repeated with more force.

Caeleb put a smile onto his face as he squeezed her shoulder and laid a hand on Aeryn. "We'll take care of her. I told you we'd look out for each other, didn't I?"

Aeryn reached for and found Theo's arm. "You don't have to be afraid anymore," she whispered. The sell-sword's eyes slipped closed again.

"Aeryn? Aeryn. Open your eyes." Theo's lip quivered.

She shook Aeryn gently, but the sell-sword did not stir. Theo shook her again, harder. Thystle touched her arm and whispered her name, but Theo pushed her hand away. She looked down at Aeryn while Loric bandaged her and Colin prayed.

Theo moved forward and rested her head on Aeryn's body. She listened to the ragged breaths enter and leave her. Tears rolled down Theo's face, soaking into Aeryn's shirt. She closed her eyes as sobs wracked her small body.

Don't leave me alone again, Theo silently begged.

68

When Aeryn was fourteen, she witnessed her first real battle. She did not participate in the fighting—Derrick forbade her to—but she helped the other soldiers collect the wounded and the dying when the fighting was over. Her father put her in charge of the care for one of the wounded soldiers, saying it would be a good experience for her. He told her to keep the man's wounds clean and dry and make sure he had fresh water whenever he asked for it. Aeryn followed his instructions to the letter, but the soldier never woke. On the fifth day, he died.

At the time, she could not understand why. *"I did everything I was told to,"* she said to her father, trying hard not to let him see her cry. Her heart felt broken somehow for this man who never even opened his eyes to look upon her.

"Sometimes we do everything we are supposed to and things still don't turn out the way we think they should, Aeryn," her father explained to her, his arm around her shoulders as they watched the sun set over the man's funeral pyre.

Aeryn took his words and locked them inside herself to remember, like she did with everything he told her. Then, she asked, *"What is death like?"*

Her father did not answer for a long time. She looked up at him finally and found him staring into the bright orange and red clouds that surrounded the descending sun. He looked deeper in thought than she had ever seen him. Then, he met her gaze and said, *"It's a question I've often asked myself, and I still have no answer to give you."* It was the first time he had admitted that he did not have an answer for her.

"The teachings of Morghell say that how you are in this life determines where you will go when you die. Fortesis tells us that all

warriors who fight well for a cause they feel is righteous will go on to fight again in his Afterlands and dine in his great hall each night. I suppose other religions have other theories, too."

"*But what do you believe, Father?*"

"*I don't know that, either.*"

"*When I die, do you think I will see you again?*" she asked him.

Her father smiled down at her. "*Of course. Wherever it is we go, I will be there, waiting for you. I promise.*"

But he was not there.

Everything was black. She heard nothing and saw nothing. For her, death was empty and still.

69

Sunlight landed on her eyelids, intruding on her repose and forcing them open. Aeryn groaned. The light struck her eyes, blinding her. With effort, she raised her hand to shield her eyes, but then, too tired still, she let her hand drop and sufficed with turning her head slightly to the side to get at least one eye out of the path of the sunlight. It was then that she noticed someone was next to her.

A small face rose into her view, blocking the light and casting a shadow over her face. She realized the light was coming from a window directly across from where she lay. Now that it was blocked, the rest of the room started to resolve around her. It was painted white. Even the window coverings were white.

"Hello," Theo said.

At first, Aeryn just stared at her. "What are you doing here?" Her throat felt dry as a desert, and her voice cracked when she spoke.

Theo's face clouded over. "I've been waiting for you to wake up."

"Wake." Aeryn frowned. She had avoided death after all.

Her frown faded as relief found her. Aeryn realized that her survival meant being forced to put off her reunion with her father, but she decided this was for the best. She knew she would see him again when it was her time, and this was not it.

She asked the girl, "How long?"

"Four days," was the answer.

Aeryn felt baffled. She did not remember a single one of them. Her last full memory was of completing the binding spell. An explosion and a blinding light. Her friends' voices around her. A voice telling her to sleep.

"Caeleb, Allemar, and Colin did everything they could, but for a while, your injuries didn't respond to their prayers or spells and wouldn't heal. No one could say why. Even when they did, though, you didn't wake up," Theo told her.

"Tynan tried to help you, too, but you still didn't wake. Colin said it might have something to do with the binding spell, like it drained you, but Allemar said you were on the edge of the Great Gap, deciding which way to go. I was worried you would . . ." Theo's voice trailed off.

Aeryn saw the hard exterior that Theo tried to keep melt away. In its wake, a young girl frightened of being abandoned again remained.

"I'm still here," Aeryn told her.

Theo nodded. She quietly asked, "Would you like some water?" When Aeryn nodded, Theo handed her a cool mug.

As she sipped the soothing liquid, Theo said, "You scared me shitless."

Aeryn smiled, but she told her, "You shouldn't say things like that, you're too young." She was starting to feel stronger.

She finished the water and gave the empty mug back. Theo set it on a table near the bed. It was painted white like the rest of the room.

Theo frowned. "I don't feel too young to say it."

Looking into Theo's eyes, Aeryn found she could not argue with her. She saw more maturity in the girl's eyes than should ever be forced on someone so young. Aeryn reached out a hand to brush a strand of Theo's blond hair out of her eyes. It and the rest of Theo was clean again. All the dust and filth from The Harbinger's lair had been washed away.

Aeryn pushed the girl's hair back from her neck, where her own dagger had cut Theo. There was no mark there. Aeryn wondered what reminders lay under the surface, unseen.

"It's okay," Theo told her, knowing what Aeryn was thinking.

"It's not," Aeryn replied.

She remembered all of it, even though she watched it through a cloud of darkness. She remembered The Harbinger taking control of her during her lapse. She remembered him making her say those things to Theo and raising the dagger to cut her.

"I let his darkness take over." Her hand shook slightly.

Theo took it. "It doesn't matter anymore. He's gone. He almost ended all of us, but he didn't."

Aeryn nodded and took a deep breath, letting it out slowly. She closed her eyes a moment and then pushed herself up into a sitting position, leaning against the mountain of pillows that were behind her head. Her arms and shoulders still ached, and she was still covered in bandages.

"Who did this?" she asked.

"Colin mostly. I helped sometimes."

"I should thank him." Aeryn glanced toward the door on the other side of the small white room. "Where are the others?"

"Downstairs with Allemar. They're helping to put the worship hall back in order. The refugees have all gone," Theo replied. "I think Tynan will want to talk to you now that you've woken up. He's been anxious for you to get well again. He's leaving us."

Aeryn said, "I'm not planning on staying either." When a renewed look of fear passed over Theo's face again, she added, "I'm not suggesting that I'm going to leave you here. I'm just saying that I don't plan to stay in Pius. I feel well enough to travel, and to be honest, I'd like to be gone from this city as soon as I can."

"Running off again, are you?" Thystle said from the doorway. Aeryn had not heard her come in, and judging from the way Theo jumped when Thystle spoke, she had not either.

"I finished what I came here to do."

"I hope you were planning on at least saying good-bye first. I think Caeleb would be very disappointed if you didn't. All those nights by your bedside wasted." Thystle smirked at her, but Aeryn sensed something hidden behind her words. Hurt over her sudden departure

347

maybe.

"Of course I was going to say good-bye to everyone," Aeryn replied. To her horror, a flush rose to her cheeks at the thought of Caeleb by her bedside. She kept talking, hoping neither Theo nor Thystle noticed it. "Besides, you are always welcome to come with me with us, if you'd like."

Thystle shook her head. "I appreciate the offer, but I have things of my own to attend to. Where will you go from here?"

"I think I will head north again, back to Belhaun."

"Well, I've had four more days than you to hang around here. I'm not anxious to stay any longer either," Theo said as she retrieved Aeryn's clothes from a chair by the door and handed them to her.

Thystle suggested that they leave Aeryn to dress in private and tell the others that she was awake. When they had gone, Aeryn took a deep breath and carefully pulled back the white sheets and blankets. She decided that the amount of white in the room was enough to put her off the color for a lifetime.

Slowly, she put her feet on the floor. Her statement to Theo that she felt well enough to travel was a small falsehood. She still felt somewhat weak and tired, but this city was not the place in which she wanted to recover. As kind as Allemar and the rest had been to her, she felt anxious to put some distance between her and the city where The Harbinger had almost killed her. She had to admit she would miss her new companions—she just could not resign herself to the thought of one more day in Pius.

Aeryn dressed herself, mindful of the bandages as she slipped on her leather leggings and woven shirt, both of which had several cuts in them that were now mended. Aeryn wondered if the mending was Colin's handiwork as well. By the time she had pulled on her boots, she felt strong enough to walk around and did so with small steps.

There was a light knock on the door, and she looked over to see Colin hovering in the doorway, his back to the room. She could not help but smile.

"Come in, Colin."

The young cleric came into the room. "Theo said you were getting dressed, so I didn't want to barge in."

"It's fine. I was going to come downstairs soon."

"Oh, well, I thought you might need some help with your bandages."

She smiled to cover a wince as she bent to pick up her belt and baldric from the chair. One of the cuts across her ribs was not quite healed and let her know it. "No, they're all fine. I wanted to thank you. Did you mend my clothes, too?"

He blushed at her thanks. "It was really a group effort. The clothes, though, that was Theo. She's rather adept with a needle and thread." Colin paused as his pale eyes looked around the room. Finally, he asked her, "Can I help you downstairs? I mean, if you do not need help, I understand, I just thought I would offer, in case."

At first, Aeryn was going to politely refuse his help, but as she put on her cloak, other wounds quietly complained, so she accepted. "Thank you. I'm stiff from lying in a bed for four days."

He nodded and put his arm around her waist. Aeryn put her arm over his shoulder and let him support some of her weight as she made her way to the door. She felt silly leaning on the young cleric for support, but realized she would feel even more embarrassed if she collapsed.

"What about Ferrin? Was there a memorial?" she asked, to take her mind off needing his support.

Colin did not respond for a moment, then he said, "His body was mutilated in the explosion, so they burned his remains in the courtyard of Symon's ruined temple rather than let Allemar see what was left of him. They brought his ashes back. We blessed them and then buried them here on the grounds."

"It was probably for the best that they brought only his ashes back."

349

The young cleric agreed as he helped her down the marble staircase. "They managed to get his body just in time, too. Loric told me that the rest of the temple collapsed as they were riding away. The Harbinger's tunnel and chambers must have caved in. There's nothing but a crater now. No one else can go down into that accursed place. I have to say I'm pleased."

Aeryn was relieved as well.

70

Near the bottom of the stairs, she withdrew her arm from his shoulders, thanking him for his help. Colin nodded and let go of her waist, but stayed close to her the rest of the way down. The others waited for them in the worship hall. Caeleb smiled when he saw her, and she found herself smiling back, even as she realized that Tynan was not among the group.

Allemar came forward and took her hands in his. He looked better than he had the last time she saw him. He said to her, "I am pleased you are awake finally. Are you sure you should be up so soon, though?"

She nodded. "I feel well enough, and I would like to be on my way again as soon as I can. I hope you understand."

Sadness touched his eyes as he replied that he did. "I cannot imagine that our city holds a good place in your heart. You have gone through much suffering these last days, and I do not doubt that you would prefer to put it behind you as quickly as you can."

"Coming to Pius was not all bad for me. But yes, I think it would be good for me to start fresh. Please accept my thanks for all you have done, I greatly appreciate it, and my deepest condolences over the death of your son. Ferrin fought well against The Harbinger and died heroically."

"Caeleb has told me so as well." He let go of her hands and clasped his own in front of him. For a moment, she thought Allemar was going to pray, but then he said, "I have faith that Ferrin has earned his place at Aephis's side, and that someday we will see each other again."

Unsure what else to say, Aeryn only nodded. Looking around at the others, she asked, "Where is Tynan?"

"He told me he would wait for you outside in the stables," Allemar answered. "If you will excuse me, I must stay here and finish readying the hall. I will have my first sermon since The Harbinger's attack tomorrow at sunrise. The rest of you, please go and say your good-byes to Aeryn and Theo."

Aeryn said good-bye to Allemar again and headed outside. The others followed her as she walked toward the temple stables. Caeleb walked beside her.

"I know I can't change your mind about leaving, but I hope you'll consider visiting us again," he told her.

"I'd like that," she said.

The others stopped outside the stables and let her walk the rest of the way on her own. She saw Tynan standing by Rowan's stall. He had shed his borrowed body and now stood facing her in his ghostly form. The way he looked at Aeryn told her that his leaving was going to be final this time.

"I wanted to give you a chance to see all of your friends before you had to talk to me," Tynan told her as she entered the stables.

The smell of the hay and dirt and wood brought her back to life a little more. She looked at Tynan for a moment and then swallowed past a sudden lump in her throat. "You are one of my friends."

He smiled. It was the most genuine smile she had seen on him since their first meeting. "That gladdens me to hear. I had wondered if it was possible for me to win back any of your trust."

"You did." Aeryn searched words. "I . . . I know that I was angry with you for a long time, and I cannot forgive your deceptions. However, I realize now that you really were doing what you thought was right at the time."

"Perhaps. Even I have my doubts about my actions in certain instances."

"I don't want you to go," she quietly said. It occurred to her that it was his voice that she had heard, telling her to sleep when she was injured in The Harbinger's lair. He had kept his word to be with her all the way to the end. "You helped me to defeat The Harbinger. That means a lot to me."

Tynan shook his head. "Allemar's orb and Aric did most of the work, and your strength and the strength of those with you did the rest. As for leaving, however, I am afraid that I must."

He stepped toward her and pointed at Aric standing against the door of Rowan's stall. "I have left Aric here for you. Its powers have been spent, and it is little more than an ordinary sword now, but I would like you to keep it, to remind you of me from time to time. Caeleb was kind enough to sharpen it and polish it to refresh its shine, and he did a marvelous job."

It was true. The sword shone like never before. Even the scorch mark left by the binding orb was no longer in evidence.

"I will do that." She looked from Aric back to Tynan. "Where will you go then?"

"To whatever lies beyond life and this half-death I exist in now. In Valis, Sevnor told me I would be unable to move on until I let go of the lure this mortal world held for me. I was angry at the time that he said that. But, over the last several days, watching you ride off to fight The Harbinger without me and then sitting by your bed with the others, waiting for you to choose to live, I realized that the material items and accomplishments I collected in life mean nothing once life is gone.

"It is a gift to have people around you who care for you, Aeryn. All the impressive stories about my deeds and the items to prove the stories are worthless now. Friends, family, love. Those are the only ways to true immortality. With all that I gained in life—Aric, the gold, and the Black Caverns—I died a poor man.

"I believe I was close to realizing that before I died, but I forgot all of it quickly enough. Egotism was my true downfall. You helped me to remember that lesson. For that, I thank you from the bottom of my heart. You showed me the way home again." He looked at her and said,

"It saddens me to leave you, but it is time for me to move on finally. And Theo . . ."

Aeryn looked over to see the girl lurking nearby.

Theo raised a hand to stop him. "Don't say it, I've said enough good-byes lately, and I'd rather not say anymore. How about we just settle for see you later?"

Tynan smiled. "As you wish, little one. I will see you later, as you say." He looked at Aeryn again.

"See you later, Tynan," she said, choking on the words.

"See you later, Aeryn." He laid his hand on her shoulder, but she did not feel its touch. "Thank you again for freeing me from my self-made prison. Live well."

Turning away, Tynan walked to the door of the stables. He stopped at the entrance to look back at them once more and then walked out. Aeryn watched him go, wanting to say more, but knowing that she had to let him go.

With each step, his ghostly form faded a little, until he faded completely away. She walked to the doors and stared after where she saw him last, waiting to see if he would reappear. He did not.

"The man sure knows how to make an exit," Thystle said, a sad smile on her face below her dark spectacles.

Devil stood next to her, and his reins rested in her hands. She mounted and looked down at Aeryn. "I'm not one for long good-byes, so I think I'll take his exit as my cue and leave as well."

Aeryn nodded and embraced Thystle when she leaned down. "It was good to see you again," she said to her friend. "Be careful in your travels."

"I always am," the vampyre said with a laugh. To Theo, she said, "Try to keep Aeryn out of trouble."

"I will."

Thystle turned Devil and nudged him into a canter down the street. Aeryn did not watch Thystle until she disappeared from view as she had Tynan. She wanted to hold on to the idea that they at least would see each other again in the near future. She turned to Caeleb, who was leading Rowan out of the stables, fully outfitted.

"And then there were five," Caeleb said with wry humor. He handed Aric to her along with Rowan's reins.

Aeryn sheathed Aric in its permanent home next to the sheath holding her father's sword. "I want to thank all of you for all that you have done. Especially you, Colin, for taking such good care of me while I was injured." Aeryn gave the blushing cleric a brief embrace.

Loric was more stoic as she clasped his wrist in a traditional adventurer's farewell. "I'd gladly fight by your side again, Aeryn. If ever you need us, you know where we'll be."

"I know. The same to you, Loric."

Caeleb smiled down at her as she came to him last. "Remember what I said about coming to Pius again. I didn't say it idly."

She smiled back. "I know."

Before she had a chance to think better of it, Aeryn leaned toward Caeleb and kissed him on his cheek, resting her hand lightly on his shoulder. She murmured in his ear, "Thank you for staying with me. If you ever find yourself in the north . . ."

"Definitely," he said as she pulled away again.

Aeryn turned away quickly. As she turned, she caught a quick look of jealousy in Theo's eyes. The look was fleeting though.

"Come on," Aeryn said, laughing quietly.

Theo waved to the three men as Aeryn led Rowan out of the stable yard.

Walking eased the ache in her muscles. When the temple had passed out of sight, Aeryn chanced to take a deep breath of air and relax. She pulled her cloak tighter around her. It was still cold, but this cold seemed less ominous to her. Aeryn smelled a hint of wood smoke in the air, and it brought to mind warm hearths for once, rather than a burning city.

"Well, I see the weather hasn't improved with the slaying of The Harbinger," Theo complained while looking up at the now gray-white sky. It began to snow.

"I disagree," Aeryn said. She watched sporadic snowflakes collect in Theo's hair and realized that for once, the snow was just snow, and not another reminder of her father's passing. She smiled at the thought.

When she noticed a smithy on the street ahead, Aeryn decided they should stop to buy Rowan new shoes before they left Pius. She told Theo, "After the way we pushed him, I think he deserves to have something nice done for him."

Theo nodded and patted the stallion's shoulder. "Caeleb taught me how to care for Rowan and how to ride a little, too. I hope that's okay."

"It's fine. It was probably good for Rowan to get a little exercise."

The smithy, a short man with a blond mustache that curled on the ends, told them it would take at least the afternoon before he could shoe Rowan. Aeryn suggested to Theo that they restock their supplies while they waited. Theo readily agreed, and they set off for the marketplace near from the smithy's shop, packs in hand.

Merchants belted out sales pitches for their wares, each promising the best quality, and musicians played soft strains of music to attract a coin or two from the passersby. As they circulated among the various carts and stalls, Aeryn quickly found that Theo had the same affliction as most children and was easily distracted by the vendors selling brightly colored but useless trinkets. She had to extract the girl from the stalls of several such merchants. Surprisingly, she did not notice the young thief trying to steal from a single one of them.

Normal life seemed to have returned to Pius. The survivors of The Harbinger's siege on the city moved through the market in thick crowds. The resilience of people never ceased to amaze Aeryn. If any of them knew what she and Theo had been a part of below the city, they gave no indication. Pius's citizens kept their attention on their work and their errands, and only a few met Aeryn's gaze, and then only long enough to smile a greeting before they moved on.

After the third time Theo strayed from her side, Aeryn turned to tell Theo to leave the vendors' carts alone or they would return to wait at the smithy's shop. Something caught her attention as she did so, however. She turned her head to get a better look and froze. She squeezed Theo's shoulder to get her attention.

"Ouch, that hurt. I wasn't doing—" the girl's voice trailed off as she saw Aeryn staring.

A small gray figure with black eyes and leathery gray skin tottered toward them, arms outstretched. One of The Harbinger's body gatherers.

"It can't be," Aeryn said. A chill went up her spine as she watched the little creature stalk toward them.

Before she could reach for Aric, the wrinkly creature tripped over a rock and fell forward. It started crying. A man in blue and purple velvet ran up to the sobbing creature and grabbed hold of him. The image of the creature faded away, nothing more than an enchantment, and a little blond-haired boy was left in its place.

Aeryn released her vise-hold on Theo's shoulder as the man helped the boy up and held him. The man tucked the silver wand in his hand into his belt and picked the boy up, murmuring to him. There was a small cut on the boy's nose, but otherwise, he appeared unharmed by his fall.

Then, the man turned and noticed Aeryn and Theo staring.

He gave them and unsure smile. "My son Petr wanted to try out his costume for the Festival of Masques. It's still a month away, I know, but you know little boys."

Aeryn could not find her voice, so sure was she that nothing was over after all.

Theo replied for her. "It was a great costume. He had me totally fooled."

Finally, Aeryn nodded. "Completely," she agreed.

The man smiled again and turned away, bouncing Petr a little. The boy laughed and hugged his father's neck. As she watched them walk away, Aeryn took a deep breath and let it out. She had to relax, she told herself.

"I knew it wasn't one of those things," Theo said as they started walking again.

Aeryn allowed herself to laugh.

"Maybe I thought it was for a moment. But, *just* a moment." The girl looked around as if she expected another little creature to jump out from behind one of the vendors' carts. "You know, I'm sure it's been an hour. Rowan must be ready, don't you think?"

Aeryn agreed. "Let us get a couple more things and then we'll see if he's ready."

When they finished gathering supplies and were headed back to the smithy, she asked Theo, "What would you say about us not returning north the way we came? How about we follow the coast instead?" She had no need to see their route south again, even with The Harbinger gone. She wanted to put those memories aside for now and move forward.

"Sounds like a great idea," Theo replied. "I've never seen the ocean."

Aeryn smiled and reached out to ruffle the girl's hair.

Ducking her hand, Theo said, "Hey, I'll race you back to the smithy's shop. Last one there has to buy the winner supper." She added, "From someplace other than here."

Aeryn paused before she replied, wondering how that would work, seeing as how the young thief had no gold or silver of her own.

Theo then said, "I guess that'll be you either way, but . . . *Go!*" The girl took off.

Aeryn just stared after her. She took her saddlebags off her shoulder and tucked them under her arm. Once Theo realized Aeryn was not following her, she stopped and turned back.

"What's the matter, afraid you can't catch me?" Theo called out.

Aeryn said nothing. Theo started to walk back, asking if she was alright.

She let the girl get halfway back and then started running. Theo let out a delighted squeak and almost tripped over her own feet in her haste to turn back again and keep Aeryn's long strides from closing the gap between them. Laughing, Aeryn chased after her, telling herself that she would be damned if she would let the young thief beat her. Her father had taught her better than that.

SPECIAL EDITION BONUS MATERIAL

I: THE FALL OF TYNAN SELVANTYR

The story of Tynan's demise, as told by Tynan to Theo, without too much embellishment . . .

Author's Note

In the original printing of the book, the story that follows appeared as a prologue (minus Tynan and Theo's interactions). With the new edition, I decided to remove the prologue, since readers don't need to know how Tynan died in order to understand the larger story in the novel. However, I decided to still include it as a short story in this edition, because I think it's a story worth telling (and so does Tynan, of course). I think it works even better in this format. — *A.M. Rycroft*

The Fall of Tynan Selvantyr

Theo tossed about under her blankets, the night too quiet now for her to sleep. She opened her eyes to see Tynan still awake, poking at the fire. Aeryn was asleep nearby, and she guessed the others were, too. The dead man looked over at her when she sat up.

"Can you not sleep, little one?" he asked her.

She shook her head.

"Shall I tell you a story?"

A slow smile spread over her face. "Tell me how you died."

"Ah." A similar smile touched his face. "Settle in, young Theo, and I will tell you that tale most interesting."

Theo gathered her blankets around her. He began.

A chill hung on the late summer air, imparting the promise of an early and cold autumn, and yet the sky still remained true. Tynan Selvantyr turned and shielded his eyes, the same shade of sapphire blue as the sky, and looked up at the sun high on the horizon. Its rays simmered against his deep red cloak, despite the coolness in the air. He studied the sun's position behind him and determined that, with the steady pace of his golden stallion, Duraden, they would reach the top of the mountain ridge by midafternoon and arrive at Nightstone Peak soon after. Tynan lowered his hand and turned back at the mountain pass ahead of them.

He looked around at the dark rock of the Black Mountains, and as usual, he saw no one. Few people traveled through the winding passes, and no one other than he called them home. Their terrain was simply too treacherous and the environment too inhospitable. For the most part, Tynan did not mind the solitude, as he liked to brag whenever he could about the uniqueness of his home in the Black Caverns, buried deep

1

within the Black Mountains' Nightstone Peak.

Today, however, the solitude did not please him.

Everyone knew his name: Tynan Darius Selvantyr, the illustrious adventurer who wielded both great magiks and a great sword. He had personally made sure of it. Born sixth in the line of eight children, Tynan learned at an early age to prove his uniqueness to garner the attention of his father, Scanlon Selvantyr, a prominent armor merchant in the southern city of Acantha, or anyone else.

This proved difficult, considering the family's merchant business and their involvement in Acantha's politics was everything to Scanlon, but Tynan had little interest in either. He expressed this to his father at a young age, much to Scanlon's fury.

Unlike other men of noble birth such as he, Tynan's passions fell in the realms of travel and the rough life of adventuring. When his abilities as a sword-wielder and magik-wielder fully bloomed, Tynan set off with his best friend Rimen, son of Scanlon's elven gamekeeper Trion Orinthwend, and headed north, leaving his family far behind.

He and Rimen quickly formed their own adventuring group, the Company of Seven Strong, and after two decades of adventuring, the bards of Cathell sang Tynan's name in every tavern and noble court across the northern regions and beyond. He loved the fortune and renown he had gained in the pursuit of his passion for high adventure. But, he was alone.

For all the fame and fortune he amassed, friends were few and far between. Jealousy and rivalry earned him more enemies than true friends. Even Rimen, the only one who truly understood him, was no longer in his life, having been killed in battle two years ago. He'd even managed to alienate the rest of the Seven just a few days ago, and he was not welcome as member of their group anymore. Tynan wondered if being pushed out of his own adventuring company was a humiliation he could survive.

Not for the first time, Tynan also wondered what had become of the rest of the Selvantyr family since his leaving. He never returned to Acantha. In the beginning, he sent letters to his mother, and his mother sent letters to him through the Bronze Helm Inn in Valis. He sent letters less and less frequently over the years, however, and eventually those from his mother ceased altogether.

Sighing, Tynan looked around at the steep rock walls on either side of the mountain path in an attempt to distract himself from thoughts of his family and of Rimen. It did no good. He looked at the other mountains in the Black Mountain Ridge rising into view. The black peaks he saw seemed to glare, condemning him as a fool, and looking at the walls and the way they hemmed in either side of the path just served to remind Tynan how he increasingly felt toward his life of late: closed in.

Now that he thought about it, only wide enough for two riders to pass each other, this path was the perfect spot for an ambush or a trap. Tynan shuddered as a chill rose up his spine. He wrapped his cloak tighter about his shoulders and waited for the chill to pass. Spurring Duraden on, he encouraged the stallion to climb faster.

His thoughts trailed back to Rimen. No loss ever hurt him as badly as Rimen's death. It happened when Tynan got the idea that the Seven should take on a large group of orcish bandits terrorizing a small town. When Tynan heard of them, he decided that the Seven should rid the poor town of its problem, even though the other members of the Seven protested that they might be in over their heads. Nonetheless, they accompanied him and Rimen and tracked the bandits to their den in the highlands. During the battle, Rimen was fatally wounded, and not even Tynan could save him.

Angry at these memories, a scar on a life that should have been only stellar, Tynan gripped the hilt of his sword Aric and pulled it free of its sheath. Duraden's ears flicked back at the sound of the blade rasping loose. Tynan brought the polished blade up in front of his face and stopped, staring at his reflection. Raw grief etched his handsome

3

features; his blond locks seemed to droop. Taking a ragged breath, Tynan rearranged his face into a more dignified expression of quiet sadness.

His blue eyes traced Aric's lines. The sword was beautiful, shining steel from point to grip. Although he loved Aric, sometimes the sword was a painful reminder. Vortenthas, the dwarven swordsmith god, gave Tynan this sword as a reward for saving the life of one of Vortenthas's favorite clerics. He also promised Tynan one favor from the dwarven gods, to be called upon at the time of his choosing. When Tynan tried to call in the favor after Rimen's death, however, asking that his friend be returned to life, Vortenthas denied him. The god told him that the life of an elf was not his domain. Such was in the hands of the *elven* gods, and he would not offend them by crossing that boundary uninvited.

To cope with this second loss, Tynan dove back into his adventuring life, and guilted the Seven into the same—for Rimen, he told them—but he never felt himself again. He certainly did not smile as much. In life, Rimen had been quick with a joke and often entertained people with tales and songs he wrote. He could stir up an entire common room in an instant. But the joy that Rimen brought to Tynan's life died with Rimen, and adventuring with the Seven became harder with each quest. Unbeknownst to him at first, the rest of the company blamed him for Rimen's death, a secret they had let him in on only recently.

When Tynan looked around again, he realized something was wrong. So deep was he in thought, he did not notice that Duraden had reached the top of the ridge and had stopped behind a large boulder, blocking Tynan's view into the valley. Tynan untied Duraden's reins from his saddle pommel and took them in hand. He nudged the horse with his boots and clucked at him, but Duraden did nothing. A gust of wind blew some of Tynan's blond locks into his eyes. He swept them away with his hand and gently nudged the horse again. Still nothing. Tynan nudged harder, but still the golden stallion did not budge.

Frowning now, Tynan asked, "Do you sense something?" The

horse only snorted.

He looked around but saw nothing unusual ahead or behind them in the mountain pass. Tynan dismounted. Duraden whickered and tossed his head. Yes, something was wrong; Tynan felt it now. The hairs on the back of his neck stood up. Frowning more deeply, he took a small spyglass from his saddle bag and scaled the rock wall. Once atop the wall, he crawled onto his belly until he could see into the valley below.

Tynan brought the spyglass up to his eye, careful that the sun did not reflect off the brass tube or the lens. There were men in the valley, at least half on horseback, and all of them wearing armor. He counted thirty men, all dressed in black from head to toe. Even the horses were armored. The men stood about as if waiting for something to happen, and as Tynan identified several in their ranks, he knew they were waiting for him.

The men he recognized were members of the Black Order, a band of "adventurers" renowned for their infamy as mercenaries and thieves. They stole from and killed honest adventurers and terrorized anyone who opposed them. In recent years, the Black Order grew and broke into sects that spread out across the Northlands like a disease. Tynan and his companions had butted heads with all of them. The two groups despised each other and did not mind showing it. The Company of Seven Strong bested the Black Order on a number of quests, taking home substantial amounts of treasure that the Black Order made clear they felt should have been theirs.

Lowering the spyglass, Tynan rolled over onto his back to think for a moment. He had one idea why the mercenaries would be camped out in Night Valley, lying in wait for him, and that was that they were trying to get at his fortune of gold and silver and the magik artifacts he had collected and stored in the caverns on the other side of the valley below. The location of his wealth was widely known.

Tynan let it be known to anyone who asked; however, that his hordes were guarded by a complex system of magikal traps and wards. A few people had lost their lives proving it. Other than himself, only Rimen could pass through the cavern unscathed. He made an amulet specially for his elven friend at the time he put his magik traps in place.

Tynan did not know what made the Black Order decide to make such a move on him now. Perhaps news of his break from the Seven had already spread, though how they arrived in the valley before him was unclear. No doubt they used magik to expedite their arrival. Whatever the cause, the ambush was important enough to have drawn at least one high-ranking member of the organization: Zentin Thrace. Tynan and Thrace felt a particular animosity toward each other, and Thrace sat at the head of the group of mercenaries awaiting Tynan now.

Tynan slithered back over the top of the rock wall and down to the path once more. Calmly, he placed the spyglass in his saddlebag as a hard spike of indignation rose inside of him. Tynan decided he would rather die than allow the Black Order access to his caverns, though he felt confident it would not come to that. After all, he was a famous fighter and sorcerer, and they were little more than common thugs.

Placing a boot in the stirrup, Tynan got into his saddle once more. "Are you up for a battle, my friend?" Tynan asked Duraden.

His stallion stamped a hoof in the black gravel and tossed his head, causing his bridle to jingle violently. Tynan took that as an affirmative and drew on a pair of doeskin gloves before loosing Aric from its sheath again. He leaned back and sliced cleanly through the ropes that held the small litter tied behind his saddle. Taking Duraden's reins in his other hand, Tynan quickly called to mind three battle spells— wind, dust, and fire—and then turned his horse toward the path down into the valley.

As they cleared the cover of the steep rock walls and boulders, Tynan kicked Duraden into a fast gallop, holding his head and his sword high as befitted someone of noble birth. They were more than halfway down into the valley before anyone called attention to Tynan's charge down the mountainside, a long cloud of dust and gravel streaming behind

Duraden's hooves. A collective shout rose from the base of the valley, and Zentin Thrace called his men into formation. Mercenaries scrambled to mount their horses and fall into line. A grim smile fell into place on Tynan's face. He spoke the words to his wind spell and then the dust spell, combining them.

Seconds later, a full-blown dust storm swept across the floor of Night Valley ahead of him. Winds howled and debris blinded the men waiting for him. Chaos ensued.

Men shouted and horses neighed in fright. Tynan squinted and urged Duraden to plunge directly into the heart of the storm, hoping to ride right past the mercenaries through to the other side of the valley and up Nightstone before anyone was the wiser. He did not have far to go up the side of the peak to the entrance. A mere hundred yards separated Tynan from freedom, and he felt confident that they could make it. He realized too late that he could not have been more wrong.

As soon as Duraden carried him into the storm, visibility dimmed almost to nonexistence. Flying dust and dirt clung to Tynan's eyelashes, threatening to blind him altogether. Duraden skidded to a stop so suddenly that Tynan was nearly thrown from the saddle. When he opened his mouth to shout at the golden stallion, dirt blew down his throat, choking off his words. The grim realization that he had made a mistake by entering the storm settled into the pit of his stomach. Vaguely, he heard someone chanting the words to a spell. A moment later, a crosswind blew much of the dust clear.

The Black Order controlled their mounts faster than Tynan thought possible. Arrows and magik spheres rained down on Tynan and Duraden, only to be thrown off course by the winds of Tynan's first spell. Fortunately, this allowed Tynan to better guide Duraden. He wiped as much of the debris from his eyes as he could with his sword arm and pulled on Duraden's reins again. He jerked the horse back around in what he thought was the direction of Nightstone Peak, not caring if the bit cut the stallion. Then, he kicked Duraden hard in the side.

The golden stallion leaped forward, but Tynan saw their escape route disappearing. Men were closing in to flank them on all sides. Duraden did not get far enough to clear the still-raging storm before he reared up, narrowly avoiding a collision with the ranks of riders blocking their escape. Tynan grabbed wildly for his saddle's pommel to keep from falling.

Men on foot rushed in to strike at Tynan. Several of them were struck by Duraden's flailing hooves as he spun around, and others were crushed when he planted his hooves back on the ground. More men advanced to take the place of their fallen comrades. Tynan swung his sword about wildly, trying to keep the men at bay as long as he could, and coughed on the dust and dirt still choking the air. He knew he could not cast spells if he could not talk. In a desperate attempt to regain his voice, Tynan dropped his reins and ripped free the canteen of water strapped to his saddle. Half the water he poured out went down his dust-coated throat, the other half he spit out at a man grabbing hold of Duraden's loose reins.

Duraden danced backward, but the man planted his feet. As he did this, Tynan coughed once more and then croaked out the words to his fire spell. Blazing, orange fireballs sprayed out from Tynan's hand in all directions. The man holding Duraden's reins became a human torch and dropped the reins as he staggered backward. Several of the Black Order's horses emitted eerily human screams as more fireballs struck home. Burning mercenaries joined the macabre chorus.

The acrid smoke caused by the fireballs cleared just long enough for Tynan to see Nightstone, and he turned Duraden in that direction. Spurring the stallion into a gallop once more, they charged for the opening. Men stumbled into their path, and terrified, rider-less horses reared up as Tynan and Duraden bolted through the renewed chaos. Tynan masterfully steered his stallion past the obstacles. As the daylight became visible again, Tynan saw his victory in sight. He congratulated himself and turned back to laugh at the mercenaries still stumbling about.

Tynan never saw the ax that struck out and buried itself in Duraden's side and sliced open Tynan's lower leg as well.

Duraden listed to the left without so much as a dying scream while Tynan struggled to free his feet from the stirrups before Duraden fell. He landed hard on the ground, and Aric skittered out of his grasp and out of reach. Turning over, he gasped for breath. Tynan was greeted with the dead eyes of not only Duraden, but also the man who had felled Duraden. Unable to get his ax and himself clear before the horse toppled over, Duraden's weight had crushed the mercenary. Tynan hissed with disgust. The stench of burning flesh that floated through the air stung his nose as he struggled to his feet, only to cry out in pain from his injured leg. He fell to his knees. His head turned when he heard a low chuckle behind him.

A mercenary hefting a heavy maul came out of the miasma of smoke and dust. Towering over Tynan, the man hauled his weapon over his head and brought it crashing down. Tynan dove forward, toward his sword lying some feet away. The maul powdered the black rocks it hit in place of Tynan. The soldier turned and raised the maul to strike again. Frantic, Tynan dove for Aric a second time. His fingers grasped the hilt. Rolling out of the way as the maul's iron head fell a second time, Tynan muttered the words to a minor energy spell. Healing spells were not something Tynan kept at the ready, as he rarely needed them, and the spell he cast gave him only a small boost of energy. It was enough to get him moving, though.

Rock shards pelted his face and arms as the maul just missed him again. He ignored them, using his sword to lever himself to his feet. The mercenary swung the maul a third time, aiming for Tynan's midriff. Tynan brought Aric around to block the flying maul, but mistakenly braced himself on his injured leg. His leg buckled, and Tynan was unable to block the blow. He only slowed it down. The maul landed a blow to Tynan's right side, and he felt several ribs break on impact. He fell to one knee, gasping for air.

9

Laughing, the mercenary reached for Tynan. When he got close enough, however, Tynan used his left hand to thrust his sword forward into the man's gut, putting all of his strength behind it. The man looked surprised for only a moment before his eyes rolled back in his head, and he fell lifeless to the ground. Tynan pulled Aric free of the mercenary's corpse after he staggered to his feet and headed in the direction of Nightstone again. Then, his wind spell faded out. Tynan went pale as he looked over his shoulder and found at least half of the Order's forces still standing.

Zentin Thrace's eyes locked with his. "Get him!" he screamed, spittle flying from his mouth. The remaining mercenaries turned in unison.

Tynan's mind went blank except for a single teleportation spell. Without delay Tynan spoke the necessary incantation and pictured the entrance to the caverns. He disappeared in a brief burst of blue light. The arrows meant for him pierced empty air. Tynan reappeared partway up the side of Nightstone Peak, in front of the giant boulder that served as the entrance to the Black Caverns. It was high enough and wide enough to admit a man on horseback.

Tynan wasted no time to see what reaction the mercenaries had to his reappearance. He faced the boulder and muttered the words to open the door. A deep rumbling rose as the boulder rolled back. Tynan fell into the caverns as a slender opening appeared, without waiting for the boulder to roll back all of the way. He immediately spoke the word to reverse the boulder's direction. When the boulder shut the opening again, he leaned against the cavern wall of black obsidian and slid to the floor, exhausted. His broken ribs caused him enough pain that he saw spots, and Tynan crumpled onto the floor on his uninjured side, gasping. The gasps became sobs, and he slammed his palm into the stone floor with frustration. This was not how his life was supposed to end.

A moment later, his sobs ceased when he became aware of the rise and fall of spellcasters chanting a spell outside. Tynan wanted to laugh—any spell they tried would be useless—but he could hardly breathe, let alone laugh at their folly. He was dying, his strength failing.

It saddened Tynan that this was how his end would be met: bloodied and alone, without friends or even family to carry on his legacy after he passed on to his final destination. Tynan reflected that the bards of the land would undoubtedly write ballads about his final hours. Tynan only hoped they did his struggle justice.

Then, he wondered how those people would even know what had happened in the valley this day. Without a doubt, the mercenaries outside would have a jolly time recounting their own version of events, with Tynan turning tail and running to the caverns to die at the end of the story. Tynan groaned. His immortal reputation was doomed.

Anger followed on the heels of his humiliation. Not only had the Black Order attempted to rob him of his riches, but they planned to rob him of his dignity and his reputation as well. They would keep the people from knowing that he, Tynan Darius Selvantyr, had fought bravely against them and held his own until he was mercilessly outnumbered.

Tynan pushed himself upright out of the pool of blood that collected underneath him. Great men did not die lying down, he told himself.

Using the last of his magikal energies, Tynan cast another teleportation spell, bringing to mind the tower at the center of his caverns. He reappeared on the lowest level of the tower, leaning heavily on Aric for support. He looked around at the cream-colored stone walls. Tynan sighed. It was the only part of the caverns not made of obsidian rock, and it was Tynan's favorite place in all of the Black Caverns.

The tower interior was bright with lanterns and candelabras that burned continuously with magikal light. To one side was the comfortable seating area where he and Rimen had spent hours debating Valisian politics or discussing what quest the Seven should take on next. Across from him, a spiral staircase led to the upper floors, and next to the staircase lay the stone with a slot in its center where Aric rested when not at his side.

As he looked around, Tynan felt robbed by Death, knowing there was so much more for him to do in the world. Limping to Aric's stone, Tynan felt like breaking down again, but the wave of emotion was derailed when the caverns suddenly shook. Tynan uttered a curse as he was almost knocked off his feet. He grabbed the stair railing next to him. The caverns trembled a second time and the lantern lights flickered as they swung crazily back and forth. Stone dust drifted down from the ceiling.

"Those thrice-blasted bastards! Do they wish to shake my caverns to pieces?" Tynan growled. "*Fools.* They will accomplish nothing that way. There will be no bounty to take away if the mountain caves in on top of me."

It occurred to him that they did indeed know this and were acting merely out of spite.

Then, another thought occurred to him, and he remembered of a debt still owed to him. A grim smile touched his bloody features. Closing his eyes, Tynan summoned his will and stood straight, without aid. He raised his arms, fingers locked around Aric's hilt, and brought the sword up in front of him, point down. His blue eyes opened again, and he stared into the blade's reflection of his face, still handsome beneath the dirt and the blood.

In a clear voice, he said, "Hear me, O Dwarven gods of Blood and Stone. I demand my final boon of thee. Call down your wrath upon those that seek the destruction of this place! Bring fire and Hell down upon them who use their evil against me now." He paused for a ragged breath. "I close these caverns from safe entrance for all time. May all but the one whom you might deem worthy of safe passage perish within these corridors."

"Smite them all, O Dwarven gods of Blood and Stone! Smite the unworthy in my name."

Tynan slammed Aric's point down into its slotted stone. The last of his strength spent, he collapsed into a heap on the stone floor, staring upward. He felt a tremor rising up from under him and smiled. At last, he let the darkness take him.

Outside, a deep tremor shook the ground, and the sky turned black as pitch. The mercenaries and spellcasters fell silent, staring at the sky. Nothing was heard but the rumbling of the ground and the panicked neighing of the horses. Forks of red lightning sliced the sky. The earth cracked, and fire and smoke rose around those that still remained, barring their escape. Then, the skies opened and brimstone rained down from above, burning those that stood in Night Valley below.

All but one man perished in Night Valley that day. When it was over, he crawled through the smoking remains, his hair white and his limbs shaking. On his knees, he begged the gods to forgive him for his crimes. A whisper on the wind told him to leave Night Valley and tell all what he had seen. Whether in his head or the voice of a god, the man heeded its words.

He left the valley on foot and swore not to stop until he had reached Valis and relate what had happened in Night Valley that day. He would warn everyone to stay far away from Nightstone Peak and Tynan Selvantyr's accursed caverns. The dark gods themselves guarded his tomb.

When Tynan finished the story, Theo just stared at him. "That was some tale," she finally told him.

He looked satisfied at her reaction. "I think, though, that now would be a good time for you to sleep. We have another long day ahead of us."

Theo yawned and nodded. She laid back down and pulled the blankets up to her chin. As she stared at him on the other side of the fire, she wondered if ever there was a man more pompous than Tynan Selvantyr. She supposed not. She also wondered why had he told the story all in the third person, like some bard relating someone else's story.

It was strange. As she drifted off to sleep, Theo decided he was just quirky that way, and she was alright with that.

II: THE WORLD OF CATHELL

Ever wonder what is the difference between a mercenary and a sell-sword? Or why isn't Morghall called Morghell? Go deeper into the larger world of Cathell and its history.

What is Cathell?

Cathell is the name of the land mass that extends from the Sea of the Crescent Moon down to the region just south of the Golden Peaks.

The Gods
While you may think that the pantheon of the human race is overly complicated in comparison to those of the elves and the dwarves, know that all three pantheons have one thing in common: they rarely interfere in the lives of mortals. This might seem arrogant to some mortals, however, maintaining the balance in the mortal world holds the most value to them. To avoid upsetting it, they are reluctant to get involved in the affairs of mortals.

Races of Cathell
Beyond the humans, elves, dwarves, vampyres, orcs, and goblins mentioned in the pages of *Into the Darkness*, there are also demons, centaurs, faeries, imps, nymphs, and a mysterious race of beings called Immortals, first referenced in *The Taming*.

The Elves
All elves are born with inherent nature-based magikal abilities, however, with study they are just as capable of achieving high levels as general spellcasters and mages. It is not uncommon for elven casters to rival or surpass the White and Black magiks of human spellcasters.

There are two commonly recognized subsections of the elvish race: woodland elves and frost elves.

Woodland elves—These beings consider themselves the stewards of the Forever Wood and many other woodlands. They are extremely arrogant and insular. Humans, for the most part, are regarded with disdain and are considered the Great Destructors. The elves of Alethia are protective of the woodlands at their borders to the point of outright hostility toward non-elven outsiders.

Frost elves—The frost elves differ greatly from forest and woodland elves. They are nomadic and much less insular in comparison. Frost elves are wary of outsiders but do not treat them as unwelcome. Frost elves have been known to mix with many of the other races of Cathell, whereas many fewer woodland elves do.

The Dwarves
Much like woodland elves, dwarves tend to be an insular race, often preferring underground dens to aboveground living. Some dwarves are content living among the other races. All dwarves worship the four elements in nature: earth, water, air, and fire.

The Vampyres
There are many myths about vampyres in Cathell—they're undead, they're immortal, they're evil, sunlight kills them. Few of these rumors are true and many are based on half-truths. New vampyres are created when the blood of an existing vampyre is consumed by a non-vampyre human.* Through this process, the parasite that causes vampyrism enters the non-vampyre, turning them into a vampyre as well. The parasite doesn't change the personality of the host, but it does give them a strong urge to consume the blood of other living beings, especially humans.

In exchange for the consumption of blood, the parasite confers certain superhuman abilities upon the vampyre, such as longer life, increased speed and agility, increased strength and stamina, faster healing, and heightened senses of sight, smell, and hearing. It is this heightened sight that causes vampyres' difficulty in bright sunlight; it simply hurts their sensitive eyes. Some vampyres cope with this issue by spending the daylight hours indoors, while others have found a way around the problem, like with a pair of dark spectacles, as Thystle has.

While the increased pallor of the vampyre makes them seem undead, the vampyre is a living being and can be killed. However, a complication to killing a vampyre is the parasite's overwhelming sense of self-preservation. Reaching a state of near-death will cause this self-preservation instinct to go into overdrive, and the creature that exists within the vampyre tries to override the will of the vampyre itself. Vampyres must take care not to reach this stage and thus enter a battle of wills with the creature inside, for once the vampyre is taken over by a state of blood rage, the parasite does not willingly relinquish control until it has been allowed to consume enough blood to begin the healing process, avoiding death. In rare cases, vampyres seized by blood rage have awoken from its throes to discover they have killed close friends.

*In extremely rare cases, intercourse between a young male vampyre and a non-vampyre female may produce a child, which may or may not also become a vampyre. The mother is never turned in this scenario, for reasons unknown to vampyre kind. Non-vampyre children born in this way are almost always rejected by vampyres and humans alike, and are called the Nameless.

Purpose of a Sceptor
A sceptor is no mere cleric or priest. The title of sceptor is only bestowed upon a cleric that is favored most by their chosen god. When a cleric achieves the elevation of Sceptor, they have as direct a line to their god as a mortal may achieve. They are given guidance by their god, and their opinions may be considered by their god. The sceptor knows when their god is happy, sad, displeased, or, on rare occasions, in pain.

The Eternal Sleep
Gods, at least in the human pantheon, do not last forever. If they fall out of favor or simply tire of watching over the balance, a god will enter the Eternal Sleep. Although it is not impossible for a god to be awakened from the Eternal Sleep, it requires an act of true devotion and sacrifice to reenergize a sleeping god.

Rillenvair
The land of the gods is both beautiful and terrible, full of things both light and dark. Rillenvair is divided into kingdoms that house the various races' deities. Iritor is the kingdom of the human pantheon, ruled by Aephis, the High Father, and Cira, the High Mother. No mortal has ever set foot in Rillenvair other than in their dreams and nightmares.

Morghell and Morghall
Morghall was established as the center city of The Fang after the time of the barbarians, to honor Morghell for sparing the survivors of the barbarians' tyrannical rule. You may ask, however, why the city whose patron god is Morghell is then called Morghall, rather than Morghell.

The truth is that once upon a time, it actually was, or more accurately, it was called Morghell's Hall.

In time, however, people with some very broken Common ran the two words together often enough that outsiders thought the city was actually called "Morghelall". This morphed again into just Morghall.

The bastardized name caught on, and no amount of correction by the people or governors of The Fang was able to shake it. Eventually, with his god's permission, the fifth governor of Morghell's Hall declared the city renamed Morghall.

Paladins
In a nutshell, paladins are holy fighters. They fight for the glory of their chosen god in return for the god's favor. If deemed worthy, their god grants them certain magikal powers, and strength and stamina beyond that of other normal men and women.

Rangers
A ranger is part naturalist and part fighter. Rangers are often solitary individuals, preferring to range alone across the woodlands, plains, and mountains of Cathell. They typically find companions to be difficult to deal with and illogical, compared to the logic and order found in the plants and animals that popular the world.

The Differences Between Sell-Swords and Mercenaries
While both are considered swords for hire, for war or other physical tasks, the distinction comes down mostly to motivation and morality. Mercenaries are typically in the business of fighting for whomever offers the most money, regardless of the motivation behind the employer hiring them. However, sell-swords choose their work based on factors beyond how well a job pays. The motivation of the employer is often a consideration prior to a sell-sword signing on to a job.

What is The Fang?
The region known as The Fang starts at the westernmost edge of the Forever Wood and juts out from the main continent of Cathell into a spit of land shaped like a wolf's fang. The Fang, unlike many other parts of Cathell, is ruled equally by the governors of a six city-state collective,

with Morghall serving as the center city for The Fang. A centralized Fang army provides law and order for the region.

The History of The Fang

Centuries prior to the events in *Into the Darkness*, the region now known as The Fang was an unruly place ungoverned by any one person. Inter-settlement skirmishes were commonplace and violent to the extreme. Then, a horde of barbarians from the Wastelands crossed the Sunset Seas that separates the Wastelands and The Fang and invaded Cathell.

The invaders were not able to go farther east or south due to severe resistance from the elves of that region, but they contented themselves with settling in for a long period of tyranny against the people living on the peninsula. The general lack of order inherent to the region meant there was no army to put up any real resistance to the barbarian invaders. The barbarians remained the overlords of the region for over two decades before those enslaved by the barbarians began to organize a rebellion to overthrow their captors.

When the resistance succeeded and the barbarians were pushed out of The Fang, the survivors came together to form a collective government. The region was divided into the six modern city-states, and The Fang has existed in relative harmony ever since.

III: THE GODS OF CATHELL

Into the Darkness mentions several of the gods worshipped by the people of Cathell. Learn about them and others in this detailed list of the gods of humans, elves, and dwarves, along with their qualities and quirks.

The Gods of Man

It seems to elves and dwarves that there is a god for almost everything in the human pantheon, even murder and vengeance. Some gods fall out of favor from time to time, sometimes to be replaced by new gods, perpetuating a cycle of renewal.

Aephis
God of Sun and Heavens—Eldest son of the old gods and current ruler of Iritor, the kingdom of the human gods in Rillenvair. The title of High Father passed to him when the old gods stepped down for their children to take their place in the pantheon of humans. Travelers often pray for benevolence from Aephis prior to beginning their journey, in the hopes of fair weather. His symbol is a white ring or a white disk to represent the sun.

Cira
Goddess of Stars—Eldest daughter of the old gods and co-ruler of Iritor with Aephis. The title of High Mother passed to her when the old gods stepped down for their children to take their places in the pantheon of humans. Cira is also considered the goddess of guidance for travelers who might otherwise lose their way without her. Her symbol is three stars in a triangle formation.

Anora
Goddess of Love—Anora is both the mender and breaker of hearts. When she is smiling, your life is filled with the joy of new and everlasting love. When she is unhappy, however, your life may take a very dark turn indeed. Women often pray to Anora not only to find a suitor, but for fertility as well. Her symbol is a simple heart or a small child.

Rohbaron
God of Justice—Patron god of the just and bane of deceivers. Rohbaron is the strictest of all the gods, and only the most pure of heart will earn his favor. His symbol is a hammer.

Juliandar

Goddess of Wisdom—Part scholar, part healer, and part spellcaster, Juliandar is the patron goddess of the learned. She is a goddess of the sciences and humanities alike, and she is the patron goddess of healers. Some spellcasters and mages pray to Juliandar to allow them to achieve higher levels of magik use. Her symbol is a book or tome.

Oleandar

Goddess of the Harvest—Patron goddess of agriculturists. It is only through Oleandar's love and favor that the farmer may yield bountiful crops. If she is angered, your fields may never produce another good crop, and all the crops you grow will be tainted with a terrible blight. In addition to farmers, women who are with child pray to Oleandar for a healthy child and easy childbirth. Her symbol is a wheat stalk.

Wersal

God of Benevolent Magik—Wersal is considered the patron god of White spellcasters. When magik users pray to Wersal, unlike with Juliandar, they seek to achieve greater power behind their spells. His symbol is a lightning bolt.

Lilleth

Goddess of Music and Revel—Lilleth is the most cheerful and laid back of all the gods. She is found wherever song and dance and general revelry happens. She is considered the patron goddess of bards, playwrights, actors, minstrels, and barkeeps. Her symbol is a fiddle.

Aspen

Goddess of Forest and Nature—Considered one of the most beautiful of gods, second only to her sister Anora, Aspen is stewardess of the forests and woodlands. Though pragmatic in her own way, the needless death of even a single tree or flower saddens her. She is the patron goddess of rangers and naturalists. Her symbol is an elderwood tree.

Cerapis

God of Seasons and the Wind (Land)—Husband to Aspen, his work goes hand in hand with hers and Oleandar's alike, although sometimes, he falls more with Ireteah. He is changeable and moody, and may bring clouds and great storms whenever he is angry, but Aspen always knows how to charm him again and get him to pull back his clouds. He is worshipped by many in combination with other gods. His symbol is a simple cloud.

Heldanic
God of the Seas and the Wind (Sea)—Patron and bane of sailors alike. Heldanic is changeable in the same way as Cerapis, but without anyone to temper his rages. A sailor in Heldanic's favor can sail from Mirror Bay to the Sea of the Crescent Moon in just a few days. But, fall out of his favor and that same sailor may have to break out the oars to paddle his way home without any wind. Anger Heldanic outright, and you'll find yourself meeting Morghell at the bottom of the sea. His symbol is three wavy lines.

Penthea
Goddess of the Hunt and the Lost—Where Aspen is the stewardess of the forests and woodlands, game falls under Penthea's watchful eye. She loves the thrill of the hunt, but don't go killing off her animals just for sport, or you may find the tables turned. Wise hunters ask permission for a kill when they enter her realm and offer thanks to Penthea and the fallen animal after a kill. Travelers lost in the woods also pray to Penthea and Aspen to guide them and keep them safe. Penthea is also a patron goddess to rangers. Her symbol is a strung bow and arrow.

Tempes
Goddess of Fate and Time—Though some see her as cruel, Tempes is the most neutral of all the gods. She cares not for the pleadings of the unfortunate nor the thanks of the fortunate, though it does not stop her worshipers from offering either. She cares only for maintaining balance and order in fate and time. Her symbol is three straight lines to represent the threads of the past, present, and future to come.

Morghell
God of the Underworld—Like Tempes, Morghell remains a neutral party with an eye for balance. He welcomes those felled by Fortesis, Symon, Ireteah, and Kayen and Raen all the same and passes judgment upon the soul before him, weighing its merits and detractions. The sick and dying offer prayers for mercy to Morghell. He is also the patron god of the city of Morghall, whose land once saw much torment and death. His symbol

is three faces: the tormented, the neutral, and the satisfied.

Symon
God of Luck, Chaos, and Madness—The most changeable of all of the gods. Symon is prayed to by merchants, travelers, gamblers, adventurers, soldiers, and thieves alike. Without his favor, your luck may run out in an instant. His symbol is that of a three interlinked rings.

Fortesis
God of War—Fortesis cares little for the reasons behind war, he cares only for the thrill of a good campaign and a bloody battle. If you are skilled with a sword and feel just in your heart for the war that you make, Fortesis may well shine favor on you. He is the patron god of soldiers, though some mercenaries and sell-swords also pray to him for fortune in battle. His symbol is a sword placed across a round shield.

Ireteah
Goddess of Strife and Hardship—Though she is considered a dark god by most, Ireteah considers herself neutral, bringing plague, famine, strife, and hardship to the rich and the poor, the good and the evil. Pray that you never attract her attention, for you may never escape her clutches alive. Farmers are often seen leaving an offering or two at an altar to Ireteah to try to ward her curses away. For that reason, her symbol is a farmer's pitchfork.

Kellen
God of Thieves—Kellen is a favorite in Rillenvair for his fanciful stories. A trickster after the heart of any thief or con man, Kellen grants those who pray to him quick hands, sharp wits, and a winning smile. His symbol is a hand.

Xenephon
God of Dark Magik—The polar opposite of Wersal, Xenephon is the patron god of the Black. His worshipers seek only power and dominance over any kind of wisdom. Xenephon's symbol is a staff with a pointed tip.

Kayen and Raen
Gods of Hatred and Torment, Murder and Vengeance—The twins Kayen

and Raen are the least amenable or liked of all the gods. Even the High Mother finds them distasteful whenever they're around. They delight in all of the darkest of human emotions and motives. They share the symbol of a black square divided corner to corner by a gray line.

The Gods of Elves

The elven pantheon is all the things that the human one is not: simple, nature-based, and generally on the side of good, or so the elves think. Within the elven pantheon, there is never a changing of the guard like in the human pantheon, and their gods may be seen as both male and female or neither. Elves, they like to say, are not nearly as strict or changeable as humans.

Mana

God/Goddess of the Four Elements, Nature, and the Seasons—If there was a god or goddess who served as father or mother to the elven people, it would be Mana. Without Mana, there would be no land, no trees, no animals, no sun or moon or stars, and, ultimately, no elven people. Mana's symbol is a golden ring, symbolizing the unity of all things in nature.

Solinarae

God/Goddess of the Sun—With the rising of the sun, Solinarae blesses the land, making plants grow and purifying the world from the darkness the night brings. Solinarae's symbol is a multirayed sun.

Luminarae

God/Goddess of the Moon—Though seen as slightly darker than his/her counterpart, Solinarae, without Luminarae, the tides would not change, the land would not cool at night, the night blooms would not come out, and Hianara's stars would never be seen. Luminarae's darkness is necessary. Her symbol is that of a silver disk.

Hianara

God/Goddess of the Stars and Magik—Only seen at night, Hianara's stars guide travelers and light the night's sky even when Luminarae's moon is absent. She is also the patron deity for spellcasters and mages. Hianara's symbol is a group of four black stars.

Oriya

God/Goddess of Love and Joy—Oriya is the most positive of all of elven deities. She embodies all that is great in the elven people. Her symbol is an arch of sunbursts.

Hahlimarend
God/Goddess of War and Death—While Hahlimarend may seem to an outsider to be a dark god, this deity embodies the strength of the elven people in the face of adversity and hostility. Also, the elven people, who live many centuries, do not see death as an end, but rather as the beginning of a new stage of life.

The Gods of Dwarves

The dwarves have even fewer gods than the elves, with just five caring for the well-being of the dwarven folk. This suits the dwarves just fine, as they like to keep life simple in any way that they can. They have no time or patience for fanciful things, unlike those humans and elves.

Bracktoll

God of Earth and Stone—All things originate from the earth in the dwarven mythology, and so Bracktoll is the most respected of all the dwarven gods. Without him, plants cannot grow and there is nothing to mine and nothing to mold. His symbol is a maul crossed over a pickax.

Ferrima

Goddess of Wind—Ferrima is greatly respected by the dwarves. Her winds bring fresh air to the mines, fuel to their fires, and power to their windmills and turbines. If angered, she might blow down your house and all of your crops. Her symbol is a soaring eagle.

Terrimina

Goddess of Water and Life—Terrimina is the sustainer of the dwarven people and of nature. She is the embodiment of the bountiful harvests from the fields and fertility for mothers. Her symbol is a pair of wavy lines.

Vorthenthas

God of Fire and Metal—The god of smithing and swordcraft alike, Vortenthas is the embodiment of both strength and artistry. His symbol is a heavy smithing hammer.

Graydor

God of War and Death—Though dwarves would rather stay home, they are fearsome fighters who are not to be angered, lest you find them on your doorstep, swords and axes in hand. Graydor is found at the frontlines of any dwarven battle, and he shall escort the fallen to their final rest and lay honors at their feet.

ABOUT THE AUTHOR

A.M. Rycroft is a dark fantasy and horror writer in Pittsburgh, PA. She holds a B.A. in English from the University of Pittsburgh, and she has been a technical and creative writer for over 10 years. *Into the Darkness* was her first dark fantasy/horror novel and the first set in the world of Cathell.

Follow Rycroft's blog at www.writinginadarkroom.com to get updates on her new projects and giveaways. You can also subscribe to her newsletter. She also posts regular updates on her Facebook page (www.facebook.com/amrycroftwriter) and on her Twitter feed (@amrycoftwriter).

If you still find yourself with a burning question about the World of Cathell or its characters not answered in the bonus content, fear not. Rycroft's website will soon have a dedicated World of Cathell page, where she'll add new tidbits of information about Cathell as they develop.

PRAISE FOR THE TAMING

"I was hooked from the very first chapter [...] It features a small range of characters including the love interest Lilla, her maker Wiat, and a villain that makes your blood boil. I couldn't put this down and read it all in one sitting." – Tilly Booth, book blogger (tilly-and-her-books.tumblr.com)

"This is a dark fantasy with colourful well-drawn characters. We leap from one danger to the next always one step behind Thystle. [...] The question on everyone's lips is – when's the next one coming out?" – Fiona Cooke Hogan, book blogger (ww.fionacookehogan.com)

"The Taming is a quick and easy read, but doesn't leave out any of the details. A well written Dark Fantasy full of action, and characters with depth that you can love, or hate. I loved Thystle, a vampyre, with a sarcastic nature, and her need to find out the truth. [...] This was my first dip into the Dark Fantasy genre and I must say I will be getting a copy of 'Into the Darkness, by A.M. Rycroft,' the first book, in this interesting and fantastical world of Cathell." – Emma T. Gitani book reviewer for *Our Write Side* (ourwriteside.com)

33795607R00247

Made in the USA
Middletown, DE
27 July 2016